MW01514423

Brad, Congratulations and all blessings on *The Melting*. You know the secret, it's courage. We need you and your work.
— ANNE RICE,
author of *Interview with the Vampire*,
The Witching Hour, and *Angel Time*.

Brad is a talented and serious writer. I am a fan.
— RALPH COTTON,
author of *While Angels Dance*,
Blood Rock, and *Escape from Fire River*.

Brad, you're a hell of a writer. You've got too many good ideas.
— GARY RAISOR,
author of *Less than Human*,
Graven Images, and *Sinister Purposes*.

'The Melting' Rocks, Brad! A truly frightening book from one of the great new Authors of this generation.
— ROBERT PRESTON WALKER,
author of *Mr. Smoke*.

THE MELTING

BY

BRAD RIEMAN

THE MELTING

Copyright © 2010 by Brad Rieman. All rights reserved.

This book is a work of fiction. People, places, events, and situations are the product of the author's imagination. Any resemblance to actual persons, living or dead, or historical events, is purely coincidental.

No part of this book may be reproduced, stored in a retrieval system, or transmitted by any means without the written permission of the author.

Cover Design by Brad Rieman
Back Cover Author's Photo by Pamela Rieman

Printed in the United States of America.

ISBN # 1449589308
UPC/EAN-13 # 9781449589301

First Edition:

10 9 8 7 6 5 4 3 2 1

I would like to dedicate the completion of this work to the almighty power of hope. I owe a debt of gratitude to the legs I stand on; My Wife, My Children, My Parents, My Family and Friends - if I knew you, then you're at least partially responsible. Thanks!

With a special thanks to
my lovely wife, Pamela, for working *around* me.

And to my mom, because, you know, ...she's mom.

Okay, and now a group hug with just the kids.

Thanks to everyone involved!

For Tracy

Stop the World
Melt with me!

Brad R   8/6/11

"When Evil rises..."

OLD FRIENDS

Chapter 1

Sunday morning...

It was 10:00 a.m. and all who were going to Church had gone, while those who weren't, namely - Janie Dugan, lay in her front yard, observing herself and the entire neighborhood...melt.

IT'S MELTING, MY HOUSE IS MELTING!
Her face grew long, her mouth dropped in slow motion. The bottom lids of her eyes were stretched; pulled down by some unseen force. There was an uncompromising grip tugging at her jaw and forehead, pulling her skin to the back of her skull.

She filled with panic and dropped to her knees. The house in front of her, her house, was no longer solid. The concrete, stucco and wood, all sagged and stretched out of place. Whatever was happening to her was happening to everything.

The roof ran in sludge-like drips over the wood siding. The chimney bricks liquefied and oozed into each other. The windows and doorway, the mailbox on the wall, flowerpots and rain gutters were all dripping...melting. Everything, everywhere, wavered in a wall of clear and rippling gas.

Janie's brain exploded in screams, echoes in her head. *It's melting. My house is melting!* But no voice came to her mouth. The fears devouring her could only be found in her eyes, eyes that grew wide as her mind spiraled out of control. She was victimized by complete incomprehension and disbelief as she watched her house pooling up like melted ice cream.

In an attempt to crawl to the door, she found that moving her arms and legs was as arduous as lifting dead weight.

She tried rocking herself, to roll over, accomplishing no more than teetering back and forth like a bug flipped belly up.

Her dissipating condition would only allow her to stretch, then fall. She tried again to scream, only causing a puddle of saliva to form in the back of her throat and she gagged.

As her stomach came up on her, before she could swallow it down, the burning lumps of acid singed the base of her tongue with a vile taste.

Drained of all energy, she rolled to her side and lay like a quadriplegic fallen from a wheelchair. She was terrified and unable to move, waiting to die...or worse. But as she watched her house transform, she noticed, though it seemed to be melting, it never dissolved. It never became a puddle on the ground. It swirled and revolved continually, but never came down.

The weight of her body was heavy like lead, persisting to stretch and fall as gravity kept sucking her over.

"Uuuugghh!" exertion burst from her in anguished moans, while her mind flashed with images of her life:

She saw herself, seven years old, deciding after washing her pet Guinea Pig, *Blitzen*, that the quickest, easiest way to dry him off would be in the microwave. She would never forget watching her little pet puff up like a bag of popcorn, lumping out in all directions, with bulging eyes, until finally exploding with guts and glory right in front of her.

He popped so hard his head slammed the door and snapped the latch open. Red and yellow ooze had mixed with patches of fur and dripped from the edge to the counter.

All the houses in the neighborhood flipped upside down as Janie looked over the top of her head. Her neck was arched in the middle, her throat was stuck in the air, and all the houses were melting. The few cars in the driveways were melting. Her body was like a slab of rubber left in the desert sun on a barren highway, and no sign of rescue.

Then...with the impact of an unexpected slap in the face...as if a light suddenly came on, something thumped her on her lower forehead, near her left eye, and she could move again.

The sky is blue, she thought. Her body dropped. Her neck relaxed. Her face looked up directly into smooth blueness.

"The sky is clear and blue," she said out loud. Her voice rang alone in the stillness, "I can talk." Immediately she tried moving her arms and legs...no problem. *Thanks for the oil can, Dorothy. I can move again.* As rejuvenated as the Tin Man in 'The Wizard of Oz,' she could move like nothing had ever happened.

Rolling over, onto her hands and knees, the vision of melting houses burned in her mind. But when she lifted her head and opened her eyes, there, like before, it was a beautiful Sunday morning on Fable Street.

Was this her punishment from God for being the *only* one in the neighborhood not to attend Church that morning? Then, something (confirmation perhaps) ran into her eye from where she'd been thumped. When she wiped at it she thought it felt too thick to be blood, and when she took her hand back to look at it, she found herself staring at a gray and white lump of gooey bird droppings.

Her stomach turned and started back up, but she was quick to hang her head and take several deep breaths. Sweat beaded profusely and rolled down her face until the nausea subsided.

"What do you want, God?" her eyes rolled. "What did I do to deserve this?" she spat out the words in short, jerky gasps. "Whatever it is you think I did, God, I didn't do it!" and she stretched the end of her sleeve over her palm to finish wiping her eye.

What the hell was that? The question buzzed in her brain like loud radio static. *Did I have a Stroke, and now I get to up and walk away as if it never happened?*

She got to her feet. *No way, I couldn't stand if it was a Stroke.* Slow and cautious, she walked to the house. *I went to get the paper and...Bamm! The world spun upside down and my house melted. I didn't black out. I didn't suddenly go delusional. There are no major fires in the neighborhood. The temperature is not 200 degrees. No nuclear explosions anywhere that I know of.* She stared wide-eyed through the cosmos, searching for rationalization, but nothing came to her. *So what the hell? Was it just in my head?* she shuddered. *What the hell is wrong with me?*

There was the chill factor; she was frightened that something might seriously be wrong with *her*, not the neighborhood.

Back inside, "Dear God," she sniffed, "what if I've got a Brain tumor? What if I missed those early warning signs you're supposed to look for, and these are the final stages? What if I only have two weeks to live?" She stumbled in a panic through her brown and yellow wooden-duck-infested kitchen, to the wicker dining table. She fell into a chair and cried her own personal waterfall of tears.

With her head in her arms, she felt the soiled sleeve of her top squish against her. Pursing her lips into a scowl, and with large tears rolling down her cheeks, she jerked up, snatched her top over her head and threw it to the floor.

Like a statue, she sat alone and quiet in her agony. Until, eventually, she fell back into her sobbing.

The fear of possible near death future made her realize how lonely she'd become. She wanted to hold somebody, but there was no one there for her.

Her husband, Davis, had left her. They had no children. Her parents were virtually unavailable, living on a Yacht at sea, communication accessible only through emergency CB radio. His parents no longer spoke to her. He had told them how she cheated on him. How he decided to surprise her at work one day; showing up for lunch, only to find her in the managers office taking dictation, without a pen, without paper, and in his lap. Her blouse was open and her bra was off (his hands were her support). She was rocking back and forth, grunting between commands, "Faster, Uh!" Her cheeks were flushed, "Harder, Uh!" Sweat glazed her golden skin, "Deeper, Uh...Uh!" In walks Davis, *Surprise!*

The only thing at that moment that kept him from total devastation was, at least with him she didn't have to moan directions. Though, later he realized, with him...she never moaned at all.

"I have no one," she announced to her ducks. Her trickling tears became rivers. "I'm twenty-six years old, completely alone, and I'm dying." Her head filled with a collage of memories - visions of old friends, good friends, and her best friend when she was sixteen, Krys Sanders.

Janie and Krys; if there was trouble to be found, they'd find it. They did everything together - movies, McDonalds, boy watching. And Shawna, how could she forget Shawna Taylor, always the three of them for boy watching. Though Janie already had 'her own' boy.

There was a time (ten years before) when all Janie had to do was snap her fingers and Davis would come running.

Davis also had two best friends, Billy and Jeff. They weren't romantically linked with Krys and Shawna, but the guys liked the girls well enough, mostly because they played a decent game of softball.

But usually when Janie snapped, Davis ran – and Krys, Shawna, Billy and Jeff would all generally follow. They called themselves 'The Brat Pack of Pleasure View South Side.' Their parents conceded it was an accurate title.

Janie hated herself for what she'd done. Her lust had simply overpowered her desire to be faithful to a drowning marriage. Jason Hartman, her supervisor, was hard for her to look at without lusting after. He worked out at the spa and (she joked to herself) *he was lean, mean, and she wanted him in between.*

He worked out on lunches and three nights a week. Janie did lunch at the same time and would go to watch. She even followed after work sometimes...just to watch.

She would tell Davis she had paperwork to do, or needed to go shopping. Once, she actually had the nerve to say she was visiting a sick friend.

Then, as fate would have it, the first time she ever really cheated, she got caught.

She still couldn't believe she let herself lose control like that. It had been a very hot day, his shirt was open to avoid perspiration stains, and there he sat with pecks and biceps bulging through a thin athletic T-shirt.

Janie and Davis had had problems in the bedroom for over a year, and by that time she just didn't care anymore. She cut loose like a kid in a candy store. She closed the door and told him she wanted him.

When he looked up, she had already unbuttoned her blouse. His marriage was also rocky, he was just as hot as she was, and *damn it*...the mood hit them both at the same time. "So, come and get me," he say's.

Now why Davis picked that day to surprise her, showing up to take her to lunch, she'd never know. *He never did shit like that!* But then neither did she. So, all she could figure was that...*damn it*, it was just one of those days.

"Oh God, what did I do, I've ruined everything," Janie wept hard, her mind speared by the thought of her wickedness.

"I need somebody," she cried. "I don't have any..." she stopped, "Krys!" She'd been thinking about her for the past several weeks, *why not call her?* She'd only seen her a handful of times since she and Davis moved from Kentucky to Florida five years before.

They hadn't been married even six months when 'Red Engine,' the auto-garage Davis worked for suddenly had lay-offs. And him being the low man on the proverbial totem pole was the first to be let go.

Fortunately, his Uncle, Jesse (who owned and operated 'Jesse's Garage'), needed a fulltime person. Unfortunately, it *wasn't* located right there in Pleasure View, where he and Janie had been born and raised. It was in Destin, Florida. The move was hard, but necessary for the work.

So they packed up their meager belongings, met Krys and the gang at Pizza Hut for a last pizza jamming, beer slamming goodbye party (after which, Shawna tossed her pepperonis), and they hit the road.

The urge to call had been growing for weeks, and if ever there was a right time, this was it. She knew Krys would understand her loneliness. *Sometimes old friends simply lose touch. And sometimes you just need them back again.*

Janie relaxed a bit. It made her feel better just to be thinking about the phone call, "Gosh, I miss her," she sniffed.

Janie had no idea 'her old friend' would be the one to clue her in about her destiny with bizarre melting experiences.

Chapter 2

*N*o, *that's too close together*. Krystal Sanders stared at the setting of her eyes, reflecting back from the mirror, completely focused on even the slightest changes. *Come on, you can do it...spread that nose a little*.

Krys sat cross-legged and naked on her bed, only the flow of her waist-length chocolate brown hair served as any kind of cover.

The room, connected at the back of her basement, was dark, lit only with candle flames. She'd inherited the house by virtue of paying the second mortgage on it since the death of her parents two years before in an automobile accident.

She sat comfortably on a shimmering black sheet of satin that disappeared to the floor in the shadows beneath her. The upper walls, the ceiling, and a small covered window were all that came to light in the dancing flames.

The tiny window was in the top right corner of the room. Outside, that window was at ground level in the backyard. The glass in it had been tinted for a couple of reasons - one, so sunlight wouldn't come glaring in on her. And another; with the curtains closed, it was foolproof against possible exposure of private activities if someone tried to peep in.

The little candle-lit bedroom was her favorite room in the house; of course most endeavors that took place there involved boys. However, lately, Krys was discovering something else in that room, something

9

more personal and a bit freakish about herself, and she wasn't quite ready to share it with anyone yet.

Recently, she had stumbled upon the fact that she possessed some sort of supernatural power. And like a cat, curiosity was taking her to the edge. "Experimentation! It's the only way to know for sure," was her motto.

With a delicate squeeze on the handle of a mirror, she watched with deep concentration, like a good mad scientist, as suddenly, a grip of knotting muscles rippled through her like steel wire being coiled in a machine. Feeling the power she was trying to control, she glared at her reflection.

"Move," she ordered. And with an anxious tingling, her eyes actually began to reshape.

Slowly, they adjusted away from each other, sliding to the edges of her face, widening the bridge of her nose, "Ok...stop," she commanded. But she hadn't let up on the concentration. *"Stop!"* she shouted. And like releasing stretched rubber, they stopped and snapped back to their original form.

Her face was her own again. Her eyes returned to their designated places. She stared into the mirror and smiled for a solid minute, until eventually confessing out loud, "I have control."

Catching a glimpse of her left nipple in the mirror, she was reminded of her nakedness. She noticed beads of sweat rolling down her breasts; she was hot, surrounded by candle flames. Her chest lifted in small heaves with her breathing, "I have control," she repeated. The potential of power and opportunity quickly swept through her imagination, "I can shape things with my mind." Suddenly aware of the limitless possibilities she had access to, she looked at her breasts...smiled again...and commanded them to..."*Grow!*"

Her eyes widened, her hot face glowed red. Her insides filled with warm vibration. Her nipples ignited with an electrical charge and became erect, standing hard at attention as if to salute the day.

A surge of heat raced through her muscles. The kind of heat you feel coming in from a snowy outdoors and stepping up to a burning fireplace. Her blood boiled, she glistened with running sweat and her breasts began to...grow*!*

The burning wrapped around her ribs and filled her stomach. Vibrations raced small streams of blood bubbles through her like the fizz of Champagne.

She fought losing consciousness, enjoying the convulsing explosions of heat that reshaped her. Her blood pulsed faster, keeping time with the scattered bulges. Each burst sent a tiny shock wave of electricity, a spearing sting straight to the tips of her nipples. If a drop of sweat happened along, it would sizzle there until it burned itself away.

She watched, mesmerized, as a life-long dream materialized right before her eyes. *This is amazing.* Her pounding muscles beat like a drum. The 'growing' was erotic. "Mmmmm," she purred.

Suddenly, she saw her breasts leaving the Madonna category and racing towards Dolly Parton, *"STOP THERE!!"* she cried. And just before the next explosion, they stopped. Just like that. As quickly as it all began, it ended. Only this time...the rubber-like stretching stayed. There was no snapping back. She stared at her reflection with open mouth, slowly looking down at her perspiring body.

Nervous, she lifted a hand to touch herself. She wrapped her fingers around one breast, pinching her nipple between her thumb and index finger, and gently squeezed. "It's real," her voice was a whisper of shock.

It was true, the once semi-flat-chested, 'no brassiere necessary' girl sitting in the middle of her bed, now had D cup breasts.

The room was quiet, except for her own heavy erratic breathing, crashing in her ears. *This is a miracle.*

She was attacked with all the thoughts and emotions of reality and delusion, the morals of right and wrong, the questions of magic and good and evil, and the condemnation *and* pride of her actions. A thousand screaming voices raced through her head - sitting alone in her fiery little room. "This is unbelievable," she sighed, "and I can control it."

Excited, about to shout, 'I have to tell somebody,' she was suddenly struck with fear. *I can't tell anybody. They'll think I'm crazy (which I might be), or they'll want to use me for some sort of lab experiment.*

Suddenly afraid, for no logical reason, she laid the mirror on the nightstand, got up and blew out the candles. When the last flame died, she stepped into the downstairs living room and closed the door behind her.

Bugs Bunny and Yosemite Sam squabbled softly on the television. The TV was the one roommate Krys could shut up whenever she wanted, or turn on if she was lonely.

She leaned against the door, still trying to neutralize her breathing, "This is incredible. My boobs are beautiful." But the smile of adoration faded to confusion and ultimately the key question - *Why didn't they go back to normal?*

Slick with sweat, she peeled her body from the door, took her coffee from the end table, sipped it, and went upstairs. Still nude, she passionately fondled her newly developed chest, until eventually convincing herself they *were* real, and they were there to stay.

* * *

The tag said 'Laura Gayle,' it was the only tag she missed tearing off in the dressing room at Wal-Mart. Realizing her tops and blouses no longer fit, Krys threw on a lightweight overcoat, grabbed her purse and went shopping.

Being naked beneath the coat was not uncommon for her, she hated the confinement of clothing and would shed them whenever possible. Being an admitted exhibitionist, things like that were just daring outlets of excitement for her. Flat-chested or not, she enjoyed her sexuality and the sensuality of just being naked.

Finally reaching the front of the checkout line, she laid down a handful of price labels. "Here are all the tags."

The sales lady; a short, white haired old woman, near blind with bottle-bottom spectacles, looked confused, "Tags for what?"

Krys looked up, "Excuse me?"

"I said," the old woman scowled, "tags for what? What are the tags for?"

Krys was momentarily dumbstruck, her thought was, *Why the clothes that I'm wearing, of course. I realize you're an extremely old and most likely blind woman, but you must be able to detect that the clothes I'm wearing* are new.

But then the old woman would want to know where the clothes were that she wore into the store. And that would not be as easily explained.

Well, you see, this morning my boobs grew several sizes and I simply couldn't find anything to wear. So...I wore nothing.

"Ma'am where are the clothes these tags came off of?" And there it was, the moment of confrontation. Krys tensed, a drop of sweat rolled from her temple. The clerk, who'd started out the day already annoyed, was now agitated, "Look, young lady, just because I'm old, don't mean I'm senile."

Krys had hoped it would be obvious enough that what she was wearing came off the rack, "These clothes," she waved her hands down her body. "The ones I have on. That's what the tags are for." She stared into the old woman's face, looking for a sign of comprehension. Nothing. So she enunciated, speaking slow and clear, making sure she wasn't misunderstood, "I'm buying the clothes that I'm wearing."

The agitated clerk looked her up and down with disapproval, "Well where's the clothes ya wore when ya come in the store?"

Krys burned with the heat of embarrassment. She was amazed the white haired old hag would take the time to stand there and grill her in front of a line of hot and restless onlookers.

Then, under her breath, and between her teeth...she lied, "Lady, I lost all my clothes in a fire. All I had left was this coat. I wore it down here to get some new clothes. Is that all right with you?" her tone burned with hate.

"Look girlie, I don't care if ya wanna buy new clothes or not, but are ya telling me you came into this store *naked*? Just wearing a coat? Stark naked under your coat?" the old woman questioned, "*Naked naked*?"

Now the entire line had stopped shuffling. The song on the muzak station had ended, and most of the men were all but tearing her clothes off her with their eyes.

Krys was red and hot. She plunged into her coat pocket, pulled out a one hundred dollar bill and stuck it in the woman's face, "I hope you choke on those tags," she hissed. "Keep the change," she added, and turned and left the store.

The old woman's face was a mask of surprise, "What'd I say?"

*   *   *

Rolling down the five-mile stretch of Lancaster Lane, the car weaved as Krys reached behind herself, grabbing and scratching, fighting to yank one last tag from the back of her sweater. It had been digging into the flesh, just out of reach, between her shoulder blades.

"Aaagghh, I'm gonna get mad in a minute." Then two fingernails clamped onto it, gripped like a vice, and with a jerk, she tore it out. Of course, she slammed her hand on the car roof along the way.

"Ouch," she cried and dropped the tag, snapping her hand to her lap to cradle the pain. She cursed and stuck her knuckles in her mouth to sooth the throbbing.

"I had no idea buying clothes for bigger boobs could be so aggravating," that made her smile. Soon she was amused by the whole situation and laughing out loud, "I can't believe I literally outgrew my clothes. I finally have breasts."

But she had questions that still had no answers. *How did I do it?* Confusion clutched her emotions and squeezed. Little good and evil ghosts flew in one ear, across her mind, and out the other. She was feeling the edge between rapture and fear of the unknown. *Is it wrong? It doesn't feel wrong. It feels good.* She pulled her shoulders back and stuck out her chest, elated with power, she pushed the gas pedal to the floorboard and decided not to think about it anymore.

"Radio time," *Click!*

Prince was on, inducing sex, when Krys leaned back and noticed the bottom of the steering wheel disappear beneath her new, mystically produced and larger than ever...body alterations. And finally, no longer able to contain herself, she arched her back in a stretch, quickly riveted her eyes to the highway, and while one hand held the steering wheel, the other reached beneath her sweater to feel her new...*self.*

"This is so good. I am definitely going to enjoy these."

She came to the Lakeside Highway turn off, and time to make a decision. Lancaster Lane was a nice straight line to home, if she stayed on it she'd be there in ten minutes. But if she took Lakeside, she could cruise the country a bit and be home in twenty. This was always a rough decision, she loved the scenery on Lakeside; and she was feeling good, not in any particular hurry to get anywhere.

"Let's take the highway." She spun the wheel hard right with one finger, and turned up the radio two more notches. *Cruise time.*

Lakeside Highway (Hwy 90) was beautiful. It ran along a one-mile stretch of Marble Rock Lake, then into a small forest of trees, very green and very tall. It was a strip of road that the sun rose from one end and set on the other.

Beyond the trees lie what used to be acres of unused fields of grass. Now it was the giant black asphalt parking lot of the 'Xanorse' chemical plant. A huge ugly cold gray concrete structure that stood right in the middle of nowhere.

But at the moment...

...The wind was flipping her hair, it felt good, and the lake was beautiful. She slowed down to enjoy the view, "Man, it's pretty out here." The sun's glitter on the water sparkled in her eyes. If she squinted she could see a rainbow.

The highway stretched out long and straight in front of her. Soon she was staring at the lake more than watching her driving, until, even when she did look back at the road, the vision of the water remained in her mind; it stayed alive in her eyes.

This is odd, she thought, *I see the road and the front of the car, but it's like looking through a ghostly image of the lake. Huh...too bizarre.* Soon the road became clearer and the lake faded to traces of water ripples running through the windshield. Running.......and running.......and.......running.

The forest was coming up when she realized the ripples were more than just a thought, and not going away. In fact, it was getting thicker in its continual movement. Suddenly, streaking like a spear of ice through her veins, panic struck. *Reality check. The windshield is melting.* "Oh no, not now," she begged. "Oh, please not now." Krys hadn't experienced an *uncontrolled* melting in over a week, and with naïve dismissal, she'd hoped they'd gone away.

"I have control," she told herself. "I can stop this," her voice trembled. "I say stop." The ripples were flowing heavy and persistent now. "I said STOP!" The whole car turned soft and oozy. *"STOP NOW!!"* No use, it's not letting up. The windshield began running down over the radio, the tires bled into the highway. Everything went into meltdown mode.

Trees became giant fountains of green, the pavement ahead was a black pool of liquid asphalt and she was sliding into it. *Krys, get a grip, you know it's all in your head. If you can stay fixed on the center of the road, you've got a fifty/fifty chance to shake it off.* She hated accepting the fact that she had no choice in the matter.

Her body tightened and became very hot. She couldn't move her foot to the brake pedal. She couldn't lift her arms to turn the steering wheel. She felt her face stretch and her eyes pull down her cheeks. Her mouth tugged open; her bottom lip stretched away from her teeth.

Then a new horror struck. Her brand new and improved bosom stretched down and rested in her lap. This pissed her off. Nobody was going to mess with her new boobs. *I have control,* she thought. She directed every ounce of concentration on the road. *I can see the white line. I'll stay fixed to that and hope no one's coming the other way.*

The radio dripped with an obscure little tune called 'Dry County' by *the B-52's.* The words to the song formed in slabs of hot street tar that were melting and flinging themselves like mud onto the windshield. They came at her face and splattered on the glass. But she maintained concentration and stayed close to the dashing white lines.

In the corner of her eyes she could see the trees, tall and green, with branches smothered in melting leaves. They formed pools of dripping sap that flowed into itself and swirled with a constant blend.

She strained to looked away from the road for a moment, just long enough to see the green tree melt reshaping itself and taking on a form. The manifestation was quickly identifiable as a bubbling mass in the shape of a human body. *Oh God!* The spear of ice pierced again. *That's* my *body! My new body!*

The pools had become large bubbling replica's of her own figure, from her firm and round 'behind,' to the nipples of her new breasts.

One tree after another turned to the oozy melt. Not just two or three, or even ten, but a hundred or more. Then she noticed the swirling mass leaning in toward her. A hundred green breasts all floating in at her from the side of the road.

A highway of boobs, she thought. If it hadn't been so frightening, it would have been funny. But as one momentary reality followed another, panic took on new dimensions. She suddenly remembered needing to try and stay on the road. *The road!* She thought, but when her eyes tried shifting back, they would barely move. It was like pulling two lead boulders up a hill.

The move took forever. *I'm gonna die. Come on eyes.* Eventually, she strained them back into position and found the strip of white lines. *All right, there it is, stay on it.*

But the instant she locked into the guiding stroke marks, they became animated and peeled up at her from the blacktop. They rose from the surface of the road and then fell. The way goop in a lava lamp boils and stretches upward, only to drop back to the bottom. *Stay with them,* she thought. *Keep the car in line.* She imagined she was using telepathic control, and at that point wasn't questioning anything that worked.

The end of the forest approached, the once full-breasted trees were now simply waterfalls of green, running into a thick and gurgling river. *Thank God. At least I'll make it out of the forest alive. Maybe when I get to the Xanorse parking lot, I can run off the road without getting hurt too badly.*

Then she remembered 'Short Cut'. This was the road so named for the purpose it had served its whole life. Short Cut was a road that actually divided the Xanorse Chemical Company parking lot from the wall of trees at the forest line. It was once just a strip of dirt at the edge of a field. But now, it was paved and ran alongside a parking lot. *Ok, time to shift brainpower into warp drive.* In her mind she smiled, *At least I haven't lost my sense of humor.*

The tree falls were coming to an end and Krys was hell bent on turning. Her left arm was full with tension, but no muscle or coordination. She tried pulling down on the steering wheel with it - which wasn't *nearly* as hard as her *right* hand trying to push up on the other side. She couldn't believe how difficult this normal simple movement could be. Still...she *was* making it work.

As Short Cut came upon her, she put everything she had into the turn. The car slid but kept going, she was actually doing pretty good. Then the tires locked into a jerking slide and charged onto the road with a skid. At that angle, by the time the back tires came around, the G-force had seized the car and sent it spinning, 35 mph right back at the trees. *Goodbye cruel world.* Krys watched her life flash by just before she hit. Then, everything went black.

She stared into the blackness long enough to stabilize her breathing. Then she opened her eyes.

The roof needs re-upholstering. She laid on her back across the front seat, staring at the inside roof of the car, "I'm alive."

It was true, it was over and she lived through it one more time. The car was at the foot of the tree it had slammed into. She was okay, the sun was still shining, and as far as she knew, it was still Sunday.

Sweat dripped from her face. Her stomach suggested a momentary run for the border, but she quickly pushed that thought away.

Trembling with shock quivers from the body slamming she took, she pulled herself up by the steering wheel. A shining glare of light stabbed her eyes. *Thank you, Mr. Sun. I guess my favorite thing next to being melted, is being blinded.*

She slapped the visor down, threw her head back and took a few deep breaths. After a short time of meditation, she sat up straight, put the gearshift back to neutral and turned the key. With two sets of crossed fingers and held breath, the car fired up. *Oh thank you, thank you, thank you.* She tingled with relief and let herself collapse onto the steering wheel. A few more deep breath's later, and after regaining full consciousness, she nervously reached down to check her current breast size...good to go! "Oh thank you God. You must like them too."

The door creaked open as Krys dragged herself in the house. Slightly dazed and confused, she stumbled to the sofa and flopped. "I need a glass of wine," she announced to the room. But before she could take action, the phone rang, *Yes! Reality!*

She grabbed the phone before the third ring, "Hello?"

The familiar voice on the other end was truly welcome, "Hi, Krys? It's Janie. How are you doing?"

Chapter 3

"**W**ho's that?"

Kate Green, 2nd shift Head Nurse at Pleasure view Memorial Hospital, was getting the low down on the day's activities, when she looked up and saw a young man rounding the corner from the elevator to the main hall.

"That's Billy Dunes, a friend of the 'Basket Case' in 12-B, the one who gets his eyes lubed every hour," Maxi answered.

Maxi Lynn and Kate were the 1st and 2nd shift Head Nurses of the 4th floor. The 4th floor, more commonly referred to by those *inside* as the Einstein Department, and by those *outside* as the Loony Bin, was the Mental Health Ward of that particular medical facility. Jeff Blake, an old buddy of Davis Dugan and Billy Dunes, had recently taken residency in a room halfway down Corridor B.

"Oh yeah, the guy in 12-B, his name is Blake...something, right?" Kate asked, and chomped a lump of chewy, pink bubble gum.

"Yeah, Jeff Blake," Maxi responded unconsciously while checking off her duties from the day's roster, then she blew her own gum to a bubble.

Kate and Maxi could have been split from the same atom. They grew up best friends in the San Fernando Valley in California. They were both 28 years old, and both dying of boredom. So, desperately, urgently, trying to 'find themselves,' they packed up all their cares and woes, and headed south.

They had trained as nurses, and after six dozen applications, and a lot of Résumé pushing, 2,000 miles later, in Kentucky, they both found positions in the same hospital.

With only one car between them, they moved into a small apartment behind the hospital; where work was only a short walking distance. It was a nice, well-kept place, and several other nurses lived in the same complex. Maxi and Kate enjoyed it, and had no more compelling notions to move. Not to mention; working opposite shifts of each other, whoever was home, was usually home alone and had all the privacy they needed.

"You know that Billy Dunes is pretty cute - too bad about his friend," Kate said, and blew a big pink bubble. Maxi looked up in time to see it bust and smack back on her lips.

* * *

Billy turned another corner, walking swiftly past the pastel pink and concrete gray color scheme of corridor B, to Jeff's room. He looked ahead and spotted the number 12 on Jeff's door ten feet away. Suddenly, unexpectedly, as some reminder of an experience he'd had earlier that morning; the hallway, in one smooth motion, stretched out in front of him.

As if someone had grabbed the wall at the end of the walkway, like the pocket of a slingshot, and pulled it back - with both sidewalls cooperating as the stretching bands.

"Oh, not now, not here." Billy felt sick, he reached out to brace himself as he stumbled forward. Then, like a train barreling down a track, the wide pink stripe on the wall came shooting past his face. The slingshot had been turned loose and was snapping back.

Just a helpless bug in the sites of an oncoming circumstance, he watched the back wall race toward him like the bottom of someone's shoe about to splatter his entire being. His eyes stretched wide open.

There was no time to look for escape. But then, just before it hit...it stopped. Right where it should have, just where it belonged, where it most likely never left, at the end of the hallway.

Upon the instant return to reality, Billy found himself on his back. Obviously, he had fallen and rolled, and was now staring straight up at Jeff's number 12, "Oh Jesus, Jeff, I hope they figure out what's wrong with you, before it happens to me," he groaned.

Billy opened the door and slowly stuck his head in, "Jeff?" The room was dark, with only slices of outside light splicing through the mini-blinds. He could see Jeff crouched in the corner of his bed, "Jeff, it's me, Billy, I'm going to turn the light on." He didn't know if he was giving a warning or asking permission, but he paused and waited for a response. Even a moan would have helped comfort the decision. *Yes? ...No?* Nothing. *Well, here goes.* He switched the light on.

"Duuhhlleh Huuulp Mah," Jeff wrenched his neck around to see his friend. Billy was startled that Jeff hadn't changed at all. He was the same as two days ago when he'd brought him in. Only, two days ago he didn't know what was happening to him, now he did.

Billy had his own first melting experience that morning while fixing coffee. In the end, it left him sure he'd be sweeping up grounds from the kitchen floor for the next two weeks. And just now, he'd had a second, milder version out in the corridor.

"Jeff," Billy's heart went out to his friend; locked in that state of terror and helplessness, "does it look like everything is melting?" Jeff looked sad and scared. His eyes were huge, spreading way out of proportion. The lids were being sucked up into his brows. The skin over his cheekbones stretched down as tight as a drum. His whole face pulled apart, his neck had a grip on his chin and tugged at his bottom lip, exposing red tearing gums covered with drooling saliva.

"Duuuhhlleh," he had to push his tongue against the roof of his mouth to try for a B sound, which was actually more of a D sound. Fear swam vicious, jagged circles in his head, but his mouth wouldn't release a cry for help.

Billy walked in and closed the door behind him, "Jeff, I know what's happening to you." Jeff could barely function, every move he made took all his strength, and then he would ease back, gasping, exhausted and breathless.

Billy sat on the edge of the bed, "It happened to me this morning. I went through what you're going through right now." He stared in silence; he couldn't believe what he was looking at.

"It looks like everything's melting, doesn't it? Only it doesn't go anywhere, it just swirls in one place." He continued staring, scared for his friend. "Jeff," Billy was close to tears, "I came out of it. I know you can too."

Jeff slowly rolled his eyes to look more directly at him.

Suddenly, Billy was sucked back to the door, like a giant vacuum had gotten him.

"Duuuhhlleh," Jeff choked.

A long thick string of drool spilled from his mouth and landed in the ever-increasing stain of wetness covering the front of his 4th floor issued Pj's. Panic struck hard with pins and needles as the gray and white matter of his brain went haywire again.

The end of the bed turned up at him, stretching tall and wide. Then it curled over so the tiny legs that were once on the bottom were now on top, glaring down as two sinister metal eyes, glowing. The edge of the bed itself reshaped to form a giant smiling mouth, a hungry mouth ready to eat something.

"Duuuhhlleh."

Then, like hot wax, it all melted down and went back to its original shape. Jeff looked toward the door for Billy; only there was no door.

What he saw was a long green hallway with a spot of darkness at the end, a small black dot too far away to make out. But, as he stared, he realized it was moving toward him.

That's not right. Wait a minute, he thought, *is it getting closer? Or is it just getting bigger?* Whatever the something was, it was growing right in front of him...very fast.

The dot started forming, the hallway got shorter. *That's not a hallway,* he reasoned, *that's the door. The door that sucked Billy up just before the bed monster came.* He stopped just long enough to do the simple math, 2 and 2 equals...*Hey, that's Billy coming at me!* The door, it seemed, had taken Billy, then stretched back as far as Jeff's mind would let it go, and was now firing him forward in slingshot mode. *Oh No! We're going to splat,* "NOOOOO," he groaned harshly.

"Jeff, snap out of it," Billy said calmly - still sitting on the edge of the bed. Right where Jeff had left him. Jeff's eyes filled with tears when he registered the swirling image of his friend in front of him; realizing Billy had never really gone anywhere. "It'll be ok, you'll come out of it, I promise." Jeff tried pulling his eyes closed. No go. Helpless, he rested against the wall.

Jeez, what if he doesn't *come out of it.* Billy stared at the floor, slipping away with his thoughts; *Jeff was always the strong one.*

* * *

It was a hot lazy Friday night in July, when he was fifteen (Billy was fifteen, Jeff and Davis were sixteen), Davis rolled up to Jeff's house in his father's 1968 Emerald Green, Thunderbird Convertible.

The T-bird was John Dugan's pride and joy. Not a scratch on it, spit shine on the chrome, and waxed every six months. It was a rare occasion that anyone other than John Dugan would ever drive the T-bird, and on those blue moon moments, Davis and his mother were the only exceptions to even be considered.

Davis - because he really helped his father keep it in good running condition (and show room appearance), and Jennifer Dugan because, if he didn't let her, he'd be sleeping on the sofa for a week.

Once, their neighbor, Eddie Farmer (Eddie 'Farter' if you asked Davis or John. Or more commonly, 'The Farter Man') had the nerve to stick his head into the Dugan's garage while John was waxing 'The Green Machine,' and inform him that too much wax would cause a heavy build up and he'd lose the shine.

Davis, who was applying Armor All to the matching, Emerald Green, leather interior at the time, looked up to see 'The Farter Man,' with his triple roll gut hanging out four inches below an old faded Led Zeppelin T-shirt.

"No shit, Sherlock," John declared. "You have any other brainstorms today?"

Davis grinned, neither him or his dad liked Eddie Farmer, and John Dugan was the sort of man to let you know what he thought about you right up front. Eddie knew how the Dugan's felt about him, but every once in awhile he was overcome with an urge to stick his two cents in. John said Eddie had a sick and masochistic desire to be humiliated, and since Eddie insisted on annoying him, he was more than happy to oblige. He would ridicule him at any and every opportunity. Eddie would shrug (the incomprehensive shrug of an idiot), turn and walk away, sucking on a beer bottle.

But, regardless of whether it was 'The Farter Man' or 'The Pope,' John Dugan didn't like anybody telling him what he should or shouldn't do with his T-bird.

"Hey Billy, where's Jeff?" Davis yelled from the drivers seat.

"He's taking a dump." Billy was stretched out on the grass in front of Jeff's house when he heard the horn blowing all the way down the street. He sat up to watch the stylish green convertible (with top down) pull into the driveway. Jeff had also been stretched out and waiting, until an uncontrollable force attacked and he sprang up, racing to the house, grabbing his ass, screaming "Oh shit! I gotta shit!"

Billy smiled in amazement, "How'd you get your old man's car?" Davis tipped his head back and slid his sunglasses down over his eyes, "I told him we were going to check out the car show in Charlestown, and how cool it would be to show off the T-Bird."

"You are so full of it," Billy couldn't believe Davis's dad was that easy. Davis turned to face him, tugged down on the glasses and said, "Well, I promised I'd mow the lawn tomorrow too." They laughed.

"Davis, dude," Jeff was standing at the door, still tugging at the zipper of his fly, "you got the cruising machine, I don't believe it."

Davis laid on the horn and cranked up the radio volume, "Let's hit it, boys." Jeff flew across the yard, screaming *"Shotgun!"* He jumped the door and landed flat on his butt in the front seat. That was ok with Billy, he got in the back - it was enough for him just to have good friends like Davis and Jeff to pal around with.

Billy Joel's 'Its still rock-n-roll to me' blasted from the speakers, accompanied by the boy's vocal support. They tore down Ponders Lane, chugging from a not so carefully hidden, six-pack of Miller's Beer. Davis had an older cousin of his buy it for him. Davis always professed Miller's to be 'the best,' followed by, "And don't I deserve the best?"

Billy felt the beer quicker than his pals - one, because he rarely ever drank. And two, he was smaller and lighter than either of them. Though they were all close in age - in size, Davis and Jeff each pushed six-foot tall. Billy barely stretched to five,' nine".

This was only one of the many things the two older boys teased their young friend about. They both liked Billy a lot, and were never serious about it, but it was always convenient in making themselves look better, if they had someone around who was a little different, to pick on.

Billy also had thick blonde curly hair; and wasn't that always a good enough reason for a general five to ten minute harassment. Davis and Jeff, of course, had straight hair; Davis's was chocolate brown, Jeff's was jet black.

But the best teasing happened when Shawna (Krys and Janie's friend) was around. She was always a bit too obvious in her infatuation with the blonde young Billy.

If the girls happened to be talking about getting together with the boys, for whatever reason, Shawna would invariably ask, "Will Billy be there?" She'd say she was just making sure not to end up the odd 5th wheel. But Janie would mention it to Davis, and Jeff and Davis felt it expressed enough interest for them to give Billy grief about it.

They liked to refer to Shawna as Billy's 'girlfriend' ("Hey Billy, are we cruising without your *girlfriend?*" Or, "Billy, won't your *girlfriend* mind us hanging without her?" Billy didn't like any of it, and the worst was "Hey Billy, when you gotta piss, does Shawna hold it for you?")

The teasing sucked, but he never lost control, he knew they were kidding, and *he* knew *they* knew he really was not interested in Shawna. In fact, if he were to choose any of the three girls as a potential 'girlfriend,' he was much more attracted to Janie. She was calmer and more mature than the others (and she had a nice ass). But Janie was Davis's girl, so that little fantasy ended right there.

"Hey Billy, you want to pick up Shawna? There's plenty of room to stretch out back there," Jeff was being a jerk as he and Davis drank their beer. "Uh...Hey, Jeff," Billy retaliated, "you want to kiss my ass?" They all laughed.

Davis punched the gas and they shot down Ponders Lane, which would eventually meet Lakeside Highway. The houses grew farther apart as the landscape became more rural. They were getting further from 'the burbs' and more into the country.

Billy rocked with the radio, using the back of Jeff's seat as a drum, when he kicked something on the floorboard. He looked down, "Hey Davis, why'd you bring a baseball bat? If you want to play ball, it's gonna be dark soon."

Jeff looked over, "You didn't."

Davis had a smirk growing, "Billy, my boy, how'd you like to learn a new game?"

Jeff and Davis shot each other quick and wicked grins, Billy knew he was in trouble. But the smiles were contagious, and a nervous one spread slowly on *his* face, "What game?"

Davis looked directly at him from the rearview mirror, "We call it Mailbox Baseball."

The two in the front rolled with laughter. Billy's grin began to twitch, "What's Mailbox Baseball? ...How do you play?" he asked, knowing good and well he really wanted no part of a game that involved a baseball bat and...a mailbox.

The car slowed down, "Billy, ...Son," Jeff did his 'fatherly advice' impression, "you are about to learn one of the more notorious games that we, as young men, have the responsibility of surviving as tradition. It's not exactly baseball, it's not exactly vandalism, it's more...oh, a cross between the two...a happy medium you might say." Jeff stopped and looked Billy dead in the eyes, "If you'll hand me the bat, we can begin."

Billy grabbed the bat at the thick end and lifted it; Jeff took the neck and adjusted his grip, "Now pay attention," he instructed. Then just before he turned back in his seat, he looked real serious, reached out a hand to Billy's shoulder and added, "...And Billy, we want you to know, it is a privileged man who gets to learn this game in a convertible." With that, Jeff turned and stood up, one foot on the floorboard, one on the seat.

Suddenly, it was apparent to Billy what was going to happen. Twenty yards in front of them was a mailbox post at the side of a long driveway. Davis's foot pressed the gas, and he started chattering, "Hey batter, hey batter." For a short, absurd moment, Billy hoped deeply that they were kidding.

"Hey batter batter," the mailbox was now only a car length away.

"Come on guys, quit messing around," Billy's voice trembled as he tried to force out a small laugh.

...half a car,

Hope crumbled like a brick building under a wrecking ball.

...at the front fender,

"Jeff?"

"Hey batter,"

...right on it.

"Swing!"

Jeff swung full force. Billy watched with slack jaw as the little tin box crunched and tore loose, sailing across the yard like a large...baseball.

It flew through the air and smashed into a tree, a large Oak tree whose enormous size could easily claim ownership of the entire yard. In fact, it would have been difficult to *miss* the tree.

Billy had to admit it was a beautiful hit, the two older boys cheered triumphantly as the mailbox implanted itself between branches. "Once a mailbox, now a birdhouse," Davis announced.

"A home run!" Jeff shouted. "Was that beautiful or what?"

Davis and Jeff slammed beer cans together in a toast, dropped their heads back and guzzled.

For the new member of the team, however, as if the overpowering force of guilt didn't shake him up enough. Billy's stomach took an unsettling drop when he saw the bat coming over Jeff's shoulder at him. His body could not move to take it; he could only stare at it, terrified. Until his voice gained control and blurted...

"I can't believe you guys just destroyed someone's property like that."

Davis and Jeff looked back at him, their smiles faded. They hadn't considered that Billy might not find their little game amusing.

"I mean, you just drove up, beat the hell out of someone's mailbox, and drove off like you could care less how much money or trouble you just cost them," Billy kept a straight face, glancing back and forth at the two of them. "...And nobody even saw you do it."

Not knowing what to say, Davis and Jeff looked at each other, then back at Billy. "*Nobody* saw you do it." Suddenly, they were pleasantly surprised and relieved to see one of those big contagious shit-eating grins split across his face, "Give me the bat."

Davis choked on his beer; Jeff broke with laughter. Billy took the bat.

Fifty yards up the road was the next post, Davis slowed down so Billy could prepare. He stood up, one foot on the floorboard, one on the seat, and hoisted the bat into position.

"Ok, Billy boy, here it comes," Davis warned. They were moving up quicker now. Billy got himself psyched for it, he gripped the bat harder and gritted his teeth. Tense would have been an understatement for what he was feeling right then. All his muscles tightened.

"Hey batter batter, hey batter," Jeff did the chant. "Here it comes Billy, don't miss it," Davis yelled. There was a little red tin rooster on the side of the box, Billy fixed his sight on that and watched it race toward him. "Hey batter batter, hey batter," Jeff and Davis were both chattering between beer guzzles.

I better not miss this, Billy thought. And just that quick they were right on top of it.

"Hey batter swing!"

Billy had pulled back and swung like he was trying to kill something. A spray of sweat flew from his face, his arms cut through the air and the bat smacked the little tin rooster right in the belly.

Davis and Jeff were stunned as the mailbox left it's post and sailed like a rocket through the sky. A big lump of crunched metal flew into the blue yonder.

Billy watched, the way a golfer watches for his ball to fall from the heavens and land...hopefully someplace where he can see it.

"Truly amazing, Billy," Jeff was in awe. They watched the descent as it headed straight for the roof of the house. "Say, Davis," Jeff asked, "about how hard do you think that thing is going to hit?" Just then, and without hesitation, the box crashed with a loud thump, and skidded and bounced across the shingles.

"Davis?" Billy looked pale.

"Yeah?"

"Do you think we could get the hell out of here before someone comes out?"

Davis agreed, "Good idea," and he hit the gas. The car leapt forward, Billy was almost thrown out over the trunk.

Half a mile later, when they were sure they were out of sight of anyone who might have been watching, Jeff told Davis to slow down.

"I want to do another one."

Davis looked sideways at him.

"And then *I'll* drive and you can do one."

They downed the remainder of their beers and Billy handed the bat back, "We're going to end up in jail, you know," he mumbled.

"Look," Jeff's enthusiastic smile was full of excitement, "there's one coming. Slow down, let me get ready."

Davis had already eased up on the gas as Jeff took position. "Wait a minute," Billy pointed, "look."

At the house up ahead, who's landscape they were about to redesign, a woman stumbled through the front door. Not able to catch herself, she fell onto the short front porch. She was immediately followed out by the kick of a large foot and a man's hollering voice.

"Bitch, where's the rest of 'em?"

Davis slowed way down, to a crawl, trying to catch what was going on.

A large, stubble faced man with protruding beer gut was fighting his way through the front door, attempting to see how many bruises he could put on the woman.

"Hey," Davis's voice jumped, "that's old man Schuster and his wife."

Jeff looked closer; a wave of sadness rushed through him, then quickly turned to a volcano of anger. "Yeah, that's Donna Schuster all right, she comes over to visit my mom sometimes. Good looking woman..." he stopped to watch for a second before finishing, "but she's always got bruises...and cuts. She tells my mom it's from raising farm animals." They were all silent.

"I don't see any animals, do you?" Davis asked.

"Just that big ugly one coming through the door," Billy answered.

"I told you I wanted a *case*. I drank twelve last night, what am I supposed to do today?" He kicked her again, forcing her down the porch steps.

A nail sticking out a half an inch from the guardrail caught the inside fold of her elbow along the way, and cut into her. It ripped straight down the inside of her arm to her wrist. It wasn't a small nail either, and she wasn't just cut, she was ripped. Quick spurting blood streaked to her palm and off her fingertips.

"I told you to get a case, didn't I?" Gary Schuster ranted on. "I can't *believe* you only got twelve damn beers. I said..." he drew back for another kick, "...a fucking case!"

Thump!

You could hear his boot collide with her ribs from across the yard; she gasped for air as the breath was punched right out of her. Her arms flailed loosely in her stumble. Her clothes were soaking up an endless stream of blood.

Gary Schuster reached down with both hands and picked his wife up by her collar, then slammed her limp body against a large oak tree. Donna was going to scream, but when a small stumpy branch stuck itself into the back of her neck, her voice could no longer find its way out.

"Now get your sorry ass cleaned up," Schuster continued, "and get back to town, and get more beer. Before you *really* get hurt," and just as he was ready to leave her with one good punch for the road...

"Hey, Asshole," came a voice from behind.

Gary Schuster, amazed that anyone would have the nerve to interrupt him right in the middle of a good wife beating, turned around. One eye opened wide, the other half closed in a squint, and his face twisted in the most psychotic scowl he could muster up.

"Man, you are one ugly piece of shit."

There, only ten feet away, stood Jeff Blake, holding a baseball bat.

"Boy, you got just five seconds to turn your ass around and get the hell offa my property," Schuster seethed.

Jeff was shaking, but made no move to leave, "And if I don't?"

"Iffin ya don't," Schuster threatened, "I'm gonna break your scrawny body right in half. In fact, I'll probly just grab you at your asshole and start tearing till there's two of you. How's that sound?"

Jeff looked at Davis and Billy standing ten feet on the other side of him, they looked as nervous as he felt, but the ball was in his court. He looked back at old man Schuster. "Well," Jeff said, "I guess, since I ain't leaving, you dick sucking, dog shit-head mother fucker. You best get yourself to grabbing," and he raised the bat over his head.

Schuster was momentarily struck by the boy's audacity, then he filled with blind rage. Davis, Billy, and even Donna Schuster were all surprised at Jeff's courage (or stupidity, depending on the outcome).

"I'm gonna kill you, you little fuck," Schuster growled, and took a swing at him. Jeff backed up quick enough for him to miss, allowing the big Oaf to fall flat on his face.

"Come on, fat Ass. Get that lard belly up and fight like a man. Or do you only beat up on women?"

Thinking about what Donna probably had to go through every day of her life, made Jeff so angry, he worked himself into a frenzy; ready to kill.

"You little shit," Schuster huffed.

For a fat man, he was quick to get back on his feet. Glaring at the boy, he smoothly reached behind himself, and suddenly, when a pocketknife appeared, Davis lunged for the man. "Jeff, look out he's got a knife," he yelled, and jumped Schuster from behind. He had not quite anticipated the strength of the man's weight though, and with a flinging swing, Schuster sent Davis flying across the yard to land at Billy's feet.

"Stay out of it, Davis. I can handle this slimy turd." Jeff rocked and hopped back and forth with stimulated adrenaline.

"Boy, you have dug your own grave," Schuster said, and threw out a fist backed up with 300 pounds of fat. Jeff was caught off guard as the mountain of a man came right at him. And there was no time to get the bat up before..."Uuuooofff!"

Schuster landed right on top of him, knocking all his wind out. He grabbed the boy by the collar as he rolled off, took him over in a circle, slammed him down on the other side, "Uugghh!" and Jeff suddenly knew what it felt like to be a mailbox getting whacked.

Schuster got to his feet, ready to jump up and down on the boy, when Jeff rolled, took a deep breath and staggered back up.

'Jeff and Goliath' stared at each other; fire blazing in their eyes. Then, like a bear, Jeff stretched up tall and growled at the top of his lungs, and ran at the man, "AAHHGRRR!"

With the bat waving wildly over his head, he cried out and brought it down, catching Schuster before he could move, between his shoulder and his head. He thumped the old man at the inside of his neck and knocked him to the ground.

Davis and Billy cheered, *"Go Jeff."*

But Jeff forgot Schuster had a knife. And as he lie on the ground, the man reached out and grabbed the boy's leg at the ankle and yanked, Jeff went down.

With his knife in the other hand, Schuster reached out and buried the point right under the ball joint and sliced down through his shoe and across the bottom of his foot. The grass stained white tennis shoe filled with blood and turned bright red. Jeff howled a scream that neither, Davis or Billy, would ever forget.

"Gary, stop! Please!" Donna found courage enough to speak.

"I'm gonna kill the bastard," Schuster raged. "And then I'm gonna kill..."

Suddenly, in frozen disbelief, Gary Schuster watched, as Jeff, on his knees, took the bat back and brought it around, seemingly in slow motion, right at his face.

"...Oh shit..." was all he got out before the crack sounded and the ramrod of wood drove itself into his mouth. His jaw crunched and broke apart. The few teeth he'd managed to keep this far in life, shattered; flying gray and yellow stained ivory, sprayed like splinters across the yard. The pain was so unbearable, the fat man collapsed in an unconscious heap.

Jeff sat on the grass and stared at him, trying to catch his breath. There was a full minute of silence before he finally looked up at Donna, who'd been hiding behind the tree, with her arm wrapped in a piece of her skirt. Their eyes locked for another thirty seconds, and then *he* asked *her,* "...Are you ok?"

Billy remembered that was the last they ever saw of old man Schuster. It was right after that that Donna had him arrested for abuse with intent to kill. Then, word was, she packed up and went to live with a sister in Georgia.

And now, here was mister tough guy, Jeff Blake, his best friend...a vegetable in the Einstein Department at Pleasure View Memorial. Not able to swing a pencil, let alone a baseball bat. "Jesus, Jeff, what is happening to us?"

Chapter 4

The wind echoed in her ears, whipping through her strawberry blonde curls. She watched the reflecting glitter of the sun separate and scatter on the water, as the nose of her boat, 'Ladies Choice,' cut the stillness.

Marble Rock Lake was a favorite place for water-sports, or picnics, or just laying out to get a tan. On warm summer nights, at any given moment, you could easily find fifteen separate couples making out. Parked in cars or on a blanket beneath a tree. This would invariably result in *at least* one teenage pregnancy per winter.

Today, however, as for the little gold and lavender motorboat making its way from one end of the lake to the other (and back again), it was just two old friends out water skiing.

"I'm so glad you came back, Davis," Shawna said over her shoulder. "I really missed you when you and Janie moved to Florida."

Davis Dugan turned on the padded bench seat behind her, "I thought we weren't going to mention *her* name." She turned and smiled apologetically. He watched the dimples in her cheeks come to life.

"I'm sorry. It won't happen again," she promised.

He smiled back. *How beautiful she's become,* he thought. He couldn't believe he never saw it when they were younger. Their eyes locked for a moment, just to look. Then Shawna went back to her driving. Davis found himself watching her loose and silky curls blow in the wind.

As *Ladies Choice* headed into the horizon, there was only an hour left before the sun would set. Slowly, Shawna eased up on the gas and let the boat idle.

"You know, I forgot how beautiful this lake is," Davis said, relaxed and thoughtful. "Do you and Krys come here a lot?"

She turned off the motor so they could drift in the stillness. She picked up her drink (Captain Morgan's Spiced Rum and A & W Rootbeer, thank you) and went to sit next to him.

"Well...I tell ya," she said, "since Krystal and I bought this boat two years ago; during the summer, and as far into the fall as we can stand it, we practically live on this lake. In fact, if I hadn't put in a special request to have it alone today, she'd be here with us right now."

Shawna brought her glass up and drank. When she took it back down, the wetness on her lips glistened in the sunlight. Davis was captivated.

"I'm amazed, Shawna," he said. "I can't believe I never realized how beautiful you are."

She felt the blushing heat of self-consciousness, and smiled back. They'd been looking at each other for several hours by then, their eyes were full with anxious exploration - the shape of their mouths, their style of hair, the general maturity that had developed in their appearance.

The blood pumping in their hearts quickened. The electric tingle of desire raced through like liquid fire. Their lips hungered for the taste of each other, and it had been growing for the past two weeks; from the minute they reunited and laid eyes on each other. Then, after long deliberation about right or wrong, he leaned in and kissed her.

One hand went behind her head, the other around her back, and as he pulled her to him, they crushed into each other's arms for a full minute of passionately wet kisses, then slowly pulled apart.

"Mmmmm," Shawna practically purred, low and soft. The longing in their eyes and the wanting on their lips lingered for a snapshot moment. Until, they both suddenly felt wrapped in a blanket of confusion and guilt, not to mention having a big dose of good old-fashioned shyness.

Either way, it was the same feeling you get when you experiment with something dangerous or forbidden, and you find yourself attracted to the excitement.

They smiled bashfully and looked away, trying to hide from each other, yet unable to ignore the fire they'd just ignited. Eventually, they looked back.

They stared warmly but silent into each other's eyes, they knew they'd just entered a new beginning, but neither of them knew what to say. Davis tried awkwardly breaking the ice, "So..." he started, "you and...uh...Krys are partners on this tub, huh?"

Shawna held back bubbly laughter, her face beamed, gorgeously alive, listening to him fumble his way into conversation.

"I still can't believe you two are rooming together. You and the 'Wildcat' of Pleasure View South Side."

Shawna's eyebrows creased and her smile faded. Her face fell under a dark shadow of distraction.

"Shawna?" Davis caught her sudden mood swing. "What is it? Is there something wrong between you two?" He was surprised by his own concern about her quick change. He felt a jolt of emotion, unavoidably aware that it had been awhile since his heart had last grabbed him with a grip like that, and choked. The fact was, since he and Janie had split up, he hadn't let himself feel much of anything. Maybe this was a good thing, a breakthrough. It was nice being with Shawna, and not dwelling on the memories that haunted him day after day.

With the rim of her glass resting just in front of her lips, she said, "Actually, Krys *has* been uptight lately. I think its those weird mind bending trips, like that one you had, and now this thing with Jeff, only she's not talking about hers. And it's not that she's changing, really, she just seems distracted all the time." Shawna took another drink.

"You have any idea why she doesn't want to talk about it?" he asked.

"Well, I try not to stick my nose in her personal business," she paused and rolled her eyes, "you would not believe how private Krys can sometimes be. Though I have dropped enough hints that I know it's bothering her, and if she wants to talk, I'm always there for her. But she doesn't say much, just that she gets headaches sometimes and it screws up her vision, but 'she's fine.' And if *she* won't go see a doctor, what can *I* do?" She shrugged and took another drink.

Locked into her eyes, Davis sat back and guzzled a long drink of his beer, then gave her a nod of agreement, *what can you do?* "Maybe," he said, "when they figure out what's wrong with Jeff, it'll answer some questions."

Then, deciding to change the subject, he dipped into the past, "Hey, do you remember...."

Shawna Taylor burst into *Angelo's* the way she always did, throwing the glass doors open wide and posing like the goddess of some distant planet.

Those watching half expected a bolt of lightning and a thunder clap. A few heads turned and looked at her, however, not overwhelmed by her presence; they turned back to the more urgent matter at hand...their burgers.

Angelo's was the best burger joint in town, and only the coolest people hung out there (or so they believed themselves to be).

It was popular because it had atmosphere. The ceiling was decorated with hundreds of various and assorted beer bottles (domestic and imported), lined and strung up in rows; they hung right side up so you could read the label. Those over 21 knew Angelo's didn't serve that many different beers, they understood that it was just decoration, and they were content with the standard *Coors, Bud or Miller.*

All along the back, and halfway down the right side wall, were a string of video games and random pinball machines. Usually, a small group of boys gathered at one game or another, watching some local pro spend his entire weeks allowance; exhausting himself trying to demonstrate speed and accuracy (or lack of it), on a game that more specifically required memorization of a programmed pattern rather than natural ability. He would do this until he was challenged, or until his burger was ready, whichever came first.

The top half of the back wall was glass, you could easily see out onto the patio area, where large umbrellas sprouted from little round picnic tables. Next to the door that led to the patio, was a jukebox full of old *and* new radio hits.

The place was also equipped with two 57-inch screen television monitors, which ran continuously. They were placed at opposite ends of the room, so no matter where you sat, you could watch some MTV or whatever that season's ballgame was.

But, the more popular obsession at the time, was listening to the jukebox, usually something new and Billy Idol's 'White Wedding', or something old and Billy Idol's 'White Wedding.' Either way, 'White Wedding' was played heavily at Angelo's that year.

Waitresses were required to perform their duties on roller skates, wearing a body fit tank top T-shirt (brassiere still mandatory), nylons, and very short shorts (which crept their way, invited or not, up their behinds). It was all very sexist of course, but tips were incredible.

Davis and Janie sat quiet, heavily involved in devouring a couple of vanilla shakes and french fries, when Shawna stepped up to the table and sat down. She was attempting to suppress a squirm of excitement. "You-all are not even going to believe what Krys is doing."

Davis continued sucking his milkshake. Janie grinned mischievously and tuned in for gossip, "What is it? What's she doing?"

Shawna spilled her information enthusiastically, as though she hadn't told a good secret in months, "Well, you know how she's been hot for Bruce Edwards ever since eighth grade?"

Janie nodded, "Yeah...so?"

"I just saw her on the back of his Yamaha, turning off Lakeside Highway onto...are you ready for this? ...Billy's path."

Shawna sat back with a smile; glowing with pride because she was not only the one who discovered the juicy information, but the one to reveal it as well.

Janie giggled with shocked amusement, "You mean?"

"That's right," Shawna smirked, "since no one but us knows about Billy's path..."

Janie laughed, "Krys is taking Bruce Edwards to the tree house." She shrugged with a grin, "Well, I guess she's finally going to get him. She's been wanting him long enough."

"You better be lying, Shawna," Davis's voice cut through the giggles like a knife.

Both girls froze and turned; they'd almost forgotten he was there.

"Krystal is showing the tree house to an outsider?" Davis was pissed. "She has no business doing that, that tree house is our secret. She'll turn it into a *whore house*."

Both girl's faces contorted with disgust, his crude accusation was uncalled for, though they *were* aware that Krys did have a carefree attitude about sex. And they did understand the boy's rights to the privacy of their club. After all, if Davis hadn't been dating Janie, you could bet it would have remained a three-member only club. Then, Shawna felt the need to defend her friend.

"Well I'm sorry if someone finds out about your stupid tree house, but Krys has just as much right to use it as you and Janie do. I know you boys made the decision to invite *us* in, to be part of *your* 'Club,' but that should mean we have just as much right to it as you do." She stuck out her chin and sat quiet, with big eyes, trying not to look scared, waiting for his reaction.

He glared at her for an eerily silent moment...then, a purely evil smile spread over his face. Janie and Shawna felt a dark cloud come over them; they knew the wrath of any one of the boys could be a scary thing.

"You're right," he said, now wearing the Devil's grin. "We do *all* have a right to the tree house. In fact..." he pondered an idea; "I think I'll exercise *my* rights, right now." He stood up, pulled some money from his pocket for the bill and dropped it on the table.

A tingle of anxiety shot through Janie's insides. The tingle that feels like a million pins and needles sticking you all at once. It starts in your chest and spreads outward, making your head hot, then forms a lump in your throat, and of course, there's that driving force that tells you you're about to pee on yourself.

"Davis, don't," she pleaded.

He looked in her eyes, and the Devil was smiling, "This could be the most fun we have all week long...are you coming?"

Walking to his car, the girls chased behind. Shawna had her hands at her head, hating herself for causing what was about to happen, "I can't believe I opened my big mouth. Krys is going to kill me." They got in the car, a 1965 Ford Mustang, bright red with black interior. The body was in good shape, but the motor needed work. Davis fired it up.

"Please don't do this, Davis. Krys will never talk to me again," Shawna pleaded.

The Devil kept smiling, "If you don't want to go, Shawna, get out now." He stared at her and waited...nobody moved; he hit the gas. "I just gotta stop by the house first, and pick up something."

Janie felt ill, she knew Davis like a book, and she knew what he *had* to pick up.

He pulled off the road onto a thin strip of grass separating the asphalt from the trees. This particular spot of the forest lay just to the right of the middle, between Marble Rock Lake and the Xanorse chemical plant. Billy's Path was on 'The Plant' side and went into the woods in that direction.

'Billy's Path' was exactly that, a dirt trail that he half discovered, half created, and it led into the heart of the woods. Where he and his Dad had built a good sturdy tree house two summers before.

The past summer, Billy, Davis, and Jeff decided to extend it by building two additional rooms in a couple of the surrounding trees. Then connect them all with hanging walkways.

Each walkway was a row of 2-inch thick, 1' x 3' slat-boards, strung together. Each side handrail was a crisscrossing rope laced into the walk, then raised four feet, to be knotted onto a long rope they had strung up from one end to the other; it was the acting guardrail. It looked like a bridge in an 'Indiana Jones' movie. But the overall affect was more resembling the *Swiss Family Robinson* tree house.

Davis looked at Janie, who (feeling like a drowning rat) stared at the 35mm Canon Camera with detachable zoom lens; Davis's most prized possession - hanging from his neck. "Let's go get her!" he commanded, and leapt from the car.

The girls scrambled out close behind, still hoping to talk him out of it before they got to Krys...and Bruce.

Shawna slammed her door extra hard, hoping Krys might hear it and clear out. Davis turned and flashed a burning look of annoyance, but then quickly twisted back into the grinning Devil.

"She can't hear you, the tree house is half a mile in there," he snickered low and sinister. "And she's preoccupied."

Trotting through the weeds, leaves, and long stabbing brush, Shawna continued to beg, "Davis, please don't, she will never forgive me. I'll do anything you say. I'll talk with her. I'll make her promise never to tell anyone about the tree house unless you guys say it's ok first."

Davis trekked on, silently.

"I'll make sure she understands...Pleeeeese."

He could not help being amused and thrilled by the power he held. He knew he had control, and wasn't about to let up.

"Davis, I can't believe you're going to do this," Janie said. Her voice, amongst the quiet of the trees, rang through echoingly clear, almost loud. Suddenly he realized, all the girls had to do, when they got close enough, was to make some noise, and it would blow the whole event.

He stopped, "Ok look, I'm tired of listening to you two. I'm going to do this. I'm going to teach her a lesson." Again the girls looked pale, sickly, their bodies slumped with defeat. The mental anguish of Krys's embarrassment turned over and over in their heads.

"So," he continued, "since this is my idea, I want you two to go back to the car right now and wait for me. That way you won't be a party to it, and I won't have to listen to you."

"But..." Shawna pleaded.

"No," he ordered. "Go on, I won't be long. Just go and wait."

Janie glared at him, knowing there was no use in arguing, once he made up his mind to do something, right or wrong, Davis *always* followed through.

"Come on, Shawna," she said. "There's no reasoning with him when he's set his mind to being an *Asshole.*" She fired the word at him, then turned and both girls slowly headed back to the car.

Shawna turned briefly, putting on the biggest sad puppy dog eyes she could, but Davis just smiled and disappeared into the woods.

Making his way along the path, he began to visualize the scene that lay ahead. He always thought Krys was fairly attractive, a little thin to his liking perhaps, but none-the-less good looking. She was obviously small breasted, but she had a nice round behind; he imagined he would get a good picture of it while it slowly moved up and down. In fact, her behind was something he himself wouldn't mind sinking his teeth into.

He pictured her as the rider...on top. And if he were quiet, he could move around from the different rooms and walkways collecting great photos.

His mind raced with ideas about the pictures he was going to take of her jiggling little titties. He thought about her long brown hair falling over her shoulders, sticking to her sweaty body. He could see her head thrown back, as she jerked with thrusting spasms, and saliva falling carelessly from the corners of her mouth. Her long thin stomach stretched down as she arched her back and rocked on Bruce Edwards's throbbing erection.

Davis figured Krys would be a moaner; panting things like, *Uh, harder...harder,* and, *deeper...deeper. Oh please more...more. Oh...ooohhhhh!*

Eventually, he was walking blindly, his imagination leading the way (at least 7 inches in front of him). *Fu-uh-uck me. Oh...oh...pleeezze, ooohh..ooohh,* and finally, *aauugghh...aahh...mmmmmmm.*

And, while lost in fantasyland, he noticed his own *self* was now very large and hard, smashing painfully against a wall of Levi's. He found this comically amusing, but at the same time, it annoyed him that he was getting that turned on by Janie's best friend. Thinking if it weren't for Janie, he might really like to have a go at ol' Krys himself.

Okay, I need to put that thought right out of my head, he decided. Figuring he better put that thought out of *both* heads, or he could get really horny. And it wouldn't be the first time that year that he would produce an accidental ejaculation. God had shown Davis before, on more than one occasion, anything was possible.

Of course, statistics and Davis figured he was at his sexual peak. Which he hoped would be the beginning of a lifetime stretch. But for now, he reached into his pants and readjusted himself to a more comfortable position, and walked on.

As he came around the last huge Oak along the path, the tree house suddenly came into view. He would just weave his way through the surrounding trees, so as not to be seen. And then he heard her. And as he'd hoped, she was a moaner. The forest rang out with *"Oooohhhh, Fuuuuccccckkkkk Meeeeeee."*

Davis fought to keep from laughing. *This is going to be good.* He clutched his camera.

Creeping around, trying desperately to keep sticks and general growth from crunching under his feet, a part of his subconscious heard something else, it sounded like echoes of his footsteps. But when he stopped to listen, there was nothing. By the third stop, he got irritated with his own paranoia and decided to ignore it. Eventually, he found himself standing beneath the room that seemed to be exploding with moans and groans.

It was quite stimulating, the thought even crossed his mind to whip out his own 'yang' and give it a good jerking. But, he took a few deep breaths, and resumed his venture.

After sizing up the situation, he concluded his best photographic angle would be from the room they'd built in a tree off to the left of the original *main room*. The main room had one window that faced the direction of the road, and one sitting wide open to the room on the left, and since he had no possible way to get in line to see through the first one...

They had built another room off to the right, and a little higher, but to see in from there, you would have to stretch out further than he wanted to attempt while holding the camera. Though, it would've been photographic genius, snapping shots that looked down through the small sky-window they'd put in the main room.

They had cut a square hole and attached hinges to make a lid that opened or closed, depending on the weather. Odds were that Krys would have it open and the sun would be shining all over her sweaty behind.

But Davis knew it would be a lot of trouble, and he wouldn't have time to get into a well-balanced position before he'd make too much noise and get caught.

So he started up the slat board ladder they'd nailed to the backside of the tree on the left. Trying desperately not even to breathe any louder than was absolutely necessary. He didn't want to disturb 'the moment.'

Once in the room, with camera in hand, he stepped slowly over to look at the view. His blood raced, and though he was being cautious, he still almost tripped over a chair.

When the boys furnished the tree house, they decided they would only bring in the bare essentials. There was a card table and six folding chairs, (there *were* only three, then Davis hooked up with Janie and company).

They got the old sofa Billy's dad had thrown out on the back porch. They took a full length mirror with a long crack in it, that Jeff's Mom no longer used. They rounded up some sheets of plywood, and between the three of them, constructed a junk chest, containing all the incoming goods of the summer.

Suddenly, Davis's eyes filled like a dark night with fireworks. His imagination was instantly replaced with live action figures. The very naked and moist Krystal Sanders had her very hot *self* planted firmly on Bruce Edward's face. Her round behind moved slow and grinding while she lay stretched out over him, giving his hard smooth cock the licking of its life.

At least she had a blanket spread over the sofa; Davis gave her credit for that, a clever attempt to conceal her afternoon delight.

He was also pleased to see that her derriere was facing him at a slight angle. *This is a good shot*. He lifted the camera and reached into the small carrying case hanging from his shoulder. He pulled out a short, wide-angle zoom lens and snapped it on.

"Krystal baby, you do have a beautiful ass," he mentioned to himself, and clicked off three pictures of it. Then he watched for a moment as it moved from side to side and around in small circles.

He refocused and closed up on as much of her face as he could get from the side. Her wet mouth was sliding down Bruce's erection. Davis was mesmerized by the glow emanating from her face; she was apparently lost to any reality outside of those four walls. Compelled by passion, she sucked and bit and licked and swallowed as deep as Davis had ever dreamed a woman could (...or would).

"Jeeez," he licked sweat from his beading upper lip, "Janie could use some lessons from this girl," he clicked off a few more pictures. "A lot of lessons."

It would be ten more years before he would discover that, perhaps it wasn't entirely Janie's lack of enthusiasm. Perhaps it was just him and her together that didn't work.

I've got to get some overhead shots of this, he thought.

Thump!

"What the hell was that?"

He looked around for the source of the noise, and in the corner of his eye, he saw a rock fall from the table to the floor in the room with the future 'Pin-up' couple.

He quickly looked at Krys, who had suddenly stopped bumping and grinding. She sat straight up on Bruce's face, twisting slightly to look behind her for the origin of the noise.

"Oohh, now that's a picture," Davis snapped another one. This time her tiny breasts were facing directly into the camera, her face was flushed red and hot, something wet ran from the corner of her mouth, and her hair lay limp and wet over her shoulders.

Thump!

This time Davis saw it. A rock flew through the sky-window from the third room. When he looked over, he was suddenly pissed to see Janie and Shawna trying to warn their tree house abusing friend by throwing stones.

Party poops, he thought.

Krys snapped her eyes to the sky-window.

That's a good pose. Davis smiled and clicked twice.

"Krys, get on the floor," when the girls knew they were caught, they gave up trying to hide and began yelling.

Janie and Krys's eyes met, they locked and glared at each other. Then Janie's words began to sink in, *"Get on the floor."*

It suddenly dawned on her that all was not right in *Tree House U.S.A.,* and maybe she should just follow directions rather than argue.

But as she dove forward to get from the sofa to the floor, Bruce reached out with both hands and grabbed her right at the waist.

"Where the hell are you going?" he pulled her back. Her hands smacked hard on the floorboards as the top half of her body went down, while her bottom half was being held up by her hips.

Bruce was on his knees on the sofa, holding her sweaty buttocks up in front of his mid-section. Davis was losing all control, ready to roll with laughter; the moment was too perfect.

"Oh man, this is front page material," snap...snap. Two more pictures.

"Bruce, let me go," Krys grunted, trying to wrestle free. "Don't you see Janie and Shawna out there?"

"Yeah, I see 'em," he replied. "You want to ask them to join us?"

He may have been laughing when he said it, but Krys had no doubt that Bruce would be more than willing to have a go at all three of them at the same time.

He looked up at the two in the other room, "Hey girls, come on down," he yelled. Then he clutched Krys tighter and slid his rigid cock back inside her.

Considering the position she was in, all bent over, hands on the floor and her ass up in the air, the pressure of his already large penis felt twice as big as before.

"Aaauuuggghhh," she moaned. Her neck arched up until her head almost touched her back.

"Yet another great pose," Davis laughed and clicked off three more pictures.

Krys had a momentary rush, thinking it actually felt incredibly good. Under other circumstances she could be having an amazing orgasm or three...or five. But, Janie and Shawna were outside watching, and something, she still didn't know what, was wrong. Then she looked straight out in front of her, and found herself looking directly across at Davis in the other room, laughing and taking pictures.

"Aaahhh," she screamed. "Davis Dugan, I'm gonna kill you!" Bruce looked up and saw Davis with the camera; but not having a single modest bone in his body, and as much of an exhibitionist as *he* was, this was not a problem.

"Hey, Dugan get one like this," while holding Krys up with one hand around her waist, he reached out with the other, grabbed her left arm and pulled it back. Then with that hold to keep her body against his, he let loose of her waist and quickly reached forward with that hand to grab her right arm and yank it back as well. He moved fast enough that her chin didn't hit the floor, and suddenly Krys was hung, suspended in mid air.

With both of her hands in his and her arms stretched back behind her, she sprouted straight out and stiff off his mid-section; if Bruce had been an automobile, she would have been his hood ornament.

Davis looked at her face staring straight up at him, her eyes glared red, burning with hatred. He could see down her chest, her little pencil eraser nipples pointing straight out at him, and her stomach curving back into where their genitals came together. Bruce's legs stretched down from between where hers were wrapped around his sides, and she looked as if she might come flying off at any given moment.

"Outstanding!" Davis exclaimed, and clicked away. *Snap. Snap.*

"Bruce Edwards, you shit-head!" Janie screamed at him. When he turned to look up at her through the sky-window, he saw a much larger stone than the previous one's, coming straight at him. His reflex action of fear, watching the rock descend upon his face, made him loosen his hold on Krys just enough for her to slip one arm free.

"You Bastard," she yelled, and grabbed his wrist with the hand he was still holding, then dropped her other shoulder, turning all the way around, her legs twisting his groin, and just as Janie's rock plowed into his skull, Krys's fist shot into his mouth like a cannon ball.

The impact sent him from the sofa, through the air, and up against the front wall. His head went out the window and drove the ledge above the wall into his throat. This caused a momentary loss of air in the windpipe and he dropped breathlessly in a clump.

Krys herself fell and slammed to the floor, leaving her momentarily stunned and flat on her back. Then, while laying there absorbing the pain...she remembered she was still naked; she quickly rolled over and scurried to her cutoffs and bikini top, and slipped them on with lightning speed.

"Oh well, photo shoot's over." Watching Krys scramble, preparing to come kill him, Davis shrugged, "I guess it's time I get outta here," and he ducked through the floor hole and down the back of the tree.

Hastily, Krys scanned the room for the *big* rock Janie threw in; "Ah!" it was at Bruce's feet. He looked like he'd been on a weeklong drinking binge and was trying to remember his own name. She figured he was too messed up to try anything, so she reached over and picked it up (it took both hands).

Heading for the forest, Davis had just come out from under the room she was in.

"Davis, *You Mother-Fucker*," she yelled and let loose with the boulder, hefting it with all her might.

While picking up his pace, he looked over his shoulder at her and a moment of sheer dread came to life. He saw the huge stone falling from the sky. *Man, I can't believe what good aim she has. She's definitely on my team next time we play softball.*

Then...*Shit! It's going to hit me*...and he made a heroic dive to escape the mutilation about to impound him. It did almost miss him...*almost*. But when all recourse to escape had finally vanished, it caught him flat on his left ankle, tearing away the skin and any meat that may have come between it and the bone.

In a single flash, like the snap of a picture, one quick and throbbing moment, he was left a large gaping hole just above his foot; exposing an inch of bare bone, some torn tendons, and a steady flow of blood filling in a swamp of broken veins. His white *Nike* sneaker was suddenly red.

He wondered, for a fleeting second, if he had worn socks that day, would it have softened the blow? Then a rippling wave of excruciating, mind torturing pain washed through. He felt as if his foot had been fed through a meat grinder.

"Jeeessuuuusss Charrist, Krystal! Aauuugghhh!"

He wiped at the blinding water welling up in his eyes and tried to focus through the pain. Only, when he started to make things out again, he looked up and saw Krys...*the Devil Woman*, holding three more rocks *that Janie and Shawna had supplied*, and was reaching back ready to let one go.

"I gotta get out of here." Davis worked his way back to his feet (what was left of them), and hobbled into the forest. He left a long trail of blood, and if you looked close enough, a line of tears beside it.

Krys watched the first rock disappear into the forest along with Davis. She knew she missed him; she stood motionless, watching. Maybe she wanted to make sure he wasn't coming back, or maybe she was just too shook up over the whole incident, but she wasn't moving.

"Ooohhh, my head," Bruce moaned. Suddenly transporting back to reality, Krys turned, and remembering why she was there in the first place, quickly became very sympathetic.

"Oh my gosh, Bruce, are you all right?"

Davis stumbled, falling through the forest, trying to stay as much on the path as possible, there were less stickers and brush there to stab at the bloody muscle swelling from his ankle. He saw Janie and Shawna cross twenty feet in front of him. They were heading out of the woods toward *the plant*, where they could cut down the Short Cut that lead in the direction of Krys's house.

"Janie, come back," he yelled. But the girls kept running. "Janie, I'm hurt. I need help." There was no response. *Damn those girls.*

He decided he would never be able to drive in this much pain. *I'm going to have to catch up to the little shits just to get them to drive me home,* he thought. So he parted from the path and began to cut through the trees after them.

Just then..."*Davis! Help!*"

First he heard Janie call out, he couldn't tell if she was mocking him or what. Then he heard Shawna..."Heeellllppppp!!!"

"That was Shawna," he huffed, hacking his way through the brush. *Shit, maybe they really are in trouble. Why else would they call for me? They must know I'm just going to kill them.*

Then he saw them up ahead, but one of them wasn't standing.

"Davis, hurry," Janie saw him closing in and motioned him over. The pain in his ankle throbbed like a slamming jackhammer. He bumped and scraped past the twigs and sticker brush.

"Damn it, Janie, this had better be real. My foot is now mutilated thanks to you two." He looked down where Shawna had fallen *through* the earth, "What the hell is that?" he asked.

She was crying, "Please Davis, please, you've gotta get me out of here." He was still pissed at them, but he felt sorry for her and leaned over to pull her out, while Janie rambled on about what happened.

"We were running, mostly to get away from *you*, when all of a sudden the ground gave away and she fell through."

"It's weird," Shawna said, "I can move my feet underneath like there's nothing around me."

Davis hovered over her and reached to grab under her arms, then gave an urgent tug. Fortunately, she was easily pulled out. But then she fell backward, pushing him off his feet, and she landed flat on top of him.

"Ooppff"

"Thanks, Shawna, but I really don't need a rupture today."

"Sorry," she mumbled.

"Look," Janie whispered and pointed at the hole.

They crawled around to look.

"It's a tunnel," Davis said. "It's an underground tunnel."

Shawna stood up abruptly, scrunched her nose and turned away, "Well, I don't know what it is, but it stinks like crap in there."

Janie's face blocked off most of the hole, only a thin beam of sunlight sliced through, "There's a pool of something down there."

* * *

Just the mention of *The Pool* brought memory lane to an abrupt dead end. Shawna was intense with a chill factor when she said, "Let's not go *there* today, okay?"

Davis stared back just as emphatic, "Yeah...let's not."

A moment later, she stood up, "Well, you want to ski one more circle and call it a day?" again, inflicting her adorably cute dimples and pearly white teeth on him.

"Yeah, sure, why not," he stood up beside her and grabbed a quick kiss.

Slowly she pulled away and stepped to the captain's seat, "Ok, slick lips, man your life jacket and hit the water." He smiled agreeably and put the jacket back around his neck. Shawna revved up the engine.

He climbed over the edge of the boat and lowered himself into the water, "I notice it hasn't warmed up any in the past half hour." She detected a slight shiver in his voice, "It stimulates the blood," she replied.

She turned to face him; her back was to the orange and red sunset. A beautiful glow cast from behind her strawberry blonde curls as she watched him get into the skis.

"You want to jump the ramp?" she asked.

At the opposite end of the lake there was a man made ramp for ski jumping.

"Yeah, sure, why not," skis on, rope in hand, he was ready to go.

"Ok, get a grip on your trunks," she told him (not a hundred percent sure how much she meant it), then she turned in her seat and hit the gas.

The boat took off and Davis rose swiftly on the water, crouching and gliding over the smooth surface. Lost in a world of *perfection*, Shawna smiled from the wheel of her boat, with Rum & Root beer in hand, racing into the horizon.

Water sprayed from the nose of *Ladies Choice* (the name was emblazoned on both sides of the front and in large letters across the back) as they cut through on a golden strip of sun reflecting glitter. She thought the end of the gleaming trail, where the hills cut the light short, would be a good place to turn and run for the ramp.

Davis had done his share of water skiing in his lifetime, but it had been several years since he'd done it last. Shawna turned, they smiled and waved at each other, eventually he yelled at her to keep her eyes on the road.

When the boat came to the designated turning spot, she thought it would be fun to run him around in a few circles. She threw the wheel into a sharp left turn and held it. Davis took a wide right sweep of the lake, power sliding nicely, sending a million drops of liquid sunshine to spray out a shower.

When Shawna turned to look back, she saw a rainbow stretch over the water.

Davis was having the most fun he'd had since he and Janie went rafting down the Colorado River two years before. *Aaah, Screw Janie! I don't need to think about that lying, cheating,* (he never felt comfortable calling her the 'B' word) *Witch!*

The unexpected surprise memory attack was enough to raise his blood pressure a little, but then he looked at Shawna up ahead in the boat. She raised her glass and toasted him, threw her head back, her wavy hair bounced softly on her shoulders, and brought the glass to her lips. She tipped it bottoms up and poured long and slow down her throat.

Jeez, she's beautiful.

By the third circle Davis was yelling at her to straighten up. "I'm getting dizzy," he shouted. Laughing about it, she turned the wheel back and headed to the ramp. The sun felt good on their backs.

Shawna gunned the motor a little and watched straight ahead as *Ladies Choice* skipped and jumped over the waves they had created. Davis was twenty-five yards behind, taking the same skips and jumps, and holding his own very well. First he would lean in, then out, then in again. Eventually, the waves ceased and they were back to slicing a smooth surface.

Shawna sped up another ten miles per hour, grabbed the three quarters empty bottle (a fifth) of Captain Morgan's and took a straight swig.

The boat looked like a shooting arrow. Davis felt the sting of water biting his ankles and the increasing pressure on his muscles to keep his legs from buckling.

"Hey," he tried yelling again.

"Here it comes," she screamed back, smiling with delight.

He looked ahead, *Oh yeah...I forgot.* It had been too long since he'd skied last, and even longer since he'd jumped a ramp. Suddenly he wondered if they should have talked about this a bit more before actually attempting it.

Too late, even if he had screamed at her, she could no longer hear him over the roar of the motor. And at the moment, she was concentrating more on her driving than on his skiing.

Oh well, if we're going to do it, let's at least pretend we know what were doing, he thought. Then he lowered himself closer to the water.

60

'75 yards'

There were signs posted along the lakes edge, to let you know how close you were to the ramp. Seconds later...

'50 yards'

"This is going to be good, Dav..." Shawna's mouth suddenly went dry, her head flooded thick and heavy with mental incapacity. It was like trying to hold a bowling ball with her shoulders. She dropped into her seat. Her mouth could no longer form words, but the thoughts that raced in the back of her mind pulsed very distinctly with fright; *Oh my God, what's happening to me? What's happening?*

Her arms dropped to her sides like sandbags. Her legs and feet were immovable. She remembered that this degree of limpness was called 'dead weight.' And the dead weight in her right foot pushed the gas pedal to the floor.

"Shawna, what the hell are you doing?" Davis screamed again. Then he saw her head drop back over the seat and her arms swing lifelessly at her sides. *Oh God. Something's wrong with her.*

The boat was ripping through the water. The signs shot past, *20 yards...10 yards.* "Oh no, the ramp. I'm going to eat it for sure."

Panic seized his heart as he watched the smooth angled surface, surmount the water. He felt wind ripple over his body, and watched the front of the skis meet the long, climbing ramp.

Suddenly, Shawna's foot fell off the gas and the pedal sprang up. Davis was flying up to about mid-ramp, then the towrope went slack in his hands and he lost the pull of the boat. At the top, his feet went off, but he had no balance and his body fell back.

Crack!

He heard his own head hit the top edge of the ski jump. The solid board burrowed straight through his hair, split the skin beneath it, and continued on its quest for skull. Once there, it struck a thick reserve of blood.

The whack knocked him semi-conscious, his body was in mild shock and didn't feel much of the six-foot drop back to the water, where he bounced and skidded like a skipping stone.

Fortunately, the skis automatically popped loose and broke away from his feet. Unfortunately, they too were traveling as fast as he was, and beat him about the arms, legs and face along the way. Suddenly, the water came alive with floating driftwood particles. Strategically placed there to scrape and tear at his skin by the 'all knowing God,' in an anticipative wait for one: Davis Dugan, to come rolling through.

His mind wavered with concussion; his nose sprang loose with profuse bleeding. When he couldn't breathe in he tried blowing out. And as he stopped bouncing and came to rest, floating still in the cool water, the pain of the nose blowing brought him back to harsh reality.

He didn't have to see himself to know he looked like he'd just had a bad dream with Freddy Krueger. He felt his left eye swell from where a ski had popped him; it turned all shades of purple. He could feel gaping lacerations in the bottom of his feet; they stung viciously as he tread the water. He tried to keep himself moving, not really sure where to or why, or what day it was, or his own name.

He felt all the cuts and bruises pounding unceasingly through every inch of his flesh. Then, from the corner of his eye, he saw the water surrounding him was red.

Oh jeez, I'm lying in my own blood. Man, I hurt. Thank God for life jackets! Then another jolt of fright hit him, *What if this isn't my blood?*

"Shaawwnnaa," he cried. *Oh Jesus, where's Shawna?*

Lifting his head, his brain washed over with a rush of white blindness. He almost passed out. Then he saw the boat, it was idling slowly. It had run down the lake a short way, turned around, and was heading back toward the ramp.

Davis sat quietly watching, listening. He found his hearing had become ultra sensitive to any sound breaking up the silence of the evening. He heard the low hum of the motor, the clanging of his skis bumping together in the water, and a small choir of chirping crickets. That was it, but that was enough, it rang volumes in his aching head.

He watched the boat get closer and knew something was missing. There was no sign of Shawna. *Where the hell is she?*

In a clump on the floorboard of *Ladies Choice*, Shawna's mouth hung open in the midst of a voiceless scream. Long strings of saliva hung from her lips and created a small pool of slimy thickness next to her head. The drool ran into her hair and encircled her ear, causing it to suction to the deck.

Her cheeks pulled down, her forehead pulled up; her eye sockets stretched wide open to an enormous size. She had no point of reference to compare the experience.

Shawna had become the same stretching slab of meat the other's had all been; Janie on her front lawn in Destin, Krys on Lakeside Highway, Jeff in the Einstein Department at Pleasure View Memorial.

She could hear Davis calling to her, she tried raising her arm for him to see. Looking down the center walk from the front of the boat to the back, she saw the short white base and purple cushions of the lounge seats. Beyond that, she could see the corner of the motor rising from the back of the boat, the red burning sky, and the edge of the sun sinking in the horizon, all...melting.

Oh God! Her mind screeched a cycle of echoes; *it's melting. The world is melting,* over and over. Panic had a choke hold on her throat. Her adrenalin pumped full speed, but her body wouldn't move. *This is it, we've had a nuclear explosion, the whole world is melting and I've become paralyzed.* Terror pounded in her heart, her fear had taken to new depths, tears streaked from her eyes.

"Shawna?" She heard Davis again and grasped for a way to make him come to her. With all her strength, she tried raising her arm to signal him. Her stretched out eyes watched her fingertips as she concentrated on the lift. They would not move. She did sense, however, that her shoulder maybe jerked a little...and her arm *had* twitched, but her hand lay lifeless on the deck.

Aaahhh, crap and other expletives (oh shit, damn, hell...) echoed loudly in her head. She could actually hear the words bouncing off the walls of her brain, with that thin tinny, over-inflated basketball slap on the gym floor sound, *shbang*!

I have to...Then, full with anger, and a little help from racing anxiety, she threw out her arm and...in a moment of amazement, it worked.

Her body turned, her arm went straight up, then slowly over...pulling her over with it. *This is good,* she thought. Until it went all the way over, and with bad luck being the only luck going right then, her hand caught on the steering wheel and pulled it down. The boat suddenly went into a hard right turn.

She had also managed to roll onto the gas pedal and accelerate the speed by about ten miles an hour.

Davis had just reached the boat when it suddenly took off in a circle around him, "What the hell?"

As it passed, the suction pull from the propeller yanked him under water, then the boat darted away.

Gurgling, he resurfaced snorting and coughing, and yelling "Shawna, what the hell is wrong with you?"

Tortured with confusion, he watched the boat circle. It came very close to him. *She's gotta be sick or something. I have to get to her.*

He had no idea how to get close enough to get back on board. *Maybe I could swim around with it, build up enough speed, grab the side and pull myself up???? ...No way, my arms are about broken as it is.*

Watching the boat in its continual circle was making him dizzy. The pulsing pressure of water that entered and left his sliced foot throbbed uncontrollably. *Auugghh, I'm not going to last much longer before I pass out.*

He watched the boat go around again...and again, wracking his brain for an idea. Then it came.

With one eye on the boat, he glanced down at the strap of his life jacket. Naturally, it had knotted up and had to be untied before he could pull it loose. His arms ached from shoulders to fingertips as he tried to take the thing over his head. "Nice day for water skiing she says, huh!"

When the jacket was completely open in his hands, he looked at the boat's motor, "Now, how the hell am I going to do this?" There was only a ten-inch gap between the water and an opening to the motor. He knew whatever he did would have to hit in *that* ten inches. And there was no way he was going to go *under* water to try to stop it.

Maybe, if I hold one end and swing it around, it'll catch, wind itself in, and burn the engine out.

He raised one hand from the water, kicking hard to stay afloat, and began swinging the life jacket around over his head, waiting for the boat to get close enough to catch.

Ok, ok here it comes. The boat zoomed past, Davis swung the loose end at it and missed by three feet, "Jeez," he rolled his eyes, "that was good." He waited and watched as it came around again. *Ok, ok, I gotta get serious now. I don't have much strength left...make this one count.*

Ladies Choice came shooting up next to him, whizzing past, and as soon as he was directly behind it, he thought out loud, "Now!" and swung the jacket strap, snapping the loose end and catching it in the exposed section of rotor. Luckily for him, rather than being pulled in with it, it was snatched out of his hands.

The belt, jacket, and buckles...all of it, wound itself into the motor with some disturbing snapping and popping, then it frayed and shredded itself into the gears.

The boat jerked and tried not to stop. Davis smelled the burning oil that suddenly sputtered and blew out a cloud of gray smoke. And with one hard clunking knock, it came to an abrupt stop.

The boat was dead in the water; everything became calm. Davis was silent. Ripples sloshing against the watercraft seem to be the only movement. And with the sun slipping away, it had become dark and still.

Almost too afraid even to speak, his voice was a whisper, "Shawna? Are you alright?"

No answer.

He swam to the boat, grabbed the side and pulled himself up. Cautiously, he peered over the edge; he could see her body down the center walk.

"Shawna?"

He climbed inside, carefully walking only on the toes of his one foot that looked like it had been cut in two. He had a sudden flashback to the boulder flying through the trees at him, only to crush and tear its way through that *same* foot. *Jeez, I'm gonna end up a cripple one day.*

He came up the walkway and looked at her. Shawna's face was jumping out at him. All her features were grotesquely distorted. Her cheeks had an invisible force tugging and stretching them down to her neck.

Her brows were pulled way up into her forehead making her eyes look three inches in diameter. Her mouth stretched open in a frozen silent scream. Her body didn't move, only her pupils struggled to look up at him.

"Duuhveess, Huullpp Mauh."

She knew it was him standing in front of her, though she couldn't make him out very well, everything was oozy and melty. He was just a tall fleshy monolith of dripping skin; she couldn't even make out his face. Behind him, the lavender seat cushions were pools of purple soda pop flowing over the sides of their base.

Saliva covered her chin and neck and streaked over her shoulders. The pink, normally moist under skin of her eyelids was drying out, becoming red, stinging...and burning.

"Oh my God! Shawna?" Davis was overcome with fear; he knew exactly what she was going through as he watched the incredibly beautiful woman he'd spent such a wonderful afternoon with become an extremely distorted mutation.

"Shawna, can you hear me?" He leaned over, reaching out to pat her cheek, hoping to get a response.

She watched the mound of dripping, bubbling flesh come at her face. Fear beat furiously in her heart, then...*Slap!* He smacked her.

The cushions stopped dripping. The tension in her cheeks let loose and slowly drew back to their normal position. Her eyebrows came down; her eyes resumed their original size and shape and were now only dry and irritated.

She sat up, scared with a fear that was unmatched in her lifetime. Davis gave her a towel to wipe her chin. They stared quietly at each other, absorbing the shock. Then he sat on the deck and leaned against the seat. She grimaced when she saw his foot.

The silence was long before they, at the same time, asked the same question, "Are you all right?"

THE
HAGGER'S

Chapter 1

P leasure View Kentucky, 1980, your average 20th century town in the southern midwest. All levels of schooling were available - Nursery through College, or *Trade* if you preferred, with contemporary technology and access for completion of your desired education. Close enough to any type of social activity you might look for; Dining, Theater, Sports...etc. The local residents could even behold an evening of 'Shakespeare In The Park' if the bug bit 'em.

But, the *local* community was small, small enough that if you were in need to find someone, you could usually track them down through a relative or friend, or perhaps a friend of a friend (as was the case on occasion).

In most circles of conversation, the names of several people, mutually known, would generally come up. The town was so small, you really had very little privacy; and consequently, anyone you knew, usually knew anything they wanted to about you. Including things, perhaps, you didn't necessarily want known.

Then...there were the outskirts, the edges, the hills that surrounded the town. From where farm folk and *Hillbillies* came, where Rednecks originated. These were people and families who, for the most part, didn't associate with the rest of the townspeople, except for *necessity*. *Necessity* being, if they were building a new shack for storing a broken tractor or possibly a liquor still, if they came to town for lumber, that's when you might see them. Occasionally, you might remember the name of one that made an impression on you (amazing you with some grand display of a lack of education, or sophistication...bad manners...smell).

One such person as this would be Jimmy Hagger. Jimmy was sixteen, same as Davis and Jeff, with one significant difference; Jimmy had never had any formal schooling...in his life. He was raised and *educated* by his parents, Bobby and Opal Hagger.

Growing up in the sticks, farming vegetables and raising cattle and chickens, was where Jimmy attempted developing his brain. But, learning to read and write, soon proved to be more of a task than he wanted to spend much time at. He could piece *some* written words together, but it was a struggle.

The Hagger's were not an ambitious bunch, most of the farming they did...or cared to do, was just enough for themselves, with only small extras on the side for basic survival money. To them, this was life, liberty, and the pursuit of happiness.

The Hagger house (such as it was), for most of its existence, was not much more than an oversized shack. It had been built so long ago, that originally; there had been no foundation put beneath it. It was just plank board over the ground dirt.

Somewhere along the way however, Bobby's dad (Jimmy's Grandpa), Ray, had decided to dig under the planks and pour a six-inch thick slab of concrete. His reasoning was to enforce the insulation and help keep out spiders and other crawling things that previously had an open door invitation. Then he replaced the boards with new ones. This adventurous move lasted throughout the year of 1940.

The walls of the house, inside and out, were slats of wood two inches thick, ranging anywhere from six to twelve inches wide, by eight feet long.

There was an outside wall, an inside wall, and six inches of insulation between (another innovative move by the industrious Ray Hagger). After this particular home improvement, the general upkeep of replacing the insulation would occur each time a first child was born to the *previous* first child born. And with the cracks in the slats gaping as badly as they did, exposure to rain and other elements of the weather each year, made it more or less mandatory.

There were four bedrooms in the house, each one the same as the others. The parent's, however, had a bed with a mattress and box springs, while everyone else had a mattress on a coiled wire metal frame.

There were some homemade, handcrafted dresser drawers and matching clothes cabinets (no closets) scattered throughout the house.

The kitchen was very much a part of the living room. The sink in the kitchen was well equipped with cold and cold running water. When hot water was needed, it was heated on the stove. They had a water heater, but it was small, and there were lots of little Hagger's, so it was only used in dire need. The Hagger's thought the faucet was a big step in modernizing (there were no complaints over the removal of the *hand pump*).

Bobby had also invested in a huge generator; he kept it under a shed roof out back. Once a month, he went to town and bought forty gallons of gasoline for it. This generator was their entire source of electricity.

He also purchased large blocks of ice for their Ice Box. It was jammed full of only the *necessary* items they needed to keep cold, like milk (their own personally processed cows milk), meat, and home-made ice cream (when they had it). They picked their eggs fresh daily; there was usually plenty to go around.

Their oven was a wood burning, old black stovepipe. It was also the heater for the house, which was why it sat in the middle of the living room. In the winter of '68, Bobby was inspired to make sure that where the pipe came up through the hole in the ceiling was sealed *solid* all the way around. The inspiration was *sparked* after watching the insulation catch fire one night and burn up half the roof before they could put it out.

The roof was another one of those things that would be replaced every five to ten years, simply because they used cheap materials.

The pipe, stemming tall outside, also served as a marker to identify location. The house was very much a blend with its surroundings, and times when the family would picnic at the lake, or Grandpa Ray and Bobby (then later, Bobby and Jimmy) would go hunting, if they miscalculated their direction on the way back, they could look up, spot the tall black pipe with bold red letters down the side that spelled out 'Hagger,' and find their way home.

Around back was a small barn made of the same materials as the house, only without insulation...and no floorboards. Inside was a lot of dirt and hay. There were a few not very healthy looking cows, and a twenty foot by twenty foot wire cage with fifteen chickens clucking about inside.

Just beyond the barn, was a small pasture where the cattle would graze. This was the same *cow pie* riddled pasture the children played in.

It wasn't the most romantic setting, but the Hagger's called it home and they were proud of it. A not so lovely estate, handed down from generation to generation. Grandpa Ray's daddy, Earl Hagger, had built it when Ray was just a young boy. Ray inherited it when he met and married Verna Skagg...then passed it on to his son Bobby when Bobby married Opal Slander. And Bobby had every intention of passing it on to his first born, Jimmy, when he took a bride. That *was* his intention.

When Ray Hagger was thirty four years old, and had already decided to leave Bobby the house (and surrounding property), he started thinking, if the house was going to be the family legacy, then...shouldn't they have their own family graveyard on the grounds somewhere?

After long and thoughtful consideration, he decided it was the only respectable thing to do. So one evening, while his *daddy*, Earl, was relaxing on the front porch...shot gun in hand, looking for jackrabbits, Ray moseyed out, took a seat on the overturned washtub and presented the idea.

The thought of all future generation Hagger's buried side by side, together in death as they were in life, brought tears to Earl's eyes. This was the most thoughtful honor of family unity he'd ever known. So choked up, he could hardly respond. Finally, there was a nod, and giving Ray a big hug, he said, "Ray that there's the most loyal thing you coulda ever thunk up. I b'lieve it's a wunnerful idear."

Now, many years later, fifty yards from the vegetable garden, off to the right of the barn, lay the family cemetery. There were plots and headstones for the entire Hagger clan, including some of Earl's wife Trudy's relatives, Ray and his wife Verna, a lot of their brothers and sisters, aunts and uncles, and in-laws and cousins all down the line.

By the time Bobby was a father with a brood of his own, the family burial grounds was well established. It had become as natural a part of the landscape as the barn, or the vegetable garden, or cow pasture, or the family's underwear strung out on the clothesline.

The cemetery was formed on slightly inclining ground, where Earl and Ray had actually dug up trees to create a more squared off space, and leveled it out (as much as possible).

When they finished, they found that if they looked close enough and hard enough through the remaining trees, they could see the small concrete chemical lab that would one day become the monster known as 'Xanorse Chemicals Inc.'

The Hagger's lived to the right of the laboratory (if you were viewing from Lakeside Highway), on a large clearing of land that was virtually impossible to see from the road because of the encompassing woods.

The outside tree line formed a wall along the edge of the Xanorse parking lot behind the building. On the left edge of the lot, trees had been cleared to help create the narrow road that went from the highway, straight through to Honeysuckle Lane. This paved strip was the easy access road known as *Short Cut*. To the left of that strip, the trees flourished again and completed the rest of the forest. It was in that section of woods that you would find 'Billy's tree house.'

Bobby and Jimmy knew of the tree house. In fact, they knew every inch of the forest, front-to-back and side-to-side, from their hunting expeditions. They figured, however (as peaceful people do), if they didn't want folks messing with *their* privacy, they most likely shouldn't go snooping in the business of others...where they didn't belong...and were most likely not welcome.

So, when they would get that far out, and came across the tree house, they simply smiled and walked past. Jimmy did remark one time though, "You know for a buncha city kids no older'n me, they did a helluva job on that there house." Bobby and son were both im-pressed.

Then Bobby would spot a scampering jackrabbit and instruct Jim-my to "*Shoot it!*" And with the speed and precision of a well-trained gunman, Jimmy would smoothly swing his rifle up, bring it to a dead stop in his hands, steady as a rock, and squeeze the trigger...

Blaaast!

The rabbit's head would depart from the body, leaving a ruffle of meat protruding from the neck, and spraying a bright red discharge of blood.

"That's a fine body of meat there," Bobby'd say, and they would watch the headless form, alive with severed nerves, jump and twitch in the grass, coating the greenery like an abstract artist radically flinging paint to a canvass.

Chapter 2

J immy had several brothers and sisters; in fact, the Hagger's were a good size family. There was the youngest, still a baby, Sally Ann, she was two years old. Then there was Ernie, and though Ernie was five, he refused to give up drinking from a bottle. Then Darrell, he was seven. Then Becky - nine. And Patty - ten. (Bobby had endured Opal's constant moaning about being fat, sick, and pregnant for two years in a row with Becky and Patty). Then Cassandra (Sandy), she was thirteen. And finally, Jimmy - sixteen.

Though, not a conscious decision, Bobby did spend more time with Jimmy than with the others. One reason was because he was older. Another was, he was a boy. And a third, because being older, it was more like spending time with another adult (whatever that meant in the Hagger clan).

Every once in awhile, Bobby and Jimmy would go for walks through the cemetery, where Bobby told the boy stories about his deceased relatives. Jimmy would stare at the headstones, struggling to read the inscriptions as he listened.

One comfortable evening in June, a mild breeze blew as father and son sat on the cool green grass, looking at the writing on the marker in front of them. Some were carved in wood, while others were simply crosses made of two sticks tied together and had a chiseled plaque nailed to them.

The one in particular they were looking at was made of stone. It read...

Here Lies
Trudy Hagger
Born 1901 Died 1961
Beloved Wife
Of
Earl Hagger
And
Mother
To
Charles, Lila,
Cynthia, John,
&
Ray

"You know," Bobby said, "I was only twelve years old when your Great Grandma died." He never took his eyes from the headstone. "She was the best Grandma a kid could have."

The two *men* sat, each chewing a long stick of grass.

"Yeah?" Jimmy could always sense when his *daddy* was getting ready to tell a story.

A moment later, the corners of Bobby's mouth turned up in a smirk and he grunted, "Hmmpff." Jimmy turned, studying his *Pa*. Then a grin slid onto his own face, baring the twelve teeth he had, and exposing the gap where a rifle had kicked back on him once while holding it too close to his mouth, knocking out a couple of seriously deteriorated gray and yellow teeth. "What's funny Pa?"

Bobby looked at the boy, and asked thoughtfully, "I ever tell you 'bout the time your Great Grandma Trudy decided to wage war on City Hall?"

Jimmy's face twisted with confusion, "Watchew mean, Pa?"

* * *

"Beat it lady!"

The gruff voice of a leather skinned construction worker rumbled in Trudy Hagger's ears like a hillside rockslide.

She had planted herself right on top of a carefully stacked supply of dynamite at the edge of the forest; just off from what would one day be Lakeside Highway.

Behind her were flagged areas and posted signs warning that, 'Beginning April 12, 1936, This Section Of The Lakeside Forest Will Be Under Construction.' The state had approved the area of trees to be ripped out in order to construct a new chemical research building called 'The Lakeside Testing Lab.'

Trudy had spent her life growing up amongst the trees and (what she called) *beautiful forestry*. And she was not about to let some *city fellers* go tearing into it to build some *poison* research building that might spit some weird wood killing chemicals into the air. Trudy Hagger was an environmentalist even before there was such a thing.

In her mind, since the birth of gas powered automobiles, the human race was slowly going to destroy itself with the smoke it poured into the air. Of course nobody at that time thought there was any sense to what she said.

But there they were, and what 'Brenner's' construction crew had not anticipated on that monumental ground breaking day, was the appearance of Trudy and her clan of Hagger's.

"Lady if you don't get off them boxes right now, I'll be forced to drag you off," the rumble voice bellowed again.

The air was clear and quiet that day when the man in the metal hat finished giving orders, and with only a split second of silence between, everyone froze at the sound of a rifle cock echoing through the trees. It was Earl, looking straight through the sites of the shotgun pressed against his shoulder.

"You touch that woman, boy, and I'll shoot you a new hole for pissin outta." He spoke direct and piercing, then spit a wad of tobacco at the man's feet.

The entire Hagger family had gathered for Trudy and *her cause.* They didn't all necessarily believe in it the way she did, in fact, some said they'd rather be out hunting deer, or fishing. But those who felt her *vexation* was justifiable talked the rest of them into it.

All of Earl and Trudy's kids were there, even young Ray. Earl's brother, Don, and his family were there. Trudy's two sisters, Angie and Carol, and their husbands and families were there. And, as the societal icing on the cake, some nearby townsfolk, concerned about the ruination of their woodland landscape, showed up to lend support. This was the 'Home Team.'

'The Visitors'

...Consisted of eleven construction workers, three from nearby towns, the rest from nearby states where, in 1936, not being able to find work in their own hometown, they went to where the work was.

There was a Foreman and an Assistant Foreman. Two Building Engineers (the suits) with blueprints in hand, checking boundaries and such. And a seventeen-year-old girl named Sheila, hired by the city to supply food and drinks (sandwiches, coffee, lemonade...). And they really hadn't planned on having to face a showdown before collecting a paycheck.

Charles Hagger snorted a laugh over his daddy's comment about the *pissin hole.* And when 'The Man' turned to see who was laughing,

Charles was right there with his own rifle up...barrel to nose, and cocked, "Don't you touch my Mama."

Joe Brennen was *The Man* who now had the scent of gunpowder coming at him from both sides. This made him both angry and nervous. The mentality of the people he was dealing with was starting to sink in.

"Look folks," Joe said, "I'm not trying to start any trouble, I'm just doing the job that was given to me."

Spat!

Earl spit tobacco again, "Well, I suggest you give it back then."

Charles pig grunted more laughter, "Give it back (snort, snort), that's a goodun, daddy."

Earl smiled.

"Bill?" Joe called to Bill Black, standing next to a pick up truck. Bill straightened up, eyes wide. "Take the truck to town and get the Sheriff, before one of these trigger happy fools hurts somebody."

"Yes sir," Bill replied, and went to get in the truck. But as he hit the seat and the key slid into the ignition...

BANG!

Bill dove down on the cushion; he figured one of the 'Hillbillies' had just blown Joe off to another dimension. Then he felt one side of the truck sink, and realized it was a tire that had been shot.

Trudy's Brother-in-law, Jack Sawder, grinned big (showing off his random selection of yellowed ivories). His rifle was still smoking, "Jes cleaned it this morning, Earl. Hoped I'd get to use it." This brought more snorts from Charles.

Joe Brennen was getting pissed off, "Lady, I appreciate what your trying to do, but would you please ask these...these...uh...*gentlemen*," (he'd never felt so foreign using such a common word), "to put their guns down so we can talk about this."

Trudy's eyebrows lifted, "They ain't stupid, mister. They can talk and hold a rifle at the same time." Joe looked at his men; they looked back and shrugged.

"I tell you what you need to do," she continued, "you-all boys need to load your carcasses back into them there vehicles of your'n, and high tail it outta here. That's what you need to do. Afor ya git hurt."

Joe felt his jaw clench, "How do I know," he said, "that once I get in one of *them there vehicles*, you won't blow out another damn tire...or worse?"

Charles started moving from side to side and walking a half circle around Joe, "Uh oh, Ma. I think we got us a live one. I think I smell a rumble comin."

"Drop your gun, hillbilly, I'll rumble with you. I'll kick your ass from here to the lake, you ignorant piece of shit," Joe stepped closer to the boy and spoke directly into his face.

Suddenly, as if two mosquitoes from hell had decided to wage war, Joe felt the biting sting of something pierce the back of his neck, "Aaahhh!" And at the sound of laughter, he turned to see little Ray and Johnny, Earl and Trudy's youngest, with peashooters in one hand and a load of small rocks in the other.

"Ray! Johnny! You put those away and git back over by your Pa, we got business to tend here," Trudy scolded the boys.

Ray and Johnny ran behind Earl, even Charles backed off a little, he may have been ready for a rumble, but he knew the tone of his Ma's voice when she meant business.

Joe looked at Trudy, still pissed, but relieved that she was at least willing to talk. He really didn't come there to fight; he came to work. However, if the situation came down to it (and there were no guns involved), he could, and most likely *would*, single handedly, beat the hell out of each and every one of them.

Joe Brennen stood six foot, four inches tall, and weighed 260 pounds...all muscle. This was in no small part due to his life of physical work. If he wasn't digging ground or moving steel, he was lumberjacking. And if field activity was slow, he would be on street repair in the city.

"Ok, lady, you want to step down from that dynamite and talk business?" he asked.

Trudy sat clutching her rifle, one hand on the barrel, the other on the butt, and a finger on the trigger. She paused a moment to size up the man in front of her. He was tall, his body was massive, he wore a thick leather tool belt loaded with potential weapons, and stood in steel-toed construction boots. Eventually, her eyes came back to meet his.

"Start talking, Worker Man," she told him.

Joe glared at her, suddenly not real sure what he could say without getting shot, "Lady, I don't know what to tell you," he started, "I've got a work order here to cut down five acres of trees and level this land we've roped off. Now these work orders come from the Government's Chemical Research Department and are signed by Mayor Deilher. So if you have a problem with that, your problem is with them, not us." Joe felt a small rush of authority, trying to say all the right things to get through to these *back hill's* people.

"Well, Worker Man," Trudy said, and hacked out a wad of spit, "I don't rightly care about what all dealings you got going on with the folks in the Government. Alls I know is, you're here with a load of tools, ready to tear up this beautiful forestry, an I ain't gonna let ya."

Joe was hot, his temper flared, "Well, dammit, lady, I've got orders to follow, what the hell do you want me to do?"

Trudy smiled, "I'm glad you finally asked that question. You see, I know this here part of the country like the back of my hand, and I happen to know that over in Colvert, about four mile west of here, there's a section of land that got burned up last Fall. It's all dead timber, an I don't figure anybody would take unkindly to you building your chemycal buildin over yonder," (fortunately for any Dental Hygienist who might have been watching, as big as she was smiling, she kept her lips together).

Joe had locked his irritation behind clenched teeth, trying to convince himself that she really was trying to help, "Lady, don't you think this entire area has been checked for the best location? Colvert is too far from any decent sewage outlets, there is no access to electrical power, and the road leading in is too narrow, there'd have to be road construction before we could even start the ground work." He had reached the limit of his annoyance at not being able to get started on the long job ahead, and knew he was only going to last about another minute before getting fed up and grabbing every one of them by the back of the neck, guns or no guns.

And now Trudy was pissed too, "Well, you ain't cuttin into *my* forest," she snapped. He'd taken what she thought was a perfectly good idea, and torn it apart. "This forest is mine and my family's and you can't have it." She stood and pointed her rifle squarely at him, "Now git yourself the hell outta here mister, afor I commence to blastin." And raising the gun to the sky, she took a shot to show she meant business.

The blast echoed through both, the trees and Joe's ears.

Everyone - the crew, the family, and the townsfolk were silent...frozen. Earl's mouth dropped, he had never seen Trudy fire a gun before. He knew she could *talk* up a storm, at times even use the rifle for threatening purposes, and would usually get her way with it. But she'd never actually pulled the trigger.

"Oh Jesus," Earl muttered, "she ain't never been this stirred up afor."

"Are ya gonna leave, ya Bastard?" She glared at Joe.

Joe looked over at Bill Black, Bill had grabbed a few sticks of dynamite and some matches from the back of the truck, he was waiting to see if some shit was going to hit a fan. Then Joe looked back at Trudy, "No," he announced, "I ain't." And without taking his eyes off her, said, "Bill, why don't you light one of those sticks and toss it there in the trees next to those three toothless pieces of hillbilly shit."

Without pause, Bill lit a fuse and let one fly. He knew they had just crossed the line; the game had gone too far, it was now going to be a battle of wills.

The three *hillbillies* in the woods were Don Hagger and Carol and Jack Sawder, and they made a mad dash from the area, barely clearing out before the stick hit and blew up two thin trees.

The explosion startled Trudy and caused her to squeeze off another shot.

"Wait!"

The cry was from Tom Dayton, one of the Building Engineers. The collar of his white button down cotton shirt was a sponge of nervous sweat...and he was near ready to drench his drawers, "There has to be a better way to deal with this." Tom looked pale as a ghost, scared the next shot would be at Joe Brennen, or...possibly...himself.

There was fire in Trudy's eyes when she turned her aim on Bill, "You best drop that other stick right this second, you sumbitch, or you'll be wishin you were *only* dead."

Bill found himself staring straight down the barrel of a cocked shotgun. The dynamite hit the ground.

Tom spoke impulsively, not knowing what to say, "Ma'am, please, if you'll come down to the courthouse, I'm sure we can work this out."

Trudy's voice was cold and steady, "You jes ain't understandin, are ya?"

"Ma'am we are not the one's who have control over this matter," he said.

Joe looked at Tom, Tom was sheet white, fearing that the woman was going to pull the trigger and blow one of them off to the spirit world.

Then...the cock of another rifle echoed in Joe's ears. And from a mouth whose teeth may never have seen toothpaste, let alone something as foreign as mouthwash, a stench reeked out with low and slow, calmly spoken words, "You do what my Mama says, and get yourselves gone from here, or I'll be scraping your brains offin the trees for dinner tunight." Charles was only nineteen, but ignorance armed with a loaded gun can be a mighty scary thing.

"That's it!" Joe blurted, and swung around, throwing his fist into Charles's gut, forcing the air from his scrawny body. The boy doubled over gasping for breath.

Joe took advantage of the moment and seized the rifle, then pulled Charles up by the hair at the top of his head. He held him out in front of himself for protection, pulling back hard on his head, facing him to the sky.

And with his hand low, Joe brought the barrel up under Charles's sweaty chin, "Come on, you redneck sons-of-bitches, give me an excuse to blow his head right-the-fuck off. I fucking dare you."

Charles was regaining his breath, but the sudden turn of events got him all jittery and he was breathing in quick short gasps, jerking his body back and forth. His ignorance however, went undamaged and shone through like a star, "Shoot him, Pa," he yelled. "Shoot him!"

"Let go of the boy," a townswoman cried.

"Yeah, let him loose," came another.

Joe and Trudy glared into each other's souls. You could hear the murmur of a revolt growing louder and louder as more comments cut through.

"Get the hell out of here. Go back to the city."

"Let the boy alone."

"We ought to beat the hell out of *all* of 'em," said Trudy's Brother-in-Law, Jack.

Then, after a short moment of silence…

"Yeah, that's what we ought to do." Joe heard the voice behind him and turned around. It was one of *his* men, Alan Hardesty. "What do you say, Joe? Let's just beat the hell out of all of them." There was an uprising cheer of agreement from the crew.

"Come on, Joe, you hold the kid for insurance, and we'll go kick their stupid hillbilly asses," Dick Braun, a large and muscular crew-member spoke, stepping away from the truck.

Then Alan bent down and picked up an axe, "Better yet, let's just cut 'em up," he swung the axe up over his shoulder and smiled.

Trudy's eyes widened twice their normal size and she raised her rifle to shoot at Alan, when she saw both her brothers-in-law were already going for him.

Maniacal grins twisted their faces, and their eyes were crazed. If Alan was caught, he was surely a dead man.

Another of Joe's men, Larry Walden, picked up a cross cut saw and was slicing the air with it.

Alan saw the two men coming at him and began swinging his axe back and forth.

"No, no, this is crazy," Tom was yelling.

Everything was suddenly very intense and violently dangerous. Joe wasn't the only one surprised by the abrupt turnabout, Earl and Trudy both looked shocked. In fact, Earl was so dumbfounded and scared for Charles; he froze with his mouth hung open. His rifle seemed to be stuck in an invisible holster, resting rigid in mid-air.

Trudy looked to Earl for guidance. It took two seconds for her to realize he'd taken temporary leave of coherency and she'd have to figure this one out on her own.

Instinctively, she raised her gun and took aim for another crewman, Ron Roberts, who'd also started swinging with a crosscut saw in one hand and a hatchet in the other.

She personally had no previous experience firing a gun, and was shaking, but everything happened so quick, tension and reflex caused her finger to squeeze the trigger.

The explosion sent a bullet, like lightning striking, into the saw blade. It shattered in a dozen pieces. Slivers and shards of metal flew and lodged into Ron's face. One jagged piece an inch and a half in diameter sliced down through the left corner of his mouth and straight into his tongue. His bottom lip peeled back in a flap and blood spurt over his face. It sprayed out so far; it shot into the face of Dick Braun standing next to him.

Another piece buried itself in his forehead and some gray matter oozed out. Still another fragment shot through the bottom lid of his right eye, above the cheekbone, and at an upward angle, pushing the eye completely out of its socket.

Ron's screams could be heard all the way to the lake. He dropped to the ground holding his head, but so lost in pain and shock, he passed out. Small bubbles of blood pumped from his face.

Trudy's Brothers-in-Law, Jack Sawder and Henry Gunner, approached Alan, who maintained a serious and steady swing of his axe. Jack and Henry had rifles, but they were more interested in a simple good ass whipping than anything else.

So, rather than shoot him, they turned the guns around to the butt end and tried beating the weapon out of his hands. It was almost amusing, them swinging at Alan (and missing), and him swinging back (and missing).

Joe looked down at Ron Roberts, his face covered with pulp and a red pool spreading around his head. Joe's stomach turned, *Jesus,* he thought, *this is insane.* He turned to Trudy, "If that boy is dead, I'll see to it you hang."

Trudy stared at Ron, her face shining with surprise at the damage she'd done. She was speechless. Fortunately, Earl had come back to his senses and could speak for her, "You let my boy go, you sumbitch, or he ain't the only one who's gonna git his face blowed off."

Joe sunk again with continuing disbelief; how did he get involved in this whole situation? And why do these stupid hillbillies keep on with it?

"You *Asshole!*" he was enraged with hatred for these people. He took the barrel of the rifle down from Charles's chin, and brought it around to the back of his right leg, behind his knee, "*Fuck you,*" he shouted, and pulled the trigger.

The impact would have thrown Charles off to the trees, but Joe had a tight grip on the boy's hair (greasy as it was). So, even though his body leapt into the air, it fell right back into place. Only, when it came back, the right leg, from the knee down...was gone. Completely blown off.

Charles hung there for all to see, as Joe held him up like a protective shield.

The upper portion of his leg stuck out, dripping shredded meat from the blown away pant leg, while severed nerves slapped at the torn flesh, and blood streamed down the protruding bone that stuck out two inches further than of the rest of the leg. Charles passed out.

Jack, Henry, and Alan, all stopped battling to look at Charles. He hung from Joe's fist like a wet dishrag. For a moment, time came to a complete stop. Nobody moved. Nobody spoke.

Then...the shriek of one townswoman running off into the forest, echoed like a kind of screaming death cry. Like an emergency siren, warning everyone that their lives were all about to change. And as the scene settled in, another scream hailed that all hell was about to break loose...and it did.

"Holy Jesus! He blew cousin Charlie's leg off," said Jack Jr.; only a year younger than Charles, the two had grown up together, best friends. Jack Sawder Jr. ('Junior' as he was called) never carried a rifle; he claimed they were too awkward. But he did like the damage a gun could do, and was partial to pistols, a .32 caliber to be exact. He also liked knives, his favorite, was a silver handled, 10-inch stiletto that he wore in a side strap. Never left home without it. That day he had both.

"You blew cousin Charlie's leg off," Junior repeated in disbelief. Then, in more of a reflex, not consciously aware, he reached for the stiletto. And, with years of throwing experience, had the blade out, in his hand, and arm back for a thrust before Joe could even blink. In fact, when he did blink that was all he saw, a pointed strip of metal coming at him like a darting bird.

He tried to duck, but in doing so he only lowered himself to catch the blade in his left collar. It stuck deep through his upper chest, sliding between the bones.

The cutting pain pounded horrendously with the penetration. Joe wavered momentarily, bordering unconsciousness, grasping at flashes of clarity.

"Aaaggghhh!" he screamed. *"Sonafabitch!"*

He dropped Charles to the ground and reached to pull the blade out. The first tug pulled the skin back and blood squirt his face. The second tug pulled out the knife, more blood, some oozy white stuff, and swollen muscle.

The pain blocked all rational thought from his mind while his body numbed with shock. Apparently, though, nothing vital was severed, and his focus then became to stick the blade back into the little bastard that threw it at him.

Alan saw this as the go ahead to start swinging again, he swung the axe around hard and fast...into Henry's gut. Henry tried to jump back, but not before the cutting edge had a chance to slice into his belly. Henry went down grabbing the gaping wound, blood shot between his fingers.

Trudy and Earl raised rifles and fired on the crew; who were either looking for weapons, taking cover, or both. The *young* 'Hagger kids' ran and hid behind trees. Most of the townsfolk were *already* hiding; they had come to save a forest, not participate in a family feud. The exploding and ricocheting bullets off metal, was not only ear piercing, it was extremely nerve shattering. Bill Black damn near crapped his pants when a shot blasted out the windshield of the truck he was in.

"That's it," he muttered. He turned the ignition, stomped on the clutch, threw it into gear, hit the gas, and charged toward Trudy...still on top the boxed dynamite. He figured it wouldn't be a good idea to ram a pile of explosives, but he could put a scare into her.

At the last minute she looked over, and scared she was. So startled in fact, she fell off the stack backward and landed on her rump.

Earl was caught up in the gunfire and commotion, and *thinking* Trudy had things under control, he went weaving his way through the trees, closing in on the other truck.

"Don, go 'round the other side," Earl told his brother. Don was older than Earl and a lot grayer, but Don had a keen eye with a rifle, "I gotcha, Earl," he called back. "Come on, Chrissy." Don hunched down with his oldest daughter, Chrissy, and the two of them circled through the trees to get to the other side of the truck.

Chrissy was in a class all her own. She was twenty-four years old, and the only good looking Hagger in the entire clan. Cynthia (Earl and

Trudy's youngest daughter) wasn't bad looking either, but Cynthia was still a child, fourteen-years-old, not quite the woman her cousin was.

Chrissy had been described, even by people outside the family, as beautiful. Her hair was waist-length, thick, soft, and blonde. She wore it parted in the middle and swept back behind her shoulders. She stood five feet, seven inches tall, with a figure of 36-25-36, which was already more curves than any three other Hagger women had combined.

To Don, her daddy, she was not only beautiful, but a crack shot as well. Pistol, Rifle, Knife, Slingshot, Pea Shooter, Bow and Arrow, you name it, Chrissy could not only shoot it, but she could put out the eye of a snake at a hundred feet.

Jack had finally knocked the axe out of Alan's hands. Alan watched his only defense drop away, then looked up at smiling Jack Sawder, baring rotted old black and yellow teeth encased in chewing tobacco. His face covered in dirty brown sweat, running over his lips and beard stubble. Alan could smell the words he spoke as they fumed from his mouth, "Ok, shit-head, it's jes you and me."

Fear ran like acid through Alan's veins, "It's not fair," he cried, "you've got a gun."

Jack's grin got bigger; he put his face right up next to Alan's, winked, and tossed the rifle over his shoulder. Then he brought up two ragged looking fists and said, "Come on chicken boy, I'll jes give ya a good ass whoopin then."

Alan stared at him, panic pounded in his chest. Jack threw out a rabbit punch and tagged him square on the jaw.

Alan's head flew back, his face flushed red with pain; a growling moan erupted from his throat. And though the punch itself hurt, his anguish came when, being unprepared, he chomped down on his tongue and nearly bit it in half.

The surprise of it shot-gunned a rage within him and he snapped back, spitting blood in Jack's eyes, "You muhver fufver," he cursed through busted lips, and thrust a heavy booted right foot flat into the man's testicles.

Jack's eyes popped wide open as an agonized scream ripped loose from his throat. His hands plunged between his legs, his legs buckled, and he fell face first into the dirt. Alan hovered, debating whether to kick him again or move on; feeling suddenly charged up to go on a hillbilly elimination spree.

Joe finally cleared some of the blinding pain from his head, and with stiletto in hand, searched for *Junior*, "Where are you, you bastard?" Then he saw two other Hagger boys, Johnny (Earl's 11 year old) and Frank (Don's 22 year old), both moving in on Bill, who was preoccupied trying to reverse the truck away from the dynamite so he could go around and get Trudy.

Joe saw Johnny holding back to cover Frank. Then noticed Frank already had his rifle lifted to the back of Bill's head. He knew if he didn't do something quick, Bill was dead. So, reaching back with the stiletto, he snapped his arm forward and flung it.

It breezed by Johnny's ear (the hairs on his neck stood up), and Joe and Johnny both watched the knife implant itself into Frank's back. It slid in as smooth as if it had been greased. His arms flew out from his sides and the rifle fell to the ground. Blood spattered the truck as little Johnny watched his cousin turn with a tortured grimace and spew thick red liquid from his mouth. Frank was wide-eyed as he looked from Johnny to Joe, his mouth stretched open for a silent scream, then he looked back at Johnny. Then when his eyes rolled up, he dropped to the ground, twitched a few times...and died.

Apparently Joe's aim was better than he thought, he'd pierced Frank right through from the back of his heart. Johnny turned to Joe, "You killed him." The two stared at each other.

Earl and Junior came around one side of the other pick up, while Don and Chrissy circled the back; they could see each other, and between them was three crew men (each with a pick or an axe of some kind), crouching next to the truck, trying not to be seen. It didn't work.

"Time to die, boys," Don announced, and raised his rifle. He took quick aim and fired. One of them caught on quickly to what was happening and dove behind a nearby tree. The bullet missed and whizzed past Junior's ear, "Sorry 'bout that Junior," Don apologized.

Then Earl squeezed off a shot and hit another of them (a boy nineteen years old) in the left shoulder. He spun around; his back slapped against the truck and he slid to the ground. A red jagged trail streaked the side of the gray truck.

Chrissy stepped out in front and raised her rifle to the third man. Their eyes locked just for a second, long enough for her to notice his desperation. He noticed only her coldness. And when he turned to run, she pulled the trigger.

He never heard the blast; his head blew clean off. As if somebody had taken a sledge-hammer to a ripe tomato, skull and brain matter spattered the shrubs. His body ran on in reflex for a moment, until his legs figured out what had happened, eventually, he stumbled and fell.

The one man, who'd darted for the trees, looked back to see what had happened, and was suddenly overcome with anger. He stepped out with his hatchet, brought it back, and flung it ferociously at Chrissy.

She saw it coming, with just enough time to step out of the way. But Don was right behind her. The axe buried itself dead center into his face, blood shot from every opening in his head. He dropped to the ground with arms flailing, trying to grab the handle and pull it out, but then his body went limp.

Chrissy froze, "Daddy?"

Larry Walden, who'd been dragging a handsaw and axe around, while dodging bullets that Trudy's sisters, Carol and Angie were firing, turned a corner of the pick-up and came face to face with Earl.

"Stand back Junior," Earl warned. And the two began batting at each other with rifle barrel and axe handle.

Walter Stone, the boy shot in the shoulder by Earl, crawled over to where Don's rifle had flown, and picked it up. He struggled a bit, unable to move his left arm very well, took aim as best he could, and without anyone noticing or trying to stop him, shot and nailed Junior right in the ass. Junior yelped like a wounded dog and ran for the trees.

Chrissy heard Junior's cries and saw him disappear into the forest, when she turned to see who had shot him, she found herself looking straight into the chest hairs of Dick Braun. He was three times her size, all muscle, dirty, sweaty, and appeared to be salivating, "Come on, sweet Bitch. What say you and I show the jackrabbits how to fuck," and he picked her up by her arms. He shook the rifle loose from her hands, turned her around, and in a bear hug...headed off to the trees.

Earl decided he was going to have to knock the damn axe out of Larry's hands before he could get the gun barrel in position to shoot him. So he took a hard and deliberate swing with the rifle, the axe slipped from Larry's sweaty palm and flew away. That would have been good for Earl, except that Larry panicked and started swinging with the saw blade.

He swung frantically like a loose power line whipping back and forth. The saw came around and cut into Earl, then pulled out in a drag, ripping over his wrists, then in again, and back out. Sawing back and forth. Pulling away, then in again, and again, until Earl's arms began to look like a hungry dog had chewed them to the bone. His hands were covered in gloves of blood when he dropped his gun, howling with the pain. Larry was momentarily satisfied, and seeing his chance to run, he vanished into the trees.

Dick threw Chrissy to the ground and yanked his belt out to tie her hands. "Let go of me, you pig. Let me go!" she screamed.

"Yeah, you think *I'm* the pig, little girl, but *you're* the one that's going to squeal," he grunted.

He tied her wrists tightly behind her. Then rolled her on her back and began tearing her clothes off. First to go was the *body fit* under-shirt she had on...there was no bra.

"Nice tits, Bitch!"

She spit in his face. She cussed him. She screamed and growled, but the more she did, the rougher he got.

"Spit all you want, girlie, I'm gonna to fuck you till you bleed," his grin was evil. He started tugging at her jeans and found she wasn't wearing any underpants either, "Well shit, girl, you're making this easier by the minute." Then he began to slobber on her.

Though she screamed and kicked her legs, it was to no avail. Dick had them pushed up and apart with his massive body wedged be-tween. Most of his weight rested across her naked stomach and breasts - holding her down, sliding back and forth with dirty, gritty sweat.

As he sucked and bit on her neck he could hear the grunt of his own breathing. But...there was something else. Every time he breathed out, a second exhale followed right after. It was like an echo, only distant, from somewhere back in the woods.

At first it didn't bother him, he was too busy drilling the girl. His cock was large and in charge, in fact, the girth of his petrified penis was splitting the young woman in two. She was tearing and bleeding down the insides of her legs.

Finally, Dick got irritated with the echo and had to know if someone else was out there. When he pulled off, Chrissy started to lift up with what strength she had left. "No ya don't," he snarled, "you're not going anywhere," and he punched her hard in the jaw. He knocked her out. She fell back and lay motionless as he climbed off. He pulled his pants up and went to look behind a cluster of nearby trees.

There, in the tall green grass, only fifteen feet away, was Sheila Corter (the coffee girl), in basically the same position as Chrissy, with most of the same kind of bruises on her. Only, Sheila was gagged so she couldn't scream. And there, furiously pumping away on top of her was Erwin Gunner, Henry and Carol's boy.

Apparently, Erwin (who was all of seventeen) considered himself more of a lover than a fighter, and had stayed away from the feud. No one even noticed when he grabbed Sheila and took off.

"I'm going to kill you, you shit-head little hillbilly!" Dick growled at him.

Erwin looked up and saw the wall of a man coming at him, fixing to kill. He almost released his bowels. His face turned white, his eyes grew wide, and he leapt to his feet in a scramble to get his own pants up, while trying to run away at the same time.

Suddenly, a cascade of gunfire thundered through the forest.

Boom! Boom! Boom!

The heavy sound of shell blasting ripped through the air. Dick heard one tear into a tree next to him. Joe heard two puncture the truck behind him. Alan heard two burst the gas tank of one of the trucks.

Earl saw the windshield explode out of the pick-up that still had one. Everyone froze, looking for the source of the gunfire. When the fighting finally stopped, and everyone was still...the shooting stopped as well. The sudden silence was deafening. Then...

"All right. That's enough!" ...It was Trudy, from twenty feet above. Everyone looked up to see her standing on a large sturdy branch of the tree she'd climbed. Her rifle was aimed directly at Joe Brennen. Below her were Angie and Carol, each armed with shotguns pointed directly at the two building engineers, Tom Dayton and Paul Storm; they'd been captured and tied to other trees.

Trudy was quiet as she looked around at all the blood and disgrace. And in that moment of silence, everyone looked around with disbelief; no one was able to quite comprehend what they'd let themselves get caught up in.

"Earl?" Trudy called, "We need to go home now. There won't be any tree ripping here today, I can tell ya that fer a fact."

Joe looked from Trudy to Bill, and was struck with surprise, *When did that happen?* Bill had been shot through the chest and was hung over the steering wheel in the truck. He was as dead as Frank Hagger, who lay with a knife in his back, on the ground behind him. Then Joe looked at Trudy, "Lady, this is not over. First they'll arrest you, then they'll lock you up and throw away the key. Then they'll come back and build here anyway. Whether you like it or not."

Trudy glared at Joe, "Let's go home, Earl."

* * *

Bobby stopped talking; he stared hard at Trudy's grave. Jimmy was completely engrossed; he sat unmoving, hanging on every word, "What happened then, Pa? Did they arrest Grandma?"

Bobby looked sideways at the boy, "Nope," he said and looked off thoughtfully, "I reckon they coulda. But the way it was told to me; at the trial nobody was able to say fer sure, one way or ta other, which side actually threw the first punch, or took the first shot, them or us.

So, the Judge said, since as many of us got wasted as them, he figured it was all evened up. And as long as he never heard a peep more outta your Grandma, he would let her go back home."

Jimmy's mouth hung open, "And Grandma didn't try to stop 'em the next time they come out?"

"Well, from what your Grandpappy Ray told me, she mighta tried, but the next time they come out, they brought armed guards with 'em and surrounded the outside of the land back there. Wouldn't let nobody in or out until all the trees was cleared and they were laying down cement."

Bobby was quiet for a moment, and then he looked up in the direction of the 'Xanorse' plant. "We lost a lot of Hagger blood that day...thanks to that chemycal buildin."

ATTACK ON PLEASURE VIEW

Chapter 1

It was spring of 1989 when the attacks began that would bring Pleasure View to its knees.

One such event occurred on a dismal June evening as northern Kentucky was having another of its infamous thunderstorms. Lightning tore up the sky, exposing the blinding whiteness of Heaven, while the thunderclaps of God sounded like dynamite exploding on rooftops. Shutters, trashcans, and whistling trees played background to an orchestra of gushing wind and rain.

Electricity was cutting off and on throughout Pleasure View and surrounding towns. Television viewing (if your television didn't zap out) was a continual annoyance of beeps, signaling you to read the caption at the bottom of the screen. Notifying you that there was a thunderstorm happening in the area (the assumption being, that you weren't intelligent enough to figure it out for yourself). The warning was to stay away from windows and doors, in case a blast of wind or rain, or possibly a tree suddenly decides to push its way in (again, the assumption was, you couldn't figure that out for yourself).

Sarah Maples had stayed home that night, alone. Sarah was nineteen years old and had been on her own for a year. The last years at home with *The Folks* had gotten to be too much for her. She and her mother were in constant battles...

"Clean up your room..."

"Mother, I'm seventeen, and it is *my* room."

"...And turn down that music."

"The music's not loud."

And, "Sarah, will you make dinner tonight, dear? I'm so tired."

"Well yeah, you've been drinking all day."

And, "The laundry needs washing," and, "The grass needs cutting," and, "Have you vacuumed this week? ...Remember, dust first." Then, "Sarah, I think it's time you start paying rent. $150.00 a month would be reasonable."

"Excuse me? Hold on. Back up right there. Rent???" Sarah ranted swear words the whole time she was packing; but when it's time to go, it's time to go.

She moved in with Veronica (Ronnie), a friend from work. They were waitresses at the 'Won Ton Express,' a local Chinese restaurant, which was remarkably popular considering the owners were real Chinese, and in that area of the south, in 1989, there was still the occasional 'Whites Only' sign lingering outside certain dining establishments.

Ronnie was twenty years old, and most likely would have stayed at home with her parents another year or two if Sarah hadn't pushed so hard for a roommate.

They both had night classes at the Community College, and were both in complete agreement that full time school could wait. At the moment it was more important, if for no other reason than preserving sanity, to be independent.

On this particular evening, neither girl had any classes. And with the storm eliminating any reasonable business at 'Won Ton's,' (it just wasn't safe driving in that kind of weather), their Boss, Ti Lee Wong, called and said the restaurant would be closed, they had the night off.

Then, Ronnie (refusing to be held captive by *a little rain*) decided to spend the night at her boyfriend, Scott's house. This left Sarah home alone to enjoy her privacy.

She was psyched for a pleasant evening, curled up at the end of the sofa, watching TV, until *all* the power finally went out. At which time, she broke out the candles she kept in the drawer of her mahogany, roll top desk; the one piece of furniture she treasured. And as she lit them, she placed them strategically around the living room. Then she went to the bookcase and pulled out her hardback copy of Stephen King's 'The Tommyknockers.' She sat down, with book in hand, and a glass of ice tea (hold the lemon, heavy on the sugar), and began to read.

The wind howled through the partially opened windows in the bedrooms. And though stormy and wet outside, this was still June, still Kentucky, and no matter how much wind and rain there was, it was still 80 degrees outside with 90 percent humidity, so yes, the windows were open.

Sarah couldn't help thinking how perfect everything was. The rustle of leaves on the trees outside, the rain slapping the concrete patio, the glow of flickering candle flames, the ice tea, the crackling thunder. All while becoming spellbound in a good scary book. She had no idea that by morning, her life could very well have been inserted into a Stephen King novel.

It was almost 9:30 when she thought she heard one of the potted plants on the patio tip over. She had been so engrossed in the book, she wasn't sure if it was just nerves overreacting to the storm, or possibly a cat outside knocking things around in search of shelter. But after a studious moment of concentrated listening, she dismissed the notion that anything was wrong and went back to the book.

Then she heard a crash in Ronnie's bedroom. The leaping spring she made from the couch was very similar to the last bursting shower of a Red Devil firework...just when you think it's over; an unexpected shot of flame and noise makes your heart skip five beats. If she were a cartoon (she thought) she would have been the cat who shoots to the ceiling with fully extended claws, rigidly nailing herself to the plaster.

After a long and quiet period of speculation, she decided she should try to find the source of the noise. *Perhaps,* she thought, *it was that cat outside breaking something, and the sound just echoed through the window.*

"Yeah, that must be it." Now she was talking to herself.

Sarah picked up a tall candle and, trailing her light through the darkness, slowly headed down the hall.

Her heart was beating three times its normal rate, inching her way to Ronnie's room. When she turned in through the doorway, lightning ripped the sky and lit the room brighter than any bulb could have.

The sudden flash snapped a picture of an open window whose screen had been pushed in; knocking over a glass kerosene lamp that Ronnie kept on the nightstand, breaking it into a dozen large pieces on the floor. Then she was immediately cast back to darkness; again, the candle flame her only light. But the image of the screen and broken lamp stayed with her.

Now how does a screen blow in like that? she wondered. But her tension had eased a little, thinking she'd solved the mystery.

Slowly she crossed to the bed, next to where the broken glass had scattered, and lowering the candle, she stopped just short of the first piece. *I guess it would not be wise to venture any further, barefoot,* she thought, and she sat in contemplation on the edge of the bed.

So, how did that happen?

Relaxing for a moment, judging the situation, she brought the candle around to see if the screen was still in one piece. Half of it was under the bed, but what she *could* see, had been ripped down the middle. Astonished by the damage, she sat quietly in the dark, speculating.

Eventually, the silence began to fill with the sound of her breathing, the swooshing in and out in her ears. *In...and out, in...out, in...out, in..in...out..out, in..in,* she was suddenly aware of an echo each time she inhaled or exhaled.

That's odd.

And then...fear rippled through her soul, *Oh God! There's someone in the room with me.*

Her eyes grew wide, she would have done her 'scared cat spring' again, but fright had her planted to the edge of the bed.

The wheels in her head spun a thousand miles a minute. *What do I do? What do I do?* Finally, a decision; *If I remain calm, just slowly get up and walk out like nothing's wrong, he'll figure I didn't realize he was here, and leave me alone...yes, of course, that's what to do.*

Sarah looked down; *come on legs, move!* Fear held her in a tight grip - it was all she could do just to stand. But, one at a time, her feet inched toward the door.

Hearing the second person's breathing grow anxious, she thought perhaps he was scared too. Then she miscalculated her foot placement, and her left one came down directly onto a thin sliver of glass, which made no hesitation slicing into her. The pain was instant and merciless. The sliver went through the front ball of her foot, circled around inside, and poked out through the thin web of flesh between her big toe and the one next to it.

The scream within never actually found vocalization, it caught like a baseball wedged in her throat. Not daring to cry out, tears pooled in her eyes.

Instead, she stopped stiff for a moment of acceptance, shook off a shiver of repulsion and nausea, then leaned over, lifting her foot at the same time, and grabbed the bottom of the glass (resting a good inch and a half into her), and tried to slide it out.

The first attempt was unsuccessful, her fingers slid off with the oozing blood, *Fu-uck!* Her mind was momentarily psychotic with excruciating pain.

Finally, at the end of her patience, she yanked up the corner of the bedspread, twisting her one hand into it, while using the other, still securely gripping the candle, to guide the light to see by. And clamping tightly onto the glass, she pulled. She felt every movement the sliver made inside, twisting and squeezing through swollen, throbbing meat. Until, with a muffled grunt, it was out. The release from the pressure was so great it actually felt good. She blew sweat off her upper lip, and realized her whole body was wet with perspiration.

Relieved the crisis was over; she stood straight up, with candle in hand, and found herself looking into Ronnie's 3' x 4' dresser mirror. And, just above the flame, directly behind her, she saw two glaring yellow eyes, and heard...*breathing.* Only, now it sounded more like water slurping its way through a clogged drainpipe. Like snot sucking up.

Her mouth opened when a hand rose over her right shoulder, and her overflow of suppressed screams finally released in full throttle to the silence of the dark apartment.

CRAAACK!

Another bolt of lightning tore through the sky, again lighting the entire room. This time she saw in the mirror, right behind her...the face of death.

The lightning engraved the image of a face not even a mother could love – something, once human...maybe. But now, the form surrounding the yellow eyes (eyes that didn't quite glow, yet somehow radiated in the dark) had the appearance of something long gone and rotten.

Between the sunken eyes and blackened red skin, were decayed nostril fragments. Long openings where the cartilage, except for a few dripping particles, was gone.

The flapping remainder of what was once a lip, peeled back, exposing six corroded teeth floating in boiled, blistered, and disintegrating gums. While threads of a tongue lay black and limp behind the bottom jaw.

One ear consisted of a lobe and shredded flesh up to the middle, and then it was gone. The other ear was completely missing, leaving oozy bubbles of puss and red leaky blisters surrounding the hole.

The entire body, from the hair down, dripped with thick greasy purplish yellow oil. Long black hair was plastered in dripping strands of the oil, drained onto a slick and shiny dead face. Slime coated the entire body, covering the skin that remained, and the jutting bone where it didn't. The bone itself looked as if termites had feasted there.

Sarah looked in the mirror at the hand above her shoulder, at fingers where flesh had pulled away and torn loose from their tips and now bones poked through. Then she saw oil run down one skeletal stem and drip off onto her nightshirt. It bubbled and fizzed and ate through the material, then fizzed again, and burned into *her*.

That scream could very well have ripped vocal chords. Immediately, she took the hand still wrapped in bedspread, and hit at her shoulder, at the spot of ooze. Then shook free of the spread, dropped the candle, and darted for the door. Her only guide being, the dim glow of light timidly reaching down the hall from the living room.

Sarah's foot stuck to the carpet each time she slapped it down and squeezed out blood. Coming from the bedroom, she grabbed the doorjamb to swing herself around, holding on so she wouldn't fly into the wall on the other side. And in that whirling second, she looked back into the dark, and could see the grotesquely mutated face of the creature close enough behind that she could smell the stench of its breath.

"Oh God!" she cried, and threw herself into a run down the hallway.

"You're mine, Darlin!" it spoke. The voice was a deep and raspy gurgle.

In the living room, she looked quickly for some kind of weapon. Her eyes fixed on the fireplace, *The Poker!* She leapt for it, yanking to rip it from the holder, the shovel and brush banged into the wall. Sarah turned quickly to fend off her assailant, who was now three feet in front of her.

Then an all-new fear came to light, she noticed shooting sparks in the blackness behind the creature. *Oh my God!* Her mind was an explosion of lucidity. *The candle, I dropped the candle. The place is on fire.*

And *the thing* came at her.

In her disjointed observation, she realized, *it* was either *covered* with the weird oil, or the oil was soaking through from the body underneath. Its pants were an old pair of jeans, ripped and frayed at the bottom, holes rotting through everywhere, clinging to a pair of oily legs and held up by a piece of rope. And its shirt was an old T-shirt in the same condition.

She could see patches on its arms and legs where the skin had disintegrated, exposing bone and muscle. There was thick red-black blood mixed with oozy yellow pus running and blending with the body oil. She could see toe bones sticking through where the flesh was eaten away, same as the fingers.

"What do you want?" she screamed. *"What are you?"*

"I want to show you how I feel," it said, and came closer.

A burst of flames suddenly shot down the hall, spreading high and wide behind *him*, but his eyes were fixed like lasers on her.

The fire quickly grew to be a surrounding wall. The heat was so intense; she was forced to keep her eyes nearly closed, while backing away, bumping into everything.

She jabbed out with the poker, seeing him coming at her. She missed. The back wall was closing in; soon she would have nowhere to go. Then...another jab, *Bulls eye!* But...

She hit him dead center in the stomach, but there was no pressure, no puncture, no force; it just slid through, like a sewing needle through silk.

He smiled.

Sarah's face was chalk white. She stared at the heavy rod stuck in his stomach, then up to his face and the insane grin of jiggling teeth floating in red boiled gums.

Her stomach was coming up and her head was drowning in a flood of horror. *I've got to maintain,* she thought, *I've got to get out of here.*

The creature stuck out its right hand and grabbed her upper left arm.

Sssssss!

She burned instantly; first feeling the absorbing heat, then...the sting of fire. She looked and saw yellow oil squeeze out between the fingers wrapped around her. It was fizzing, bubbling. She could smell flesh searing away, and his hard, greasy grip closed tighter, burning all the way through.

She jerked to get free, but before he let go, he gave a last hard squeeze and completely disconnected any meat between her upper arm and her lower arm. All that remained was a five-inch gap of bone.

Sarah threw herself to the side; numb with shock, except for the burning that engulfed her shoulder and dead left arm. She tried grabbing the edge of the loveseat to pull herself up, but only her right arm would lift. Her terror was blinding as she realized she had only one working arm.

The awareness of her condition took only a moment too long to sink in, before the creature reached out and grabbed her thigh. Her mind was a kaleidoscope of distortion.

"Aaaagggghhhh!!!"

And while sending out the echo of a fresh scream, more of her burned. This time, however, she rolled away before it could melt through. Sprawled on the floor, belly down, she lifted her head and saw the sliding glass door in front of her. It was open...

It was *open!*

It Was Open!!!

Only the screen stood between death and freedom. And in the reflection of the glass side, she saw the entire apartment in flames behind her.

With her one good arm, she pushed up onto her knees and was about to crawl away.

Slap!

Two slimy hands came down, one on each hip, and that was about all the confirmation she needed, to realize she was going to die – followed by cremation.

She tried to pull away, but the grip was tight, and then...a nightmare beyond the realm of comprehension. A pain so sharp she slipped in and out of consciousness. The creature behind her, holding her, had taken out whatever it was that was left of his penis, and began poking and prodding between her legs, trying to find an opening.

First it was a jab to the thigh, then one to each buttock. Sarah felt the branding of a burning iron missing its mark, over and over, until...Bulls eye! It hit.

His oil covered, blood blistered, penis erectus, plunged directly into her. Scorching and tearing through her vaginal walls with the ungodly burn of chemical fire.

So overwhelmed with violating pain, she erupted with an anger she had never experienced before. Her body reacted with the numb, unexplainable strength that perhaps only someone doing PCP might understand.

From her knees, with one arm, she leapt forward away from him; rolled, and climbed to her feet.

"Where ya goin, Lover?" he demanded. The fire was at his heels. Sarah ran into the screen door, knocked it out and went down with it, only to have to struggle to her feet...again. She turned to check *escape status* and saw the creature walking slowly from the roaring flames that consumed the apartment behind him. He stepped through the open doorway into the rain.

Not looking back again, she turned and ran blindly into the black stormy night; the rain slapped her face, a dead numbness was in her left arm, a bleeding puncture in the bottom of her foot, and an unconscious blackout swiftly coming on with the indescribable pain and hemorrhaging between her legs.

The creature disappeared into nearby trees, not to be seen again that night. Sarah finally reached the road, but with no strength left, she dropped to the ground and fell into a dark slumber.

The sound of Fire Engines approached in the distance.

Chapter 2

With the attack on Sarah Maples, the entire community of Pleasure View went on guard; an edge of fear had everyone looking over their shoulder. Windows and doors were closed and locked on hot days and at times that would normally never happen.

Sarah lived long enough to make it to the hospital. A passing driver saw her stretched out along the side of the road and phoned for an ambulance. Once she arrived, however, she mumbled only a few delirious words about a monster, and something about burning oil, then she doubled up with convulsions, grabbed at her groin, made a long whining cry...and she died.

The autopsy showed that her insides had simply melted away, as if someone had poured acid into her from between her legs; burning through the uterus, into her abdomen, and eventually through both, her stomach and back. There was no genitalia left, and just too many vital organs were missing to even try to save her.

Three and a half weeks passed before local residents would begin to ease cautiously back to the comfort of their own homes. Randomly, a door or window would be left open during the *day*, though a watchful eye was kept.

The police were baffled, and an all out manhunt was conducted during the first two weeks. But when nothing turned up and no clues were found, they decided whatever it was that attacked Sarah, was gone. So the search, more or less, faded to a back burner.

Then in late July, Fred and Debbie Peterson of 1329 Barkley Street, just off of Lancaster Lane, returned home from a two-week vacation in Florida. They had spent five full days at Disney World, then drove to the coast and spent the rest of the time on the beach. As usual, Fred was already dreading the return to work on Monday. He claimed the vacation had worn him out and now he needed more time to rest up from *that*.

Fred and Debbie each grabbed as much luggage as they could and tread up the front porch steps, acutely aware of the heat descending upon them after a fifteen hour ride in an air-conditioned automobile.

Fred sluggishly pulled out his house key and went to stick it in the lock, when he noticed the knob didn't look right. It was...rusty...or something.

"Did the doorknob look this bad before we left?" he asked.

Debbie was tired and hot, and at the moment didn't really care, "Jeez, I don't know, Fred, open it up will you, it's hot out here." He shut up, shrugged and opened the door. Inside, Debbie noticed an odd smell. Her first assumption was, with the house all closed up for two weeks, it was just musty and needed airing out.

"Gosh, it smells like dead fish in here," she moaned.

Fred turned, fighting a grin, "Debbie?"

"Yeah?"

"Close your legs and see if the smell goes away," he laughed.

Her mouth tightened, suppressing her own amused smile, "That's cute, dear, you ought to be a damn comedian."

On the way to the bedroom, they sensed something wasn't right, nothing really outstanding, just little things exposing themselves one at a time. One noticeable item was that everything seemed to have a film of dinginess over it, not dirt exactly, but...just not clean.

Fred also noticed that all the doors; bedroom, bathroom and closets, even the little daisy yellow shutters hanging in the serving window between the kitchen and the living room, were shut, "I don't remember closing all these doors," he said, "do you?"

Debbie looked puzzled, "Well, no I don't. But I guess *you* must have. *I* didn't do it."

They continued on to the bedroom, scrunching their noses at the smell that lingered. "Debbie, why don't you open the back windows, while I get the front ones, and let's air the place out."

He dropped the luggage at the foot of the bed and turned to walk out. Debbie dropped hers next to his and then flopped (collapsed) on the bed.

"Alright."

Fred went back down the hallway to the kitchen and to the window above the sink. When he reached for the latch he found it was already unhooked...and open. *No way. I wouldn't have left this open...would I?* As he stared at it with disbelief, he saw dried brown crusty film on both the lock and the frame. "That looks like the same crap that's on the doorknob out front," *and that latch looks deformed.*

He scratched his head and shrugged. "I guess its just time to do some spring cleaning and see what all needs fixing."

Then he went to the living room windows. Now, if there had been even a slight breeze that day, the curtains would have been moving and he would have seen that they too were open. But there was no breeze, and he was right up on them before becoming aware of it. And they too were covered with the crusty brown stuff.

He turned and shouted, *"Debbie?"* ...She was standing directly behind him. They looked at each other, Fred felt the quick infiltrating heat of embarrassment, "Uh..sorry."

"The windows in the back were already open," she said.

Fred grew nervous and pale, "Did you notice any weird brown stuff on the latches?"

"Yeah," she said, "how'd you know?"

His worry was suddenly obvious; "I think someone was in here while we were gone. I know I didn't leave all these windows open. One maybe, but not all of them."

Then concern began to gnaw at Debbie, "So what are you telling me, someone's come into the house? And as far as we know..." her voice lowered, "...could still be here? Right now?"

Their eyes locked. An icy chill wove itself through their bones.

"Ok, ok, don't panic," he told her. "Pick up the phone and call Krys. See if they ever caught that maniac that killed Sarah Maples while we were gone."

Debbie was pale, "Oh Fred no, you don't think..."

"Just call her, Debbie."

Debbie picked up the phone to call Krys Sanders, friend and neighbor for the past three years, down the street at 1342 Barkley.

While she desperately waited for the ringing to end, Fred went to the coat closet next to the front door; he reached in and grabbed a small .32 caliber pistol from the top shelf. Then pulled down a box of shells, took out six, shoved the box back into place, and proceeded to load the weapon.

After the tenth ring...Debbie put the phone down, "Not home!"

"Well," he told her, "let's have a look around."

Debbie's eyes were wide. On one hand, she was afraid to move. On the other, she thought the whole damn thing was crazy, just their imagination, they wouldn't find anything. She tried to convince herself that maybe they *did* leave all the windows open. Maybe the place did just need a good cleaning...

'BANG!'

...Maybe she just imagined that loud crash in the basement just then. "Oh shit! He's in the basement!" she cried.

Fred began to shake. He held the gun up in front of him, "That Bastard. How dare he come into my house."

Slowly he inched himself into the kitchen and to the basement door.

"Fred, please don't go in there," Debbie was sliding into a good solid panic."

"Don't worry," he told her, "I'll definitely shoot first and ask questions later. You go call the police."

She went back to the phone, picked it up and started pushing buttons, *9...1...click*, the phone died.

"Fred, the phone is dead!" she screamed to the kitchen.

Fred suddenly felt a grapefruit size lump in his throat, and an instant urge to urinate. "You bastard," he mumbled, and grasped the knob of the basement door. Debbie grabbed the nearest weapon she could find; a metal encased, foot long flashlight they had magnetized to the side of the refrigerator. She stood in the kitchen doorway with it (keeping a safe distance).

"Come out of there," Fred shouted down the darkened basement stairway. Then he reached over to turn on the light.

Flick...flick. Nothing.

Damn, he thought, *that light is always out.* The only other light he had to see by was the fragmented 8:30 p.m. sunlight, streaking through dancing tree leaves outside and entering a small 1' x 2' window at the back of the basement; making weird shadows on the walls and causing everything in the room to appear much larger than normal.

He looked over at Debbie, "I'm going down."

"No, Fred, don't. He'll kill you. He's a murderer," her voice trembled.

He turned back to the basement, "Yeah well, somebody's got to stop him before he kills again. And now we can't even call the police. And they couldn't find him *last* time he got away. I've got to try to stop him here and now."

He took the first step down.

Krys and Shawna pulled up in Krys's driveway, "Hey look," Shawna said, "Fred and Debbie are home. That's their car, right?"

Krys looked over, "Yeah, let's go and see how the trip went," she turned the motor off and got out.

Wham! The heat nailed them like a slap in the face.

"Jeez!" Shawna said, "give me back the A/C before I melt."

Krys laughed, "Come on, wimp."

Debbie was shaking, clutching the flashlight like a baseball bat, while Fred disappeared into the basement. Descending the stairs (which were feeling weaker than he remembered), he grew keenly aware of everything around him; like the slight movement of air from the house fan crossing the back of his neck. He could hear his own breathing. He felt his heart beating its way up from his chest into his throat.

"Are you down here, slime ball?" (He had no idea how on target his description was). Very slowly, one step at a time, he reached the bottom. When his right foot hit the floor and his left was on the last step, he stopped to listen. All was quiet except for his breathing.

Then, a sound he did not expect, a sound so terrifying, he experienced a near loss of bowel control. It was the deep, raspy, gurgling voice of the same creature that killed Sarah Maples, now concealed in the darkness of his basement.

"You're a fool. And you'll die the way they'll all die."

The sudden scare caused Fred to squeeze the trigger. He fired a shot at the concrete wall in front of him, the bullet ricocheted two times, once streamlining so close it grazed his left arm, creasing hairs.

He froze, listening to gurgling laughter, "Ha ha ha. Now you're dead...Fred."

Spinning on his heels, Fred looked into the darkness for...for...*It!* Desperately trying to zero in on the voice echoing around him. Then, in the back corner, behind the staircase, he saw two cold beaming yellow eyes looking right at him, piercing his deepest fear; death. Fred jerked the pistol up and fired.

"Ha ha ha ha ha," more laughter.

What? He was confused. *I couldn't have missed.* It was damn near a point blank shot. Then, he fired again, and again, but the creature continued to laugh. Fred saw its eyes move, they were coming closer. It was walking toward him. He fired one more time.

Blast! ...Nothing. It kept coming.

Shit! Fred's heart was beating him up.

That's not human. "What the hell are you?"

Then he saw oily strings of slime stretch across its gaping mouth, "I am your creation."

And as it came from the shadows, it was more visible. And the more Fred could see, the more he wished he couldn't. *Well, I don't know what the hell "creation" it's talking about, but I'm not sticking around to find out.* He lunged for the steps, taking two at a time, until suddenly, halfway up, a bony hand shot through the space between the boards. Fingers clamped around Fred's ankle like a vice. His pants sizzled with tiny oil bubbles.

He looked down and was shocked with horror to see his ankle burning away. *Jesus Christ! This is insane.* And when the pain finally kicked past his confused amazement, he felt his skin searing...melting. With a hard jerk, he pulled free, *"Run, Debbie, Run!"* he yelled, and speed crawled up the remaining stairs.

The excruciating pain in his ankle slowed him way down, and the creature came around at the bottom. Each step it took left an acidic engraved footprint bubbling on the wood, where it would eventually dry and become brown crust.

Fred hobbled and pulled his way to the top, then threw himself out onto the kitchen floor. He turned quickly, slammed the door shut and backed up against it.

Debbie was in the living room, peeking through the entryway, "Fred, what is it? What's down there?" He could only stare at her.

Then, two words…"It burns."

Debbie stepped cautiously back into the kitchen, "What do you mean? What burns?" Then she saw the pool of blood around his ankle, "Oh my God! Fred, what happened?"

He was terrorized with disbelief, "It grabbed me and…I started burning. It hurts Debbie, it hurts bad." She knelt down to see how much damage there was. The impression of a hand was melted into his flesh. It was red and mutilated, but only deep enough in a few spots to release the blood that was running onto the floor.

Bamm! The basement door pounded against his back.

"Aaagghh!" Fred and Debbie both screamed and jumped. Fred put more pressure on to keep the door from opening, and braced for another pounding, but it never came. Debbie backed out of the kitchen. There was a moment of dead silence.

Then…'*Ssssss,*' a quiet sizzle on the other side. "Oh Jesus, he's melting his way through!" The sizzle grew louder. The creature was pressing its entire body to the door and burning the wood.

Fred sprang to his feet (foot and a half), turned the lock on the door (seemed like the thing to do), and ran (hobbled). He had only made it to the entryway when the last splinters of wood dissolved and the creature's body began to appear.

"Fred, where's your gun? *Shoot it!*" Debbie screamed.

"It doesn't work, the bullets go right through him."

She helped him down the hall to the bedroom. The creature reached the entryway. "Run, rabbits, run. Maybe tonight we'll have rabbit stew," he laughed and kept walking.

The bedroom door slammed shut, a chair slid up under the knob, but, again, it was a wooden door, and this one was hollow.

"We've got to do something, he'll be through that in no time," Fred said.

Debbie looked around for a place to hide, "This is ridiculous, we've got to get out of here." She pointed to another chair in the corner, "There...put that up to the window and let's climb out."

Fred's face was a sudden expression of thankfulness and love that he had married such a smart woman; if he'd had time he would have kissed her. Hell, if he'd had a minute longer he would have screwed her brains out. He picked up the chair and took it to the window. Debbie was on it before it hit the ground.

Bamm!

They both turned. The creature was tearing its way in, and it wouldn't take but a few good beatings to break through that lightweight, *piece of shit,* door.

"Quick," Fred yelled at his wife, *"get the hell out."* She knocked the screen off with one hit and threw herself over the windowsill.

'Ding...Dong!' The doorbell rang.

"Fred? ...Debbie? ...Are you guys home? It's me, Krys."

The creature stopped.

Fred stopped.

Unfortunately, the bedroom faced the back of the house; Debbie couldn't see the girls at the front porch.

The slime-ball started back for Fred. Fred stared at him; his brain said, *go on, get the hell out of there,* but his body was busy listening to his eyes; *wait, I'm not done looking at this gruesome thing in the daylight. With its gaping flesh and rotted face, and the oily dripping purplish yellow goo.*

"Jump, Fred, Jump!" Outside, Debbie was screaming at him. Eventually, his eyes came out of the trance and told the body *Okay, time to go!* And he climbed onto the windowsill.

Now, if Fred had been smart and dove out the window the way Debbie did, he might have stood a chance. But he screwed up and started going out one leg at a time; for a moment, he was basically straddling the window. And as he pushed his backside through, trying to pull his other leg and head out at the same time, the creature reached up with both hands, and grabbed the sides of his face.

...'Sssssss'

"Aaaaaggghhh," Fred screamed with torturous pain.

Debbie grabbed the leg hanging outside and pulled, as the creature's melting grip slid down Fred's head to his neck (leaving burn tracks like tire skids). Fred's last view of life was the hideous face of his killer - followed by the pain of his head coming off.

"Did you hear that?" Shawna asked. "Jeez, either someone's hurt, or their sexual exploits have reached a new high."

"Yoo hoo, Fred, are you ok?" Krys's voice trailed down the hall. "We knocked and the door came open, and you always told me 'an open door is an invitation.' You-all are not having sex are you?"

As Debbie pulled on Fred's leg, the creature squeezed into his throat. The screams racing from Fred's brain to his vocal chords had already been stopped. He was dead!

"Oh my gosh, Krys, look at the door."

Krys and Shawna saw the busted up bedroom door and felt goose bumps race down their bodies. They were suddenly empty of thought, and speechless; but their eyes had to know what happened. They crept forward and looked around the corner.

The Oilman turned and glared. His grip on Fred held tight.

"You're just in time for dinner, ladies," then Fred's neck burned through and his head came off in the creature's hands, "...Brain casserole."

The girls shrieked, long and loud, and turned white...then green. Shawna grabbed Krys's arm, *"Run!"* she ordered, and they flew down the hallway.

Debbie fell back to the ground, Fred landed on top of her, "Fred? ...Are you all right?" She could not yet see that her husband had no head. Then she rolled him off of her and sat up, grabbing his shirt to pull him over. "Fred, are you..."

She stared at the empty space above his shoulders. Her mind spiraled down low enough to see a smiling red faced Satan standing amidst fire in the pit of hell, and her screams echoed through the air, so piercing, it chased birds from trees.

"Shawna, that's Debbie! In the backyard." Krys was taking deep breaths as they came from the house to the porch. "We have to help her."

They circled the side of the house and found Debbie, on the ground, crying, holding what was left of Fred in her arms, rocking back and forth.

The side door of the house slammed! All three girls looked over and watched as the creature crossed the open yard to the tree-line edge of the forest. They could not move, they could only stare, until he was gone.

Finally, Shawna spoke softly to Krys, "Do you know who that looked like?"

Krys glared at her, "Yeah...but it can't be...he's dead, remember?"

Their eyes locked with a fear that reached to their soul.

Chapter 3

The Pleasure View County Sheriff's Office issued an APB on *The Creature* for the next two months, it read: *Be on the lookout for a Caucasian male, age uncertain due to physical deterioration, skin blistering and decay. Some body features are actually missing, including; right ear, nose, all fingertips, and portions of arms, legs, and lips.*

Suspect is covered, head to foot, with thick oil. This oil is laced with several forms of acid. <u>DO NOT,</u> *for any reason, make physical contact with suspect!*

He is wearing old ratty blue jeans, an old ratty shirt, and reeks of toxic stench easily detectable for long distances.

He has killed two people and is presumed responsible for the deaths of three others originally thought to be accidents or suicides. Traces of brown crust that proved to be the dried remains of the oil that covers him were found near each of the five victims. This 'crust' was also found in the vicinities of fifteen other homes and commercial establishments.

He is believed to be on a serial rampage, targeting certain designated individuals. In linking the deaths of Sarah Maples, Fred Peterson and the others, we've discovered that four out of five of them worked for Xanorse Chemicals.

(That was no surprise, half the people in town worked for Xanorse. It was Pleasure View's primary source of employment).

"Jeez, that description kills me every time I hear it," Alex cut in. Trevor was reading the report again for the umpteenth million time. Alex Keene and Trevor Bolton were two of the cops cruising the area, looking for the one now referred to as...*Oily*.

Trevor and Alex had been partners for nine months, they shared a lot in common - partly by coincidence and partly they just rubbed off on each other. Either way, they had a good working relationship. They knew what to expect from each other in most situations, whether confronting a wife beating husband...or facing a shoot out.

Harassment opportunities were their favorite; it gave them a chance to show off the smart-ass they could each be. Throwing power and position around was not a problem for either of them.

"Is there nothing in there about where this *Oily...thing*, comes from?" Alex asked.

Trevor flipped through the report, "Only that he shows up out of nowhere, disappears into nowhere, and so far, never in the same place twice."

They both shook their head with disbelief. "Wonderful," Alex said, and punched the gas. The squad car shot down Lakeside Highway.

It was early evening when they reached Marble Rock Lake. Fall was upon them and the nights were cooler. The leaves on some of the trees were already changing color. A lot of the summer's fun at the lake had ended. *Except for the die-hards who refused to give up the boat and go home.*

Alex pulled off onto Sand Rock road, the old dirt road that inter-wove itself through the trees along the back of the lake. Sand Rock ran the entire length from one end of the lake to the other, and back out to the highway.

Somewhere in the middle of it, another little dirt road too small to have its own name, branched off and wound up to the top of the hill.

The hill had no official name either, but it was often referred to as *Ghost Hill,* for several reasons, one; anytime a fog rolled through, even though you could still see the lake, the hill would seem to vanish. All that was visible was an occasional tree poking through, sometimes several at different levels, like they were floating in the mist.

Another reason was; through the years, several children on family outings had gotten lost in the forestry of the hill and were never found. It was suspected that Wolves frequented the area (they were heard but not widely seen).

People say that on foggy days, if you saw one of the occasionally visible trees poking through, that it wasn't really a tree at all, but the ghost of a lost child...*hence the name*, 'Ghost Hill'.

The hill was also the protrusion of earth that separated Pleasure View from the small, almost microscopic, one horse town known as Colvert. For a short time Colvert *was* bigger, the locals actually referred to it as a separate county. But then it dwindled again back to a small community of about eighty. Not really big enough to warrant having its own name, but...it did. If you were to look on a map, a local map, Colvert showed up less and less.

It had only one general store for clothing and such, one grocery store - with only one or two brand names of anything. It had *one* gas station, with *one* pump, and there was *one* place to eat - 'Colvert County Kitchen.' There were, however, three or four family owned shops strategically placed between the central stores on *Main* Street.

There were four or five dirt roads branching off of Main Street, each with four or five houses on them, and not much else. Not really a nice place to visit, and you sure wouldn't want to live there. But for those who did, it was home and they were content.

Alex came to a stop at the top of the hill, he and Trevor got out to look around. From where they stood they could see most of Colvert, half of Marble Rock Lake, the forest where Billy's tree house was, and the top half of Xanorse Chemicals.

"So where do you suppose this murdering bastard is camped out?" Trevor's voice cut through the cool hilltop breeze with the question that was quickly growing to nagging status.

Alex had no answer; the deafening sound of silence on the hill was response in itself. There just wasn't much to go on, and a lot of the area had already been covered.

They stood scanning the countryside, listening to the wind in the trees, while the orange burning sun slowly dropped behind them. The lake was calm and still, with portions of it hid in the black shadows of trees.

Lakeside Highway was vacant, quiet, except for one old Volkswagen that sputtered by a few minutes earlier. The trees on the other side of the highway swayed in the breeze, flickering the leaves that had already turned - amongst the majority of ones that were still green.

The sky was clear, crisp and blue as far as you could see, disrupted only by the huge white billowy clouds of smoke coming from the three stacks at Xanorse.

"Keene?" Trevor finally spoke.

"Yeah?"

"What's that?"

Alex looked where Trevor was pointing, "What?"

"There," he said, "that line of smoke."

Alex looked bewildered, "That's the Xanorse Plant. Those are smoke stacks. Hello."

Trevor stared off beyond Xanorse, "No, no, behind them, to the right. There's a long thin cloud of smoke there in the trees."

Alex squinted.

"You see it?"

"Yeah," his voice was low, "I see it."

They were quiet for a moment. Finally, Trevor asked again, "...So, what do you think it is?"

Alex stared hard for a minute then said, "That's where those Hagger people live."

Trevor nodded with instant acknowledgement, "Right...I forgot about them. That *is* about where their place is, huh?"

"Well," Alex shrugged, "I'm pretty sure. But I guess there's only one way to find out, and...*ain't nothing happening here.*"

Dirt kicked up a cloud from the back tires as they coursed down the hill. The ride *down* was the main reason Alex liked going up the hill in the first place.

He considered himself a good driver, a bit of a daredevil perhaps, and the road he was on gave him ample opportunity to prove it. It was full of narrow snake windings, with a cliff edge side that dropped straight down into the trees. And the road itself was only a consistency of loose gravel and dirt.

"Want a rush?" he asked, but didn't wait for an answer, he punched the gas.

Though he was used to the excitement, Trevor still got nervous. He braced himself, clung to the door handle and the bottom of the seat, and prayed.

Alex twisted and fishtailed (with the shit-eaters grin), and took the first two curves...no problem. Then the back end started swinging further out, until...eventually, halfway down, he started to lose the back driver side in the gravel.

The rear of the car did a quick drop just before the tires caught hold again and pulled them back up.

"Hey, Keene," Trevor finally spoke, "you're fucking up."

Alex rolled his eyes, "Come on now, you ain't chicken are ya? I did that on purpose. That's the *mid-point-scare*. It's there to keep you on your toes."

Trevor looked sideways at him, "Yeah, well let's just make sure I still have toes to keep on to when we get to the bottom." Then he braced himself again.

At the bottom, in the turn back onto Sand Rock road, Alex punched the gas one more time and shot himself into the straightaway. Then, at breakneck speed (Trevor's eyes widened) ...he hit the brakes and spun the wheel in the opposite direction. The car went into a 360 spin and made a complete circle.

Both men watched the world pass by sideways, until finally coming around to stop pretty much in the forward position. Alex touched lightly on the gas and drove Sand Rock road back out to the main highway, like business-as-usual. "Nothing like a drive in the country, aye Bolton?" he grinned.

They passed and waved at the last couple to dock their boat and leave the lake that day, and then pulled onto Lakeside and cruised in the direction of *the smoke rising from the trees*.

They drove past where Billy's path used to be...

(*Where no one from the gang had been in at least five years. The walk to the tree house had grown over with shrubs, reducing the size of the path to a simple line of dirt.*

The tree house itself had rotted quite a bit through the years; boards had broken loose and dropped, gaping holes came one after another in different sizes like floats in a parade. The remaining wood had gone soft. The sofa was moth eaten and stunk of rot. The entire fortress had become a den of spiders and webs.)

...and they turned on to *Short Cut*; barely a two-lane blacktop that went through to Lancaster Lane. Alex took the sharp left, passing the Xanorse parking lot on the right, and drove a half a mile through the forest, until he came to the long and winding dirt road/driveway that led to the Hagger house.

He slowed for the turn, then slowed even more, eventually, he got down to 10 mph. Trevor looked over, he didn't think he'd ever seen Alex drive under 35 mph before, even coming to a stop. "What happened, Speed Racer?" he joked, "You just discover the brake pedal?"

Alex wore a tight smile and kept both eyes watchful through the windshield. "Well," he said, "if this Bobby Hagger is anything like most Hillbillies, *living-in-the-sticks*, we'll need to come up on him real slow and friendly like." He looked at Trevor and smiled. "You know they'd all just as soon shoot you as look at you. As far as they're concerned, we're trespassing." Trevor's smile faded.

"You ever hear any of the stories about the Hagger's?" Alex asked.

The fading smile slid into a worry line, "Well, I guess most people have heard the story about what happened that day back in the thirties, about the *feuding massacre* they had with the construction team that showed up to clear the land for Xanorse."

Alex nodded, "It was the 'Lakeside Testing Lab' then."

"Whatever," Trevor shrugged. "Why? What else is there?"

As Alex drove slowly through the trees, his tone grew serious, "Oh, a few things have happened through the years," he started. "Like...well actually, starting with that day, in fact. I don't know if you know it, but there was a girl there that day, working for the construction team, her name was Sheila Corter; she was the coffee and sandwich girl.

Well...once all the commotion got started, one of the Hagger cousins, Erwin Gunner his name was, grabbed this girl, Sheila, and hauled her off into the trees and raped her. And, well...to make a long story short, nine months later, she had a kid."

Trevor looked grim, "You're kidding. That's disgusting."

"Yeah," Alex agreed, "the girl was so mentally messed up over it; she raised the kid telling him stories about *Hill Monster's*. She told him his father was one, and that the world should be rid of creatures like that. But not to worry, she told the boy...she loved him *anyway*."

Trevor blew a sympathetic sigh, "That could mess up a kid's psyche."

Alex continued, "You ain't kiddin. By the time the kid was eight years old, he had such hatred for *whoever* his father was; one day he got a hold of the pistol his mother kept under her mattress, and went out hunting. Guess what for?"

Trevor was in disbelief, "An eight year old kid? Did he know where to look?"

Alex smiled, "Oh yeah, he knew. His mother made sure that the boy *knew* where his dad came from, and *who* he was, and *where* he lived. She said she wanted him to always be sure to know where *not* to go, even by accident. The psychiatrist didn't believe his going there was any accident."

Again surprised, Trevor asked, "Psychiatrist? You mean they actually caught him trying to do it?"

"Oh he did it all right. They found the boy four days after he'd disappeared from home, sitting in a tree at the lake, with the gun in his hands. He was staring at an old rowboat in the water, two fishing poles hung off the side. And the bodies of Erwin and his younger brother Dale were lying in the bottom. Each had three bullets in them. Not only did the kid know *what* he was doing, *he knew how to do it*."

"How did he know it was Erwin in the boat?"

"Said he snuck up to the Hagger place a couple of nights before," Alex went on, "and just listened. Once he figured out who was who, he heard Dale say that him and Erwin were going fishing the next day. The psychiatrist seemed to think that the kid's mother, Sheila, was actually an accomplice; that she set him up. Because she was...like I said ...messed up."

Both men sat quiet for a full minute, until Alex eventually finished, "Anyway, they ended up putting both, mother and child, in an institution. She didn't speak for five years. Then one day she got access to a metal butter knife and killed herself. First she sawed through her wrist, then she plunged the round-headed thing into her stomach. ...Fun, huh?"

Trevor scowled, "What about the kid?"

"The kid? I heard there was a lot of reprogramming and he straightened out pretty good. Eventually he was released, grew up, got married, and actually has a family of his own."

Trevor smiled, "Another happy ending," they laughed.

Turning with the bend in the road, Alex flicked on the parking lights. The sun was almost down and very little shine was coming through the trees. But it wasn't dark enough to go full on with headlights yet.

"Know any other good stories?" Trevor asked.

Alex glanced sideways at him, "About the Hagger's?"

He shrugged, "Yeah."

"Well, there's all kinds of stories about that family," Alex said. "But I guess the saddest would be the one about Bobby's mom, Verna, and his sisters and brother."

"What happened to them?"

"It was back in 1961," Alex went into another tale. "Due to the process of elimination, as I understood it; the first born of the family is the one to inherit the Hagger home. For Earl and Trudy, that would have been a boy who was one of the one's killed that day at that standoff back in the thirties.

The next two in line were girls, I think they got married and moved away. Then there was another brother, barely two years older than Ray. *He would have* gotten the home, but he met a girl in Colvert and decided to move in with her. This left, the remaining members of the household; Earl, his wife Trudy (the one who *started* all that crap with the chemical plant) ...

Trevor nodded.

"...their last remaining child, Ray, his wife Verna, and their kids. Bobby was the third child born to Ray and Verna, but the first *son*; he had two sisters older than him, one younger, and then a younger brother.

Anyway, it was in the spring I believe, and Earl and Ray had decided to take Bobby on a two-week hunting trip. This, apparently, didn't sit well with Bobby's oldest sister, Marie. Marie, they say, was a tomboy, and insisted that she go too. The other sister, next closest to Bobby's age, June, had no longing's for hunting or camping.

I guess there were words exchanged between Bobby and Marie about it. But she *was* old enough, and she was as tough as any of the *men* in the family, and in the end...Marie went on the hunting trip with her Grandpa, her Daddy, and her Brother; who, upon their return, were most grateful that she did.

While they were gone, it seems; Trudy and Verna thought it would be a nice surprise to have a couple of cows butchered and ready to eat when they got back. Normally, Earl and Ray would handle that, but Trudy and Verna were countrywomen; they'd done it several times themselves, they knew what they were doing.

So, they finished one cow; they slaughtered it, cut it, packed it, and wanted to be finished with it before starting a second one. And they had done just fine. But when they decided to cook *themselves* up a nice dinner, they noticed the meat had an odd taste.

...I guess it was the middle of the night when they realized something was seriously wrong. Bobby's little brother, Alvin, woke up crying with a bellyache. This in turn woke up Molly, the youngest girl - who also whined about not feeling good.

Within a half an hour they were all up, and Trudy and Verna were pouring castor oil down everybody, including themselves.

Trudy figured out almost immediately what the problem was; the only reason they would all be feeling the same thing, was that they all ate the same food. Then she remembered the taste of the meat - and she knew.

In the next few hours, everyone had chills and nausea. And before the sun even came up, Trudy and Verna were out back checking the other cows.

They were on a straight path to the cold wet grass of the pasture, when they passed the barn door and stopped suddenly, to stare at the chicken coop.

Through the wire mesh, they could see a blanket of white; every chicken in it was dead. Some were on their backs, some were slumped over their nesting, in one corner; six of them had crowded together as if to protect themselves from something.

Nobody had paid attention to the poultry for a couple of days, so no one saw it happening. Then, at the door they saw *Old Red*, the Rooster, on his back.

Trudy and Verna bounded to the pasture, to the fence gate, and stared. Two cows were down, two others wobbled, their legs folding beneath them. Trudy dragged the gate open and rushed to the two that were down. They were dead.

Their hides were patchy with large festering boils. Maggots had already accumulated, their mouths frothed vomit.

Trudy looked at Verna; darkness haunted her eyes, "Anthrax," she said.

They took only a moment to let it sink in, then back to the house and the children. Inside, the kids were all bunched together on the sofa with five blankets over them, trying to keep warm. But their little bodies shook with chills and fever. Trudy and Verna came in to see them all holding each other.

Chickens crowded together to protect themselves from something.

The children looked up, sweat glazed their tiny faces and their teeth clenched and chattered.

Verna had to grab a chair and sit before she fell. She and Trudy were feeling the impact of the fever. Trudy went to one of the bedrooms and came back with two more blankets. She gave one to Verna and wrapped the other around herself.

If she had thought about trying to get to town, she would only have had an old tractor to do it with, and she was too weak for that.

Earl wasn't due back for another five days - heavy black silence.

Eventually, she pulled the children apart and put them in their beds, wrapping them up tightly. Then she put Verna in her bed and wrapped her.

After closing up the house, she pulled the curtains together and shut out the light. Then she took a blanket and pillow, and a note pad and pencil, and went and laid down on the sofa.

She wrote Earl a letter with all the words she knew, trying to explain what happened. Then she dropped the pencil to the floor and placed the paper on her chest, laid her head back and closed her eyes.

Four days later when the men...*and Marie* returned home early, that's how they found them."

Trevor's mouth hung open, "That's horrible. How do you know all that?"

Alex shrugged, "A lot of it was in the note that Trudy left Earl. Earl had to get someone out here to investigate and take precautions against the spread of the disease. The note was put in the report. The rest was basic deduction."

"Did they know where the disease came from?"

"Not really," Alex said. "Earl and Ray tried to claim that it was brought on by pollutants in the air from *The Chemical Plant*."

Trevor stared at him, "What do you think?"

"Don't know what to think," Alex muttered, "but I believe if it *had* been something gone airborne from the plant, a whole lot more people than just the Hagger's would have died."

"Look, there it is." Trevor pointed ahead to the Hagger's old shack house, standing just as natural amongst the trees as...the trees themselves.

"Sure looks rundown."

"Yeah," Alex agreed. Then pointed to the stovepipe coming up out of the roof, "But there's the stream of smoke. I guess that solves that mystery." The car crept slowly in on the house. "Let's talk to 'em, see if they've heard anything about our *oily* friend."

Bobby Hagger came out to greet the men. There was a tobacco pipe in his mouth that he held with one hand, and a shotgun in the other. The squad car stopped and the two Officers got out. Alex left the parking lights on.

Bobby squinted, watching his visitors carefully. "What kin I do fer you fellers?" his voice was dry.

Alex and Trevor smiled, "How are you this evening, Mr. Hagger?" Alex asked.

"I'm jes fine. What kin I do fer ya?"

They looked at each other and realized they should get to the point quickly. "Well, Mr. Hagger," Trevor began, "it seems there's been some trouble in town and the surrounding areas during the past couple of months. We were just checking to make sure everything's ok out here."

Bobby looked at them and scratched his head. He couldn't decide if they really had come all the way out there to warn him about trouble, or accuse him of causing it.

"You say trouble in town?"

They nodded, "Yes sir."

He scratched at his beard stubble thoughtfully, then…"Well, what say you-all boys turn them lights off an come inside an tell us what it is you're looking for. I'll have Opal serve ya up a cuppa coffee."

Trevor was just about to beg off when Alex elbowed him (good manners keeps folks from wanting to shoot at you sometimes).

Both men had seen other houses in the woods (built by the curious *Hill People)*, and they more or less expected the kind of termite ridden, wood rot decay that a lot of them had; maybe some insulation poking out through cracks, and cockroaches slipping in and out of corners.

…And, if they had come to visit five months earlier, that is what they would have seen. But this was different.

The inside of the house was actually dry-walled and wallpapered. The floor was all new wood; each slat cut perfect and straight, with a good tight fit. It was even waxed. There was an overhead light (probably 60 watts) hanging in the living room, and another in the kitchen, the glow lit the areas nicely. Bobby had apparently re-established his generator.

There was an almost spotlessly clean sink and counter area. And just on the other side of the stove, was a beautifully hand carved dining table and six chairs.

The sight of an almost modernly civilized interior, against what was near a shack outside, threw Trevor and Alex for a loop. "You been doing some remodeling, Mr. Hagger? The place looks real sharp," Alex commented.

Bobby stiffened slightly. He hadn't been expecting any visitors, so he wasn't thinking about anybody noticing his latest handy work. He glanced around, taking in all the changes he'd made, again, "Yeah, I...uh, the old wood was getting jes a might too old an needed replacin. And somewhere's, the wife had seen some pitchers of this here...new fangled...stuff and talked me into it. I personally think it's kinda sissy, but the Missus likes it."

Opal took coffee from the stove, "You boys want some sugar?"

"Oh, no thanks ma'am, just black," they both responded.

During the next half hour, the three men sat at the table while Alex and Trevor told Bobby about the recent attacks on Pleasure View. About Sarah Maples and how her insides were burned away. And the head splitting experience Fred Peterson had suffered. And how, what must have been the same creature, came up from the back seat of Sue Ann Walden's Mustang, probably showing his nasty face in the rear view mirror and scaring the Bejesus out of her, just before her unexpected and sharp right turn into the river...from the second street bridge.

The police had hoped that the *thing* had drowned with her, and just floated away. But two weeks later, Sam Stallworth was found out near Ghost Hill, his body at the base of a tree, his brains on the branches above. At first they thought it might be a hunting accident, then they thought suicide, then they found traces of burned leaves with the dried brown crust on them and they *knew* it was something else.

Then, there was the latest incident; Morgan Newton, 'Personnel Manager' for Xanorse Chemicals - found floating in an old metal rowboat out on Marble Rock Lake; not only floating in the lake, but floating in the boat as well. It had been filled with liquid waste, the kind Xanorse disperses every day in their subterranean disposal pool.

Liquid that would eat the flesh and organs of the one soaking in it. Morgan Newton was eaten right down to the bones, only identifiable through dental records.

When the storytelling was over, the three men sat quietly. Trevor and Alex waited for a response from Bobby. All he had to say was, "How do you-all know this creature person was in the car with that girl what drove offun the bridge?"

The obscurity of the question, after the stories he'd just been told, took them by surprise. They said that when the car was fished from the water, the reports indicated that there were large areas of the backseat burned away by some type of acid. That was all the connection they needed.

Suddenly realizing how gruesome their topic of conversation was, Alex quickly looked around for any children who might have been listening. There weren't any.

"So where's all your kids Mr. Hagger? I thought I remembered you having a whole slew of them out here?" he smiled, trying to lighten the conversation.

"Well sir," Bobby said, "Sandy done went an got herself married to Walter; a cousin on Opal's side. An you know we lost Patty a couple a year ago to that pneumonia that was going around."

Alex and Trevor hung their heads, "No sir, I didn't know that, I'm sorry," Alex offered.

"Yes sir, an we damn near lost Becky to it too, but she pulled through ok. Now, her an Darrell got rooms of there own out back. Built 'em themselves, about halfway from here to the outhouse," Bobby laughed. "Built 'em there because that damn Darrell has to piss so much of the time. I reckon he jes wanted to be closer to the hole if ya know what I mean," they all laughed.

"An then Ernie and Sally Ann," he continued, "they already done gone to bed for the night. They gonna get up early an go fishin tamarra."

Then Bobby got quiet, and thoughtful, a distant smile settled on his mouth and he scratched lightly at his whiskers.

Alex stared at the scraggly man. Bobby felt it. He cocked his head to look at the stranger in his home, knowing what the next question would be.

A few seconds later, Alex asked it, "You...uh...ever hear anything from Jimmy?"

Bobby's smile never flinched or faded, and then his mouth cracked open, "Nope." When he talked, Alex noticed how worn his face was, how dry and slow his speech was, the rigid jerking of yellow and gray teeth moving up and down. "I figure by now he's probly done made friends with the Aliens that got him. Probly built hisself a house on their planet, living peaceably with 'em. Wherever he's been took to." He spoke with the conviction of a man who's believed a lie for so long, it's become his reality.

The two officers looked at each other, and then back at Bobby. "You say Aliens got him?" Trevor asked, with a tone of...*Excuse me? Did I hear you right?*

Bobby craned his head to look at Trevor, "Had to be Aliens. Why else would a sixteen year old boy just up and disappear one day for no reason, an nobody able to find him for ten year?"

Neither officer had an answer; they remembered there were days and days of searching for Jimmy...and nothing came of it. Not a clue was ever found. Eventually, the search was called off; the disappearance of sixteen-ycar-old Jimmy Hagger remained one of the unsolved mysteries of Pleasure View. *But, Aliens?* Trevor thought.

The two men shrugged, finished their coffee, and rose from the table. "Well, Mr. Hagger, if you'll just keep an eye out and let us know if you see anything suspicious, we'd sure appreciate it," Alex told him.

"Sure thing," Bobby agreed.

The two visitors bid goodnight, stepped outside and walked to the squad car. Bobby closed the door behind them.

Alex was just about to man the driver side, when he noticed a pile of timber off to the left of the front porch. It wouldn't normally have caught his attention, but it was such a big pile. "Man, look at all that wood."

Trevor looked and was also surprised at the amount. "That's a lot to burn. But it can't be just tree timber. It's probably a lot of the old insides of the house."

Alex stepped closer for examination. "Yep, that's what it looks like. I wonder what triggered him off to go and tear it all out and rebuild. I mean these people are not the most industrious bunch you'd ever meet."

They took a slightly closer look and could see just by the light from the window, the wood was badly deteriorated. Termites had eaten a lot of it, and there were places where large holes had almost worn through, like the wood was thinning, disintegrating in spots.

They inspected a moment longer, then turned back to the car.

When they pulled away, the full white moon floated high above in front of them. The sky was dark with a mystic blue shadow beyond the forest, the trees appeared black all around, except where the headlights hit.

Alex used more speed to leave with, than he had coming in, but he still kept a slower pace than usual, since he was not overly familiar with all the bends and turns in this particular road.

The quiet drive, disturbed only by the background static of the two-way radio, was more than Trevor could handle. "Hey, I'm sorry, but I'm a little spooked by this whole evening; talking about Aliens and shit. You mind if I turn on *my* radio?" He had a portable radio he carried with him most of the time. Alex didn't mind; he appreciated the distraction, "Do it."

With the first *click* came *Cat Stevens* 'Moon Shadow.'

"Oh this is good, this is comforting," Trevor mumbled. Then began to sing along about losing hands and losing eyes.

"You know, this song is kind of morbid," Alex said.

Trevor smiled and agreed, "Yeah, can you imagine Fred Peterson singing this? *'If I ever lose my head, I would bleed, I'd be dead.'* That was all it took, the tension broke with laughter, and it was big. "Aaaaahhhh, that's *sick!*" he said.

They turned a sharp curve, and the headlights caught a glimpse of something that suddenly vanished behind a tree...

"What the hell was that?" Trevor asked.

Both men stared hard into the trees, but nothing moved. "It was probably a deer," Alex told him - his driving slowed to a crawl. Their eyes shifted, looking for movement.

Then, again, in the beam of the headlights they saw bushes rock sharply back and forth as if something was walking through them.

"Something's out there, Alex, I can feel it." Then bushes were moving on both sides of the road, "Look, they're all moving...everywhere! Something's out there!" Trevor jerked around excitedly.

"Yeah, there's something there all right, maybe we should stop and investigate."

Trevor looked at him like he was insane, "Are you insane? What if it's that *Oily* thing? Or what if it's Aliens or something?"

Alex looked blankly at his partner, "Aliens?"

"Hey," Trevor defended himself, "stranger things have happened."

"Stranger than Aliens?"

There was a sharp bend in the road, and when the car came around and straightened out, they saw *it* - in the road directly in front of them, in the headlights; Oily...*The Creature.*

"Shit!" Alex cried, and slammed on the brakes.

They watched it slowly coming at them, beneath the full Moon floating overhead. "Jesus Christ! What is that thing?" Trevor whimpered.

"Beats me," Alex's voice trembled, "but it looks dead."

Both men froze in their seats, too shocked to move; watching the half fleshless thing with burning yellow eyes and coat of thick slimy oil, walking right at them.

"Well shit, Alex, what are we going to do?"

Then they heard the deep, rumble of its gravely voice, "We're coming to take you away, ha ha, he he..."

The sound was hammer-driven fear - through their spines. "We've got to kill that thing," Alex said.

Then another sound faintly filled the night, the Officers hadn't even picked up on it yet. Trevor was squirming to pull his pistol. "So, what? We shoot him, right?"

The small noise suddenly got louder, "What the hell is that hissing sound?" Alex turned to his side window...

'Sssssss.'

...and saw a hand - open palmed, melting through the glass, coming at his face.

He was stunned, and tried to jump back, but the hand was large and suddenly through, and had a grip on him. The hand was not oily like the creature in the headlights, but a second later, he felt his face...melting. His skin was suddenly hot, the burn of a branding iron swept in and pressed down - he locked up, terrified, in pain.

"Aaaahhhhh!" Alex screamed and threw the car door open. The creature was knocked away.

"Oh my God!" Trevor looked into the road ahead, there were three more of them standing with *Oily*. "What the hell are they?"

Their burning yellow eyes reflected the glare of the headlights like mirrors. "They look dead," Trevor mumbled. *Dead and rotted,* he thought. Missing skin and hair, with thick black-red blood dripping slow like melted wax from the holes in their arms and legs, holes deep enough to see bone. Their eyes were sunk in on either side of where their nose *used* to be - now only a large gaping hole, exposing brain rot.

Some were men, some were women, some were old, some were young, and they were all as decayed as Oily, the only difference was...they were dry.

Trevor pushed his door open, barely taking a glance to see if he was going to be leapt upon by Mr. or Mrs. dead person.

He saw more of them coming from the trees, but figured, as slow as they were moving, he had time to get out. And he knew if he stayed inside, he was dead for sure. So he bolted, racing to the back of the car to join Alex, who had his pistol out and was shooting at everyone.

The two cops, with guns out, slowly backed themselves down the road, like two gangsters backing away from a shoot out. Like Butch Cassidy and the Sundance Kid.

Trevor looked at Alex with panic stricken eyes, "Jeez, Keene, how's your face feel? It looks like you got a third degree sunburn."

Alex maintained a sense of humor to keep from going into shock, "You mean my face is still there? It feels like an egg stuck to a frying pan, the one you can't scrape off. Jesus, Trevor, what the hell is going on here, did we just step into the Twilight Zone? Do you see Rod Serling anywhere?"

Eventually, the creature count got up to ten, as they came from the woods (and Rod Serling nowhere in sight). They walked from the beam of the headlights and sides of the road to form walls on either side of the car.

Apparently, the leader, Oily, decided to walk *over* the car, from hood to trunk. Leaving burning footprints in the metal.

Trevor and Alex could hear their gravely mutterings grow more intense and clear.

"We warned you."

"You can't stop us."

"Death to the creator."

"What are they talking about?" Trevor nearly screamed.

"I don't know. But I'm not waiting around to find out." Alex began firing.

Bang! Bang! Bang!

Then Trevor opened fire. They were both good marksmen, they knew they were hitting their targets, but nothing was happening. The bullets were flying right through them.

"Oh this is good," Alex said, "we're out here with *Night of the Living Dead,* and we can't kill them because *THEY'RE ALREADY DEAD!* Well, Fuck that. I'm out of here," and he turned to run.

Unbeknownst to Alex, four more had come up directly behind them - and he ran right into the arms of a dead man/creature. Looking into the face of the thing, he went limp; he saw a bullet hole in the rotted forehead of its skull. Alex was confused, "I didn't shoot yo..."

But he didn't get the chance to finish, the creature folded his arms around the officer and squeezed.

"Alex!" Trevor yelled and was about to run to the rescue, when a hand came down on each of his shoulders. But by that time, he was so frenzied and spastic, he automatically started swinging...violently.

The arms of the man holding Alex - melted through. His body didn't burn and sizzle the way the other victims had though, he went out more like a large wax candle, running in long drips.

As the creature slid into his flesh, Alex oozed over himself and puddled on the ground. Until the creature's arms came through and it was virtually hugging itself. Alex's torso became a thick and multicolored pool. No more than two legs and a head remained.

Trevor was twenty yards down the road when he looked back and saw his partner, his best friend, now...beside himself...dead. He was hyperventilating even before he turned to run, but he *did* run, stopping only long enough to shower his shoes with puke and wipe sweat from his eyes.

Then he figured he would be safer moving randomly through the forest rather than sticking to the road, where 'the dead' were on a steady course.

Somewhere in the night, a rainstorm blew in, occasionally filling the sky with bolts of electricity and exploding groans of thunder.

The ground became soft and muddy beneath Trevor's feet, as he stumbled and crawled through the brush and darkness.

The following morning, he was found soaking wet, staggering down Lakeside Highway, in shock. He didn't even know his own name. He had gone deep within himself...and could not be reached for comment. He mumbled the name of *Oily* a time or two, and cried out about, "They're dead. They're all dead." But that was the most anyone could get out of him.

Reports from the investigating team sent to the area, said they had found Alex and Trevor's car (what was left of it), and there were traces of brown crust in a melty trail down the length of it. Twenty-five feet ahead was the remains of Alex Keene.

They also detected a lot of sliding tracks in the road, but that could have just been skids from the car, after all, Alex did have a certain, well-known, driving reputation.

There were no other signs of life...or death.

Chapter 4

Within twenty-four hours, the Pleasure View Police were all over Hagger land; looking for a mob of dead (or possibly *undead*) killers, led by *The Oily One*. They combed the pasture and barn, and searched the house from front to back; Opal was not pleased, she had just cleaned the day before, and *not all* Officers bothered wiping the mud off their shoes. Bobby's boots may have been just as muddy, but they were sat, respectably, at the front door.

The pile of wood at the side of the house was pulled down; no dead people there. Just old chewed up wood with holes in it. It was peculiarly clean though. It had rained the night before, and many other rains had come and gone prior to that, but this wood was *too* clean, as if somebody had taken a brush and scrubbed it.

They moved on to the back...way back, to the family cemetery. Nothing there was outstandingly odd, except that there was *no* grass growing over the plots. When asked about it, Bobby said that the grass had died years before, most likely due to the chemicals seeping into the ground from the Xanorse waste-pool (or as Bobby put it; *That chemycal plant's septic tank*).

This was actually a reasonable explanation. And the Hagger family's feelings about the chemical company and how close it was to their land, was no secret. No one pressed the issue.

Most of the day was spent at or around the Hagger place, but nothing turned up, other than a short trail of crust remains, halfway down the road to *Short Cut*. It came from nowhere; it led to nowhere, and it dissolved abruptly in the shrubs and trees of the forest.

The 'PVPD' did a last sweep through the mile and a half that led back to Lakeside Highway. Baffled, they returned to their respective squad cars and drove away.

The search continued extensively for a while throughout surrounding counties, but no leads were found, and the number of officers available for search, began to dwindle. After a few more months of absolutely nothing, the search for *Oily and Company* took a backseat to daily priorities.

Until December 22nd, three days before Christmas...

People started believing that, either the creature's had been drained of their life force and they went back to where they came from; gave up the ghost and died. Or, they moved into the woods, or on to some other town further away.

And didn't Trevor (currently doing time in *The Einstein Department)* every once-in-awhile mention something in gibberish about Aliens?

Whatever people believed, or wanted to believe, they tried to suppress it, tried not to think about it. Then, on December 22nd, 1989, they got a wake up call. And this time the horror was amplified ten times over. This time it was more than just *one* of them, or even the handful they'd heard about, this time it was *a lot more*.

Xanorse Chemicals was having their annual Christmas party at 'The Griswald Hotel' in one of the banquet rooms; *The Gold Room*.

The Griswald was the most luxurious hotel in the area. It was twenty-five stories high with fifty rooms on each floor. The lobby was forty thousand square feet of plush, royal-red carpeting, and the Front Desk was hand carved walnut, trimmed with ribbed drapes of burgundy leather.

The desk stretched fifty feet across the wall facing the glass front of the hotel. There were two waterfalls, one on either side of the lobby, with water running over rock hills descending the edge of the stairways, leading from the Mezzanine to a small pool at the ground floor.

The ceiling was covered with square plates of gold chrome, outlined in red crushed velvet. Hanging from the gold plates were crystal chandeliers; when the sun came through the beveled octagon windows of the Mezzanine in the evening, a reflective shower of small diamonds sprayed over the walls and carpet.

Hallways reached back from each side of the desk to where the elevators were, and next to the elevators was a single hall crossing that led to the ground floor rooms.

The Banquet rooms were on the second floor. Each room had its own color scheme. 'The Gold Room' was exactly that, a *gold* room. The walls were soft gold wallpaper, textured with velvet burgundy leaves. The carpet was plush and dazzling, a brilliance of shimmering yellow-gold.

There were four large Bay windows facing out the front of the hotel, each had long gold glittery drapes. They were pulled together at the top, and opened just above the middle where they were tied back with gold tasseled ropes.

There were large gold-framed mirrors five feet apart from each other, lining the back wall, opposite the windows. Linen, and all trim; on tables, chairs, light fixtures, each set of double doors, the scattered lounge benches, and the steps and handrails that lead to the stage area, were all in gold. Even the curtain over the stage was a beautiful shiny gold satin. All wood trim was mahogany and handcrafted in a Victorian style – and freshly polished for the event.

The Hotel Staff had been preparing for weeks. The *Xanorse Christmas Party* was the biggest event of the year; it had been taking place annually since 1973, when *The Plant* was officially recognized for its contribution to the state's economy.

Chemical research directives and nationwide contracting with scientific affiliates had risen to such drastic heights, that Xanorse was forced to expand. This created a whole new job market in Pleasure View.

At last count, Xanorse Chemicals currently employed thirty seven percent of the Pleasure View and surrounding town's working population. On the evening of December 22nd, most of them and their spouses gathered for the highlight of the year.

David Maples, Personnel Director, was the first to arrive. David was next in line for his current position, when came the tragic death of his predecessor, Morgan Newton; the man found dead and dissolved in a row boat on Marble Rock Lake. Ironically, it was David's own daughter, Sarah Maples, who had been killed by the same creature that got Morgan.

David was there early to inspect; to make sure every fork and knife was in place, to see there was no lint on the carpet, to insure the band was set up, and to have servers ready to serve.

Once he was satisfied, he placed himself at the bar stationed in the right side corner. There were several portable bars furnishing the *free* liquor, Xanorse was picking up the tab. There was one in each corner and one in the middle along the side.

In one corner: the bartender was an older, gray haired, black man, whose name badge said *Nathan*. In the other corner: was a much younger man, with bad acne, his name was *Drew*. But the Bartender in the middle of the side wall was a full breasted, tan young redheaded woman named *Ingrid*. Ingrid would be the topic of conversation between many of the men that evening.

Dave Maples got a Long Island Ice Tea from Nathan, and then signaled for the doors to be opened.

It was 6:45 p.m.; the party was scheduled to begin at 7:00. Most employees were off at 5:00 (the later shift at 6:00), and most of them were racing home that night to *shit, shower and shave*, throw on their *good duds* (or gown), and prepare to party; or for the Pleasure View folk...*get shit-faced and fall down.*

At 6:55 the first guests showed up. David tried to get the band to do some light instrumental background music for early arrivals. The band, who did mostly top forty Rock & Roll, was...disturbed by the idea. Then Dave pulled out a roll of fifty's and suggested they compromise.

The band came up with something close to easy listening versions of Beatle songs. It worked. No complaints.

By 7:45 the party was well under way. There were nearly a hundred people in the room, fortunately, this particular Banquet Room happened to be the largest one in the hotel. The crowd steadily increased, about ten newcomers every five minutes. Of course, the bigger the crowd got, the more Rock & Roll the music became. By 8:30 they were doing *Aerosmith's* 'Dude looks like a Lady'.

This was the event where *Executives* came together with the *Laborers*; the evening was usually a culture shock for both sides. The phrase, 'I had no idea people like that really existed,' could be heard from one end of the room to the other, accompanied by the glazed expression of amazement.

However, everyone from both ends of the spectrum agreed; the meatballs made the evening. Italian sausage meatballs, some sautéed in Barbeque sauce, others baked in dough and cheese wrap; and all, going fast.

Another universal agreement was that the dance floor was definitely the place to intermix the classes. Every type of personality was out bumping and grinding with every other type.

In *contrast* to that liveliness was; off in a back corner, far from the dance floor, a small group of executives discussed what to tell the county water department about the new underground piping - *that led from the waste pool to some of the local reservoirs.*

Another group was having conversation about how much longer Saturday overtime was going to last.

Husbands and wives began mingling *away* from each other, and *into* the unexpected mingle of wives and husbands of someone else. It was all very out in the open, yet there was a growing undercurrent of secrets rippling through the crowd.

Eventually, Sue Ann Walden's widower came face to face with Sam Stallworth's widow, their spouses both killed by the infamous *Oily*. The conversation went...

"I'm sorry to hear about your husband."

"I'm sorry to hear about your wife. I know exactly how you feel. If there's anything I can do, please, call me".

"Thank you...I will."

The food was laid out buffet style; you could get whatever you wanted, whenever you wanted it. And it was out most of the evening (from 8:00 to 10:00). They'd had sit down dinners in the past, but people either didn't like the food, or they couldn't make it to the dinner on time, or they were just not ready to eat when it was served.

So, this time, they decided to have a two-hour Smorgasbord that consisted of meatballs, shrimp salad, pasta salad, cheese cubes, and fruit cocktail...that kind of thing. Then, finger sandwiches; roast beef, ham, turkey, and vegetables and potatoes. And for desert, there were French pastries, fruit tarts, pudding, and of course - cake and ice cream.

At the end of the table sat a punch bowl; it was eventually spiked. There was a Champagne Fountain, four tiers with a couple dozen spouts. The *company supplied* open bar served beer *and* hard liquor. The Company only splurged once a year, but it was always memorable.

Originally, a drawing for door prizes had been planned for 10:00 when the food was taken away. Unfortunately, they never made it to 10:00.

It was 9:23 when an outside security guard stumbled into the lobby, gasping for breath, the desk clerk ran to his aid. The guard could not seem to breathe, he dropped to the ground, reaching and clutching with his arms, pulling at the air, turning blue.

The desk clerk leaned his head back in his arms; trying to understand why the man couldn't breathe, then he saw his neck; there was the sunken impression of a hand burned into it. The man's neck had been squeezed and....melted shut.

It was like a solid trunk of muscle, drawn tight, splitting open with streams of blood. The man's windpipe was closed off forever. A minute later, right there in the lobby of The Griswald...he was dead. The desk clerk was stunned speechless.

The switchboard suddenly came alive with calls about power failures throughout the hotel; Televisions were dead. Room lighting flickered off and on and finally...off. The calls that were coming through, were ultimately asking the same question, "What was the Hotel doing about it?" Then the phone lines went dead.

Ted Travis - the Desk Clerk/Night Manager on duty, broke into a sweat. He'd never been faced with a situation this extreme. Authoritatively, he stood up, letting the dead guard drop to the floor, and he began barking orders.

"Hit the emergency alarm and get the police here. Page...*locate* the *House* electrician and get him on those circuit breakers, *pronto*! Page...*locate* the House Medical Staff to...."

Ted stopped when a hotel guest came through the automated glass door from the inside pool area. The man was dazed and confused, "They're dead," he said flatly. "They're dead!"

Ted turned a whiter shade of pale, "Who's dead?"

The man in the Speedos was not overly coherent, "They're dead. They're...melted."

Ted shouted for coverage, "Jenny you're in charge," he ran to the pool.

The bodies of three women lie on the concrete, their eyes wide with terror on dead faces. Ted saw nothing wrong with them from their head to their mid-section, but then their stomachs caved in - to the ground. They had been melted like thin plastic under a hot sun, onto the slick wet pavement.

The condition of their upper legs on the pavement was flat, as if something had sat on their laps and dissolved them. Then, at their knees, the inner muscle rose back up into the calves of their legs and feet, lying lifeless at the edge of the pool.

"Holy God, they *are* melted." Ted fell back and stared, unable to move.

The lights in the lobby began to flicker. Jennifer Steele was on the phone, frantic, "Hello? Hello?" She kept tapping the connect button, trying to reach the police, but the phone was a casualty of the evening. "Hello? Hello?"

As lights went out and the lobby darkened, employees went into silent hiding. In the quiet they heard shuffling feet drag over carpet, toward the emergency stairways; basically fire escapes, but used a lot by those with claustrophobic fears of elevators. This night, that would be the pathway to a Christmas Party Massacre.

In the Gold Room, the band was pounding out a rocking rendition of 'If Looks Could Kill' by *Heart*, completely unaware of how appropriate the song was.

David Maples, Stanley Levitz, and Rhonda Toush (the men just called her Tush) were engaged in a small group discussion near a set of double doors to the right of Ingrid; the bartender, when the doors opened.

People had been going in and out of those doors all night for one reason or another, so no one paid attention at first, there shouldn't have been any need to concern themselves. Until, Stanley Levitz felt a grasp at the back of his neck.

"What the hell?" he mumbled, and turned to see who grabbed him. Even his *last* expectation would not have been one of finding himself face to face with a man who'd been dead for forty years. But there he was.

Under normal circumstances, Rhonda's shrieking scream might have been heard in the next county, but thanks to the amplification of the band, the only ones who heard her at all was David and Stanley. And at the moment, Stanley had a few of his own screams to contend with.

He suddenly felt the hand at his neck sink into his flesh. The two were becoming one with each other. The burning shot up and down his spine, filling his head with shock and unbearable pain, until...he passed out.

David and Rhonda watched Stanley's reddening face flood with sweat. Suddenly, blood streamed out from his nostrils and ran over his mouth. Then more blood from his eyes...and...*pop!*

If David and Rhonda's legs were in working order, they would have turned and ran, but the fascinating thing about horror is how well it holds you in place, keeps you unable to think, to move; and they stood and watched as Stanley's mouth burst open and spewed a chunk of bloody throat muscle. It caught Rhonda in the center of her chest and slid into her cleavage. She screamed and bent over; head down, wriggling her body convulsively until the meat flopped out.

The hand that closed on Stanley's neck went all the way through, until Stan Levitz's head severed and dropped to the floor in front of Rhonda, his blown eye sockets staring up at her.

Rhonda sprang back with continued screams, and as she and David looked for a way to run, there were three more *undead* visitors right behind the one in front of them.

"Oh Shit!" David jerked and turned to run, *"Run, Rhonda, Run,"* he cried.

He need not ask her twice, she was in sprint position. Unfortunately, there were a lot of people, and not a lot of room to run, especially if you weren't looking where you were going.

David turned head-on into the group behind him and plowed down two women, while making three other guests spill their drinks.

"Hey man, I think you've had enough," one of the men commented as David himself went down flat at their feet.

His eyes bulged with terror, "They're here. The creature's are here."

"What? I can't hear you, man, the music's too loud?" The man towering over him laughed and looked back at his friends for support. Only, his friends weren't laughing, they were still with fright. Then one of them screamed.

The creature's piled into the room, one after another. Raggedy fingers grabbed one of the women David had knocked down. And though it looked like she might be getting pulled up, the unimaginable truth was, she was about to lose a hand; her wrist was melting through. And when it happened, and her hand came off, the creature holding it tossed it away; it landed in the champagne.

One by one, people noticed the uninvited guests; the ones not quite dressed for the occasion. With stunned panic, Xanorse employees were backing up to the nearest windows and doors.

The walking dead moved among them, clutching at whatever unsuspecting fool hadn't seen them yet. Billy Dunes's mother; test tube coordinator, for whom the party was an excuse to buy a new dress and shoes and get her hair done, was sitting with her back to the situation, sipping *another* glass of *the bubbly*, when one of the uninvited grabbed her hair and yanked.

She found herself suddenly looking straight into the face of a rotted skull, with only patchy flesh and one eye. Her mouth opened to scream, but was silenced as the creature leaned over and stuck his tongue down her throat.

The decayed and blistered tongue of the monster, penetrated so deep, Martha Dunes gagged and vomited into its mouth. The vomit swished back and forth between the two while he sizzled her tonsils away. Then his grasp at the back of her head started burning through, until eventually, she dripped from his hands in fleshy bubbles.

The screaming grew, as doorways were blocked by incoming dead; the rotted mutations who's immediate purpose in life (or death as it were), was to bring on a Christmas meltdown.

Two of the younger creatures; one male, one female, came up behind *fat* Wendy Rigley, a thirty-five year old Sample Analyst. *Fat* was not actually appropriate for Wendy, *obese* was more appropriate for Wendy.

The male creature reached around Wendy's thick, triple fold neck with his bony arm; holding her, while the female bent down in front of her and pressed the top of her head into Wendy's stomach.

Those in the immediate vicinity were awe-struck by the sheer obscenity of what the two little monsters were doing. They watched as bubbling innards oozed out around the head of the one at Wendy's stomach, melting itself right into her.

Then the other one's arm, at her neck, began sliding upward from beneath her chins, into her jaw; her flesh dripped all over itself. A quick, sharp, squealing cry shot from the small opening of her mouth, and then cut off when the arm rose through her jawbone.

The head of the one at Wendy's stomach was deep into her abdomen, slowly melting a path to her crotch. The fat woman was as dead as her voiceless screams, sitting in a crimson pool of blood, emitting the sound of a shifting slurp.

One unthinking man reached out to pull the stomach-eater off. He clutched its skinny, patchy fleshed waist, and yanked. With a slimy sound of wet suction, the creature snapped its head out, irritated by the interruption, "What's wrong, dead man, you never eat her from the top down before?" the voice was raspy and gritty. The words sounded garbled, like something was clogging her throat, vibrating thick and gooey as she spoke. Then she smiled, blood dripped from her teeth, she put her hand into Wendy's gaping hole and withdrew a ball of sizzling intestines, "Care for some tube steak?"

The man dropped to his knees and puked. The crowd backed up and ran away. Screams filled the room as loud as the band. Guests stumbled over each other to get away, *some* slipped through the doors, but the doors were essentially blocked.

The creatures moved in small groups. A crowd, who had backed up to the stage, got cornered. One hysterical woman took a running leap through a large plate glass window (they were on the second floor).

The band too, had suddenly become aware of the invasion, and the music faltered to a stop. Each band member froze, seeing the onslaught of dead beings.

The lead vocalist, Roxanna, screamed and turned to run backstage, but then stopped in her tracks when she saw Tommy, the drummer, pulled from his padded stool by none other than *Oily* himself.

As the Creature's hands gripped the young man, the burning was instant. Oily lifted Tommy over his head by his throat with one hand, and his crotch with the other.

Tommy tried to scream; got out a small piercing yelp, then his throat closed. Overcome by that and the pain of an acid melt into his pecker (burning it to a nub...then off, and moving into his asshole), he died. But before Oily lost his grip, he lurched forward and threw Tommy into a nearby amplifier.

The drummer went through the front of a speaker and halfway out the back, tearing through live wires. He jolted and bounced with convulsive electrocution. Sparks snapped and popped and sprayed onto other speakers *and* the stage curtains; the curtains caught fire.

A small fire at first, but it spread quickly. Then other speakers began to pop, until loose wires were sending out random shots of firebombs. Eventually, the chain reaction exploded all over the stage and fed the engulfing bonfire.

Oily pushed the drums aside and went for Roxanna. Her brain raced wildly with panic, she was suddenly searching frantically for some form of weapon. Then she stepped back and bumped her microphone stand. *The Stand*, she thought, and reached back to grab it, working her hands down to the base. Oily had just reached out to her when...she brought the stand back and swung it at him.

Her swing was sure and accurate; she caught him at the neck. And the force of the swing (combined with her hold and follow through) allowed the stand to cut straight across. She sliced his rotten head right off his slimy body.

Roxanna screamed and dropped the stand. Another band member, Sean, grabbed her and pulled her off the stage, "Come on, lets get the hell out of here."

"Wait!" she cried. "Is it dead?"

They stopped and turned to look back. Their jaws dropped with unrelenting disbelief as they watched the brainless monster kneel down and grope, in search of his head. And when he had it, stood up and placed it back on his shoulders.

He slid and twisted it into position. Roxanna and Sean were frozen with horrid fascination; the creature melted himself back together.

Then *It* smiled at them, they saw wet flaps of throat muscle through holes in the underside of its chin, and it spoke in a deep and gravely voice, "If it's not attached, I might lose it!"

Anyone near the stage, trying to escape through a rear exit, was now cut off. Forced back by fire that billowed over that entire wall. The only other escape routes available were plate glass windows; and there was little consideration to the safety of that.

The creatures had scattered through the room, disintegrating at random, those in their path. One small group of *dead* had taken Mike Stuns; the Marketing President, and his secretary; Allyson Lofton, and melted them together…in the middle.

In an irrational act of playfulness, they melted down one side of each of them and put them together - half man/half woman. If it weren't so completely appalling, it would've been Art.

Another group had burned off several sets of legs, dismembered their victims at the knees and stood the severed limbs in an assemblage together. Then they burned off heads and used them like bowling balls; thrusting their rotten, bony fingers into eye sockets, and their thumb in the mouth; and then threw them at the legs.

The walking dead were on a killing frenzy; vile atrocities took place all across the room. The *invited* guests were leaping from windows.

Eventually, Oily had worked a path to the entrance side of the room, collecting his party along the way. They stopped whatever they were doing and followed him.

At the windows were a couple hundred Xanorse employees. Some hung on the ledge, others fell to the snow and ice covered asphalt below.

The entire wall behind the stage was a roaring blaze that had stretched to the ceiling and curled over, it was torching the walls on either side of it. On the other side of the room, blocking the doorways, the creatures had formed a line. Linking a hand to the shoulder of the one next to them, weaving their arms together.

Oily stood in the center, alone. The closest person on each side of him kept that arm down, leaving him unlinked. He took a step toward the astonished Xanorse crowd, as they gaped at the ghoulish lineup, watching incredulously as the arms of the dead melded together - creating an inseparable unit of one. Like paper dolls connected in a long string.

At one end of the line was a decomposed man, fairly tall, he looked about fifteen years dead, and old when he died. Most of his jawbone and two teeth were showing, you would have seen more teeth, if he'd had them, but there was just an empty gap showing through to the inside of his throat. His nose cartilage was half gone; dark red leftover brain lurked about inside behind burning yellow eyes. His body slumped like an old person, bone and muscle poked through in places covered with thick yellow pus.

Next to him was an old woman, more or less the same age, but more decay, as if she'd been dead longer. Her entire nose cartilage was gone, but she had more teeth than him. The rest of their physical characteristics were about the same.

Next to her was a decayed young man, whose difference was, one; he looked to have been dead much longer, like forty or fifty years. And, two; one of his legs was missing a foot, in fact, from the knee down it looked like the leg had just been stretched to meet the ground, closing off in a stub to walk on.

Then, there was a middle-aged woman, and another older woman. Then a younger man, who looked as though he too had been dead forty or fifty years. His biggest difference was; half his face was caved in, cut right down the middle, like someone had chopped their way into his skull. There was no nose cartilage or upper jawbone, he was missing an eye, and the socket it used to be in was no longer round, was no cheekbone beneath it. Other than that, he looked as pleasant as the rest of them.

Next to him was a young girl in her teens, then another girl even younger, then a boy. The last three didn't appear to have been dead nearly as long as the man with the caved in face.

Next to the boy was *Oily*. To his left was a middle aged man whose claim of significance was that most of his gut was missing, like it had been chewed away, leaving remnants of torn out intestinal tubing.

There was a middle-aged woman, then two more men; one in his teens, one in his twenties, both dead about thirty years and each with obvious bullet holes in their heads.

There were a couple more young women, one with powerful hatred on her rotted face. Another man, another older woman, and on the end, a young man who had a hole in his chest big enough to pass a baseball bat through.

David Maples, initial organizer of the eventful evening, stepped out from the crowd on the other side, with the fire blazing behind them, and cried, "What do you want from us?" He directed his question straight at the oil-covered creature in the middle.

Oily, with his gruesome grin, looked from side to side at his dead entourage, then back at David, "We just wanted to let you know we're here. We wanted to thank you for bringing us together." There was almost a chuckle behind his deep and gravely voice.

David suddenly got the idea that these horrible creatures were planning on being around for a while, "Who are you people?"

Oily smiled at him, "We are the nightmare of your dreams," he laughed low and grisly.

Then, one by one, the creature's arms separated, melting back to their original form, and Oily turned and walked from the room. He was followed, in slow procession, by each of the dead party members, as the Xanorse crowd watched with silent shock.

Eventually, David was brought back to coherency by the sounds of approaching Fire Engines; he began shouting for everyone to get out of the building. By then the ceiling was coming down and they would have to run for the doors to make it in time, which, just by the grace of God, most of them did. Still, too many people died that night - not necessarily by fire.

Chapter 5

T he following Sunday, December 24th, 10:30 a.m., Krys's doorbell rang. She was still in her satin pink nighty (the short one, with lace trim) and matching pink robe and slippers. She'd been having coffee at the kitchen table, reading the morning paper, glued to the front page, entirely consumed by the story of Friday night's bloodbath.

Apparently, a lot of guests had cameras that night and were able to escape with good clear photographs. The one that made the front page was of Oily himself, after he'd lost his head and then picked it up and stuck it back on.

He stood center stage, evil incarnate with a grin, and dripping. The entire setting behind him blazed in roaring flames. The photographer had obviously used a zoom lens, because anyone who got as close to the monster as what this picture implied, was no longer living. It was very close up and exceptionally clear, perfect front-page material.

The doorbell rang again, this time Krys heard it and jumped, aware that she'd completely ignored it the first time.

Jeff Blake stood with his hands in his pockets, looking at his shoes. When the door opened, he looked up to see Krys in her untied robe, loosely open, exposing her long slender legs.

Krys and Jeff had never really found the inclination to become romantically involved, but there was definitely a playful attraction.

"Morning, Krys," he said.

"Good morning, Jeff."

"I see you're wearing my favorite outfit," he commented, "I mean, really nice legs, you know, really really nice. ...Too bad about your tits."

They laughed. Krys's breasts had been the butt of many jokes, Krys made most of them herself.

"Yeah, well, you know what they say," she offered, "anything more than a handful's a waste." She smiled and shrugged, *C'est La Vie*, and waved him in.

"Yeah," he smirked, "but I think they meant *adult* hands."

She slapped the back of his head on the way to the kitchen.

"Want some coffee?" She asked and stepped around him to the cabinet for another cup.

"Only a lot, thanks."

She picked up the pot and poured, leaving it black like he liked it, and they made themselves comfortable at the table. "Shawna up yet?" he asked.

After Krys's parents died (leaving her the house and two mortgages), as close as she and Shawna were, it only made sense financially, for them to room together and split the bills. "She's sleeping. She's still pretty shook up over the other night."

"That's right!" Jeff suddenly felt a mental slap in the brain. "I forgot; she works for Xanorse. So she was there? At the party where it all happened?"

Krys nodded, staring into her cup, her eyes wide with fright.

"Is she all right?" he asked.

"Yeah, she'll be fine, I suppose. Just shook up."

Jeff blew a low whistle, "I can imagine. Guess who else was there?"

A spear of ice rippled through her blood stream, "Who?"

He looked in her eyes, close to tears, "Billy's Mom."

She stared at him for a full thirty seconds. Neither of them spoke. Her eyes darted back and forth, waiting for the bomb. Finally he told her, "She didn't make it, one of those...*things* killed her."

"Oh Jeff, I can't...How's Billy taking it?"

He looked down into his cup, "Not good. I went to see him and his dad yesterday, and again this morning. They're both pretty wiped out." He sipped his coffee quietly.

Eventually, Krys broke the silence, "So, what brings you here? I haven't seen you *or* Billy in a month."

He stared at her, cold and blank, then he picked up the paper and turned it around to face her. The iciness in his eyes made her shiver.

She sat her coffee down slowly and looked at the paper, she went pale. He pointed to the picture on the front page, "You know who that is, don't you?"

She stared at the photograph and shook her head, "No, no, it can't be. He's dead." Tears of hard reality rolled down her soft face.

"Well, it is," he told her, water filled in his own eyes. "That's Jimmy Hagger!"

Krys started shaking, "It can't be, Jimmy Hagger is dead, you know it and I know it. We buried him together...remember?" She cringed, her eyes pleading for him to take it back.

Instead, he reached over and held her hand, "Krys, I wish I were wrong...but look, look at the picture, they don't get any clearer than that. Look at the other pictures on page two. It's him."

"It can't be," she cried.

Then a third voice cut the air, "But it is."

Standing in the entryway, Shawna was up. "It's Jimmy Hagger, I was there; I saw him. Thank God he didn't see me, or recognize me." She walked in slowly to get a cup of coffee, "Hi, Jeff. I figured you'd be showing up."

Jeff didn't know what to say, Shawna looked bad, pale and fragile. "Are you okay?" he asked.

She stared at them both, taking her coffee to the table, "What, you mean considering there's a man out there who's been dead ten years, and suddenly decided to get up and go melt down the town? Merry Christmas! I'm fine, how 'bout you?"

Jeff and Krys stared and waited, anticipating an explosion.

"I'm sorry," she apologized. "This is just too crazy." Then a horrible memory rolled in and hit her, "Oh my gosh! I'm sorry, Jeff, I didn't even think. I was there when, I...uh, I saw what happened to Billy's mom. How is he?" As the words left her mouth, an unsettling look of reality crossed her face. Perhaps it was the numbing shock wearing off, but suddenly she burst into tears. Until that moment, she'd been a walking zombie.

"Jesus, listen to me, asking how he is. I'm so sorry, Jeff." He got up and went to sit next to her, both he and Krys held her while she finally went to pieces.

"It's ok, Shawny," Krys said, "somebody'll stop him."

But who? was the question that spun in their minds. *Maybe if the police knew where the creatures camped out, they could sneak up on them while they slept (or whatever it is dead people do when they get tired of...tired of...well, when they get tired). Only* the police *don't have a clue who they are or where they came from.*

"Do you suppose all those creatures with Jimmy were family?" Jeff asked.

The girls looked at each other, "I guess they must be," Krys said, "you know that cemetery of theirs was right there where we took him."

There was a moment of silence, then Jeff finally stated what they all knew, "You know we can't tell the police who it is, they'll ask how we know." There was more silence.

Eventually, Jeff mentioned, "I heard Davis is moving back home in a month or two, you know, since he and Janie split up."

"Did you talk to him?" Krys asked.

He smiled, "Yeah. He didn't want to talk about him and Janie much, but he told me he was starting a new job back here in Pleasure View as

Chief Mechanic at Dayton's Transmission Shop. That guy, Monroe, is quitting and moving away, but he said he couldn't swing it financially for another month or two, so he's kind of on hold."

"And why is Monroe moving out of Pleasure View?" Krys asked.

"Well," Jeff went on, "he say's his wife is really schizzing out about the attacks. Say's she can't deal with it anymore. So they're leaving."

"And does Davis know about the attacks?"

Jeff studied her for a second, "Well, he knows about some of them...not all of them."

"And what do you think he's going to say when he finds out about *all* of them, and finds out we didn't tell him about it before he moved back?" she asked.

"He'll know," he told her. "I wrote him a letter last night, I'm mailing it Wednesday, after Christmas, with a copy of today's paper."

"Did you tell him who the picture of the thing is in the paper?" Shawna asked.

Jeff looked back into his coffee cup for a second, then lifted his eyes, "Yeah, I told him, I told him everything."

Shawna and Krys looked at each other, eyes wide and questioning. "You think he'll still come back?" Krys asked.

He lowered his gaze again, "Yeah, he'll come back." Then he mumbled to himself, "He has to, someone's got to help us figure out what to do."

By "*what to do*," Jeff meant, be able to find and destroy Jimmy Hagger before he found and destroyed them. They never dreamed their deepest darkest secret would come back to get them. But here it was in *un*living color, and they knew it was just a matter of time before Jimmy would center his focus of vengeance, and come after his killers.

THE
SECRET

Chapter 1

The regular hang out, in 1980, for the six members of *The Pleasure View Brat Pack,* was Billy's tree house. If they weren't in school, you could usually find one, if not all of them, there. This particular Saturday was no exception.

The day was warm and sunny; spring had finally kicked in full throttle. School was almost out, and anybody who had even a *remote* connection to someone with a boat, was suddenly establishing a deeper friendship.

For *The Pack,* that would be Jeff. His parents had an eight-seat speedboat, and since Jeff had recently turned sixteen, he was given his own key and privileges without adult supervision.

He'd been driving it since he was fourteen, so that was not a problem. All he had to do in return was to put gas in it when he used it, and keep it clean.

It was 11:00 a.m. when Jeff and Billy trod down the path to the tree house, "I can't believe that jerk, Davis, driving out here and not picking us up," Jeff griped. "I think we should go back to the road and let the air out of his tires."

Billy smiled, "Yeah, but then we wouldn't get a ride back. And one of *us* would end up having to ride double with *him* on our bikes."

Jeff raised an eyebrow, "Yep, that's about how it would go."

Up in the tree house, you could hear grunts and groans overriding heavy breathing, as Davis and Janie got passionate on the sofa.

"Uh...uh...oh...oh Davis that's good," Janie moaned low and breathless.

Davis grinned as sweat rolled down his face, his hair was soaked, his body was slick on hers. "Ooh Janie, I love you sooo much." His thrusting cock may have been putting the smile on his face, but at sixteen, his heart was truly filled with emotion, holding her close and kissing her neck.

The sofa springs in motion made a nagging, rusty squeal. "Here, let's try this," she said, and wriggled out from under him, pushing him into a sitting position so she could climb on top.

She sat gently, positioning herself on his hard throbbing penis, and slid it deep into her, until pelvic bones met, then she rocked back and forth on him.

Years later, when he thought about it, Davis realized how few and far between these bursts of Janie's initiative or desire ever were. But on that day...

He leaned his head back and closed his eyes, "God, that's good," he breathed. It wasn't long before Janie had worked herself up to an explosive orgasm. The moans and groans stretched out longer and longer - her grip on his shoulders tightened, as her rocking became almost violent.

"Oh...Oh...Davis, aaahhh...aaaahhh...I'm going to cum...mm...mmm ...ooohh Davis..." Her body contracted tight as a drum, her nail piercing grip on his arms actually drew blood, and though her eyes were closed, her brows lifted as she threw her head down and pushed for a flow of love juice.

She shook, uncontrollable tremors, before collapsing on his chest, suddenly weak, and with an odd desire to suck her thumb.

Davis had been holding off on his *second* orgasm long enough to coincide with her big one, and in that last explosion - they came together. "It just doesn't get better than that," she sighed. They exchanged wet sloppy kisses and fell silent in each other's arms.

The quiet only lasted a couple of minutes before they heard the approaching crackle and crunch of leaves and brush along Billy's path, accompanied by the faint voices of Jeff and Billy.

"Shit!" Davis cursed and pulled Janie off carefully, "It's the guys."

Janie flopped back on the sofa, naked and covered with sweat. Her bottom lip stuck out in a pout, "But what if I wasn't finished yet?"

He grinned, "Well, you are now," then he pulled the towel out from under her; first wiping himself off, then handing it to her. "You better dry off and get some clothes on, they'll be here in a minute."

He was already pulling his pants up, when she leapt from the sofa to the floor, on her knees, and took his still semi-erect penis in her mouth, she wrapped her lips around it, and slid her tongue all over it, then slowly pulled away from it to let off with a kiss, "Ok," she said, "I'll get dressed, so you can go play with *the boys*."

"Man, those guys have shitty timing," he mumbled.

Davis and Janie weren't paying attention to how quiet things had become as they finished dressing. Davis was about to pour a couple of ice teas from their cooler when, suddenly, the door flew open and both boys yelled, *"Surprise!"* Expecting to catch the couple engaged in some heavy sexual activity.

When they looked in and saw nothing happening, their smiles dissipated. They looked at Janie and Davis at the table having tea; Janie giggled, "Surprise," back at them.

Jeff walked in shaking his head, "Jeez, Janie, you are no fun at all. I know if Krystal were up here, she'd at least have left her top off and flashed us, just for the thrill of it." Billy and Davis laughed.

Janie smiled, "Sorry, Jeff, but I'm not Krystal."

"Man, that's for sure," he said, then added, "but then Krys really doesn't have much *to* flash." They all laughed.

Billy plopped down on the sofa and began screwing his face around, sniffing at the air, "What is that weird smell?"

Davis and Janie looked at each other with blushing smiles.

Jeff was searching through his cooler, smiling to himself and shaking his head again.

"So," Jeff said, "what's on the agenda for today?" There was a short pause, and then he pulled a key from his pocket and held it up, "Perhaps a cruise on the lake?" and with a grin, held out a bottle of *Jack Daniels*, "Perhaps a nip at ol' J.D.? Till we're trashed?"

Jeff and Davis both had ways of obtaining alcohol that none of the rest of them even wanted to know about.

They looked at each other and shrugged. "Sounds good to me," Janie agreed.

"Well, all right," Jeff said, and twisted off the top of the bottle, "I think I'll get started on *this afternoon* - right now. Anybody else want a drink?"

Davis was the only one to decline, claiming he needed to eat something first, to soak up the alcohol intake from the night before. And as Jeff pulled a few cokes for mixing from the cooler he and Billy brought, Davis pulled a few sandwiches from the one he and Janie had.

"Billy, turn on the radio," Janie said.

They had a small jam box that took eight D batteries and was way too heavy. They kept it in the corner on an overturned crate that was generally used as an end table.

Pink Floyd's 'Have A Cigar' strummed softly in the background. And in the following moments, each of the four present members of the brat pack slipped into a thought-pondering world of their own.

Billy picked up an old acoustic guitar he kept there. He had it at the tree house because that's where *he was* most of the time, and usually all he really cared to do was pick at it; searching for whatever random notes he could match to whatever song was on the radio. He was actually pretty good at it, and Pink Floyd seemed about the easiest to play along with.

Jeff had a stack of old Batman comics that, once he got into them, it was next to impossible to get him back out. That day he was carefully following Mr. Freeze in an attempt to turn Batman into a human Popsicle.

Janie had been slowly sipping her Jack Daniels and Coke, kicking back in her chair. She had one leg up on the table, daydreaming and gazing quite contentedly out the window, unconsciously rubbing lightly on her crotch.

Davis wolfed down a second sandwich; ham and cheese on wheat bread, with mayonnaise, and some potato chips for texture. His eyes were focused on Janie's crotch, watching her gentle massage, chomping on his food. He had to shift a couple of times to allow growth room in his pants. Her silent masturbation was re-igniting his fire.

This was the scene in the tree house for the next half hour, until it turned to boredom. Finally, Jeff looked up from Gotham City, "Well...are we going to the lake? Or, are we waiting on Krys and Shawna all day?"

All eyes went to Janie.

She looked up, '*Why are you looking at me?*' written all over her face, followed by the classic, '*Must I always be the one to make the decision???*'

"Go!" she said. "I'll wait for them. Krys can bring us over in her car. Just be careful driving that boat if you're going to be drinking."

"Yes, Mom," they chorused.

Davis kissed her goodbye. Jeff *tried* to kiss her goodbye; Davis pulled him off. "Later," they said, and climbed down the tree.

Chapter 2

It was another hour before Krys and Shawna showed up. "About time," Janie said. "I was ready to give up on you two." Then she noticed Shawna had a bag with her, "What's in there?"

Krys grabbed the bag and took out a bottle, "Coolers," she announced. "*Peach* wine coolers." Krys and Janie both had a weakness for…

"*Peach coolers?*" Janie echoed excitedly. "I love Peach wine coolers. Give me one of those."

Krys handed one over and pulled out another for Shawna, then one for herself. Popping hers open, Shawna absently began sniffing at the air, "What's that weird smell?"

Krys sniffed, it took two whiffs before she was quite aware of, and well acquainted with, the vague *odor*. She and Janie looked at each other and smiled. "So, Janie," Krys asked, "was Davis here this morning?" The two of them giggled. Shawna looked at them both and shrugged; *another joke over my head,* she thought.

"So, *was* Davis here this morning?" Shawna seconded.

Krys and Janie's laughter subsided with respect to Shawna's naiveté. "Yes, Shawna," Janie told her. "Davis and the other boys were all here this morning. And now they're all at the lake on Jeff's boat, waiting for us."

"Hmmm, all three of them, huh," Krys teased.

Janie rolled her eyes, "Billy and Jeff showed up an hour after Davis and I got here," she set her straight. "So, how about we down a few of these coolers and go join them."

They smiled and clinked bottles together, then threw back their heads...and poured.

Shawna was the first to finish, "Wimps!" she exclaimed, then headed out the door and down the tree.

At the bottom, Janie grabbed the bag, "How many more you got in there?" she pulled it open and saw three more 4-packs.

"Is that enough?" Krys asked.

Janie smiled, "I don't know, let's start on 'em and see how it goes."

"We got them for *all* of us, Janie," Shawna nagged.

"Shawna, dear," Janie informed, "by now the boys are probably half trashed on Jack Daniels; they'll never miss these," and she handed Shawna another bottle as they walked the path through the trees.

Along the way, they sang, and talked, and stopped to look at interesting bushes, they even tried to catch a squirrel or two. And after two more coolers, they were having a pretty good time. The walk was half a mile to where the car was parked, and thanks to the wine (and the bourbon Janie had already had), she was feeling no pain, "Man, I feel great!" she announced.

"Krys?" Shawna whispered, "Janie's acting like she's drunk or got laid or something."

Krys whispered back, "I think both."

It wasn't long before they all three caught dance fever and began doing circles and cartwheels, right out of the woods and up to the car.

Krys had a 1972, bright yellow, Volkswagen Beetle. It had a few rust spots on it, and a good percentage of upholstery was torn, but it ran; got her where she needed to go, and kept the rain out.

They crawled in, "Are you sure you can drive?" Janie asked.

"Of course I can drive," Krys told her, "I have a key and a license, remember?" They laughed.

"Krys?" Shawna called from the back seat...she was ignored.

"You know, maybe I should drive," Janie suggested.

"Oh, Krys?" she said again.

"Janie, I'm more soberer than you are," Krys responded.

Shawna didn't like being ignored. *"Krys?"* she repeated...much louder.

"So relax and enjoy!" Krys instructed.

"Kuhryyyss?" Shawna finally shouted.

Both girls in front turned around. "What is it, Shawna?"

Shawna was red with frustration. "...Do you have our swimming suits?"

In a moment of revelation, they all took a quick look around, then at each other.

"Don't look at me," Janie said, "I've got mine on," she pulled up her top and showed them.

"Well, shit!" Krys slapped the dashboard, "I guess they're back at my house."

There was a moment of irritation...then acceptance...then a smile... and finally, more liquor induced laughter. "Well, let's go get 'em," she said, threw the clutch into first and fired up the engine.

The *Bug* did a few sputtering jerks when she let the clutch out too quickly, but then she punched the gas and the little Beetle shot onto the highway, weaving a bit; trying to find the right lane. And when she found it, she pushed the gas pedal to the floor, floored the clutch, and took the stick straight through second and into third gear.

"Hey, watch this," she told them as they approached Short Cut.

"Krys, you're going to fast," Shawna warned.

"No I'm not, just watch."

When she reached the turn that would put her onto Short Cut, she was doing 30 mph, and suddenly she hit the brakes and the clutch at the same time.

She turned the wheel hard left, spinning the car halfway around, and slid onto the adjoining road. She did some fishtailing, then shifted back to second, slowly let off the brake to regain full control, and cruised straight ahead.

"Was that good or what?" she laughed. Janie laughed too and took out another cooler. Shawna was plastered to her seat, wiping sweat from her brow, "Uh, next time," she said, "just give me a knife and I'll take my own life, thanks. ...Jesus!"

Krys and Janie laughed hard, Janie's eyes watered, "Oh, I think I'm going to pee my pants."

"Not in my car you don't," Krys giggled back.

They were halfway up Short Cut, Krys was doing 45 mph, and trees were surrounding them closely on both sides. Suddenly, there was a loud *'Bang!'*

The girl's attention shifted when they saw a rabbit pop up and spin in the air, spraying out a stream of blood and land on the other side of the road. They were just about to speed past it...

"Shit, somebody's out hunt..." Janie started to say.

"Krys, look out!" Shawna's scream cut her off.

...When The Hunter emerged from the trees to claim his prize and suddenly found himself smack in the middle of the road; where Krys's yellow Beetle was about to change all of their lives.

Krys stomped on the foot pedals, both brake and clutch. But the attempt was futile; they were too close and going way too fast. And then, *'Baaamm!'* They hit head on.

His body lifted with the impact of the bumper, smacked the hood and flew into the flat windshield; the one that cracked his head open. Then he spun up over the roof, twirled down the backside and slammed to the ground. He rolled and skidded, and after both arms and his neck had broken, finally bounced to a *dead* stop.

The Beetle pulled over, off the pavement. Krys and Shawna were screaming hysterically, Janie reached out and turned off the ignition. "Krys, stop screaming," she yelled, but to no avail. "Krys, *stop it! ...*Shawna, *shut up!*"

It was obvious to Janie that the other two would not be able to rationalize themselves of their own accord. So...*(a man's gotta do what a man's gotta do)* she reached back and swung around with a good hard slap in the face to each of them.

Silence.

It worked! She was pleasantly surprised. They both shut up and looked at her; rubbing their faces.

They stared at each other for what seemed like a very long time, until, between sniffles, Krys finally stuttered *the question*, "Whu...what are we guh...going to duh...do?"

Janie fought to hold back the alcohol distortion in her brain and come up with an answer. "First," she said, "I guess we need to check him out and see if he's alive or not."

Sometimes reality just has a way of punching with both fists. "You mean he could be dead?" Shawna was about to ignite with more hysterics. "We just killed somebody?" Janie glared at her with more potential face slapping in her eyes, Shawna shrunk quietly back in her seat.

Eventually, both side doors of the Beetle opened and they all stepped out. Janie and Krys walked back to the person lying in the road, Shawna stayed next to the car. She rested her hand on the roof and stared at the body. A moment later, her hand was sliding, when she looked to see why; she found she'd laid it on a thick slick spray of blood. She jerked away and stared at it in horror, then turned and heaved up that mornings breakfast and a few wine coolers.

As Krys stood over the body, Janie knelt down to examine it.

"Is he dead?" she asked.

Janie didn't say anything; she was wide-eyed with shock by the mangled body with its back to her. She reached out slowly, trembling, and put her hand on his shoulder, giving a slight tug to pull him over.

The body, however, was lying at an odd angle, so it didn't take much, and rather than a slow roll over, it fell flat, hard, and open. One tug was all it needed to flop down with full weight. His arm landed on Janie's foot, both girls jumped and choked on a short scream before they realized that was all the further this boy was going to go, he was most assuredly...dead.

The asphalt and gravel chewed him up pretty good; he had small rocks embedded in the ripped gashes on his face and mouth. His bottom lip had torn half off, revealing his lower teeth like small seashells floating in an ocean of blood. His eyes had locked open with a glazed gaze of terror, staring directly at Krys. His head had turned so far around; blood seeped from the torn skin where his neck broke. Both arms were twisted; even if he were double jointed he couldn't have gotten into such a position. His legs lay limp, along with the rest of him. And as were many possums and rabbits before him, he was yet *another bloody casualty* out on Short Cut.

"His whole body seems to be broken," Janie said. "I guess...in the long run...he's better off dead."

Krys started to cry, "Oh, God, I killed somebody, this can't be happening."

Janie stood up and put an arm around her, "It was an accident, Krys, he shot out, out of nowhere."

"Yeah, but tell that to a Judge, especially after we've been drinking, they'll lock me up and throw away the key," she cried on Janie's shoulder.

Janie looked around, searching for an answer, she knew Krys was probably right about a Judge. "Listen," she said, "let's go back and get the guys. They'll know what to do."

Through Krys's blubbering, she agreed, "Yeah, they'll know what to do." She looked, painfully, at the body, "What do we do with him? I mean I know it's not a real popular street, but people do use it."

Shawna watched while the other two dragged the dead body into the trees along the side of the road.

"He'll be ok here, nobody will see him," Janie said.

"Are you sure?"

"Come on, Krys, let's just get the hell out of here. The quicker we get this over with, the less of a chance we have of getting caught."

Shawna got in the car, the others followed. Krys fired up the engine, did a jerky U turn, and headed back to the lake.

Chapter 3

"So what time was your dad here?" Davis asked. The three boys were cruising the lake, drinking and howling at the bikinis on shore.

"5:00," Jeff told him. "He came down for some fishing, then left about 8:00. Said he'd be back around four or five to pick it up."

Davis grinned curiously, "He just left it tied to the pier? Isn't he afraid someone will steal it?"

Jeff felt the heat of guilt, "Well, I told him I'd be here between eight and eight thirty, so he really didn't expect it to be alone for more than about 15 minutes. And I really didn't think it would be this late before we got here. Besides, it's a small town, who's going to steal it and not get caught? Besides that...it's insured."

Davis shook his head, "Better not push your luck, my friend."

Jeff looked straight ahead and sped up, the wind blew through his hair, "Leave me alone, will ya." They grinned and took a hit on their drinks.

Davis leaned back and looked at Billy. Billy was staring off at the beach, looking directly at Debbie Renfrow (who would later become Debbie Peterson, whose husband would lose his head one day to the boy Krys just killed).

Debbie was one of the few girls around, built good enough to get away with wearing a string bikini, and she knew it, and took advantage of it.

Billy was staring hard at her, lying on her oversized 'Budweiser' beach towel, twenty feet back from the water. The sun glistened off the light coat of lotion that covered her body. Davis noticed Billy was hunched over, and then he saw why. Billy, in his daydreaming, had become aroused enough to cause his fifteen-year old pecker to rise up and salute Miss Renfrow.

"Damn, Billy, you don't need water skis," Davis said, "you could just ride the waves on that tent pole you got there."

Jeff looked around to see what he was talking about, Billy looked down at himself. Davis and Jeff laughed, which embarrassed Billy and he turned away, trying to situate his stiffened *self* into a *not so obvious* position. "Fuck you both," he told them.

"Hey, it's ok," Jeff said, "look at her. She's worth getting hard for."

Then Davis stood up and yelled across the lake at her, *"Hey, Debbie, there's two horny bastard's here that got a hard on for you. You got Billy's dick big enough to..."* he never got a chance to finish; Jeff hit the gas and took off. Davis was thrown to the floorboard.

"Jeez, what an asshole, Davis," Jeff said. "I mean, I can be an asshole, but you give it a bad name."

Davis lie on his back, laughing, "Yeah, that's what Janie tells me," his laughing made his eyes water. Then it became contagious, they all laughed. Back on the beach, Debbie sat up, using one hand as a visor to shield her eyes from the sun, and looked to see who was yelling at her.

The boys took another shot of Jack Daniels and were passing the bottle around, when they heard Krys's little bug; 'beep beep,' in the distance.

"About time," Jeff said.

The guys watched the car race through the one aisle parking lot on the other side of the beach. Apparently, she was in a hurry; she overshot the gravel covered parking slot she pulled into, overran the grass onto the sand, and almost hit the water itself.

"You think Krys has a license?" Jeff asked.

Davis looked at him, "Passed the test by one point. You should see the picture on it, looks like she just crawled out from under Bruce Edwards."

As the girls stumbled over each other, piling out of the car, they were already screaming for the boys to come to them.

"You think they're horny or something?" Davis asked.

"Well if they are," Jeff said, "I'll take Krys."

"I don't know," Davis commented, "Shawna's got a lot nicer tits."

Jeff looked at Billy, Billy was looking down and shuffling, trying to make sure whatever was left of his erection was not noticeable. "Yeah, but Shawna's Billy's girl, remember? She likes those curly golden locks." Davis and Jeff laughed again.

"Did you guys just start out the morning with your head's up your ass's or what? I told you to lay off me about Shawna." Billy was already tired of the days joking and suddenly they were aware of it. Both, Davis and Jeff looked away, their smiles faded.

"...And besides," Billy went on, "I'd fuck Janie before either one of them two, any day."

Jeff and Davis looked back with surprise. "Touché," Davis said. There were more laughs.

Meanwhile, the girls waved and screamed frantically.

"Let's go see what they want," Jeff said and turned the boat around.

Only minutes after a very brief conversation, the boys had the boat docked and tied up. Then everyone piled into Davis's car and they raced away from the lake.

On the way, as the girls filled them in on details, Krys kept having outbursts of hysterical crying. For the most part they could calm her down; except once, and Janie had to slap her again. Of course, by then

Janie was pretty fed up with Krys all together, and the slap had more sincerity to it. The ride was relatively quiet after that.

"There!" Janie pointed to the side of the road, "That's where he is."

The Mustang slowed, coasting onto the thin shoulder of grass that ran in front of the trees, and rolled to a stop. One after another, each of the six teenagers; high school kids who shouldn't have any more worries than homework and a Friday night date, emerged slow and sickly from the car. Setting out to confront the reality of the *accidental* killing of a boy their own age, and decide what should be done about it.

As Janie pointed through the trees, "Over there!" Davis and Jeff were the first to see Krys's bloody road kill.

All three boy's mouths dropped wide open. They knew the girls would not out and out lie about something like this, but maybe, somewhere in the back of their minds, they hoped it was some bizarre mistake.

No mistake. Here they were, face to bloody face, and the body was just as torn up and dead as the girls had said, only now it was attracting flies.

"I do not believe this!" Davis exclaimed. They watched flies crawl in and out of the dead boy's mouth, occasionally stopping to rub their spidery little arms together, enjoying the meal.

"I think I'm going to puke," Billy said, and darted off into the trees.

"I think...me too," said Shawna, and shot out in the opposite direction.

"Jesus, Krys, didn't you see him coming at all?" Jeff blurted.

That was all it took. Krys went off, "Well, shit, dammit! How many times do I have to say it? He came out of nowhere. One minute I'm driving along, singing a happy tune. And suddenly there's this ignorant fucking redneck idiot standing right smack in the middle of the damn road, tempting the saints to *go ahead and march him on in*. And Wham-Fucking-Bamm, there I was to oblige. I didn't blink. I didn't look away. I was not sight seeing. He was *just-the-fuck* there. And that's all there was to it. I'm sorry. I'm Fucking Sorry, all right? He was just there!"

Janie pulled her over for a hug, and Krys collapsed into some heavy sobbing.

I'm sorry," Jeff said, "I know it wasn't your fault."

They looked back at the body, Davis bent over to examine him closer, "You know who this is don't you?"

Jeff looked down and mumbled a quiet, "Yeah."

The girls looked at Davis with terror in their eyes, they hadn't even thought about the fact that they might actually *know* the person they'd killed.

"It's that Hagger kid; Jimmy."

They looked startled, "Jimmy Hagger? The boy you guys say is always lurking around the tree house catching birds and tearing off their heads? The boy you said takes his thirteen-year-old sister into the forest for sex? The boy who's never seen the inside of a schoolroom? That Jimmy Hagger?" Janie rattled loud and fast the credits of local folklore.

"That's the one," Davis admitted.

They looked at the body. Billy and Shawna returned from their upheaving and stared along with the rest.

* * *

"Hey, bud?"

Davis looked around to the voice behind him. He was heading to the tree house on a Wednesday afternoon to pick up some homework he'd left there the day before.

"Yeah?" he answered; surprised that anybody else was out in that part of the woods right then. But the surprise went away when he saw the face.

Before him, stood a standard example of backwoods humanity, a life form generally referred to as 'Hillbilly.'

"Hi," said the boy, "Mah name's Jimmy, what's your'n?"

Davis's jaw dropped slack in amazement of the kid's interpretation of the English language. "I'm Davis."

They stared at each other, respectfully cautious, not sure but what shaking hands might be a contaminating venture, waiting for the other to make the next move.

"So," Davis continued, "What can I do for you?"

Jimmy ignored the question, "Say that's a real nice clubhouse you-all got out there betwixt the trees."

"Thanks," Davis said, suddenly hoping this kid wasn't going to ask to be a member. That would be all they'd need, sitting around trying to do homework, or Davis trying to *do* Janie, and have this toe picking, butt scratching Hillbilly at the end of the sofa, snorting and stinking and telling stories about which cousin was humping which.

In fact, Davis decided to turn right around and head back *out* of the woods, toward the highway, steering the kid's interest away from the tree house.

"So, I guess that's you I hear sometimes, out hunting with your rifle. Get some good rabbits do you?" Davis tried to make small talk while changing the direction of their stroll.

The Hagger kid turned, keeping up step, "Yeah, some rabbit, some quail, some squirrels, a couple snakes, you know, anything you can eat."

Davis's stomach took its first turn of the day. "So," he repeated, "what can I help you with?"

"Well," Jimmy began, "I tell ya, I was out here 'bout a month ago, an I seen you doing something that got me thinking maybe you an me wasn't so diffurnt after all."

Davis wracked his brain to figure out what the kid could have seen that would give him that impression. "Oh? What was that?"

"Well," Jimmy continued, "I was out here with my little sister, Sandy?" he said as if to imply that Davis *knew* his sister. Davis nodded. "We was over by some bushes not too far from your-alls place out there, just bird watching you understand."

Davis smiled to himself, *bird watching, yeah, right!*

"An we heard this grunten noise? Well, at first we couldn't figure out what it was, soze we started looking around. That's when we detected it was coming from up in that tree house of your'n. And, well, curiosity got the better of us you know, an we climbed a tree to see what was goin on inside. That's when we seen that one girl that hangs out with you fellers, up there with some other feller we ain't never saw b'fore. We seen 'em through the winder, and they was...well, you know...(Jimmy smiled, baring all twelve gray and yellow teeth)...humping like two dogs with the blood a burnin."

Davis looked surprised by his blatant admission. And when Jimmy got to the part about the grunting, he knew what was coming. The memory of a month ago came back quick enough, even before the boy got to the heart of it.

"Well...uh...anyway," he went on, "I admit we did watch fer a little while. That's when we seen you out there with that pitcher camera. And we just kinda stayed hid and watched."

Davis decided this would be a good place to stop him, he knew the rest of the story. "Yeah, ok, I remember that day, so what about it?" he kept walking, his speed picked up a little, then he felt Jimmy's hand on his shoulder. He stopped and turned to face him.

"I seen ya takin those pitchers," Jimmy said. Davis glared at him. Silence. Finally, Jimmy spit it out, "I sold some hogs last week, an I got some money; ...you want to sell somma them pitchers?"

Davis stared while the light of awareness fell upon him. *That's what this is all about?* he thought. *He just wants to get his hands on some dirty pictures?* He smiled, "Is that what you want? Some naked pictures of Krys?"

Suddenly Jimmy looked starry eyed, "Is that her name? Krys? That's a purty name."

Immediately, Davis realized it could be a mistake throwing the girls names around like that. After all, he didn't really know what kind of grip this kid had on sanity. So, he changed the point of interest.

"Well, Jimmy, I gave all those pictures back to her," he lied. "I felt bad after I did what I did." Jimmy looked puzzled; he didn't understand what it was Davis felt bad about. "But, I tell you what," by then they had reached the highway and Davis's car. "I can let you have this for free," he reached into the back seat, where he remembered Jeff had stuffed an issue of last months Playboy, pulled it out and handed it to the backwoods boy.

Jimmy's eyes lit up as he flipped through the pages, "Are ya kiddin?" Jimmy had a new hero...*Davis*.

"Naw, go on, take it, it's yours," Davis told him.

Jimmy's grin stretched from ear to ear, and when he came across the centerfold, Davis noticed his right hand going directly to his crotch.

"Well, I have to be going now," Davis said, and climbed into the car.

"I sure thank ya," Jimmy said, and turned and faded back into the forest, one hand on the book and one sliding down under his rope-belt.

Davis headed up Lakeside Highway laughing crazily to himself. He'd come back later for the homework.

* * *   * * *   * * *

"Yep, that's Jimmy Hagger all right," Davis repeated.

Jeff looked at the boy's mouth, where the side of the bottom lip that *hadn't* torn off was all puffy and swollen like he was sucking on a golf ball. It completely buried six of his twelve teeth. The other six, on the lipless side, stood out fully exposed, protruding from bloody mangled gums and surrounded by cracked jawbone.

* * *   * * *   * * *

Jeff had worked part time as a lumber salesman for Lowe's home center store during the summer of '79, when he experienced his first encounter with the Hagger boy. Jimmy and his *daddy*, Bobby, had come in to get some wood and chicken wire for a coop they were building.

Jeff remembered how Jimmy had first walked up to him and said, "I need ya'll ta git me enough tree timber an wahr ta build a chicken coop." Then smiled a large grotesque display of yellow and gray chipped and rotted teeth, loosely planted in a bad case of pyorrhea.

Jeff tried to bring words from his head to his mouth (suddenly a near impossibility), too dumbstruck by the...(missing link?)...*person(?)* who now stood in front of him.

Bobby Hagger pushed his boy aside to give a more defined request of what they needed, "What the boy means is that we'll be needin eight strips a 12' x 12" B-grade pine, and a roll a chicken wire, and some nails." Then he stood back and stared into Jeff's eyes to see if he was a salesman who knew his supplies well enough to help them. Jeff nodded; he understood.

Bobby hooked a thumb onto one strap of his overalls and opened up with *his own version* of the same smile Jimmy had.

"I'll need to write up an order slip so you can go around back and pick up the materials, if you'll just step over to the counter, please." Jeff finally reunited with his thoughts and motor functions. But as he wrote, he felt the slap in the brain reminder that, *Yes, people like this really do exist...they do exist...they do.*

He couldn't help but look up every five or six seconds (just checking) to make sure it wasn't a hallucination; this father and son duo, both wearing identical raggedy overalls, and old, old work boots that had seen their better days about five years before.

The only difference between the two, really, was that Bobby wore an old greasy, smelly T-shirt, where as Jimmy had on no shirt at all, just his own greasy, smelly self. They were both scrawny and thin, and their hair was oily and unkept, as though it hadn't been washed in a year...or two. Bobby was sprouting a five or six day growth of beard stubble, while Jimmy simply populated his face with an ever-increasing number of blackheads and pimples.

There was an obvious display of deep-rooted snot and easily pickable boogers infesting their noses, while small chunks of something, which actually looked like food, grew in their ears. Large flakes of skin crust seem to be holding their eyebrows in place.

Jeff's stomach turned a little, but he maintained tolerance, until the two...gentlemen (?) smiled. The mess that went on in their mouths was enough to bring his lunch to his throat.

As he wrote up the order, Bobby stood next to him, looking at the form (as if he could read), not saying a word, just breathing...heavily. Jeff knew it would be rude to just walk away, but the stench coming off the man's body, and seeping through his slightly parted lips, was enough to choke a sewer worker. Jeff walked to the other end of the counter, pretended to search through some papers for figures, recaptured his breath, then walked back holding it, and wrote some more.

Meanwhile, Jimmy wandered through the store touching, picking up, and examining everything he could get his grimy hands on. Eventually, he found himself lost in a sea of mirrors, face to face with...himself...in full-length reflection.

First he smiled at the boy in the glass; pleased or amused, no one would ever know. Then he made faces and laughed...out loud. And, as if he wasn't goofy looking enough, he reached up, grabbed a handful of his long black greasy hair, pulled it back, puffed out his cheeks, stuck out his tongue, and proceeded to cross *one* eye. A minute later he was blowing out snorts of laughter. This, for Jimmy, was entertainment.

Jeff looked down the aisle at him, trying to keep his own bewildered amusement from busting loose, *what an idiot this kid is*. Occasionally, Jeff accidentally let a snort slip out, trying to cover it with a cough.

"Take a shot o' some good moonshine, boy; it'll fix that cough a your'n right up," Bobby told him.

"Yes sir," Jeff replied.

Jimmy's amusement with his face only lasted a short time before he moved on to other parts of the store. Jeff eventually finished the order and told Bobby to take it to the cashier. That she would ring it up for him.

He said, "Thanks," and turned to look down the aisle Jimmy had disappeared into, then he turned to look behind himself, finally he looked back at Jeff, "Well, I don't mean ta sound like a fool or nothin, but I don't recollect which way the check out counter is from here."

Jeff thought for a moment, he knew he could have just given directions, but he was curious about what Jimmy might be up to, so..."Here, follow me, sir, I'll show you where it is," Jeff led the way.

Along the walk there was no sign of Jimmy, until they reached the cashier stand and saw he was already there.

The boy had found his way to the front and was making himself comfortable in the back of a shopping cart. He'd folded closed the front 'baby seat' section of one of the carts that was only a foot deep. Then he crawled in and laid back; his left arm hung over one side, both legs went over the front, and his right hand was in his lap.

"So...uh, you ladies work late hours do you?" he asked Marcie, the cashier who was blocked into her stall by the cart. Jimmy used his most *suave* speaking voice, which, with all the snort laughing he was doing, sounded like a cross between Mr. Haney from *Green Acres*, and the pig; *Arnold.*

"Jeff?" Marcie called in a plea for help; her voice was on the edge of panic.

"Here," Jeff said, "Marcie, this is Mr. Hagger's order form if you'll just ring it up, they'll be going out back to get the materials."

He told her all she needed to know in one breath, to keep her cool and doing what she had to, to get the hillbillies out *A.S.A.P.*

Marcie snatched the paper from his hand, "Thank you," she said, and punched the appropriate numbers on her Register.

Jeff stayed for the transaction, making sure there were no complications. Then gave Bobby directions around to the back of the store from the outside.

Jeff and Marcie watched with silent amazement, as Bobby pushed his son out the front doors, still in the cart, and head back, smiling at the sky.

"He said his name was Jimmy Hagger, but I could call him *Baby*," she uttered. Her face was nervous, quiet, repulsion.

* * *

"So, are we going to stand here and stare at him all day, or what?" Billy blurted.

The air was quiet and still, you could almost hear the snap of their five heads, as they whipped around to look at him. The question was a wake up call, they knew they had to do something, but nobody knew what. Slowly, they turned from Billy to each other.

"Davis, we've all drank and drove before," Krys said. "And I was not being negligent." She started shaking again, with tears welling up in her eyes.

Davis and Jeff glanced at each other, they knew the others would look to them for an answer simply because they were older and *the men* in the group.

"What about," Jeff started, "if we called the police and reported, anonymously, that there was a dead body out here on the Short Cut, and let *them* figure out what happened?"

Everyone froze, as if the idea was too good and simple, they had to think about it a moment. Then Krys put her hand over her eyes, hiding from the glare of the others, and said, "Somebody could have seen us leaving the scene, we were driving a little crazy on the highway coming to get you-all, and you know, that piss yellow color of my Volkswagen *Beetle*," she emphasized that it was an easily identifiable car.

"So," Jeff retorted. "So what if somebody did see three girls out joy riding on a weekend afternoon, so what if they even saw you turn off the Short Cut. They can't prove anything."

Krys was stone quiet and looked at the ground, shuffling her feet. Davis looked at her, "Can they?"

Angry and hot, she looked up, "Well shit, Davis, I hit the kid at forty five miles an hour, don't you think that did just a little bit of noticeable damage to my car?"

Everyone's mouth dropped.

"And, where's the car now?" he asked.

"I parked it behind the Coppertone sign at the lake while you-all were tying up the boat. No one will see it."

Silence.

Each member of the P.V. brat pack began pacing the boundaries of their own psychological bubble. Finally, Shawna stopped and looked to see if there was even a glimmer of idea on anyone's face before she opened her mouth. After hesitating as long as she could stand it, she creased her eyebrows in disgust, huffed a loud sigh, threw up her hands and said, "Well, would anybody really notice if he just never returned from his little rabbit hunt?"

Everyone turned, except Davis; staring at Jimmy, he brought his hands to his temples and rubbed, "You're saying, just get rid of him? Like, make him disappear?"

"Well, what else can we do?" she asked.

Heads snapped from Shawna to Davis and back again.

"What do we do with him, Shawna?"

She was trembling, her voice was shaky, "I don't know, I can't even believe I'm talking about this," her eyes filled with tears.

"I know," Janie mumbled low.

Snap, all heads turned again.

"You know what?" Davis asked.

She took a deep breath and said, "I know what we can do with him."

The anchor finally hit bottom, they each felt a last crash of resolution. They had killed somebody, and now they were about to dispose of *the body.*

A haunting quiet fell over the group as they looked at ripped up Jimmy, his six tooth smile and one open glaring eye staring back...watching them.

"A few months ago," she started, "Davis, Shawna and I were out in the trees near the edge of the road. It was the same day Davis caught you and Bruce Edwards up in the tree house with his camera, remember?" Janie looked at Krys.

Krys turned six shades of red and looked down, "Yeah, I remember." Then she looked at Davis, reached out a hand and slapped him on the back of the head, "Shit-head!" He took the slap without a word.

"Well," Janie went on, "when Shawna and I were running to get away from him, 'cause he was pretty pissed you know. We were almost to Short Cut, thinking we'd shoot up the road and go hide out at Krys's house, when Shawna suddenly fell through the ground."

Jeff and Billy looked puzzled.

"There was a hole underground," she said. "The dirt was soft, and when she stepped down, it gave way and she fell through. Half her body went under. Davis finally caught up to us and pulled her out. When we looked in to see how deep it was, we saw a pool."

"What kind of pool?" Billy asked.

"It's probably toxic waste from Xanorse," Shawna said. "It stunk real bad. But we didn't hang around to investigate; Davis hurt his foot and we had to take him to the doctor for stitches."

They looked at each other again. To describe one would describe them all; exceptionally long faces, grim to say the least, covered with beads of sweat brought on by any number of things; alcohol, humidity, fear of the repercussions of Jimmy's rabbit hunting mishap, or D - all of the above.

Davis stood up, "Jeff, grab an arm."

Jeff shivered, startled by the unexpected request. "You mean we're really going to do this?" his voice wavered.

"What the hell choice do we have?" Davis snapped.

Billy and Krys looked at Jeff with wide sympathetic eyes and waited to see if he *would* do it.

Jeff looked at Davis, then at the others, then slowly down at Jimmy, "Davis, both his arms are broken and I'm really not up to swinging a dead guy through the forest by two jangling bones...can we drag him by his feet?"

The next few minutes clicked by with the speed of a group of bank robbers fleeing the scene of a crime. Davis tossed his keys to Janie and told her to open the trunk. Then he instructed Shawna to keep a look out at the edge of the road. Billy and Krys ended up behind the body as Davis and Jeff each grabbed a leg and dragged Jimmy through the trees.

"Hey Billy," Jeff called back, "let me know if his head or anything falls off."

Billy and Krys stopped in their tracks, grimacing with disgust. The body slid along in front of them.

"Great," Billy mumbled, "Krys kills a guy and Jeff becomes a damn comedian."

Chapter 4

Davis drove a half a mile back toward the highway, and Short Cut not being the best of roads, had it's share of pot-holes; he tried missing as many as possible, but took an occasional drop along the way, Jimmy bounced around in the trunk. It was a very long one-minute ride.

Eventually, he pulled over across from the Xanorse parking lot, where he remembered the hole had been. There was barely enough room between trees to inch his way in and keep hidden from passers by, but he managed. When he stopped, they all piled out.

"This way," Janie said, walking back up the road in the direction they'd just come from, "I think it's over here. Sniff for a really bad smell and look for a large hole in the ground."

"Yeah, it's the same as when I'm trying to find my way to Krys's house," Jeff joked. Davis and Billy smiled. The girls looked exasperated. Krys smacked Jeff on the back of the head.

They clawed at brush and kicked leaves around. Billy got down on hands and knees and felt his way through the grass.

"You sure this is the right pla..." Jeff started to ask, but was suddenly cut off by a quick yelping shriek. Everyone jerked around to see that Shawna had found the hole...again...the same way as the first time, and laughter finally broke the tensions of the day; it was a good release.

"Dammit!" she yelled, "will you quit laughing and get me out of here."

Billy was the first to her rescue, he pulled her up and out *by himself*; a bit surprised at his own quick reaction to her situation. Blushing, she thanked him, "I appreciate that, Mr. Dunes." And brushing herself off, she told the rest of them they could all kiss her ass and go to hell. The laughter faded to giggles.

"Well, if you're done playing around," Davis smirked and looked sideways at Shawna, "we've got work to do." He headed to the car, "We need to dig that hole out wider so we can get down there."

Get down there, is that what he said? The statement was like a knife stab to the head.

"Say...uh, Davis?" Jeff questioned...

"Yes, get down there," he repeated. "If we don't want somebody to ever *accidentally* come across him, we're going to have to take the body deep into the pool, and I'm not doing it alone. If one of us has to go down, we all go down."

Nobody said anything.

Jeff and Billy were the first to start digging, then Krys, then Janie, and finally Shawna, "And I just polished my nails," she whined.

Davis opened the trunk and reached in, he grabbed Jimmy by the legs and pulled him out over the back of the car. When the upper part of his body crossed the bumper, dead weight latched onto gravity and the body plummeted to the ground with a thud.

One of his broken arms twisted in an impossible position behind his head and tore the skin of his elbow, the bone of his forearm slipped out with a thick and unexpected squirt of blood.

Davis felt his stomach turn on him and charge up his throat, he gagged for a minute, then swallowed hard. The nasty putrid burning had made it to the back of his tongue, but thank God...no chunks. He picked up Jimmy's feet again and dragged him to the hole. "Can you see into it yet?"

The ground was fairly soft where Shawna had broken through; it chipped away easily. "Yeah, there's definitely a pool of something down there," Krys said. "And it stinks like shit! Are you serious, we have to go into that mess? I don't think I can handle the smell."

"No, we don't have to, Krys. We *could* call the police and let them handle it," Davis snapped back. "We can just sit here sipping *coolers* while they write out their report."

She didn't even look up; just squatted with her elbows planted on her knees, her head resting in the palms of her hands, and stared into the hole, "Maybe I can handle it," she mumbled.

Davis dropped Jimmy's feet next to her. "I wonder what the hell that shit is that smells so bad," he looked into the hole. Everyone else looked at Jimmy.

"Well..." Davis started,

They all turned, anticipating instructions, like unwilling students on an expedition.

"...there's no time like the present, I guess." He grabbed the dead boy and pulled him around so his head hung over the edge, then he slid him in and let him drop.

Splash!

"Hey," Jeff had a sudden realization, "that hole's too deep, we'll never get back out."

Davis stared down thoughtfully for a moment, then quietly walked to the car and pulled out some towrope he had stashed in the trunk for emergencies (this was not exactly what he had in mind). He tied one end to the rear axle beneath the car and threw the length down to Jimmy. "Ok, so now we have a way out, let's go."

One by one, without a word, they crawled around the hole and stared into the dimly lit pool of stench where Jimmy lay floating.

Davis was the first to go. He sat at the edge, estimating how long a drop it might be, figuring no more than ten feet. But he had no idea how deep the pool was, so he pulled up some rope for slack, wrapped it around his right hand, and jumped.

Splash!

The others all crammed their heads together in a circle over the hole to see how he landed.

"Hey, you're blocking my light!" his voice was a hollow echo. They backed off.

"How deep is it?" Jeff asked.

By the light of the sun, Davis could see fairly well around himself, "It only comes to my knees. But *damn!* It stinks down here." Then he became fixated on the pool; the sunlight revealed its sparkling violet color and gooey texture.

He scooped up a handful of it and saw millions of small silver flakes, each no bigger than the head of a pin. The thickness of it made him think of motor oil.

The light from the hole spread a purple glow throughout the pit that Davis was convinced must be specifically designed for toxic waste from the Plant. Then something bumped his leg. He looked down and saw Jimmy floating face up, staring at him. He shuttered and turned back to the five wide-eyed faces above, "Come on, let's get this over with," he told them.

Janie went next, sliding over the edge on her belly, holding the rope and wriggling down slowly. Davis grabbed her legs to guide her.

While lowering in, she noticed the hole was actually very near a sidewall, maybe only three feet away, and she heard chirping.

"Davis, what's that?"

He made sure she had her footing, then let go, "What's what?"

"Listen," she said, "...chirping."

They were silent and listened.

The sound came from behind. When they turned to face the wall, staring at the grooves and ledges that had formed in the wet chiseled dirt; there, perched in long rows...were rats. Big brown and black rats; dozens of them, wiggling little whiskery noses and rubbing sharp little claws together, watching the *invaders* of their domain.

Janie screamed and jumped back, unfortunately, Jimmy was right behind her and caused her to fall ass first right on top of him.

Kicking and hitting at the pool, she struggled to keep from sliding off and going under. But when her legs separated, she found herself straddled over the dead boy's midsection. If he'd been alive, he surely would have taken advantage of the situation.

She screamed again when her hands slipped off his chest and she fell forward, her head suddenly next to his six-tooth smile and one yellow pus-filled eye. This was more than she could handle; she vomited on his face.

After coughing out the last of it, Davis yanked her up, "Janie? ...Are you all right?" She plunged into his arms, convulsing with repulsion.

"Hey, Blake," Davis called to Jeff, "you might want to warn the girls there's some rats down here, ...so, not to panic."

Jeff sat straight up. His eyes shot wide open. *This is not good*, he thought. *There are rats down there, and he say's tell* them *not to panic?* He looked at the others and could see there was no need to relay the message.

"Ok," Jeff said, "who's next?"

Shawna was shaking again, "Uh...couldn't I just stay up here and keep lookout...*Pleeeze*?" She begged.

"You heard him, Shawna. We're all in this together."

Krys and Shawna hung their heads; they knew there was no way out.

"I'll go next," Billy said, "in case Davis needs help getting them down." He glanced at the girls, then back at Jeff, "You better stay till last, Jeff, they may decide they've got other things to do."

Both girls looked surprised, like being caught with an idea they thought they could hide.

Billy scooted to the edge, called a 'Look out' to those below, then jumped in the same way Davis had. He landed pretty square on his feet with just a small stagger, catching himself by throwing his hands against the dirt wall; his face just inches short of collision. He stood still for a moment, adjusting to the darkness, until, coming to focus, he found himself eye to eye with a large...brown...Rat. And the rat, at the same time, completely startled by Billy's sudden presence, squealed excitedly at him. Billy damn near leapt into Davis's arms along with Janie.

"Sheee-it!" he hissed, and shuddered.

Janie and the boys stood quiet and still in the purple glow of toxic waste, each squinting, hating every disgusting breath they took.

Their light was suddenly cut off as Krys's butt came over the opening. Davis and Billy reached up to grab it and help her down the rope. After touchdown, she looked around at the rat covered wall, the wet tree roots growing like varicose veins from the underside of the ground, and the glittering purple oil she stood in; she pinched her nose in disgust, and then saw Jimmy's body float in and bounce off her leg. Immediately she jerked her head up and called out, "I am *not* staying in this hell hole," and she was back on the rope.

Janie grabbed her, "Oh no you don't," and pulled her down. "In case you forgot, we're doing this for you. And if I'm here, you're here.

Krys hugged her, "I'm sorry. I'm so sorry. We don't have to do this, we can go ahead and report the body - I don't care. This is just too disgusting. I can't ask you to do this for me," and she started crying again.

Davis grabbed her upper arm, "Get a grip, Krys. Don't make *me* slap you. We're all in it now, and we're not going to let you get locked up for this. So chill out, lets just do this and get out of here, all right?"

She stared at him, silent, her lower lip pushed out in a pout. She nodded agreement, a tear ran from her eye.

"Jeff, I can't do this," Shawna said. She stood with her hands defiantly on her hips.

"Shawna, you *can* do this, and we don't have all day," he told her.

"I don't think you understand what I'm saying," she said. "I am not going down there!"

Jeff was losing patience and knew he would not be able to reason with her. "Shawna, this is the last time I'm going to *ask*; will you get down in that hole, right now." It sounded more like a demand than a question.

"No!" she said. "I'm not go..."

...He picked her up; one arm behind her legs, one at the back of her neck, turned, and dropped her through the hole, "Here comes Shawna."

"...iiinnnggg dooooowwwwnnnn theeeeerrrrr. Aaaauuugghh!!!" she screamed all the way. But Davis and Billy were prepared and caught her; her butt never even hit the pool. It was, in fact, the softest landing of them all.

"Damn you, Jeffrey Blake," she yelled back at him. "You'll pay for that."

She stood and became suddenly stiff as a statue; her hands next to her face, afraid to touch anything, afraid to move, frozen with disgust.

When Jeff came through the hole, he landed next to her and splashed oiliness on her legs, he also soaked her shorts. She turned slowly, glaring with complete hatred, and very calmly said, "I hope you know I *am* going to kill you."

Jeff looked at her drippy legs, "Man, I'm sorry Shawna, I swear I didn't do it on purpose," he seemed sincere. "But, you don't want to kill me, then you'd have to come *back* down here to get rid of another body."

Her blood was at boiling level; she seemed momentarily capable of emitting steam. Her eyes closed, her teeth clenched, and she...just stood there...seething. The boys grinned.

Krys stared into the unending darkness ahead of them. "How far do we have to take him?"

Davis shrugged, "I don't know, let's see how far it goes. Maybe there's a good place to bury him up ahead, instead of just letting him float around forever. I can just see this pool filling up one day and somebody go to drain it or whatever they do, and ol' Jimmy comes pouring out on them."

They huddled next to each other and looked around in wonder. A narrow beam of sunlight came through the hole and glittered off the silver specks. They were dazzled by the flickering glow of purple, rippling with their movements.

Davis reached down and grabbed Jimmy by the ankles, "Let's go," he said, and walked slowly through the thick slick oil into suffocating blackness, dragging the dead boy behind.

They tried to stay as close to the wall as possible without getting too close to the rats (considerably large rats). They knew if they went wandering off into the middle of the pit, they could easily get lost, or step in a hole and go under and drown. They really had no idea how deep or wide the place was.

Rats were no pleasant alternative, but they were a safer bet than walking into the unknown.

"I don't suppose you had a flashlight in the car, you could have brought did you?" Janie asked Davis.

"I don't suppose you remember that you lost it in the woods two weeks ago when we camped out at Rough River," he reminded her.

"Oh...yeah," she mumbled.

"Hey, try this," Jeff said. He reached into his pocket and pulled out what looked like a ballpoint pen.

"What's that?" Billy asked.

"It's a penlight, I got it in the mail the other day, some sort of promotional thing. It's got a little button by the clip. Watch…" he pushed the button and out came a reasonably bright beam of light.

Its thin ray stretched four or five feet in front of them before it tapered off to gray and eventually black. "Yeah, that'll work," Davis said, "only, save the battery for now, let's use the sunlight as long as we can."

Jeff clicked it off, put it back in his pocket, and they continued to follow the slimy back wall.

Chapter 5

C oursing through their mission, the group felt the rancid stench in their nostrils burn its way down their throats, forcing out small choking cough spasms.

"Crimony, Davis, I hope we don't pass out from that smell," Shawna moaned.

No one commented. They were all very quiet. So quiet, the rat chirping began to echo in their ears.

At first, it was like distant chatters, then it grew. It went from background noise, to *in your face noise,* to *loud obnoxious noise,* and then...got louder! What started as squeak..squeak, became Squeeeeeaakk...Squeeeeeaakkk scratching at their brains. Then SQUEEEAAAKKKKK...SQUEEEAAAKKKKK! It filled their ears like a crashing rain shower. Small black shiny eyes flickered everywhere, and below each pair of eyes was a set of long sharp yellow teeth. And *SQUEEAAA....*

"WILL YOU SHUT THE HELL UP!" Janie screamed.

Everyone stopped and stared at her, including the rats. There was ultimate silence.

"Hey, listen," Davis said, "it worked." The entire rat force had shut up, it may have only been a momentary thing, but it was a relieving moment. And they walked on.

Finally, Davis realized he could no longer see even a foot in front of him, "Jeff, I need the light." Jeff dug it out and gave it to him. *Click!*

Their legs moved slowly through the syrupy liquid, making gentle swishing sounds. Davis had one arm back, dragging the body. Janie clung tightly to his right arm.

Krys walked behind the floating body, Jimmy's head a foot and a half in front of her knees.

Billy and Shawna trailed behind her, "Billy, you wouldn't let anything hurt me would you?" Shawna asked. She had both her arms wrapped around his right one, standing as close as she could to him without stepping directly into his clothes.

"Oh, you'll be all right," he told her. He knew not to give in too much, because of the crush *they all* knew she had on him. He wasn't unsympathetic, but he didn't want to lead her on either. "I won't let anything hurt you," he confirmed.

"Then, will you tell your idiot friend, Jeffrey, back there, to quit grabbing my legs," she said through gritted teeth.

Billy looked surprised, "Are you serious? Is he really grabbing at you?"

She looked pitifully into his eyes and nodded vigorously.

Billy turned to Jeff, "Hey, shit-for-brains, quit grabbing Shawna's legs; this is spooky enough without you being your asshole self."

Jeff was caught off guard and became angry, "I'm not grabbing her skinny ol' legs, I couldn't care less about her legs," he spoke defensively in a loud whisper.

Davis turned around and flashed the light at them, "What's the problem back there?"

Shawna stopped and did her pouty statue stance; legs slightly apart, hands on hips, chest out, shoulders back, "Your pal, Jeffrey, is grabbing my legs."

"I am not!" he yelled.

Davis put the light on Shawna's legs, "Shawna?" he said, quiet and calm.

"What?" she huffed back, not paying attention to what he was looking at.

"Don't move," he told her.

Suddenly she realized it was not *a grabbing* she felt. Her eyes opened wide and her lower lip began quivering, her entire body started shaking as she looked down.

There, in the pool, was the longest, thickest black snake she had ever seen. It was sliding in and around her legs in a figure 8. Shawna shrieked.

The rats got quiet again and drew their little claws to their ears; Krys and Jeff did likewise. Billy, however, reached into his pocket and pulled out the knife Jeff had given him (Jeff got a new one). He opened the blade and began stabbing and hacking at the snake - careful not to cut Shawna while getting a few good chops in before the thing slithered away back into the black abyss.

Davis brought the light to their faces, "Are you all right?" Billy brought the knife up to the light; it was covered with blood, thick, as if he'd gutted the thing, dripping dark red and violet down his arm.

Billy looked at Shawna, "Are you ok?"

She looked right into his eyes, her hero. She wanted desperately to kiss him right on the mouth at that very moment. But she knew he didn't feel the same, and she didn't want to embarrass herself, "Yes, I guess. Thank you, Billy. Thank you so much," she said. And then she lost control, "Oh God, thank you, that snake could have bitten me. Thank you, Billy, thank you. Please tell me we can go home now."

He turned back to Davis, "Yeah, we're ok, keep moving," he said, and they moved on. Shawna frowned and looked away in despair.

They had gone another twenty feet when Davis noticed the pool was getting deeper, now tapping at his testicles. Then he heard something, far away, but it wasn't there before, and it was getting...louder. "Hey, do you hear that?" Everyone stopped to listen.

"Sounds like a plane going over," Krys said.

"No, no, it's down here," said Davis.

They listened again, it was low and rumbling and constant, and it *was* getting louder. "Maybe it's the vibration of cars going by," Jeff said.

Davis scowled at him, "Where, on Short Cut? ...On Lakeside Highway? There aren't enough cars out there to cause a breeze, let alone a vibration."

Jeff shrugged; *Whatever, Dude, just a thought. Take it or leave it.*

Davis shined the penlight out toward the center of the darkness. The rumble was growing and he noticed the pool was swishing back and forth, sending ripples in their direction. Then, in the dark distant edge of the fading penlight, he saw something rising. It looked like a wall. "What the hell is that?" It appeared to be either something getting bigger, or something coming closer...or both. "It's a wall. It's some kind of wall coming up out there," he said.

"I don't think so," Janie contributed. "I think it's a wave, like when you're at the beach and the ocean comes rolling in."

Suddenly each of them could see it, a giant wave of oily chemical waste coming at them from the other side of the pool. "It's huge!" Jeff exclaimed.

It nearly swept the dirt ceiling above them, and it was closing in quickly. "What do we do?" Krys squealed with panic.

Billy looked at the wall behind them; there were tree roots sticking out everywhere, yeah...and some rats. "Grab a root," he said. "Grab a root and hold on, so it doesn't pull you back when it hits."

"What if it's not a wave? What if it doesn't wash back? What if this shit stinking pit is just filling up and we're all going to drown, then what?" Shawna cried.

"Then it's out of our hands and it was nice knowing ya," Davis snapped. "HERE IT COMES. HOLD ON."

They each turned and reached out to the wall, with only a second to spare, and staring into the beady eyes of the rat in front of them...

Time's up!

...They grabbed a root and held tight with both hands (except Davis, who clicked off the light, stuck it between his teeth, put one hand on a root and held onto Jimmy's left foot with the other)...then...the wave hit!

They were slammed against the wall, with all its stabbing protrusions. If they hadn't been so anxious about what was next, the pain might have been intolerable. But under present circumstances, all they could do was hold out for the final outcome.

Fortunately, the liquid had nowhere to go to build up for a return pull, so rather than a long slow tug, it simply jerked back; a sudden yank on their arms, but they held on as it washed over - covering them a good two feet above their heads.

Then came the scratching and pulling of large, desperate rats streaming by, clinging to their hair and clothes. They each felt the rodents drape across their head, clutching for dear life as the wave swept back.

The whole dousing only lasted three seconds, but the oil was thick and slow to drain off. They had to blow out their nostrils to breathe again; the violet goo had clogged every resting place it could find, including eyes, ears and mouths.

They choked and coughed up what they couldn't avoid sucking down, and used their fingers to wipe out all nooks and crannies.

"What *was* that?" Billy coughed.

Suddenly, Krys screamed, "Get 'em off! Get Them Off!"

There were rats in her hair. She grabbed at them, squeezing and throwing them off. She squeezed one so hard it popped in her hand

and spattered her face with blood. Her panic was so frenzied, she couldn't let go of it; just kept squeezing until the thing oozed through her fingers.

Then they all screamed and snatched at the little pit dwellers to get them off of their bodies. The rats were weak from the wash over, so it didn't take much of an effort. But their skin would continue to crawl for at least the next two weeks.

"I think I'm going to be sick," Krys said. Everyone felt the same. But with some quick and heavy deep breathing and gasping...nobody got sick.

They looked around at each other in the dark (Davis still had the penlight in his teeth). "You know, I can almost see you," Janie said.

Davis removed the obstruction from his mouth, "Yeah, there's a faint light from the hole. I guess our eyes are making the adjustment," he confirmed, and then clicked on the light anyway. "But I'm still using this."

"You know what I think," Janie started. "I think the pool is deeper now than it was before. I think maybe they've got some kind of holding tank, and they empty it in here every so often to let it spread and soak into the ground, maybe that wave was just the flow of a dumping."

Now there was a clear and rational thought, *and* a logical explanation that they could all accept, except Shawna. "I think there's a monster out there, and he came up looking for something to eat, and *he* made the wave."

Everyone stared at her, Janie slowly stepped next to her, "Shawna?"
"Yes?"

"I'm going to slap you now."

"I'm sorry," she hung her head, "You're probably right, it's not a monster."

Satisfied, Janie turned and sloshed away.

"It could be a giant snake though," Shawna came back.

...They walked on.

"Hope there's no bats down here," Billy remarked. Krys, Jeff and Shawna, each smacked him on the head. "Well, it's possible," he defended.

Moving along, since the pit filling or giant snake or whatever it was that had knocked all the rats momentarily from the ledges, they found themselves brushing closer to the side wall. And while the ground beneath them was soft and mushy, it was solid enough that they wouldn't sink, though it did lend itself to squishy slopes and valleys, causing the oil to rise and drop on their legs.

They had walked quietly for a while when Davis suddenly jerked back to a halt.

"What's wrong?" Janie asked, startled.

"I don't know, I think Jimmy's caught on something," Davis said.

Jimmy had stopped moving, but right behind him, Krys hadn't. She wasn't paying attention (too busy looking around the dark pool), and didn't notice they had stopped.

Bump!

Her legs were just far enough apart that his head slid between them and her knees bumped against his shoulders. The sudden stop threw her forward and she slapped down on his chest. Fortunately, her reflexes were in full working order and her hands jumped out in front of her, automatically locking her arms rigid, she held herself off of him. This she *could* have handled, but then her feet slipped, her legs went out, and her crotch came down on his face.

She was only wearing a short summer dress, and very thin panties (which were soaked). And suddenly there were six jabbing teeth urging their way through to her virtually exposed vagina.

"*Aaauuugghh!*" she screamed and pushed herself off and into Shawna and Billy.

Davis watched the whole incident; *Krys falling, her arms jerking out, planting her hands on Jimmy's chest, her loss of footing* - all while trying to figure out what Jimmy was caught on. And it occurred to him that something was oddly wrong about the whole scene.

Krys appeared to be moving in slow motion. He watched her mouth open sluggishly to scream, and he heard the scream, but it droned on forever in an endless echo. While her arms, sprouting off Jimmy's chest, looked wavy, like he was looking through vapors of gas.

And as he himself braced against the wall and leaned over Jimmy, he watched Krys leap backwards in ultra super slow motion, almost like *not moving* at all. And for the little action she did maneuver; stretching her arms and legs back - her hands and feet remained stuck to the body.

She's stretching, he thought.

...Smack!

Suddenly a new thought and redirection of focus took over, staring at his group of friends. *You-all are a mess.* And they *were* a mess, covered with drippy toxic oil.

"Davis," Janie put her hand on his shoulder, "are you ok?"

Then he realized she was standing over him and he was *sitting* in the pool. *Why am I sitting in this crap?* He looked up at her, "What happened?"

Everyone glanced at each other, then back to Davis, "You tell us," Janie's voice rose. "One minute you're trying to figure out what Jimmy's stuck on, then you're staring off at Krys for five minutes."

Davis stood up, confused, "Yeah, I turned around and saw Krys falling...in fact, that was what I was seeing when...you slapped me. And what was that for anyway?"

Janie was irritated, "Davis, I slapped you because you looked like you were in some kind of a trance. Krys was up from that fall five minutes ago. Where have you been?"

Uh oh...reality check. "Something's not right," he said, still stunned. "Dude, are you ok?" Jeff asked.

He looked them each in the eyes and said, "I saw Krys fall, and suddenly everything went into slow motion. I mean I was still seeing her fall when you slapped me just now. It was like my brain power was standing still." He looked at Janie for understanding, "Is that freakin weird or what?"

It *was* weird. He started telling them how it seemed to take forever for her mouth to open when she screamed. He told them how her arms and legs stretched, but her hands and feet didn't move at all. He tried to explain how he felt that he had no control of his own body; he couldn't make his muscles move.

Then it occurred to him, he was rambling, *and nobody was stopping him.* In fact, no one even made a comment about how stupid he sounded. And when he stopped telling his story (sensing a lack of interest), nobody said anything. He could barely even detect breathing. "Janie?" No answer. Krys?" No answer. He jerked the penlight up to their faces, the thin beam of light exposing only two of them at a time, surrounded by a ghostly purple glow. "Jeff? ...Billy?" They looked like Zombies. "Shawna?"

Their eyes had rolled up into the sockets, only the white was left to reflect the light. He could barely make out the bottom rim of their pupils. "*Janie? ...Krys?*" His heart thumped wildly. Their mouths were stretched open, but no sound came out, drool yes, but no sound. Then he put the light in their eyes and yelled at them, "*What's wrong with you guys? ...Snap out of it!*" Nothing. Their pupils eventually rolled down enough for them to see him, as if they were watching him, but they couldn't move.

Jesus Christ, what do I do? They're like Zombies. His brain throbbed.

'I slapped *you because you looked like you were in some kind of a trance,'* he heard Janie's voice in his head. "She slapped me," he said to himself. "That's it. I'll just slap them. It worked on me." He got up close to each of them, hesitating only a moment before..."Ah, shit, they deserve it," and he reached back and slapped each one of them in the face...hard.

Smack! ...Smack! ...Smack! ...Smack! ...Smack!

They snapped back and shook their heads, snatched from a deep sleep and suddenly slammed into awakening. Rubbing their eyes, they tried to focus and readjust, they heard "Hello," Davis welcomed them back. Now they understood where he had been during his unaccounted for five minutes. "Pretty damn weird, ain't it? ...You guys ok?"

They nodded, "Is that what happened to you?" Janie asked. "Like everything just got hot and rubbery and stretched out in slow motion?"

He leaned over and kissed her, "Yeah...strange, huh." Then he looked over at Jimmy to see what the hang up was.

"What do you suppose caused that?" Billy asked.

"Beats the hell outta me, Billy. Why don't you take a sniff around at the toxic air we're breathing and tell me what you think," Davis smarted. "Oh, man, look at this, he's got both arms twisted up in these roots." Davis and Jeff both grimaced as they bent over and reached into the pool to push away roots from Jimmy's tangled arms.

"That's it, isn't it? It's all these nasty fumes we're breathing," Krys said.

She was given *'the look'* by one and all.

"It's probably giving us all brain damage," she finished.

Now there was a scary reality. They glared back and forth at one another, breathless, with panic in their eyes.

But then Jimmy was untangled, and Davis was determined, "Come on," he said. And they knew they couldn't let this particular task go unfinished. So...quietly...they tread deeper into the pool.

"Davis, do you have a destination in mind? Or are we just being stupid?" Jeff asked. "Can't we just drop him right here and go?" There was a round of agreement.

On the spot for another answer, Davis told them *his plan*. "I was thinking, you know that Hagger family has their own cemetery out there, just off from their pasture. And I've been figuring that this wall we're following has been heading in that general direction. Like it's going right around their property line maybe, and if we take it far enough we could end up right around where the rest of his dead family is buried. Then we can leave ol' Jimmy right there with his kin."

Jeff shook his head, they all knew they could argue the logistics of *the plan*, but, they'd come this far, and...who knew? Maybe he was right.

"So how much farther would you say it is to...More Dead Hillbillies?" Shawna asked sarcastically.

"Can't be much further," Davis said, "look for tree root overhead, then we'll know we've passed the parking lot."

"Davis?" she came back.

"Yeah?" his jaw tensed.

"Your back is covered with spiders."

Everyone stopped to look.

Janie and Krys screamed. These were not little spiders; they were rat-size tarantulas, large crawling black spots with legs; lots of legs. And they were all down his back and in his hair, and trying to crawl over his shirt collar. They were on his arms and circling his neck. *And they were on all of them.*

They hung from the dirt above, some stringing their way down, while others just braved it and jumped.

Suddenly everyone in the group (except Jimmy) jumped and screamed and hit at themselves, trying to knock the giant insects away. There was so much confusion they wouldn't even have known if they were getting bit or not. Finally, Billy dove head long into the pool and thrashed about, shaking them off. He was flinging as much spider and oil from himself as he could, hoping whatever didn't wash off would drown. Everyone followed suit.

Davis came up trying to run through the pool, the others were right behind him.

"I'm going to be sick. I can't take any more of this. This is totally disgusting. Krys, I'm sorry, but I think I hate you!" Shawna screamed.

"Billy, slap her," Davis ordered. Instinctively, without thinking, Billy reached out and slapped her. Then she started crying, a sort of hysterical screeching cry. So, naturally ...he had to slap her again.

Shawna and Billy stopped abruptly and glared at each other. Shawna was a broken, defeated person, and her eyes accused Billy of not protecting her. "Shawna, it's going to be ok, I won't let anything hurt you, I promise."

Billy could easily shoot back up to hero status with a few carefully chosen words. Allowing her to think he may actually care about her, maybe even one day would want to *be* with her. "You won't?" she asked.

"Of course not," he said. He calmed her down a little; he even went so far as to put his arm around her shoulder. He wasn't really sure how she would interpret it, but, he thought, *It doesn't feel so bad,* and he pulled her in closer. *I guess she's ok...for a squeaky little strawberry blonde haired girl.*

Now *everyone* was seriously hesitant about continuing on, and kept hitting at themselves, making sure to get all the spiders off. Of course their imagination was already creating a whole new troupe of creepy crawlers they would most likely be hitting at for the next month. When...

"Look," Davis pointed, "up ahead. There's level ground above the pool." He looked closer, "It's like an island next to the wall."

"Land ho!" Jeff yelled and ran for it.

Shawna was right behind him...then the rest, Davis fell behind; dragging *Jimmy the dead*. And Jimmy, it seemed, was getting heavier, filling up with toxic waste.

Davis caught up and handed two bent legs over to Jeff and Billy, they dragged the body ashore as Davis climbed up.

It was perfect; it was like a large platform, completely flat. Each of them crawled up, but remained on their hands and knees, breathing heavy. Finally, they gave in to exhaustion from the long journey, and dropped to lay flat on their backs.

Davis crawled in between Billy and Janie; Krys was on Janie's other side. Shawna co-accidentally ended up on Billy's other side. *Wonder how that happened,* he thought. And Jeff was on the other side of Shawna.

Their breathing and heart beatings were completely out of sync from each other, and no one spoke, they just lay staring into the darkness. Davis put his hand in Janie's and held it as they listened to the smacking of the pool against the side of the platform.

Davis had the penlight at his side, shining down between his and Billy's legs, if either boy had had a notion to look where the light was hitting, they would have seen Jimmy's twisted broken arm where the bone stuck out from his elbow. But they didn't.

Once they focused on the stillness of the moment; no longer bouncing through slime, the glow from the penlight spread dimly over a larger area of space than they would have expected.

Lost in thought about the whole situation, they stared with fascinated anxiety at their surroundings. The wall behind was wet and slick, but it was just dirt. *Its just dirt,* Billy thought. *But...it doesn't look right.*

"Hey, Jeff?" Billy spoke, "What's wrong with the dirt on this wall?" Everyone looked.

"I give up, what?" Jeff retorted.

"I don't know...but it doesn't look right," said Billy.

They stared quietly, until Shawna became frustrated with the mind tease that the question had become, "There's nothing wrong with the dirt, it's just dirt, like it's been all the way down here, nothing but dirt and roots and rats and snakes and spiders..."

Janie sat straight up, "That's it," she said. "It's just dirt, there are no roots."

There was no tree root above them while crossing under the parking lot, but there had always been plenty coming from the wall, and now even the ones from the wall were gone. They had come to a clearing in the forest. "Davis, look!" Jeff pointed. And instead of root, they saw a small 2' x 2' square flat of wood embedded in the dirt, perfectly straight, with the boards running up and down.

"Why is there wood stuck in the dirt?" Billy asked.

Davis chilled with his first thought. Slowly, he crawled over the others. They could see he was shaky as he reached up to dig around the edge of the boards.

"What is it?" Janie asked.

He was silent until, eventually, his fingernails scraped across more wood on top, then two sides. "It's a box," he said. "It goes back into the ground."

Everyone was quiet, not sure what to think, and not wanting to think what they were thinking..."It's a fucking coffin, gang. We've found the cemetery." ...But then it was said...out loud.

"I'm surrounded by dead bodies! My life is not worth living! God, take me now!" Shawna sobbed helplessly within the blackness of the pit.

Jeff turned to Billy, "Billy, slap he..."

"Billy Dunes, if you slap me one more time, I'll see to it that you are never able to have children." She glared at him...hands on hips...pouty lip and all.

"So, good, we're here. Now, can we leave the body and *get the hell out of Dodge*?" Krys expelled with desperation.

"Davis look," Billy pointed up to where the wall and the ceiling rounded to meet each other. There was the corner of another box protruding, it was dark wood and hard to see, blending with the dirt.

"Another one," Davis said.

Suddenly, coffin hunting was all the rage there in downtown Chemicalville. They were sticking out everywhere, the gang just hadn't noticed until it was brought to their attention. One box was poking out a good two feet or more, and as Krys backed away from the one in front of her, she smacked right into it.

This particular box held the body of Charles Hagger, who in 1936 had his leg blown off with a shotgun by construction Foreman, Joe Brennen. The box had been in the ground for a long time and the exposed end was now mostly rot. The only thing holding it together was *nail rust*; and Krys had just knocked that off.

The square flat headboard shook itself loose and slid down. All that kept it from dropping off, was a single nail that remained relatively intact in a sole piece of solid wood in the bottom left corner. Unfortunately, this particular box wasn't set in the ground as carefully as the others; this box sat at a fairly wicked angle, and when the end came off...out came Charles. *Afternoon ya'll, thought I'd drop in.*

Krys shrieked at the body rumbling out at her. It slid on gravel that had found its way in through the cracks. The noise caused a few rats to jump, one grabbed Krys by the hair as it flew past. She hit it away and shrieked again. The body rolled out slowly and came to a stop. Apparently, the box wasn't as badly angled as it originally appeared.

About midway out is where Charles stopped. His forty something year decayed face glared at Krys. *Hi Krys, I'm Charles.*

Krys turned and kept screaming, only stopping long enough to grab a breath, and then scream some more.

"Davis?" Shawna said, "Slap her."

Janie was the first to laugh; this was too funny coming from Shawna. Davis smiled, *yeah, that's amusing, but I'm too tired.*

Eventually, Krys stopped, but she did not find the humor in it the rest of them did. She crossed her arms and turned her back....only, she forgot the body that she had originally turned from in the first place was still there watching her. *Charles Hagger, ma'am, pleased to meet you.*

She opened her mouth to scream again...but didn't. "Can we please do whatever it is we're going to do with that boy and get *the hell* out of here...Now...Please...Thank you very much." Krys was a wreck.

Jeff was snickering when he told Davis, "Come on, let's shove that one back in his box, and...and...hey what *are* we going to do with Jimmy?"

For the next half hour, all six members of *The Brat Pack* were on their knees, filling their fingernails with dirt as they clawed a grave into the island. After thirty minutes though, they decided, for some reason the ground was too hard, they wouldn't be able to dig it deep enough to bury him.

"Davis, its not just Shawna wimping out," Billy said, "my fingers are turning to hamburger."

Everyone looked up at their *Fearless Leader* with big sad eyes, and a plea to put a cease to the painful task.

"All right," he said, "I guess this ground *is* too hard to dig in." They looked at Jimmy and wondered what they were going to do with him; resigning themselves to the fact that he could end up floating face down in waste after all, despite their futile efforts for some sort of sanctity.

Finally, Davis said, "Let's lay him in the hole..." (They'd dug it about a foot deep) "...At least he'll be out of the pool and in the ground. Even if he's not covered."

There was quiet remorse at the thought of not being able to bury him, if for no other reason than because they'd come this far and it would have been nice to complete the job. But they dragged him over and laid him in the hole. Davis stood at the head of the uncovered grave, seeming to tower over the others in the shadow cast by the penlight he'd lodged in the wall, and he delivered his first eulogy: "Forgive us Father for what we have done, but it *was* an accident. And now Jimmy Hagger has been laid to rest with his family, please watch over his soul...Amen."

"Amen," the others repeated.

"*Now,*" spurt Shawna, "Can we *please* get out of here?"

Davis smiled, "You got it, Cookie. Let's go."

They headed briskly back into the pool; lowering themselves into the repugnant, slimy, thick, oozy oil water, and marched away from the island. The walk back went much quicker than the walk out.

Back in the liquid, they were immediately reminded of its warmth, it felt almost like bath water, sloshing along next to the sidewall, which had become quite visible in their continued eye adjustment to the darkness. They kept one arm outstretched, pulling themselves through by tree root, at a much swifter pace.

Thirty-five minutes later, except for Jeff getting slithered on and around by Shawna's big black snake, and Krys, for some unknown reason becoming the target of an 'off the wall, *rat attack*', then Janie falling a few times, taking a good *root canal* drill into her behind; they actually made it back to the opening in pretty good shape.

This time on the rope, it was girls first, then Davis, then Billy, then Jeff. It was 7:00 p.m.; the sun was closing in on the earth. It was one large eye in the sky looking down at them, sad and soulful, as the Six Musketeers climbed out of the hellhole and back onto solid ground. They wiped the goo that they could off, but the stench seemed there to stay.

They circled around and gazed back into the hole, "We are *The Pack*," Davis made the statement very authoritatively. "If any member betrays another member, that person will become exiled from the pack, from the tree house, from Jeff's boat, and from all future friend-ship or verbal communication with the remaining members."

For a moment all eyes were on Davis, they each understood the consequences, they knew this would be their bonding secret, and there was a mutual feeling of profound unity...then it passed. "Davis, you are so full of shit," Janie said.

Krys and Jeff both laughed, then Jeff slapped Davis on the back of the head, "Nobody's going to tell anyone, you big chicken shit." Then he did his Al Jolson imitation, "Please massuh, please doan be a tretnin us wit yo frienship," everyone laughed.

First it was a loud and hearty laugh, but it trickled to a personal thing. Finally, slowly...they all turned away from the hole and walked back to the car.

Before going home, they went back to the lake for a swim (clothes on), trying to scrub as much of the waste pool off of themselves as possible. It helped, but they would definitely have to do some sneak-ing around at home, stash their clothes until they could wash them (or burn them), and take a good shower without appearing suspicious.

They had cleaned the blood off the little yellow beetle, after which they could see a very clear impression of a slightly bent body in the front hood.

"Tell 'em you hit a tree on Short Cut," Davis told Krys to tell her parents.

But that night, the only one who was noticed and asked to account for his day, was Jeff, "...And why was the boat left alone for so long?"

Jeff made up a story about Billy falling out of the tree house and they had to take him to a Doctor because he hurt his leg so badly.

"Well...I guess you can't just walk off and leave your friends laying hurt," Jeff heard his dad mutter as he disappeared into the next room.

* * *   * * *   * * *

Meanwhile, back in Hagger land; Bobby and Opal Hagger huddled together on the porch swing, expecting their eldest boy to come waltzing through the trees at any moment, with a sack full of Rabbits. They rocked back and forth in the sinking sunlight and watched...and waited.

THE
UPRISING

Chapter 1

There was only a half moon shining down on the dark damp grass surrounding *the hole*. Crickets sang a melancholy goodbye to Jimmy Hagger, lying deep in the recesses of a black and endless pit.

A trace of violet gas vapors rose from the opening as the singing echoed into hollow emptiness; loud and scratchy, like scraping jabs of fingernails on a chalkboard.

Moonlight crept in and reflected the pool in still slivers of purple across the dirt wall of the underground, rippled only by the occasional splash of a kamikaze rat.

The light of the moon did not spread nearly as well as that of the sun; there was only a ten-foot radius of visibility before a curtain of blackness.

The dark oily water seem to stretch infinitely with a smell all its own. If you were to, perhaps, combine some really bad smells, like skunk, rotten eggs, the city dump, and covered it with cow manure and a dash of one of Jeff's broccoli farts, you might have a comparison.

The rats and snakes crawled and slithered among tree root. The air in the pit was thick and warm, and wet with humidity. As seemingly endless as the sky, the boundaries of the pool were nearly untraceable, and yet, there, somewhere on the outer edges, in a one-foot deep grave, lie the body of sixteen-year-old Jimmy Hagger. Resting peacefully with his deceased family.

As toxic condensation and the absorbing pool itself seeped into the earth, its fumes coursed their way through the rotting bodies buried within.

Over the next five years, Xanorse established quite a dependent relationship with government contracting. In the summer of 1982 the company was under such demand for their testing and development research, they were forced to go to a six day work week, which created more jobs, and consequently produced more chemical waste to be dumped in the pool; the ever increasing pool.

Before Christmas of 1983 Jimmy was up to his eyeballs in oily toxins. The slime had risen to his platform island grave, until finally, over flowing and covering it; filling the gaps in around his body. Where he continued to soak for the following six years.

In those years up to 1989, the members of *The Pack* had pushed the tragic memory of Jimmy Hagger and what they'd done to him, far back to a locked deposit box deep in the subconscious of their minds. So far, in fact, they'd virtually forgotten the incident entirely.

For nearly ten years, Jimmy lay surrounded by the stagnant fumes encircling him, swishing him back and forth in slimy waste. Waste containing a combination of ingredients; that under normal laboratory experiments would never have been mixed together. The results of which were completely unknown...and unprepared for.

By 1989, the pool had risen two feet over his body. If not for the earth's continual absorption, it would have been a lot higher.

Chapter 2

It was a quiet night in the pit; the rats were eating or sleeping or had gone out for the evening, but made no noise. There was a low sizzle of hot wet air settling across the surface of the pool, but no sloshing, no slithering, no waves.

Maybe, just maybe, somewhere deep in the darkness there was a faint shuffling sound, almost undetectable. Like the distant *shoosh shoosh* of something moving back and forth over loose gravel or dirt. And slowly the sound increased, *shoosh shoosh*. Not that it really got much louder, it just seem to spread over more space. Occasionally, there was a 'thump!'

The pool, in its deep midnight purple, quietly began to rock. The shuffling stayed low and scratchy.

Randomly, a few crickets chirped in, eventually joined by returning rats; chattering about their evening, donating screechy squeals to the muffled noises of the pit. Then the back of a long black snake appeared in the wake of a wave, and the pool began to swirl and bubble from somewhere below the surface.

'Splash!' Dirt and rocks shook loose from the overhead ground at the top of the wall. The shuffling continued; the pool began to sway more sporadically - sloshing against the side.

'Sssssssss!' The snake raised its head and stretched its jaws wide with a hiss. It showed four very pointy fangs and a few lines of drool. And then, just as if something had bit into its tail end, it jumped.

There was a low moan emanating from behind the dirt wall...then another.

More rats squealed, shrieking with fear of something, but not knowing what. Rocks continued to fall, as the shuffling grew more prominent. The pool became violent with splashing and rocking and small cylindrical swirls. Swirls that ignited with bright yellow electrical charges in the darkness, like lightning in the underground.

The oily liquid began to glow with the electricity from beneath its surface. Bright purple illumination lit the contents of the pool. There were tall silver pipes stemming from the bottom, connected at the base to cross-running pipes that were half buried and half out of the ground. They ran the length of the pit, back to the plant. These were the pipes used to disperse waste.

There were newly created chemical creatures; formed from a combination of bacteria and waste - they crawled along the murky, slimy mud beneath the pool. There were at least half a dozen long black snakes wriggling through the purple glow. And then there was the three-foot rise in ground level, to Jimmy's island burial plot.

He was still there, the weight of his body kept him from floating away. And now, the glow that lit the pool, was emanating from *him*, casting an eerie film over his one open jellyfish jiggly eye.

Short, quick flashes of light, zapped and popped around him with jolting electricity.

His throat suddenly grew wide and his head hinged back to meet his spine. His mouth stretched open and exuded a long, slick, black snake that wound out from his guts.

When the snake left, his head fell forward and slammed his jawbone shut...*his other eye popped open.*

Jimmy had become a giant ball of sizzling electricity, sparking blue *and* gold *and* red *and* green. And with twitches and jerks...he came up from his grave, swirling in the glowing purple pool. The jolting turned his body over, face down, and the electrification continued, charging so hard that it was either going to burn him up, or spark life back to a ten-year-dead body.

His legs dropped, his feet came to the ground. The shuffling sound in the wall grew louder, more intense. The constant scraping and 'thump, thump' pounding caused more dirt to fall.

Huge electrical power bolts shot from Jimmy's body; lighting the pool so bright it went from purple to white. The charges blasted a few snakes and tore them apart. Jimmy was writhing, whipping back and forth like an electroshock patient.

Then...there was a deep rumbling.

It was like the growl at the back of a lion's throat when it roars. It came loud and sharp and grew intense with fury, and it came from Jimmy. There was suddenly a brief moment of hollow silence, then...

...Jimmy rose, with a thunderous roar. And with feet planted firmly in the mud, he stood straight up...dripping. His mouth opened, exposing twelve loose, jiggly teeth, and decayed gums. His long black hair hung over his face in strings of saturated oil. His eyes bulged; full with fear and confusion, and hate and anger, and basic malformation from a ten-year soak in toxic waste.

He roared long and hard. Rats quieted and went into hiding. Snakes slithered off to other sections of the pool. The thumping in the wall, and all but a few remaining shuffles, stopped. The jagged currents of electricity stopped and the pool slowly rocked back to stillness.

No more swirls, no more sloshing, the pit grew dark and motionless again. Only the *drip...drip...drip* of liquid running from bony finger-tips to pool.

Jimmy Hagger, Kentucky Hillbilly, killed at age sixteen by a reckless motorist in 1980, was now alive; Dead - but alive; ten years later, in the black pit of toxic chemicals beneath the ground. Waking to a new existence, unaware of the powers bestowed upon him.

Drip...drip!

Tormented by desolation. *Where was he? How did he get here? How long had he been here? What does he do now?* The questions slid around in his rotted brain, as he stood alone in the darkness.

Chapter 3

"**M**an, I can't believe we're going down into that shit," said Richard.

Richard Danson and Todd Billings were the two-man crew chosen to go into the pit to locate the source of an electrical short that had been cutting into the power of *The Plant's* 'E Sector' for the past two days.

Dressed in protective diving gear, with air tanks and bubble helmets, they were prepared to scour the bottom of *the pool* to find a broken electrical cable.

"Well, you knew it had to happen sooner or later," Todd told him. "These cables haven't been replaced or even checked in years."

They crossed the back parking lot to the manhole cover, where Richard set up an aluminum guardrail that would encircle the hole, indicating 'men at work.' Todd pulled a crowbar from his tool belt to pry the cover off. The two men knelt down to the hundred pound lid and began working it loose. "I don't understand why they gotta make these things so damn heavy," Richard griped, "like who else is going to want to go down there anyway? Ain't nothing there but snakes and rats."

The cover jerked free and they slid it off, dragging it no further aside than they had to. The sun was coming up over the trees and glistened across the morning dew covered parking lot (which had been filling with cars since 7:00 a.m. It was now 8:30). The light hit the metal stepladder that was fixed to the underside of the manhole and ran straight down into the pool.

"Man, that's a hell of a stink in there," Todd said.

They pulled their helmets on, attached them to the ring fitting at the neck of their suits, and adjusted their air tanks. "After you," Todd allowed Richard to go first.

The metal bars were slick with condensation as they climbed down, but their gloves had rubber grips; they were fine, until Todd stepped on Richard's right hand. His reflex reaction was to jerk his hand back, which consequently caused him to let go of the ladder. He cursed Todd all the way down as he fell, the words echoed in his helmet. Todd looked to see Richard land on his ass in the pool.

Splash!

When Todd reached the bottom, Richard stood, pissed off and dripping. "I'm sorry, man, it was an accident," he apologized.

Richard glared at him, "Yeah, and I'm going to accident your head with that crowbar when we get out of here."

Todd smiled, "Well, we came prepared to get wet, you just got a head start."

Richard sneered, then pushed *him* down in it, "It's ok, you're prepared, remember?"

Todd came up looking at Richard; he wiped the glass front of his helmet and they both laughed. "Let's find this cable and get the hell out of here," he said.

The sun shone through the pit opening fairly well, but it didn't spread very far. Their helmets, however, were equipped with overhead spotlights. Looking around at the purple liquid and the overhead support beams, Richard commented, "You know the pool's gotten deep. We're going to have to go under to be able to see anything."

Todd shrugged; *you gotta do what you gotta do.*

On the count of three they descended into the waste and began feeling their way along the bottom, looking for long running electrical cables. The spread of their light cut just about in half beneath the liquid, but they could still see three or four feet ahead, when they were looking. They spent most of their time, however, looking down.

The ground was dark and murky and they could see tiny crawling things slipping in and out of the mud. Occasionally they saw a snake, but it would disappear when the light hit it. Eventually, they did come across some cable and followed it, pulling themselves along its length until it disappeared back into the earth, then they'd search for another one; hoping wherever the break was, it was exposed and they wouldn't have to do any digging.

They were still into the first half hour of the search when suddenly Richard heard a low rumble. It was so distinct and clear it startled him. He shined his light at Todd, and motioned for him to come up. The two men stood in the pool, "Did you hear that?" Richard asked.

"Yeah, it sounded like some kind of growling," said Todd. "What do you think it was?"

Richard shrugged, "I don't know...but I hope it wasn't the tank preparing to dump. Have you ever seen this pool when the tank gets full and they pump it in here? It's like a Tidal Wave." They stopped and listened for a moment...nothing. "Come on, let's get back to work," Richard said. They went back under.

They were crawling over the bottom again; each of them had picked up on a new cable and pulled themselves along. Their lights shone down at where their hands were grabbing, so they weren't really looking where they were going, moving along at a consistent and steady pace, when, with an unexpected crunch, Todd came to an abrupt stop.

His helmet had rammed into something. The sudden halting shook his brain a little; it took him a moment to refocus. When he did, he was surprised to see something that didn't quite belong there in the pit. He was staring at a pair of old, deteriorated work boots.

Work boots? he thought. *How the hell did those get in here?* Then he realized the boots alone would not have stopped him like that. Then, when he lifted his head, his light shone upward, and he saw...legs.

"Jesus Christ! ...Shit!" He panicked and jerked himself straight up out of the oily liquid. His light came up directly into Jimmy's face.

"Aaaauuuggghhhh!" Todd screamed.

"Aaaauuuggghhhh!" Jimmy roared.

Richard came flying up at the sound and turned his light on Jimmy. "Holy Shit!" his mouth dropped.

"Todd, Get away from it," Richard yelled. But Todd was frozen; he was so frightened, his scream even lost power and left him voiceless.

Jimmy too, was afraid, and with his *roar*, the decayed skin around his mouth tore like wet paper on his face. Angry and confused, his eyes bulged and oil snot began blowing from his rotted nose cartilage.

"Where am I? ...Help me!" He reached out to grab Todd by the shoulder. But when Jimmy's hand met the diving suit it was like flowing electricity; throwing off sparks and smoke...sizzling.

The three of them watched his hand burn through the material and into Todd's skin. Todd screamed with pain. Jimmy was too astonished to let go; he burned straight down to the man's chest, blood pumping out around his wrist. Todd's life flashed quickly before him and then he dropped to the pool.

Jimmy grabbed beneath his other arm, in an attempt to catch him. Unfortunately, with the possession of this melting power he'd somehow acquired, his other hand cut through the man's other arm.

It burned smooth, like slicing butter, like slowly wiping the limb right off his body. Eventually, his hand slipped up past Todd's shoulder, and the arm dropped to the pool. Richard watched, shocked...amazed, "Oh my God!"

There was nothing Richard could do; Todd was dead. Jimmy's first clutch had slid to where Todd's heart was. And with his bent and bony fingers in a clutching position, the heart scraped out in an unintended grip (two more beats) and then it smoked, melted, and ran through the dead boy's fingers.

"Help Me!" Jimmy turned to Richard. Richard had turned and was making tracks back to the spot, thirty yards away, where the sun shot its rays through the manhole.

"Wait!" Jimmy went after him with a hurried and limpy walk. Sloshing in the oil, he chased the other man through the pit, reaching out to him. That's when he noticed his arms had an awkward bend, as if they'd been broken and not mended properly. Suddenly, a flash of a little yellow car barreling down on him jumped through his mind, but just as it hit, the memory jerked away. Gone. He had no idea where it came from or where it went, or what it meant; only that, at the moment, he didn't have time to think about it. He was too busy trying to follow the man who could lead him out of that dark world and hopefully into someplace he could understand. Someplace that made sense. Maybe he could even find his way back home, maybe through that hole up ahead.

Richard tripped and stumbled through little earth valleys and electrical cables and piping that lay crisscrossed over the bottom of the pit. He saw the metal ladder ahead, dropping from the light above into the purple ooze. *Oh God, it's right there. Please, I have to make it.*

Jimmy called out again in his deep and gravely voice for the man to wait and help him...no such luck. Richard was frightened and was not about to stop. So, Jimmy's pace picked up, it would *have to* to catch up, suddenly his limp was gone and his legs cut through the liquid like knives.

Richard turned and looked just long enough to see that he could very easily lose this race, but he ran with all he had, *God, only fifteen more feet.*

Finally, he was within jumping range and leapt forward. He threw himself at the ladder, clutched the bars and pulled himself up. His suit was covered with the oil and was very slick. He lost his footing a few times, but not his grip. He heard Jimmy sloshing up behind him, *God, please help me get out of here.* He pulled up another step. Then Jimmy arrived.

"Wait! Stop, you sumbitch, or I'll kill you too," the boy growled. But Richard had lost all rationality; his only focus was to *get out.* So, Jimmy climbed up right under him. Only, when *his* hands hit the metal bars, they steamed and became sticky, as if something hot had touched on something very cold. But, being metal, it didn't melt as quickly as flesh.

Richard Danson *could* have made it and gone home with a good story to pass on to his children and his grandchildren, if only he hadn't slipped that one last time. Jimmy saw his foot come off the step and drop almost into his face. He grabbed the ankle and squeezed. "I said, help me!" and again, he was astounded to see the man's foot come off in his hand.

His fingers actually disappeared into a disintegrating boot. It burned away; leaving a nasty smell that somehow seemed to belong there in the *pit of stench.* The suit burned away, the flesh burned away, the blood, and finally the bone...all burned away.

Jimmy was stunned by this new power, he watched Richard's skin sizzle as though someone held a branding iron against him. And red blood turned to black as it bubbled over his fist. *Even the blood burned.*

Richard had one hand up over the edge onto the asphalt parking lot when the pain hit, and it pierced like an arrow.

His foot dropped and splashed in the pool. *"Aaauuugghh!"* he screamed while losing consciousness. Jimmy saw him weaken and stop climbing. Then he reached up and grabbed Richard by the belt, his decayed and bony fingers folded over and pressed against the suit, his knuckles melted into the man's back.

Eventually, Richard's pain was so great; he passed out and let go of the bars.

When he dropped, Jimmy hadn't quite burned through his belt yet and Richard dangled, suspended above the pool for a second. Then, just before it snapped, Jimmy flipped him up over his shoulder to carry him out. Apparently, Jimmy wasn't getting the message yet, for as soon as Richard folded over the boy's shoulder, again, the burning thing cut through him and split the man's body in half.

His upper self fell, head down, arms unfurled, almost in a dive; he splashed and submerged with a slurp. The legs dropped and bobbed once or twice, then they lay flat, and floated.

Jimmy looked down, 'Oops' written all over his tortured face. "Something is definitely wrong with me," he muttered, and quickly climbed out as the steel dissolved between his fingers.

The Xanorse plant towered high in the sky. It was a bright and sunny late morning; the parking lot was full, except for a small five-foot radius around the manhole. Jimmy stood, turning circles, looking at the cars, then beyond them into the trees.

The lot stretched a good twenty yards before reaching the edge of the forest. So, the dead boy maneuvered his way through the vehicles, leaving sizzle skids in the blacktop, and headed, hopefully, back home.

When Xanorse Security went to check out the disappearance of Richard Danson and Todd Billings, they discovered the mangled body parts, a lot of acidic melt, and a slithery trail leading across the asphalt from the manhole. The assumption was that there might be a new and murderous breed of snake that had escaped the chemical pool from where it had birthed.

Hopefully it would be caught and killed before Xanorse Chemicals was investigated and proven to be the responsible party for the creation of some hideous new form of life that attacks and kills.

Chapter 4

B obby and Opal Hagger were outside doing chores when noon arrived and they stopped long enough to go in for lunch. Jimmy's brothers and sisters were inside laughing and carrying on, when Bobby walked in saying "Ain't it a kick in the head that no matter how long you own something, someone's always trying to take it away from you."

Opal stopped, standing fast at the edge of the living room. "Bobby?"

He almost ran into the back of her before he stopped, then looked up past her to see what the matter was, and froze. There was a wet shiny brown film covering burn marks all over their wooden floor. The edge of the sofa was...missing, the stuffing inside was exposed and covered with brown crust.

They looked around the room and saw burn marks on the walls and around a window. There was a pile of ashes on the coffee table where some old 'pitcher magazines' used to be.

The front door stood wide open and the inside handle was on the floor; the outside handle was gone. A wooden rocking chair next to the front door was *almost* gone. It was still smoldering.

There were drying patches of crust on the wall where the family pictures hung, some of them had dropped to the ground...half burned.

Bobby and Opal looked like hooked fish, the way their mouths hung open, wondering what the hell had happened. They looked to the kitchen area, following the burn marks through the room. The cabinets were burned, the counter top was burned, and dry flaky crust was falling to the floor.

A chair at the dinner table had a low smolder across the seat of it, while two charred handprints marked the table's edge, as though someone had pressed burning irons into the wood.

Then a movement caught their eye, Bobby and Opal turned at the same time, staring, in disbelief; it was Jimmy.

The silence was deafening, each stared at the other, Opal trembling, looking at the hideous thing that was once her son. Bobby looked him up and down, dumbfounded, watching oily liquid ooze from the boy's skin and drip to the floor. "Jimmy? Is that you?" His voice quivered and cracked.

Staring at his parents, Jimmy realized he didn't look quite the same as the last time they'd seen him. He was decayed, he was ugly, and for the most part...he was dead. His voice had also changed, becoming deep and gravely, "Yeah, it's me, daddy."

Opal started crying, her legs grew weak; she would have collapsed if Bobby hadn't been there to hold her up. "Oh my Lord! Jimmy, my beautiful boy," (A mother's love. Even in better days, Jimmy was not what one would call *a beautiful boy*). "What happened to you?"

He looked down at himself, a small piece of oily flesh fell from above his left eyebrow; it dropped to the ground with a wet slap, then sizzled another burn hole. He looked up and shrugged, "Don't know."

Then, (though not exactly a sight for sore eyes) Opal went to hug her boy, "Jimmy, we've missed you so much."

"Don't touch me, Ma," he said, quickly jerking back from her. Opal stopped immediately. "There's something wrong with me. Everything I touch kind of...burns up."

Both parents looked at the floor where he stood, his feet had actually burned through the wood and he was standing on the concrete beneath. Bobby nodded agreement, "Yeah, well, it does appear thata way." Then he looked back to study his son, "Sounds like your voice did some changing too."

Jimmy shrugged again, "Yeah, I guess it's part of that there puberty thing." The tension broke and there was laughter.

Then Opal started crying and sat down at the table, "Oh my poor baby, what has happened to you?"

Jimmy looked down, almost shamefully, shuffling his feet; he knew he was not looking his best right at the moment. "I'm sorry, Ma, I guess somehow or other, I musta got myself kilt. And this is what happened cuz a me laying under that chemycal plant."

Bobby became irritated, "Whatchew mean, *laying under the che-mycal plant*?"

They listened while Jimmy told them his experience of the past two days, his story of waking in the darkened pit, and wandering lost for a day and a half before finding a way out. And discovering the strange new power he had.

There was a quiet moment when Opal asked how he ended up down there in the first place. He told them he had no idea.

The three of them were quiet, resigned to not having answers to their questions. Then, "So, how ya'll doin?" Jimmy broke the silence. Bobby and Opal perked up, eventually, they were going back and forth from each other, filling him in on the past ten years.

Cassandra (Sandy) had gotten married, and Patty had died of pneumonia two years ago, but everyone else was healthy, happy, and still living at home. Then Jimmy asked what it was they were talking about when they came in. He heard something about *"No matter how long you have something, somebody's always trying to take it away from you."*

Bobby looked into his jelly eyes and said, "That chemycal builden, *Xanorse*, is tryin to git our land and kick us out, soze they can expand. Beins that they're the *number one and fastest growing research laboratory in the country.* Hell, they even got the Chinese and Mex-icans moving in, just to work *there.*"

Jimmy stared at him, "So, what'd you tell 'em?"

"Whatchew think I tole 'em, I tole 'em go to hell. I said this here's Hagger land, it always has been, always will be."

"Yeah? And, what'd they say?" Jimmy asked.

Bobby looked down at the table, his eyes cold with despair, "Ah, they got some kind of government order, served us a check payment for the land and a notice saying we had six months to find somewhere's else ta live. So we're spoze to just pack up everthin and get lost."

Jimmy felt rising anger, his jawbones began grinding; his facial muscles made a wet smacking sound, "Can they do that?"

"They're doing it," Bobby said. "I keep gettin letters askin how we're progressin, signed by this Morgan Newton person, or his assistant, David Maples. If it ain't one of 'em, it's the other. I got three so far."

Jimmy was quiet for a minute, then asked, "How long ago did you get the notice?"

"About a month," Bobby replied. He hesitated for a second, looking at the boy, and then added, "They even tole me to dig up and move the family graveyard."

Sudden reference to the graveyard sparked a light in Jimmy's dim head, and brought up a question that had been haunting him for the past two days.

While on the walk home from the parking lot, he had calculated his location of burial, and come to the conclusion that he'd been placed underground somewhere near the cemetery. He had no idea how he got there, but there he was, and his question was; *Down there in that silent pit, what was all that shuffling noise coming from the wall next to him?*

Then it dawned on him; perhaps, since soaking in those chemicals for so many years had somehow brought *him* back to life - maybe the earth around him had absorbed enough that it seeped into the rotting corpses of his buried family. Perhaps the shuffling he heard was the *coming back to life* of his dead relatives.

Fortunately, Jimmy had no formal education or he might have considered this idea too ridiculous. ...But, since he didn't???

"Daddy, I got an idear. It may sound crazy, but you never know," and he told his daddy what he thought.

Bobby stared at him for a long while from the corner of his eyes, chewing on the end of a tobacco pipe, pondering the boy's notion. "You reckon if that's a fact," he said, "they would have this same condition you got? I mean, burnin up everything they touch. Cause that's gotta be some damn powerful liquid down there to be bringing you back to life an all."

During the next few hours, Jimmy, Bobby, and Opal shared their thoughts on the situation, and some jokes, and some stories Jimmy had missed over the years. After awhile, they were tired and decided it was time to figure out where they could put him and he wouldn't melt everything.

Finally, they set him up in a small corner of the barn, where he could rest, or hide, or whatever he needed to do. Then they brought the other kids in and explained, as best as they could, what had happened, or as much of it as they could make sense of. And everyone was instructed to '*Not Touch Jimmy!*'

That evening Jimmy lay in the barn, alone and quiet, with only the roar of a million crickets singing in the woods. He stared up at the loft, thinking about the past twenty-four hours, how everything: his predicament, and all of his family's troubles seem to come from that damn chemical plant. If not for them he wouldn't be a *living dead* person, and his family wouldn't have to leave their home. And his ancestors wouldn't have to be dug up and replanted.

And the more he thought about it, the angrier he got, until his mind seriously began to warp, to...twist. The once: average, disgusting, ignorant and backward, yet...good-natured kid he was, was now having disturbing thoughts. Of course, soaking your brain in chemical waste for nearly ten years could cause a crazy idea or two, but Jimmy was going off the deep end. He was coming up with some very maniacal resolutions to a lot of his problems. His change...was continuing to deepen.

In the days that followed, he was forced to deal with new realities. He could no longer come in the house; it would burn. He could not play with his brothers and sisters, he might accidentally touch one of them, and *they* would burn. If they threw him a ball, it melted. If they played hide & seek, he left a trail a blind man could follow. If they tried to fly kites, the string would disintegrate. He wasn't allowed to help out with chores; pitchforks dissolved, eggs boiled, vegetables charred and burn away. They wouldn't even talk about what happened when he tried to milk the cow. Jimmy; was suddenly...physically challenged.

Gradually, anger and hatred ate him up; he grew consumed with the idea that Xanorse Chemicals was solely responsible for all that had happened to him. And now they were trying to take his family's land?

"Sonsabitch's!"

Within days, Jimmy's existence became a routine of walking in the woods, bird watching and hating Xanorse - or, chasing squirrels and hating Xanorse - or, hating Xanorse and hating Xanorse.

"They can't do this!" his growl was vicious. "I can't let them get away with it," he grew obsessed. He talked to his Daddy about it, but Bobby Hagger was not a violent man, he didn't know what else he could do.

"Dig up Grandpa Earl and Grandma Trudy, they'll know what to do," was Jimmy's answer. Bobby was mortified by the suggestion, but he *was* in a desperate situation.

In the few days after, while Bobby had to *think things over*, Jimmy continued to roam the grounds, "They'll die before they get *this* land...if I have to kill them myself." There! That put a smile on his broken face. "Yeah, I could kill the bastards myself," he was thinking out loud when he saw something blow over the edge of one of the old trash barrels. It was a crumpled ball of paper; it fell and rolled to a stop.

Jimmy bent down and carefully tried to open it, at least enough to see what it was; he only burned the corner edges. And sure enough, it was a letter from *Xanorse*:

Dear Mr. Hagger,

This is to inform you that there are currently five months remaining in which for you to relocate. As yet, we have not received any response on your behalf: regarding whether or not you would like assistance in finding comparable living arrangements. If we are not contacted within seven days, we will assume everything is moving along fine and you will be vacated from the premises on schedule.

Sincerely,

Morgan Newton

Morgan Newton,
Personnel Director.

David Maples

David Maples,
Assistant Director.

Of course Jimmy was not able to read all of it, but the words he *could* put together, indicated to him that this Morgan Newton person and his assistant David Maples were the culprits behind the harassment; the ones forcing them off their own property, *the ones to get rid of.*

Bobby told the boy about the other letters, and that it was either one name or the other who had signed them, but this was the first letter with both signatures. Jimmy growled low, "Well, let's see how much damage these two fuckers can do when *they're* dead. ...I bet not as much as me."

Chapter 5

J immy and his younger sister, Becky, made their way through the woods to the Xanorse parking lot. He brought her along to help narrow the search for the ones he had grievances with.

Of the entire family, Becky was the only one who ever had a calling to *enlighten* herself. As a child, Bobby and Opal were confused, pleased, but confused by her fascination with reading. Until Becky, they had all more or less bluffed their way through life. And with none of the children attending any kind of formal schooling, they pretty much did as they pleased; like hunting, or fishing, or generally following up on whatever notion came to mind. They did have to pull their own weight in farm chores though. But, only Becky had an interest in education; like reading, writing, and arithmetic.

"How can I find out which of these cars belongs to Morgan Newton and David Maples?" Jimmy asked as they strolled the parking lot. It was late afternoon and everyone was inside; he felt relatively safe to roam through the cars without being seen.

Becky took a calculated look around, "Well, it appears they've got designated parking areas." She pointed to their left, "There's a sign that says *Administration Only!* I bet they park over there."

Jimmy turned in that direction, Becky moved on ahead of him (his walking pace was not what it used to be, sliding sticky feet over sizzling asphalt).

When they got there, Becky noticed the cement stop block in front of each car had a name stenciled on it. "Jimmy, I think this is going to be easier than you imagined," she told him, and she began looking for two very specific names.

As they worked down the rows, however, Jimmy listened to the other names she called out (I.E. Fred Peterson, Sue Ann Walden, Sam Stallworth, etc.), and stored them in the back of his slimy mind.

"Where's Newton and Maples?" his patience was thinning. Then...Bingo! Newton and Maples, right next to each other.

Morgan Newton drove a shiny silver gray Mercedes, four-door with gray leather interior and a convertible top. David Maples's space was empty.

"I guess Dave took the day off," Becky deduced.

It didn't matter to Jimmy, the wheels of what was left of his rotted brain were already spinning. "Thanks for helping, Becky. But you should go home now," he told her.

"What are you going to do?" she asked.

He stared into her questioning eyes, "It's something you're better off not knowing. Please...just go."

She stared back for a moment, she told him the family still loves him and to *be careful.* Then she turned and walked back to the woods.

Jimmy stared at the two spaces for a moment, one - full of Mercedes, the other - empty. He looked around and saw that he was only two car rows away from the opposite side of the forest from where he'd come in. And with one eye fixed on the Mercedes, he walked off to sit hidden in the shrubs...and watch...and wait.

He sat quietly just inside the tree line, for what seemed like hours. He sat so still, the occasional squirrel on a food quest would be right up on top of him before noticing there was something not right about the leaves and brush. It would stop and stare, trying to figure out if

Jimmy was a living thing or some odd new creation of nature; then Jimmy would resolve the dilemma with a low "Boo!" and the squirrel would dart off in mortal fear.

At 4:30, small groups of people began emerging from the mammoth building, heading to the cars on the far side of the lot. By 4:45, most of them were gone. Except for a few men standing at the side of a small blue car, obviously discussing something very important, like how to change the world, or at least put an end to *overtime.* Then there was a couple, a man and a woman, obviously trying to hide behind someone's Astro Van, for a moment of *intimacy* before going home.

Jimmy watched intently, he grew semi-erect - busting another blood vessel and tearing flesh that would no longer stretch. Then the couple split and went to separate cars. He wondered why they didn't wait until they got home to make out. Until it dawned on him, maybe they weren't going to the same home.

Then his attention was drawn to an odd turn of events. A small automobile, he wasn't sure what kind, he wasn't too up on modern vehicles, but it looked nice, pulled into the lot and drove up and down a few rows working itself in his direction.

He watched closely, not making any sudden movements. And was surprised to see the small car pull into David Maples parking space, but the driver was a woman. Jimmy stared hard to see through the windshield. He thought maybe it was Maples's wife.

But she was very young, perhaps a teenager, maybe eighteen or nineteen...and pretty. She stopped the car and turned off the motor, but she kept the radio going. Jimmy watched her shift around to get comfortable; flipping her long orange-brown hair over the top of the seat and laying her head back. Then she stuck her left arm out the window, waving her hand around, keeping rhythm with the blaring music. It was loud enough that he could hear it from where *he* was.

He watched the girl rock her head back and forth, and could see her bare shoulders shine in the light of the sun. He felt the dangling raw thing between his legs give another twitch of excitement.

5:00, the plant began to empty. Men and women seem to pour out of every exit, like a dozen streams all flowing from one big pond. Jimmy watched them march in the direction of their respective vehicles; he kept an eye out for the owner of the silver gray Mercedes.

He watched one man climb into his car and pull out; the name revealed on the block was...Fred Peterson. "They're probably all in on it, the bastards. I might just have to kill every one of them," he muttered.

He watched them come and go for a while; he noticed that most of the people from the Administrative lot had much nicer cars than those who parked everywhere else.

After the main crowd had thinned, Jimmy noticed two men walking together in the direction of the girl parked in Maples's space. Each man wore a gray business suit; one had pinstripes, the other solid. Both had loosened their ties and unbuttoned the top button of their shirts. The man on Jimmy's left had a thick head of orange-brown hair that, in the sunlight, appeared more orange than brown. He was clean-shaven; he had only a few freckles (nothing overly noticeable), and blue eyes.

The other man was completely the opposite. He had a full beard and mustache, his hair (like his car) was silver gray, and wavy, he wore it parted on the side and swept over. And he wore dark blue tinted sunglasses.

They conversed all the way out to their cars, the Mercedes and the small...thing the girl was in. She turned down the radio.

Eventually, the men stopped in front of the Mercedes, they shook hands, the silver haired man turned to wave at the girl, she waved back, and they went their separate ways. The orange haired man climbed into the passenger side of the little car.

But just as the girl turned the ignition key, the bearded man stopped and was patting his pockets, trying to locate something.

"Anything wrong Mr. Newton?" she called out the window.

Morgan Newton had no problem dealing with *real* problems, if they were substantial concerns - but it was the little shit that made him crazy, little irritating things that should never have happened in the first place. Things like..."Dammit! I left my car keys in the office."

The girl gave a shrug of *'sorry about your luck,'* laughed, and threw the car into reverse, "See you next time, Mr. Newton."

The man with her, her father, David Maples, leaned over, "Hey Morgan, you want us to wait around in case they're lost?" (A little brown nosing never killed anyone).

Morgan shook his head and waved them on, "No, go on. I know where they are."

David shrugged and told his daughter to drive.

It wasn't until she was halfway down the row, that Jimmy could read her license plate; *Sarah M*

Now, Jimmy had never been the brightest kid in the world, but he could put two and two together. *'Sarah M' was parked in David Maples spot, were they related? Was she Sarah Maples?*

But, she was too young to be his wife. He paused...and the answer came to him, *Daughter.* He watched the car roll from the lot onto *Short Cut.* Then he turned back to the bearded man reentering the building...*alone.*

Chapter 6

"Shit! Shit! Shit! I can't *believe* I forgot my keys again." Morgan cursed himself as he walked through the aluminum security door, the one with the *'Employees Only'* sign that hung just below a small window with crisscrossed wire running through it.

He pulled his door pass from the electronic sensor, stepped inside, and slammed it shut behind him; the latch clicked and relocked. Morgan marched irritably down the metal walk in front of him.

This stretch was actually a catwalk that crossed through an open section of the chemical development area; designed intentionally for executives on the 2nd floor to be able to observe the workers below. On the other side, the walk led into a carpeted hallway surrounded by offices.

Thirty offices lined the hall, fifteen on either side. And after 5:00, was only dimly lit by the red glow of the emergency exit light at the opposite end.

Outside, Jimmy watched the cars form lines and flow out steadily from every exit in the lot. Then he stood up and cut directly across to the doorway Morgan had disappeared through. He stared impatiently at the remaining vehicles, hoping no one saw him approach the building.

Morgan's office was third from the end (the end being another metal crosswalk that led off in ten different directions). David Maples office was opposite Morgan's, and one down.

Just before Morgan pushed his door open, a very distant hissing sound flowed into the airwaves. But the creaking noise from the dilapidated hinges on his door drowned it out; it never fully registered in his mind.

Jimmy's face melted through the glass window, while his body burned through the solid aluminum. The *Employees Only* door ran in huge liquefied drips of silver, until a giant hole had formed, and with the sun shining through from behind, Jimmy appeared in a silhouette of black. He slid in and oozed his way toward the metal walk, "It's time to die, Boss-man," he gurgled in a low rumble.

Morgan shuffled into his office by the glow of the *Exit* sign phasing through the large tinted windows that each office had, he felt it was all the light he needed. In fact, he didn't believe he even needed that, he knew his special gold plated Mercedes key ring, with the special gold plated Mercedes emblem dangling next to two gold keys, was resting peacefully in his top right drawer. And he would have no trouble finding his top right drawer.

Softly, there came the low sizzle of Jimmy crossing the metal walk at the end of the hallway, leaving a trail of smoke and oil drying to a crisp brown flake. Morgan didn't notice the frying sound on the metal, but when Jimmy hit the actual hallway itself, with padded carpeting over plywood covered concrete, the snapping and crackling of wood beneath his feet made Morgan stop and pay attention.

He listened intently as the popping grew louder...nearer. Finally, he called out "Anybody out there?" then, *Shit,* he thought, *it's probably a janitor or a night watchman, some sixty-five year old man that can't get any other kind of job. And the fool who hires all the security guards in the world,* and supplies them with a pistol, *has placed this one on my path. I better do something before the idiot takes me for a Burglar and shoots.* Immediately, he began searching for the on button of his desk lamp.

After feeling all around *and missing*, he decided to grab the lamp and look for where the button protruded. But in his reach, he knocked it over and started an eventful chain reaction.

The lamp fell into the multi-tube pencil holder, which spilled a collection of pens and pencils into the metal wastebasket at the edge of the desk; where in they bounced and banged on the bottom and against the sides. The holder itself hit a square plastic file organizer, which spilled against a glass ashtray at the corner of the desk and knocked it off onto the edge of a metal-framed armchair. The ashtray broke into several large chips that decorated the office floor.

"Well, son-of-a-bitch! If they didn't know I was here before, they surely do now." Morgan filled red-hot with embarrassed anger and cursed himself again, then he found the light.

'Click', it was on.

"Hello out there, whoever you are, it's just me, Morgan Newton. I had to come back because I forgot something," he said and went around to the other side of the desk to get the keys.

But...again, he was distracted by the strange hissing sound. It was like (though still distant) bacon frying. He stood and listened.

'Snap...Crackle...'

"What the hell is that?"

His door was half open, but closed enough from where he stood that he couldn't see into the hallway.

He took his keys quietly from the drawer, not exactly sure why he was suddenly trying *not* to make noise, it just seemed like the thing to do he guessed. He dropped them into his pants pocket and gently pushed the drawer shut. Then, just before he turned the light off, he decided to look out into the hall.

Morgan stepped cautiously to the door; the sizzle sound was right outside. *Jeez, that better be the fire sprinkler system going off, or a Security Guard doing something.* This was about the extent that his current imagination could conjure up. But, he was about to enter a whole new realm of possibilities.

Reaching out, he grasped the door and swung it open.

There in the red glow, hanging dead even with, and no more than two feet away from him was Jimmy's rotten, slimy face. "It's time to die, Boss-man," he growled.

Jimmy was thin and lanky and decayed, with large gaping sores and rippling blood vessels, standing as a grotesque, maggot festering corpse, in the doorway.

"Holy Mother of God!" Morgan choked with fear. "What are you?"

"I am your creation," Jimmy informed, "and you've pissed me off."

Morgan forced his legs to move back, inching away from the thing in front of him. But Jimmy followed, leaving smoking footprints with each step.

"What do you want?" Morgan whimpered, reaching back to clutch the desk.

Jimmy didn't answer, he just kept walking; breathing a heavy oil sucking, flap slapping sound through the gap of his hollow nose cavity. While the oil draining down the back of his throat made a slimy gurgling sound that rumbled when he spoke.

Morgan knocked the light over...again, this time onto the floor, it turned up and shone on Jimmy's face, casting a sickly yellow glow. He could feel his stomach getting ready to heave. *"What do you want?"* he pleaded.

Jimmy chuckled low and raspy, then he reached out and pressed one hand teasingly to Morgan's chest. It burned for a second, just long enough to bring a cry of hurt, then he pulled away. Morgan reached up and felt where his shirt had burned, his chest hairs were singed and his skin was painfully tender.

He turned and speed crawled over the top of his desk, Jimmy walked straight at him. When he reached the edge of the Mahogany...he burned right through, laughing. Striking out like a cat, making clawing motions with his arms, Jimmy tested to see how much Morgan was willing to tango. He continued throwing out burning swipes while Morgan tried to unfreeze his shocked muscles and move.

As Jimmy melted through to the other side of the desk, Morgan tried to run around it and escape. But, at the moment the desk split apart, one half of it fell right in front of him and he hit his shins and tripped. He flew over the top, gouging his arms and chest, then rolled across to the other side. With no time to lose, he filed the pain under things he would deal with later.

Then, just as he was back on his feet, and about to spring for the door, Jimmy picked up his wood framed, metal based, leather desk chair, turned, and threw it at him.

The chair came down on the back of Morgan's head, plowing him back to the floor and into the wall beneath the office window. The chair itself continued on *through* the window, with an explosion of glass that showered over the man crouched beneath it.

Fortunately, he'd had the sense to cover his head with his hands, but then his hands were riddled with the spray of chips and slivers; blood streamed over his scalp and down his face.

Pulling his hands away, he shook them once to free any loose fragments; then he saw the open door and desperately crawled for it. Jimmy smiled, "Run, Rabbit, run."

Morgan made it through the door and into the hallway, but then had to roll off his glass grinding palms. Jimmy followed.

Morgan heard sizzling closing in on him and tried to get to his feet (pushing up with his elbows). The jagged slivers stuck out from his hands like small stones in a bloody river. The pain made him nauseously dizzy.

Jimmy came through the door as Morgan stood. He turned and faced the creature, "You Satanic, Cock-Sucking Freak!" he shouted, and threw out a bloody fist to punch Jimmy's chest.

This was not a good move. Morgan's thrust went right into Jimmy's soft rotten body, through it, and out the other side. Morgan hadn't anticipated that, and the throw of the punch hurled him forward into Jimmy's burning arms.

Jimmy knew he could just squeeze the man, melt him, and be done with it; but that was not the plan. First, he wanted to toy with him awhile - then get some information. So, rather than squeeze, he pushed him away.

Morgan's fist came back out with a slurp, and he went down to the floor...again. Jimmy's chest grew back together. "Jesus! You can't be killed," Morgan slobbered in terror.

Jimmy sneered, "Yeah, been there - done that."

Again, Morgan scrambled quickly to his feet, thinking maybe he could outrun the monster, but when he stood this time, facing David Maples office, Jimmy beat him to the punch.

He saw the name on the door, "There's another one I want. Let's go in there," and he slam pushed Morgan right through the window of David's office.

Morgan shot through the bursting glass, this time *in the midst* of a shower of slicing shards. If he thought he'd cut himself badly the first time, he would have to call this a shredding. His face split into ribbons, and the only connection his fingers still had to his hands, was bone.

Large pieces dug into his shirt and pierced his chest, invoking several spurting fountains. He felt cuts *through his pants*, prickling and tingling like a dozen needles in his testes, and the point of a thick sharp blade piercing the side of his penis. Morgan screamed like…well…like a man being murdered. Blood trickled over his genitals and down his leg.

Jimmy, on the other hand, used the door.

Morgan lay unflinching on the floor inside; not only afraid of Jimmy, but afraid he would roll over onto more glass. And at the moment, he didn't think he could take any more glass.

Jimmy flicked the light on at the wall switch. "Nice office. Almost as nice as yours *was*." Morgan could not move, his eyes were wide with terror, praying the creature would get what it wanted, and go the hell away.

Jimmy looked down at him, unmoving. "What do you want?" Morgan spoke in a husky, painful breath.

Jimmy smiled and looked back up around the room, "Well, first; I want you. But I'll give you a minute to rest before I kill ya."

Morgan wet himself. But then, figuring he had nothing left to lose, he got smart-ass, "Anything else?"

"I'm not sure," Jimmy said, "give me a minute."

"Jimmy?" A voice came from the hallway.

Jimmy turned; Morgan lifted his head and stared wildly at the door, "Help! Help me!" he cried. "Thank God, somebody's here." Jimmy stared at the door.

"Jimmy, are you in here?" Suddenly, an attractive, teenage, black haired girl, wearing overalls, came to the open doorway.

"Becky, why did you come here? I told you to go home," Jimmy was upset.

Becky looked around, "What are you doing?"

"He's trying to kill me," Morgan cried.

Becky looked at the man in the pile of glass, "Who's that?"

Jimmy grinned, "That's your Morgan Newton, the shit bag that's trying to take daddy's land away."

The cloud of confusion suddenly began to lift from Morgan's brain, "Are you...Bobby Hagger's kid?" He was a wide-eyed, bloody lump of fear.

Becky was amazingly calm, as if the situation she'd just walked into was no big surprise. "Yeah," she said, "I'm Becky Hagger, and this is my brother, Jimmy."

The name went round and round in Morgan's head, *Jimmy Hagger?* Then it hit him; the kid that disappeared ten years ago. "You're Jimmy Hagger?"

"In the flesh...or what's left of it," he replied.

That was all Morgan could handle, he passed out.

"Jimmy, what are you going to do with him?" Becky asked.

"Well, I can't kill him just yet, I need *him*, to find out where the *others* are."

Becky rolled her eyes, "There are easier ways to get *that* information, you know. You don't need him for it."

"Like what?"

Casually, she scanned the room and saw in the corner on a shelf, there were two phone books, "The phone book. It has everyone's address in it." But she kept looking around; suddenly a smile crossed her face. She walked to the desk, "Or, better yet, this," and she reached over and picked up a Rolodex.

"What's that?"

Becky explained that it was like a handy little phone directory; with all the names and addresses of the people he would most likely want to find.

Jimmy looked perplexed, "Becky, you know I can't touch that."

She looked into his jelly eyes, "I can hold it for you. I can even read it to you." She may have been more educated than the rest of the family, but she was still *a Hagger*, and wasn't about to let anybody mess with her family anymore than Jimmy would.

"Becky, I can't ask you to be part of this."

Her expression went cold, her face turned to stone, and her eyes pierced his, "I was part of it the day I was born. I'm a Hagger, same as you, and if we have to defend ourselves and our land, then that's what we have to do."

Jimmy wished desperately he could have hugged his little sister.

"What do we do with him?" she asked.

"You think you can drag him outa here by yourself?"

She smiled and looked at Morgan lying in the glass, he was bleeding pretty bad, "You know I can. But there's a lot of glass around him, and I'm barefoot."

Jimmy walked over to the man on the floor; Becky watched the glass melt beneath his feet. He looked back at his sister and smiled, "Pretty convenient, huh?" Then he laughed; gurgly and rough, but a laugh all the same.

He grabbed Morgan's feet and pulled him to her. He hadn't been holding him five seconds, when the shoe leather disintegrated and Jimmy was melting into his skin. The sharp, instant pain brought Morgan to wake, screaming. His eyes shot open, his mouth stretched and distorted, a screech tore lose from his soul and exploded through his throat. Then he went comatose.

"Can you take him?" Jimmy asked. "I'm almost to the bone."

"Let go," she said, "I got him."

Jimmy let go. There was nothing left of Morgan's feet, just bone protruding from each ankle. Becky grabbed a wrist and pulled him from the glass. "Jimmy, he's going to leave a trail of blood."

Jimmy looked around, and then walked to a glass-free section of carpet. He walked in a square around it, burning through, separating it from the rest, and told Becky to put Morgan on it.

A few minutes later, the two Hagger kids arrived at where the building's entrance door *used to be*, they poked their heads out and looked in both directions to make sure no one was watching, then proceeded around the edge of the parking lot, dragging Morgan into the woods.

"What are we going to do with him?" she asked.

Jimmy thought for a moment, "I don't know. I guess let's take him out back of the barn and throw him in daddy's rowboat till we figure it out."

Becky thought for a moment, "But what if he tries to get away when he comes to?"

Jimmy rolled an eye at her, "What's he gonna walk on? He ain't got no feet."

Becky shrugged, "What if he tries to crawl away?"

Jimmy growled low, "Ok, so when we get back I'll burn his hands off too, all right?"

That seemed reasonable and they walked on, quietly. Then Jimmy thought of something, "Hey, where's that little phone thing."

She held up the Rolodex, "Why?"

"Look and see if there's a Sarah Maples in there," there was.

Back at the barn, they dragged the semi-conscious Morgan Newton around to where Bobby had an old aluminum rowboat; abandoned and somewhat buried beneath a pile of wood. He hadn't used the boat in years, but he kept it covered well enough that it hadn't rusted through anywhere.

Becky walked around and grabbed Morgan by the bottom of his legs, her grip momentarily closed off the blood drainage. Jimmy walked up and looked him in the face, "Sorry, Morgan old buddy, but them hands gotta go," and he grasped his wrists.

Instantly, Morgan began to melt. Skin oozed and dripped from between Jimmy's fingers. Morgan jerked with another quick scream while sweat and tears poured over his face. Then his eyes shut, his body went limp, the pain was too much. Becky and Jimmy lowered him into the boat just as Jimmy no longer had anything to hold onto. Eventually...Morgan bled to death.

The following morning, when the vandalism at Xanorse was discovered, and Morgan's car was found in the parking lot...without its owner; the Pleasure View Police department sent an investigative team on a manhunt, but to no avail. Morgan Newton had simply vanished.

Then, after the attack on Sarah Maples and Fred Peterson, Jimmy decided it might be a good idea to get Morgan's body off Hagger property.

So, one night, in the middle of that summer, the Hagger kids towed the rowboat quietly out to the lake. Jimmy rode on Morgan's back for a while, until all that was left of him were bones, floating in oozy liquefied flesh. The following morning, Jimmy sat outside with Bobby. Bobby wasn't real sure he liked what Jimmy was doing, but he *did* stop getting those pesky letters about his land.

Then Jimmy pushed again for something he'd been waiting for Bobby to make a decision on..."You know, I really would like to see Grandma and Grandpa...and Patty. I know they're just as alive as I am, Pa. Can't we dig 'em up?"

Bobby knew it was going to happen sooner or later, "Oh what the hell," he said, "Ifin's they got the same power as you, they've probably melted through their boxes by now and are rolling around in the dirt. So..." he scratched at his beard stubble, "I guess we might as well."

Jimmy stretched a horrible smile of satisfaction.

POWER
CONTROL

Chapter 1

Krys, Shawna, and Jeff had another cup of coffee; Shawna drained the pot. They drank in silence, each staring at the front page of the paper, glancing up at one another, then back to the paper.

"You know," Shawna said, "I don't understand; if he wants revenge, if he wants to get the ones who killed him, then why Sarah Maples? Why Fred Peterson? Why Morgan Newton and the others? Why the whole damn Christmas party? I mean he must have seen us out at Billy's tree house a hundred times. He had to know it was us that ran him down. He even knew some of us by name, so why isn't he popping up in our basements, or the back seat of one of our cars? Why?"

The question was valid, though it *was* comforting to think that he *wasn't* coming after them.

Chapter 2

T he annual Christmas holiday schedule at Xanorse was that they shut down the Monday preceding Christmas and remain closed through to the Friday following New Years. The Company was profitable enough that, not only could they afford it, but each employee received full holiday pay as well. This year, that time off was needed more than ever, to recuperate from the tragedy of the Christmas party massacre.

During the week between Christmas and New Years, there were no sightings, no reports of any dead people walking around. Some imaginations may have gone wild; people catching a glimpse in the corner of their eye, thinking they saw a rotted body coming after them. But when they turned for a full frontal view...there was nothing - a street lamp perhaps, or a mailbox...but no zombies.

The whole city was obsessed with the Christmas party incident, and by December 31st, *most* of the New Year's Eve parties had been cancelled. Unfortunately, *most* isn't always enough.

In the nine days since the Christmas party, Jimmy and the rest of the dead Hagger clan stayed out back in the trees beyond Bobby's pasture (apparently frosty temperatures and snow didn't seem to bother the *unliving*), and by 10:00 p.m. New Year's Eve, they had positioned themselves around town according to a plan they'd concocted.

The plan was to shut Pleasure View off from as much communication with the outside world as possible. They'd separated into small groups, and stationed themselves at specific points.

At each of these points, there were tall electrical posts supporting connecting telecommunication cables that ran in and out of town. At 10:00 'Pole Meltdown' began.

The family had determined which poles they would need to hit, and depending upon its size, they were assigned, either alone or in groups, where to go. The wood poles were an easy burn; basically a one-man job, which was good, so more family members could be scattered to other areas. Some of the larger steel connectors took several *melters*, where in they would link hands and fuse together in a circle around it, to burn it down. In the end it was a success, all poles came down and wires were severed.

A lot of inner city phones still connected back and forth to each other, but the out of town cable was gone. By 10:30, the Hagger's were through *working* for the evening and moved on to certain parties they had intended to crash. It was a decent plan with only a few uncertainties, one; when they got there, would there be just a husband and wife, and possibly a few children? Or would there be guests as well? And two, if *their* party went to *another* party, would there be anyone home at all?

At 11:59, the Hagger's were in position, according to their assigned marks, and ready to bring in the New Year.

Dick Clark and the crowd from Times Square boomed from television sets all over town.

"Ten!"
...The count started.

Jimmy and his decayed sister, Patty, rotted 'ol Charles (*Limpy*), and Junior Sawder (Trudy's sister Carol's boy) began their descent upon Howard Remmington and company at the Remmington Estate.

"Nine!"

Howard Remmington was the President of Xanorse - the leading asshole, the commanding shit-for-brains running the whole show. It was nothing personal, he just happened to be the man in charge.

"Eight!"

Earl (no teeth, no nose, one eye), Trudy (two eyes but no lips to cover the five teeth she still had. Peeling skin from her cheekbones down and her jaw was...gone...to about mid-throat). And Earl's brother, Don (same general appearance, except for the five inch axe split in the top front of his skull - now blooming Brains), shuffled down the concrete walk that lead from the street to Luke Brigham's front door. Luke was the Vice-President of Xanorse; and as far as the Hagger's were concerned - as responsible as any of them.

"Seven!"

Henry Gunner (very little patchy flesh left, some yellow ooze in both eyes, twisted gristle where his nose once was, and some loose intestinal tubing hanging from the mammoth gap in his gut; split by the axe swing of a defending Construction Worker), his wife, Angie (just decayed, died of old age), and Frank (Don Hagger's boy, rotted like the rest, but baring the wounds, front and back, of where Joe Brennen had thrown a knife into him) - staggered their way across the backyard of Rhonda Toush's neatly manicured ranch style home in the suburbs.

"Six!"

Bobby's Anthraxed sisters, June and Molly (two young girls with horribly blistered skin and breath like an old septic tank), and cousin Chrissy, Don's girl, (still with a lot of skin, chalky white, baring the traces of having once been very attractive), cut through twists and turns of the apartment complex where Gene Oldham (Head of the Accounting Department, and Suspected Homosexual) was having a small gathering of close friends (all male) for the birth of the New Year.

"Five!"

Lila and John (two more of Earl and Trudy's kids who'd died unexpectedly at young ages), John, dove into a lake too shallow to grace the depth he needed for plunging from the height he'd leapt. He smacked his head on a rock and spilled his brains out just beneath the surface of murky water.

And Lila, who'd become fascinated with sex in her early teens, introducing each and every one of her male (and one female) cousins to the moist and quivering hot spot between her thighs - had caught some incurable venereal disease; first she blistered. Then she spent some time with a bout of insanity. Six months later...she was dead.

Joined by their Aunt Carol (one who had simply passed away from old age), and they were all about to bring new atmosphere to David Maples house.

"Four!"

Verna (who'd become quite sickly during her last living days with the Anthrax, and now decayed, looked as dead as the rest of them) stayed home at Bobby and Opal's with dead baby Alvin and the *living* Hagger's.

"Three!"

Erwin and Dale Gunner (Trudy's other sister, Angie and her husband Henry Gunner's boys, who'd been shot and killed by Erwin's own long lost son, Tim Corter) were the two dragging shadows that cut across Tim's front porch. The window they passed was lit only by the inside glow of a television.

"Two!"

It was the job of the various remaining Aunts, Uncles, Nieces, Nephews, Cousins and In-laws, however dead they may be, to move in on the local Post Office, to melt through and destroy the operational facilities of courier communication. Normally there would be a night crew to sort mail, but it *was* a holiday, so the lights were all off and the parking lot empty.

"One!"

"Happy New Year!"

Chapter 3

Howard Remmington had never been what you'd call 'a party man'. When he was sixteen years old and couldn't afford the type of automobile he wanted, he knew, even then, he was going to need money. He would have to be *at least* a millionaire, and that was going to take serious hard work. So, *to party*, was not on his agenda; no time for it, never was, never would be. And by 10:30, even on New Year's Eve, Howard Remmington could be found in bed, looking forward to waking early and going over The Wall Street Journal with a cup of coffee.

Laura, his wife, was accustomed to the routine and went to bed fifteen minutes later. Only, what she looked forward to was getting a decent night's sleep, without thinking (or dreaming) about last week's Christmas desecration. At 12:00, she was still awake, staring out the bedroom window.

Patty, Charles, and Junior had each found an entry door, one around back, one in front, and one on the side. Patty thought it odd that they would take the time to find doors, when, like Jimmy, they could just as easily walk through a wall.

Laura Remmington lay staring out the window at the moon listening to Howard's chorus of snores buzz-sawing in and out. And up until 12:00 that was *all* she heard. Then...there was something else. It was inhale, *snoooorre*...exhale, inhale *snoooorre*...*shuffle shuffle*...exhale, *shuffle shuffle bop, snooore*...

What is that noise, she wondered. It sounded like shuffling in the hallway. Eventually, the shuffling was as loud in her ears as the snoring. She listened to the two sounds blend, while nervous curiosity ate at her. "Well, for crying out loud," she huffed, and shot a glare of irritation at Howard for snoring so loudly.

She grunted quietly, reaching and pushing him over on his side. It was a momentary strain, but his mouth closed and he shut up.

Shuffle shuffle shuffle bump.

There was a soft thump at the bedroom door. Laura sprang up in bed. Then she heard a hissing from outside the window and turned back to where the moon had shone through.

There, in a dark silhouette, blocking the center of the moon glow was the hideous face of Jimmy Hagger, impregnating the night with his twisted self.

Her heart stopped, frozen with fear, too scared even to scream. She stared at the slimy grotesque figure burning itself through the glass, while smoky drops fell and spattered on the carpet inside. Then two strips of dark discoloration formed on the wall beneath the ledge, Jimmy's legs were coming through.

"Oh My God!" The words sucked back in Laura's throat, *"It's walking through the wall."* Then a quick crackling noise made her look back to the bedroom door and see it had become a waterfall of liquid grain melting to the ground. And from the shadows...

"How ya doin, lady, the name's Hagger, Charles. And thanks to that there company your husband runs, I got this here foot blowed clean off," he held up his stub. Then he walked in ahead of Patty and Junior.

Laura finally found her voice and shrieked.

"Better wake up the Boss, lady, you may need some assistance," Charles laughed a gravely laugh, and Howard's eyes finally popped open.

On the other side, Jimmy had come all the way through the wall and was next to Laura's side of the bed, dripping.

Luke Brigham was very much the opposite of Howard Remmington. But he'd learned, to remain Vice President for any length of time, he would have to present the image of conformity. So, while maintaining a certain amount of 'assholiness' *on* the job, after 5:00, those who knew him better, knew that Luke Brigham could party with the best of them.

This year was a smaller party than the year before, which was smaller than the year before that. But Luke always guaranteed a good time. This year was four couples; close friends who had maintained a certain degree of partner swapping. All dancing, drinking, and roasting marshmallows, on long forks, over an open fire. Then someone came to the door.

'*Knock! Knock! Knock!...Buzz! Buzz!*'

Rhonda Toush also had a small party going, it was mostly *the guys and gals* from the Marketing department. Some drank, some smoked, some slipped outside for a different kind of smoke. This was the group who liked to talk about everyone else, while denying any rumors about themselves. Most of them kept their nose high and snooty.

That night, three holes were burned through Rhonda's backyard slat-board privacy fence. And from the base of those holes, beneath a thin frost of white, stretched three strips of singed grass.

At the other end of the strips was *The Death Squad*. Frank and Angie went around to the side kitchen entrance, while Henry chose to come *through* the sliding glass door.

Ben Goulden and two others marched through the kitchen, on their way to the darkened porch to burn some of their own grass. When, at the same time, unfortunately for Ben and company, Frank and Angie happen to be reaching for the handle on the other side. The door opened and...

"Evenin, boys," Frank gurgled.

Rhonda sat between her Boss, Drake Starky, and the arm of the sofa - across the room from the sliding glass door. She was laughing and drinking, occasionally swaying to the rhythm of the music. When, in a dawning moment, she noticed movement behind the sheer day curtain. It looked like water running. Still swaying, she asked, "Is it raining?"

The question apparently wasn't important enough to pull anyone from his or her current activity. But most people in the room *did* toss a glance to the curtain.

Some paid no more attention than that. If they didn't see anything right off, they turned back to what they were doing. Others, however, watched the movement of something clear, maybe water...showering the glass door, but then it stopped. And where only a second before, it had been moving...swirling, it was now filled with colors...and a form.

Henry Gunner had melted through the glass and followed up with a burn through the curtain. Those who'd been watching suddenly went stiff. Mouth's dropped. Those who *hadn't* noticed, were suddenly noticing those who had.

Then Frank and Angie entered the room from the kitchen. Frank had Ben Goulden's head planted on his fist. His arm was stuck right up into the neck while Ben's head dripped clots of flesh. Frank grinned, "Let's party!"

Gene Oldham was sitting on his sofa next to Martin. Martin was a long time buddy of Gene's. They sat close together, a bit closer than two men normally would. Then there was Doug Procter (Ground floor Supervisor), a husky man, and his friend, Sal.

The lights in three different areas - leading from the kitchen, through the living room, and to the stairway that went to the bedrooms, were all set on dim. The Television had Dick Clark hosting the party at Times Square; it was just low background for the social gathering of four men.

Each had a glass of champagne, and as 12:00 approached and Dick counted down, the two men on the sofa stood together with the other two, raised their glasses in a toast and drank, then hugged and kissed each other...(Suspicion confirmed).

The three dead girls, June, Molly, and Chrissy watched through the window, "What's wrong with this picture, girls?" June asked.

"It's been too long since any of those boys have experienced the wrap of something warm, wet, and pink," Chrissy said. "Let's go give it to 'em." The girls stepped up to the door and knocked.

"Just a minute," Gene's effeminate voice sang merrily through, followed by the sound of unlatching latches. "Yes? can I help..." he started as the door opened. But he stopped cold when he saw what was there to greet him. And before he could run or scream or even drop dead in fear, Chrissy had him by the throat in the clutch of her right hand, while her left came up into his crotch.

"Come here, Stud," she said. "Let me show you how to work this thing, *my way*," and she licked her chalky dead lips, with a grin.

The Maples family was not in a festive mood that evening. They were all thinking about the prospect of a new year without Sarah, David and Marge's nineteen-year-old daughter, their oldest, and Sean and Jillian's sister.

It was the first *New Years* David could remember, not having Sarah around to share it with - another reminding slap that she was dead. Melted from the inside out by the rotten penis of Jimmy Hagger.

David knew Jimmy was the one who had done it; he swore if he ever caught up with him, he would kill him with his bare hands, or die trying.

Everyone at the Maples house did his or her share of shuffling from the kitchen to the living room, Dick Clark was on the TV. Most of the lights in the house were on; this was Marge's way of trying to keep things cheery. David was popping more corn and baking cinnamon cookies.

By the time the count down came, however, Sean and Jillian were no longer interested. They had placed themselves in front of a large bowl of previously popped and buttered corn at the kitchen table, and nibbled despondently.

David and Marge stood in the living room, in front of the sofa. They had one arm around each other, side by side, with a drink in hand, and stared at Dick Clark. They imagined him suddenly getting excited and announcing, "A miracle folks, a miracle has happened. The daughter of David and Marge Maples, Sarah Maples, has just been reported back to life as a gift for the New Year."

Dick kept smiling, but there was no such announcement, instead, they were suddenly jolted back to reality by the sound of Sean and Jillian screaming in the kitchen, long and painful, gut wrenching, blood curdling screams. It pierced their ears as they darted for the two children in the other room. But when they got there, they found Lila, John, and Carol at the table, with the remains of what used to be Sean and Jillian and...the popcorn.

Back at Bobby and Opal's place, Dead Verna told dead baby Alvin the story of The Miracle on 34th street.

Tim Corter slouched way down very comfortably in his favorite easy chair. A good, strong, well cushioned chair, not one of those sissy, wobbly recliner types. He had no particular interest in Dick Clark or the dawning new year, he was watching his favorite old black and white classic movie, 'Psycho'...again.

He had taped the movie off cable TV two years before, and watched it whenever he got the chance. There was just something about the idea of Norman Bates becoming his own mother that intrigued Tim.

The wife and kids were asleep in bed; he had a tall cold beer in his hand and was set for at least the next hour and a half. Then...things...changed.

Erwin and Dale were never known for their subtlety; they had each gone to the edge of the porch and took a running leap through the front window.

Glass flew in every direction, some into Tim's face, jabbing like needles. Erwin and Dale shot across the room, they rolled and came up on their feet, tall, and directly in front of Tim (suddenly urinating freely in his favorite easy chair).

"Hi ya, Timmy! Daddy's come home to give his baby boy a great big hug," Erwin gurgled.

All remaining Aunts, Uncles, Nieces, Nephews, Cousins and In-laws peeled their way through the back door of the Post Office. Clawing at it, melting their hands into it and pulling off clumps.

Inside, there were walls of square wooden mail slots, a few desks, piles of gunny sacks, rows of bin baskets, and stacks of small plastic carrying boxes...full of mail. There were a few long tables with various weight machines and packing materials on them. The windows of the place were frosted; obscuring all vision to the other side (in or out), and each window was secured with black wrought iron bars.

The front wall was more like a divider; open on both ends for easy access from the back room to the front desk. At the desk were cabinets full of forms and documents, the money drawers, and more weight and stamp machines.

Beyond the waiting area, was a glass door that led to a lobby of post office boxes, two tables with attached pens and small stacks of change forms (name change, address change, P.O. Box change, underwear change...you name it, they could change it), and three glass lobby doors, leading to the parking lot.

The undead Hagger's gurgled with laughter, discovering the ability to melt the equipment into shapes. They could form it, creating abstract art...*real abstract*. And since they were dry (didn't ooze like Jimmy) they didn't burn things up as quick. Carefully and creatively, the scales ended up being their best sculpture of the night (almost prize-worthy), and by morning the Post Office had become an Art Gallery.

Chapter 4

I n the week that followed, with the discovery of each New-Year's-Eve massacre, every day was another shocking headline on the front page of the newspaper.

The Remmington's were the first ones reported. When Howard Remmington had failed to call Dexter Harding, his Broker (*and it was not like Howard not to call*), Dexter tried calling him. When there was no answer at the house *or* the office, knowing how predictable Howard was, Dexter got worried and called friends he had on the police force, just to cruise by and investigate.

As two officers approached the Remmington estate, their dead pan 'I can't believe I'm working on New-Year's-Day' expressions began to twist with confusion. There was a hole...in the house. An opening in the wall at the far corner bedroom, where once was just a window, there was now an entire walk-through.

Inside, they found burned carpet trails leading through the house to that bedroom and right up to the Remmington's bed (what was left of it).

It was covered in red blood blotches and globs of oozy flesh pools with body chunks mixed in. An eyeball floated in one puddle, three fingers and a portion of a woman's hand in another. One of the fingers had a diamond ring on it, but the finger had swollen so badly, the skin ripped out and left the ring wrapped around the bone.

There were other skeletal chips and hair sticking out of the goop, apparently the Remmington's never even made it to the floor.

Down the hall, in the other bedrooms, there was more of the same. The Remmington's *had* five children. One young girl was found in the doorway of her closet, her bottom half was gone. Her waist was sealed shut holding all upper guts in place, but her legs had been melted to a small thick stain on the carpet. Her eyes were wide open and full with fear.

Two other children were gone, only faint white formations in their place.

Just outside of another room, lay the head of an adorably cute seven-year-old girl, with long curly blonde hair flowing down around where her neck and shoulders should have been. The head had been torn off and *not* sealed shut, it was...messy.

The officers chose not to enter that room right away; in fact they chose not to enter any more rooms at all. One of them ran to heave his breakfast...in the fire place, the other staggered back to the squad car and fumbled frantically with the two-way radio.

On further investigation, a live-in maid was discovered in her room, more intact than the rest, but still, burned away in all vital area's.

The Remmington's also had a cook, but he was out that night and missed all the excitement. He stumbled in later, after some heavy drinking, and went right to bed. He was awakened the following afternoon by a small army of police, beating on his door.

The kitchen had gone undisturbed; the cabinets and floor unmarred by dragging burn lines. The counter was clean, the sink was dry, all dining chairs were pushed up next to the table, and there in a corner, unmoving, was a small five-year-old boy. One officer locked wide and shocked eyes with the boy, "What Happened?"

The child, lost in the disconnected world of his subconscious, stared back and didn't say a word...for many years.

The only difference between this attack and the other attacks that night was that *here* they found streaks of dried brown crust, and the puddles of flesh were covered with an oily glaze.

The Brigham's home, and Rhonda's house were found in pretty much the same condition. The murderous creativity was a little different, they had twisted off heads and stuck them on things: the post of a stairway, a large bottle of champagne...etc.

Body parts in both homes were melted, torn apart and stuck every-where, in one artistic venture or another. The most interesting sculp-ture was that of Rhonda's upper torso embedded into Drake Starky's stomach, fused together just beneath where *her* breasts rested on *his* chest. Her head was back, her eyes were wide and sightless, her mouth was open but silent, and her arms had been removed from her body, leaving two bloody gaps.

Tim Corter's family got off lucky. Apparently, his wife and kids had come running when they heard the window crash, but by the time they'd reached the living room and saw what Erwin and Dale were doing, ol' Tim was already a partial meltdown. Mrs. Corter took all of two seconds to decide whether or not to try and save her husband; and on quick examination, there really wasn't much left to save.

Her first instinct was to throw things at the creatures. But then she looked at the kids..."Come on," she grunted, and they all tore back down the hallway and escaped through a bedroom window.

At Gene Oldham's place, there was a smaller mess; only a few pieces of furniture had been knocked over. Mostly what was found, were four gay men stripped naked, one missing a hand, two others missing feet ('Homicide' believed these were warnings to not piss off their assai-lants), but all four bodies lay in a row, melted at their groin to the carpet. There were burn marks all over, legs, faces, throats, upper torsos; but basically, the three girls had decided to straddle the four men and just...fuck them to death.

At the Maples house there had been a fight. When David and Marge Maples came to a screeching halt in their kitchen, staring at the three figures at their table, reshaping their remaining two children (Sean's head had been replaced by Jillians...and vise versa...and turned backward), David exploded with rage, and nausea, and heartache, and hatred. "Aaauuugghhh, I'm gonna kill you mother fuckers!" he screamed and leapt at John Hagger with a driving thrust of his right fist. It was a good surprising blow, and quick enough that David didn't experience any melting touches.

John fell back against the wall with the punch (if he had been more solid, the hit would have had more impact), and told Dave, "Good hit, asshole. Now I guess we have to kill you too."

In the following half hour, David and Marge struggled to fight back without being disintegrated - the battle was back and forth for awhile; the dead Hagger's each taking a lamp in the groin or a chair in the face, while David and Marge began...losing things.

A swipe at the hand took off a couple of fingers, blood spurt like a fountain through a pressure-released valve, then a clump of arm or leg - a gouge at the throat. Finally, Marge took a good melting poke in the eye; it popped and dropped onto her cheek.

David saw the assault to his wife and cried out, losing a moment of concentration that he really couldn't spare. That's when Lila leapt onto him, followed by John, then Carol. Eventually, David and Marge were reduced to carpet stain.

Chapter 5

T he week after New Years also brought the first phases of power line reconstruction. The Post Office was gone; the insides melted down to mounds of thick blobs.

Of course the police had two-way radios, and the roads *were* open for in and *'get the hell out of Dodge'* traffic. But snow was thick and cold, and even with all evidence pointing against it, a lot of people felt a sense of safety locking themselves up in the comfort and privacy of their own home; behind latched and barricaded doors. The small town of Pleasure View would just have to live with one eye looking over its shoulder.

What the town didn't know was that the Hagger's were finished. They had succeeded in eliminating the persons they felt were responsible for their troubles.

Bobby Hagger hadn't received a letter from Xanorse since early September, written by David Maples in late August, the day before the discovery of Morgan Newton in a little tin rowboat on Marble Rock Lake.

The letter was to inform Mr. Hagger that he had exactly two months to vacate. Then Morgan turned up dead and Xanorse administration began to shift concerns. Suddenly, after the death of Fred Peterson, Sam Stallworth, Sue Ann Walden, David Maples' Daughter, Sarah, and now Morgan Newton, the question arose, *'Why were all the victims somehow connected with the Plant? What was the message here?'*

Then, in December, when things began to function again, Bobby received another letter. This time from a Luke Brigham; Vice President of Xanorse, requesting that Mr. Hagger present his property title in Mr. Brigham's office no later than December 31st.

However, after the Christmas party, all business matters were put on hold. And after New Years, neither Luke Brigham, or David Maples, or Howard Remmington, or anyone else who could have mattered, bothered the Hagger's any longer.

The week following New Years found the Hagger's celebrating *Independence Day.*

It took several weeks to replace the melted power poles and cables. It took even longer to rebuild a whole new Post Office, during which time, mail; cards, bills and letters, had to be rerouted, and were obviously slowed down. In the beginning, the mail had virtually come to a stop (except, of course, for the endless flow of Domino Pizza coupons).

Some people had packed up and ran, for fear of the creatures. Others waited and watched...and watched...and watched...nothing!

There were no more attacks. Three weeks went by, there were no sightings. There weren't even any *false* sightings. *Had the creatures...gone? Were they just laying low? Where did they go? Why did they go? They left once before, in the fall, but then showed up again at Christmas. Why did they leave then? Why did they come back? Were they just hibernating for the winter?*

What was left of the town watched for another return, but by February, the *smaller* community of Pleasure View began to relax a little. The snow had stopped, Xanorse was having board meeting after board meeting with the remaining administration over who would fill the now numerous positions available in upper management. Not to mention the Presidency.

Meanwhile, all *dead* Hagger's were sitting among the trees out back of the pasture, watching all *live* Hagger's build them a shelter (no doors...no point!). This would be where they would soon stay until a better idea came along.

The police, in their search, found nothing. From Christmas through February...nothing! But, they never looked down in the pit beneath the Xanorse parking lot.

The weekend of February 24th, Davis Dugan moved back home.

Chapter 6

After New Years, Jimmy and company needed a good and immediate hiding place; there was only one logical solution.

The first time they went into *the pit*, they entered through the manhole in the parking lot. They had melted a trail through the snow and began searching for the cover, when they found it; they were able to pull it off with minimal burning. However, since Jimmy had damn near burned the inside stepladder away, during his awakening escape, they had to figure another way down. They were ready just to jump in - but then how would they get back out?

It was quiet contemplation for a moment, when Jimmy, in his silent stare, found himself looking directly at Charles's leg. The one that had been blown off and was now a stretched meld of flesh that reached all the way to the ground, forming the stub he walked on. *It stretches,* he thought, "Hey!" his eyes lit up (damn near glowed in fact), "I got an idear!"

The others observed as he put his legs over the edge of the hole, "Watch," he told them, and slowly began rubbing the bottom of his legs, pulling at them, working them until it was quite noticeable that they were stretching.

Everyone smiled, "Can we *all* do that?" Trudy asked.

"Don't see why not," Jimmy said, and stretched himself down closer to the pool. When he came near enough to the bottom, he hopped off the edge of the asphalt (left an impressive indentation of bony buttocks), and found himself standing in the waste with his head still above ground level. He laughed and said, "Come on in folks, the water's fine!"

They all laughed while Jimmy worked his legs down, lowering to the pool and getting back to normal size. It was good to be *himself* again, but for a moment, he thought it was pretty cool being a giant. *And that might come in handy sometime.*

The family would spend many days during January and February in the pit, while their ability to stretch and reshape became an art. They would spend hours just reforming themselves...and each other.

Chapter 7

Davis rolled into town in a small U-haul truck, towing his freshly polished, white, with black interior, 4-speed, 280 Z Datsun behind him. He was moving back in with his parents, *temporarily*.

Jeff and Billy were there to help. Krys and Shawna would have been there to greet him, but with his and Janie's split, they weren't sure how to divide their loyalties. So, they asked Jeff to extend their welcome and say 'sorry' but they couldn't make it.

Davis didn't have much to unload; he'd left most everything with Janie (including the house). Arriving at noon, he was just in time for a much appreciated homemade lunch by *Mom* (she fixed enough for all three boys). After which, it took them an hour to unload the truck.

Whatever wouldn't fit in Davis's old room went down to the basement. Nothing seem to fall into place right, the room became a stack of boxes, with the bed being the only thing that actually got placed and set up. He knew he would definitely need it at a time when he most likely wouldn't feel like messing with it.

The boys (men) looked at each other and smiled, perspiration beading up across their foreheads, Davis suggested they go to 'The Bank Shot' and hoist a few beers to Billy's Mom. They lowered their heads in respect for the late Martha Dunes, Billy's mom, who'd served these three lunches and dinners on many more than one occasion.

Nodding, Billy said, "Can't think of anything more I'd rather drink to." They threw their arms around each other and headed out to the local Billiards Bar, 'The Bank Shot'.

By March, the people of Pleasure View were breathing easier - with the disappearance of *the creatures*. They were still a hot topic of conversation, of course, and there were plenty of stories to tell.

Davis got his fill, having a rough time believing a lot of it. In fact, Jeff had to (once again) pull out the Sunday, December 24th newspaper, with Jimmy's picture plastered across the front page, for that reminding slap of reality.

"Where do you suppose they went?" he asked.

"Who cares, as long as they're gone," Jeff responded.

"You mean as long as they *stay* gone," Davis corrected.

The guys quietly lost themselves in thought. They could only imagine where the creatures might have gone. Where no one would find them, perhaps a hideout that Jimmy had showed them. A hideout that only he knew about, because of what six members of an old tree house club had done to him. Perhaps the underground waste pool of Xanorse Chemicals was now infested with a family of undead hillbillies.

They *knew* that must be where they went, but none of them wanted to be the first to suggest it.

"I don't know where they are," Jeff said. "And as long as they stay gone, I don't really care." Billy and Davis shrugged in agreement.

Though March was cold, April warmed up nicely. By mid-month there were people wearing shorts and picnicking at Marble Rock Lake.

On one particular Thursday evening, the weather was nice enough that Davis decided to stay late at the garage and work on his own car.

The transmission shop was built of brick and the roll-up garage doors were made of aluminum, there was no insulation. So on cold days, it was as cold inside as out.

Taking advantage of the warmth, Davis closed himself in alone to do some tuning on *The Z,* plugs, points, oil, lube, and a few gaskets.

The JVC radio jam box that found it's own personal resting spot among the shop's permanent fixture's, was blaring the end of a static intensified version of 'I'll stop the world and melt with you,' a song on the 70's and 80's station by a band called *Modern English.* Davis remembered the song from a movie he and Janie had seen called 'Valley Girl'.

He remembered it was one of her favorites; she was a sucker for a love story. "Yeah, Love," he thought out loud. "A whole lot of bullshit if you ask me," and he twisted another spark plug into position.

He hated those memory shots of Janie. Something in his throat would squeeze, like a rope tightening around his neck. A rope tied to his heart, choking out a tear or two and racing it to his eyes. Then he would throw up the 'Do Not Enter' sign and force the pain back with only a small indication of nerves twitching his bottom lip.

After the plugs and points, Davis laid down on the mechanics dolly and pulled himself in under the engine. "I guess I need to go ahead with a new starter too," he mumbled and reached for the box of wrenches and screwdrivers sitting next to the tire.

When the song on the radio changed, something began to distort. And what should have sounded very good and very familiar, was for some reason coming out very long and slow...excruciatingly slow. As though someone were dragging it forcibly through the speaker.

Pink Floyd? Davis could hardly imagine Pink Floyd elongating any more than their usual. He suddenly felt very heavy on the dolly, staring into the face of the motor block...unable to move.

Drip! Drip! Drip!

Something is dripping, he thought and went to reach for the oil drain plug, only to find he couldn't lift his arms, or legs, or any other part of his body. *What the hell?* And the hand of fear reached out for a shake.

Drip!

Suddenly, his insides felt thick with lifeless muscle. *I can't move.* His mind jolted with an unexpected flashback.

I saw Krys fall, and suddenly everything went into slow motion...like my Brain-power was standing still.

He was immobile and staring wide-eyed into black liquid metal. *Liquid Metal?*

Yes, it was the metal of the engine, and it was...dripping. Melting and dripping onto his chest.

'Aaaauuuggghhhh'

The scream went off in his head, but without voice. He tried stretching his mouth open to yell, but he no longer had control of the muscles in his face. And the scream echoing in his brain came to no more than muffled groans in the back of his throat.

Drip!

He watched the motor melt over him like slow flowing lava. *Hey, lava burns!* His brain shouted.

Then his rational voice jumped in and tried to explain calmly that, *yes it's melting, but it's not hot. It doesn't burn.* Of course his irrational self didn't buy it, *it's going to cover me and fry me to death.* But rational held strong, *hey, dumbshit, listen up. I said it's not hot, it's not burning you, it's just running over you, you know, like an ice-cream cone over your hand on a hot day.*

The rest of his mind quickly snatched up the concept and began hammering it in. *It's not burning me, it's not burning me, it's not...*

And the truth was, it wasn't burning him. In fact, it felt cool to the touch. And as far as covering him, well, it dripped onto his chest and ran over his shoulders, but there was no large mass of goopy metal drowning him...not yet anyway.

Then, in the corner of his eye, he saw the bottom edge of the tool cabinet; wood and metal, oozing, running, shimmering in a silver gray swirl, all over the *pool* of concrete that was once the garage floor. He saw black rubber tires become dark holes. *Perhaps, holes to escape through? ...*Perhaps not.

Then the metallic body of the automobile, doors, fenders, trunk, hood, all of it *did* start coming down around him...and he couldn't move. He strained to look down along his side; hoping, perhaps total concentration would move him? ...Perhaps not.

Jesus Christ, he thought, *I'm being buried beneath a melted lump of automobile.* Panic, ultimate fear, and loss of control of the situation had him urinating in his pants. *Now it's getting hot,* he thought. The stream warmed the insides of his legs.

Then, abruptly, the dripping eased up. Everything kept bubbling like lava, and continued swirling in one place, but it stopped flowing. Suddenly, his eyes began to widen, to...stretch. The flesh at his jowl tugged on his face, pulling it down. Pulling the bottom lids of his eyes into his cheeks, while the back of his head pulled skin from the front; from below his hairline, his eyebrows and the thin eyelids just beneath them, came up into his forehead.

With the stretching pull on his chin, his bottom lip came inside out and exposed the flap of blue and red veined geography that led to the gums, gums now pulling away from the teeth they were holding.

It was as if someone had his skin clamped in a vise behind him and was cranking it tighter and tighter, stretching and tearing. So tight it would soon rip from his skull and blood and bone would burst through his face like a giant zit.

Eventually, his entire body was covered with melted engine. The doors and fenders pooled around him. He was the center chip in a massive cookie. The runny metal filled his ears and closed in around his face. Then, one widely expanded eye caught a glimpse of a large black drip hanging directly above it, with only an inch and a half between them.

God, no, not in my eye, his mind begged, but his eye wouldn't close. Helpless, he watched the drip swell, swaying ever heavier, pulling closer. *Please, God, no metal in the eye, Please!* And then...finally, the drip bloomed, too thick and full to cling any longer, and it fell...*Drip!*

NOOOOO!

Davis's arms flew to his face and wiped at anything he could feel. When, almost as an afterthought, he realized he was moving again. Immediately, he reached out and grabbed the, *same as it ever was,* engine, and yanked himself out from under.

He shot from beneath *The Z* on the bed of the mechanics dolly, and then threw his feet out to stop it. He sprang straight up and thrust his shirtsleeve to his eye to wipe away whatever had dripped there. But when he pulled his arm back and looked, it was only *"Oil!"*

He stared at the small drop on his sleeve, "That's it? Oil? I'm practically killed by a fucking drop of oil?" Then he turned to look at the car, still there, solid as it ever was.

The car was completely intact, just as before he'd...well...before his mind had gone-a-melting. The garage was still standing. Davis was stunned to see that it had all been a figment of his imagination. Absolutely nothing had melted.

"This is crazy," he muttered, looking around. And as strange as it was...nothing had changed. But there was a kind of unnerving familiarity about the episode that nagged at him.

"...And that was Pink Floyd's *Comfortably Numb,*" the D.J. informed with a cheery voice.

Chapter 8

Bzzzzzz! Bzzzzzz!

The customer service door buzzer assaulted the silence at full capacity; buzzing at least five times before Davis could gain composure and respond. He looked over his shoulder at the car, checking its solidity as he walked to the door to see who was there.

Through a small tinted window in the top of the door, he saw it was Shawna. But, thanks to the dark tint, she couldn't see in. On her side it was more of a mirror.

Thank God, she can't see me, he thought. *I must look like shit.* He looked down at his pants, "And probably smell like piss." He looked around and saw an old cup of coffee next to a book of work orders on the desk, he grabbed it and sniffed, it was nasty with a few floating cigarette butts, then he spilled it down the front of his pants to camouflage his urinary indiscretion.

Shaking off the jitters still rattling within, he wiped the sweat from his forehead and ran his fingers through his hair (same greasy fingers he used to work on the car engine). Halfway over his scalp he felt the grit and pulled his hands back to look at them - grimy and black, "Shit!" defeated, he slumped, "What the hell else can happen?"

Bzzzzzz! Bzzz...he opened the door.

It only took him two seconds to forget everything else and become completely mesmerized by the beautiful *woman* standing in the

313

doorway. "Shawna?" he questioned for confirmation, not believing it was the same girl he used to pick on in High School.

"Hi, Davis. Long time no see," she was all smiles...and dimples.

My God, she's beautiful, were his thoughts. What came out of his mouth was, "What are you doing here?" Then his mind hollered, *Come in pleeeeeessee. Sit down, have a drink, let me look into your beautiful green eyes, I think I might be in love.*

"Well," she said, "Jeff came over to visit with Krys, they're pretty good friends you know. In fact, if Jeff weren't so hung up on big boobs, and you know Krys doesn't have any, he might realize how much he really does like her.

"You mean she still doesn't have boobs?" Davis retorted. They both laughed.

Shawna stepped into the shop, he closed the door behind her, "Anyway, Jeff said you were staying late to work on your car, and...well...I've been thinking about you, and I figured that whatever happened between you and Janie is between you two, and there's really no reason why we, you and I, couldn't...well...be friends." She looked up at him with big, questioning, sparkly eyes, waiting to see if this was an acceptable offer.

"I've missed you too, Shawna." They looked at each other for a moment and smiled, then without reservation stepped into each other's arms for a good old-fashioned reunion hug. "It's great to see you," he said.

When they pulled apart, their smiles lingered. Then she looked around, taking in all the sights and smells of tools and gadgets caked over with black grit and grime. And looking a bit closer at Davis, she wrinkled her nose in a sniff, "Uh...lovely place you got here," she teased.

Suddenly remembering to be embarrassed, he was about to dive head long into an apology for his appearance and...smell, when she noticed the car. Her eyes lit up, "Nice *Z*, Davis..." she paused, thought-fully checking out the vehicle, then turned to look directly into his eyes, "You going to be working much longer?"

He flashed back to the melting experience of only a few moments before and almost came unglued, "NO! Uh no, I'm not," the look on his face was near panic. "I am through for the night."

She grinned a full two-dimple grin, and from the corner of his eye he was pleasantly surprised to see a slight swaying of her behind...back and forth. "So...are you hungry or anything?" she asked.

He watched her gentle movement, wondering exactly what she might be suggesting to eat, then he looked back up into her eyes, "Starving," he said.

And in that instant, her cute girlishness transformed to a mature and desirable woman. Her swaying stopped and she stood receptive and vulnerable, "So how about dinner...on me?" she asked.

How about if you just be *the dinner*, he thought. "I'd love to," he said, "that would be great." Then they both looked at him, up and down. "How about giving me a half an hour to get cleaned up?"

She nodded that that would be a good idea, "Can I just sit in the car and listen to the radio?"

The sudden image of him coming out of the washroom and finding her eaten alive, devoured into the center of a melted automobile, jolted him like he'd grabbed a live electrical wire. He turned a pale shade of white and his eyes became dark and wide.

Shawna was abruptly aware of his panic, "Davis, what's wrong?"

He stared absently for a few lost seconds, then made something up, "Uh...I really need to wipe out the inside. But first I need to get myself clean so I don't spread grease around." He looked at the four lounge chairs by the vending machines in the customer waiting area, "There, why don't you sit there. It's much more comfortable, and closer to the radio." He tried to smile convincingly...still lacking an acceptable flesh tone in his cheeks.

"Davis, what is it? What's wrong? Did something happen with the car?" her glistening green eyes intensified deep with concern.

He stared at her quietly for a contemplative moment, then looked at the car, then back at her. "Shawna," he confessed, "the weirdest thing just happened right before you got here."

Chapter 9

It was just before midnight when Billy and Jeff dropped Davis off at home. He'd been out late with Shawna (again) the night before (they'd been out together two more times since the initial reunion at the shop), and he told the guys he was sorry to have to bail, but he had to get some sleep.

Billy and Jeff were wired, however, and wanted to shoot pool and drink beer.

'The Bank Shot' had existed forever. It was a good, well stocked bar, with a good, well stacked bartender, ten pool tables, two large television monitors, video games, pinball games, trivia video and electronic gambling machines were at each end of the bar, and Dartboards.

The Dartboard area was a place you had to be alert when walking through, especially if a guy named Richard Baxton was throwing. Billy almost lost an eye to Baxton one Saturday night. *"Stupid mother fucker can't aim for shit!"* you could hear Billy shout clear across the room.

Billy and Jeff took a table at the end of the room opposite the Dartboard, closer to the goliath TV monitor. Jeff racked the balls. Billy guzzled his bottle of Coors and asked, "Who's gonna break?"

"Go ahead," Jeff offered, "I've got a beer here I need to get down first," and he tipped his head back and poured.

Billy brought his cue-stick around and took careful aim on the white ball, making sure he was lined up, then... *'Smack!'* ...the balls broke off in every direction.

In the next forty-five minutes Billy won two games to Jeff's one, while each of them consumed three more beers. Then, suddenly feeling the day catch up to them, they decided to put a deadline on the night. They would play a fourth game; if Billy won they would go on and leave. If Jeff won, they would stay for a tie breaking fifth.

The video and pinball games were vacant; the bar was empty except for one sleazy looking woman who'd long given up searching for anyone to go home with. And since the place had died down for the evening, Billy and Jeff's enthusiasm had more or less petered out.

It was just before 2:00 a.m.; The Bank Shot had been empty since 1:30, and Billy and Jeff were just finishing up, when...

Jeff took a long swallow of beer, grabbed his cue-stick, leaned over the white ball, ready to blast blue #2 into the corner pocket, "Prepare to die, Billy boy," he said, then pulled back for the slam.

Billy had his own beer up, watching, when Jeff's head, in slow motion, nodded forward and dropped to the table.

Used to Jeff's antics, unconcerned, Billy lowered his bottle and said, "Very funny."

Jeff's arms slowly stretched forward, jamming the cue-stick in front of him and tearing the cloth, while his body lay flat out on the table. Suddenly alarmed, Billy rushed to his side, grabbed him and rolled him over, "Jeff? What is it?" Billy's nerves tingled with the onset of panic.

He got Jeff on his back, slightly disgusted to find his face covered with thick stringy drool from his mouth, which to Billy's shock and awe, was distorted all out of proportion. His eyes were bizarrely stretched, opened as wide as they could and then some, and pulling up into his forehead.

Billy was mortified to see the tension, straining and pulling at Jeff's neck, tearing the flesh away from his face and shrinking it toward the back of his head.

"Jesus, Jeff!" he choked, sick with fear. His best friend looked like something from a horror movie.

Jeff couldn't move, he lay like a rippling, twitching, slab of meat. Billy watched the muscles turning beneath his skin, working themselves to a frenzy and getting nowhere. The corners of his eyes were ripped, stretched *too* far open, releasing blood to run down into his ears.

"Holy Shit!" Billy looked up, white faced, and screamed for help, *"Somebody call an ambulance, my friend is hurt."*

The sleazy girl at the bar looked over; she had a drink in one hand, a cigarette in the other, and was too drunk to care. But the Bartender came running, "What's wrong with him?" she asked, taking charge.

Billy was shaking, "I don't know. It looks like a stroke or something. Quick, call somebody, we've got to get him to a hospital."

She took off to the phone, stressed and irritated, "I should have known better than to think I could get out of this place on time."

Chapter 10

...S unday evening.

Davis helped Shawna through the door, "You sure you're all right?" he asked.

"Yeah, I guess so," she told him.

They walked in and found Krys sitting on the sofa with a half empty bottle of wine. Everyone looked at each other, nobody said anything, Krys watched Davis help Shawna to a chair, then she noticed how beat up *he* was. "What happened to you two?" she asked.

"I think we've got a problem," Shawna said.

Krys thought again about the conversation she'd had with Janie earlier, "I think you're right." They knew they were all thinking about the same thing.

Their eyes glanced worriedly back and forth at each other...until their attention seem to be curiously pulled to look around the room, as if something had changed, but they didn't know what. Then...almost simultaneously, Davis and Shawna both looked at Krys. And like a slap in the face, they saw...them.

Shawna's mouth dropped, she even rubbed her eyes to make sure her vision wasn't distorted. "Krys?" Krys looked at her, following her eyes in the stare that led straight back to herself, and down at her breasts. "Do you have...Boobs?" Shawna's face was about to crack with an animated smile of amusement.

Krys grinned, excited by the fact that her body was finally a representation of her inner self. She stood straight up, chest out, "It's like a miracle, Shawna...aren't they beautiful?"

"Whatta ya got balloons in there?" Davis joked.

Krys was quick to uphold her dignity, "They're mine thank you very much. My very own, home grown breasts."

If she didn't see it, Shawna wouldn't have believed it, "Well, how did they get there? You didn't have them yesterday."

Krys settled back and said, "Why don't you-all come sit over here and let's talk."

Shawna sat on the sofa next to her; Davis took the recliner on the other side of the coffee table. Krys took a few deep breaths and tried to put it together in her head what she was going to say, but then she looked at Davis's face and saw his black eye and the dark blood clotting in his nose, and suddenly aware of the extent of his scrapes and bruises, she realized she'd never found out what happened to them. "So, what happened to you two, anyway?" she asked.

"Well," Shawna explained, "you know those seizure things you said you've been having, where you can't move and your face stretches all out of proportion and everything looks all melty to you?"

"Yeah," Krys nodded.

"...And then I told you the same thing happened to Davis two weeks ago at the garage? And now Jeff is in the hospital stuck in some kind of a mental lock with one?"

Krys kept nodding, "Yeah, yeah."

"Well," she took a deep breath...and admitted almost with embarrassment, "it happened to me today out on the lake."

Suddenly, Krys was sympathetic, "Oh gosh, Shawna, are you all right?" She put an arm around her shoulder.

"Yeah, I'm fine, I think," she said. "I think Davis got the worst of it, he was on the skis jumping the ramp when I lost control of the boat and nearly killed him."

"Jeez, Davis, are *you* all right?"

He nodded, "Yeah, I'll live. I just wish I knew what the hell was happening to us."

Krys got quiet and sat back stiffly. Davis and Shawna could see that she knew something more than they did, and they weren't going to wait long for whatever bombshell she might have to drop.

"I got a call today," she said, and paused.

They waited.

"...From Janie."

Davis was suddenly wide-eyed with concern, but held off commenting.

"It happened to her too."

Then he almost came up out of his chair, "Is she all right? Was she hurt?"

Shawna was startled by his panic, but not surprised.

"She's fine," Krys went on, "just alone and scared," then she kind of shrank back and hesitated before finishing, "So...I invited her to come stay with me for a visit. She's flying in Tuesday."

Davis sat back and didn't say anything; in fact, they were all quiet. Then, without responding to the news about Janie, he told them, "Well, we've definitely got a problem here." The girls looked up. "Billy called this morning, he said the same kind of thing had just happened to him, but he was okay, and then something about cleaning coffee grounds off the kitchen floor."

Both girls (women) felt the piercing arrow of fear, "You mean it's happened to all of us?" Shawna asked. Her voice was dry.

"And from what you say," Davis went on, "it's happened to Krys a few times."

Krys's eyes glazed over, lost in thought, "Three times," she said, "then again today, while I was driving back from town." She scowled, "I hate that old lady at Wal-Mart."

Another moment of silence, then Davis realized he was staring at Krys's boobs (again), only this time he sensed a connection; with an arrow of fear stabbing him, his stomach churned, and though he wasn't sure of exactly *what* to ask, his brain had to know, "Krys, where did you get the boobs?"

It was no longer a joking matter; their very lives were possibly on the line. All three of them were concerned about how Krys was able to develop full blooming breasts over night.

"I'm not sure," she said, "but it does have something to do with controlling this melting thing. I know it's something coming from my brain, I just don't know what."

Davis looked back and forth at the two of them, "I'm going to call Billy and see what Jeff's CAT SCAN results were, maybe that will give us a clue."

Krys gave him the phone.

Chapter 11

Billy leaned over the small round table between them, in the hospital cafeteria, and whispered to Davis, "The Doctor says Jeff is experiencing melting brain cells."

Davis sat back and scowled, "You say what?"

Billy leaned in again, "The Doctor says that different cells from all over his head are running through his cerebrum and dripping into a small pool in the center of his brain."

Davis was silent...then only one question slipped out, "Is it going to kill him?"

Billy maintained a serious positivism, "I don't think so. He said the cells weren't dying, they were just coming together in one spot, in the middle of his head, kind of a...melting pot.

"So, why is he still so geeked out like he is?" Davis stomped on his fear and grew frustrated, wanting answers. "I mean, it's happened to all of us and *we* all came out of it okay."

Billy shrugged, "I don't know, when it happened to me I only freaked out for about five minutes. One moment everything's melting like I'm in the midst of a fire or something, and the next thing I know, my can of Maxwell House is rolling off the counter and smacking me right in the face. Suddenly...everything's normal again."

Davis grimaced, "Was the can full?"

"Hell yes it was full, one of those big two pounders. Damn near broke my nose."

Davis maintained a thin grin. Then Billy told him about the incident in the hall outside of Jeff's room in *The Einstein Department*; how it started up again, and then he fell to the floor, banged his head and got knocked back to reality.

"So each time you came out of it," Davis said, "it stopped when you hit your head?"

Billy nodded "Well, yeah, I guess so."

Davis's wheels started a quick spin, "And when I came out of it under the car, it stopped when a heavy oil drop splashed in my eye." The connection wasn't clear yet.

"What about Krys?" Billy asked.

"I don't know about previous times, but she said; when it happened out near Short Cut yesterday, she slammed into a tree and flew across the front seat...hit her head on the passenger door."

"And that's when it stopped?" Billy asked

"That's when it stopped," Davis confirmed.

The wheels were spinning faster; a pattern was developing.

"What about Janie?" Billy asked.

"She came out of it when...a bird shit dropped out of the sky and splat on her forehead. That's the way she told it to Krys anyway."

This time Billy grimaced, "Dude, that's disgusting."

"Yeah it is," he agreed, "but it worked."

"And what about Shawna? What brought her out of it?"

Davis thought for a minute, then he remembered, "I slapped her. She was...well...all messed up, so, I reached out and slapped her. Suddenly, she was back to normal," he said. "It was weird, it was like ten years ago when we buried Jimmy, remember?"

"Yeah, like I'm going to forget that," Billy mumbled.

"And in the middle of it we all started zoning out, then Janie slapped me and I had to slap all of you to get you out of it."

The wheels screeched to a stop. The light went on.

"That's it!" he almost shouted, "That's why this is all so familiar. It's the same thing that happened to us down in that pool."

Billy did remember, but only because Davis brought it to his attention. Normally, something that had happened for a five-minute period of time, ten years ago, would be lost in the annals of history.

"Yeah, we were all tripping because of the fumes down in the pit, and it was the slap in the face that brought us out of it." Billy stared at Davis, wanting to make sure he understood him correctly, "So, you think if we go in and slap Jeff in the face, *he'll* come out of it?"

Davis smiled, "It can't hurt. Everybody's been treating him with kid gloves since it happened, and not being able to move, he hasn't had the opportunity to bump his head on anything."

Suddenly filled with anxiety, "So what the hell are we waiting for," Billy said. "Let's go slap the shit out of him!" and they jumped and darted from the cafeteria to the halls of Jeff's tomb room.

When they arrived, pumped with adrenalin, they burst into the room and flicked on the light. "Jeff?" Davis called out, then he saw Jeff's grotesquely distorted features, with eyes and lips stretched so far out of proportion they stayed ripped apart at the seams, trickling with streams of blood, seeping out to run down the sides of his face.

His teeth were exposed, and much more of his gums than they really cared to see. The inside tissue, *beneath* his eyelids, was peeled outward, dry and cracked and sore. Occasionally a tear would moisten them, but not often enough.

It was obvious his eyes hadn't been closed in awhile, and he'd been laying in the dark since he got there, so when Billy turned on the light, his pupils immediately dilated to pin points. A strained groan rose in his throat.

"Quick, Billy, shut those lights off," Davis ordered. Billy flicked 'em back off - instantly.

They both went to the bed and stood next to Jeff, "Jeff, my friend," Billy said, "I don't want you to take this personally, and I hope to God it works." Then he reached back and brought down the full force of a hard slap across his face, *Smack!*

"*Aaahhhoouch!*" Jeff released a cry and the flesh at the back of his head let loose like a snapped rubber band, shrinking the skin back to where it belonged. Davis and Billy heard the folds of dry skin around his eyes and mouth crinkle as they came back into position. All of Jeff's openings sang with oozing fluid. His eyes watered heavily while saliva overflowed at his lips, but it was all very welcomed to ease the pain. For three and a half days he'd felt like someone was trying to push his insides out through the top of his head.

He moaned a lot when his face made a brutal attempt at reconstruction. And except for the rips and tears, he started to look like himself again.

His eyes darted back and forth between the two friends standing on either side of him, watching with horror-stricken faces. Until, he found his voice (raspy as it was), "What the hell was that all about?" he asked.

Davis smiled at Billy, "See Billy, a good slap in the face and Jeff's back to his old self again." Then he turned to Jeff, "We gotta get you out of here."

Jeff still looked scared, "Why? What's the matter with me?"

"It's not just you. It's all of us," Billy told him.

"I think Krys has an idea of what to do about it. But we all need to get together and talk," Davis said.

Jeff looked surprised, then scared again, "Krys? ...Is she all right?"

Davis smiled, "All right? You should see her, my friend, she's never been better."

Chapter 12

By 6:00 Monday evening, the Doctors had given consent to release Jeff on his own recognizance. He doused his face with lotions and ointments to help heal the cracks and splits, then joined his parents for dinner to show them he was okay.

Janie flew in from Florida late Tuesday afternoon, and at 6:34 was greeted by Krys and Shawna at the airport. They were all excited about the reunion. Three life-long best friends together again.

On the drive back from the airport, stories were exchanged about their lives over the past few years; each ended with...*a melting.*

Davis, Jeff, and Billy arrived at Krys's house first and planted themselves on the front porch. Between Davis's battered head and Jeff's shattered face, they looked like they'd been in a fight. All three sat relatively quiet (still worn out from the weekend) and waited.

Finally, *the women* pulled into the driveway. The sun was still out and reflected blindingly from the roof of the car. Krys was the first to get out, but the driver side faced the neighbor's house and the glare of the sun prevented any decent view of her body; Jeff and Billy were still momentarily deprived vision of the recent changes.

The front passenger side opened and Janie stepped out. Davis's heart stopped, dropped, and broke for a minute, he hadn't seen her in months. And suddenly there she was, the woman he'd known since boyhood, the first woman he *Fell in Love* with, the woman he saw through thick and thin, who he'd broken up with and made up with ten times before finally asking her to marry him. The woman he lived with for five years and for five years tried to have children and couldn't. The woman who'd became bored with him and ripped his heart out by cheating with another man. *Yeah, that's her,* he thought. *Wish she didn't look so good.*

Jeff and Billy both took notice that Janie really *didn't* look too good. She looked a little haggard and worn out. Her make up was all in the right places and her hair was brushed, but she just didn't shine the way they remembered.

Janie looked at the three of them, then just at Davis. She could see the crease line between his eyebrows, the one he got when he wasn't too happy about something. She could see it from the car. She'd heard about 'the boating accident,' yet, despite the scrapes and bruises, she whispered softly to Krys, "I wish he didn't look so good."

Krys still had her sunglasses on, so Janie couldn't see, but sometimes 'concern' gave *her* the *same* crease. And right then she was thinking about that Shawna had been dating Davis for several weeks now, and *Janie didn't know that.* It was never mentioned on the drive from the airport, and, *has Shawna thought at all about the repercussions of this meeting?*

Then Shawna opened the back door and stepped out. Until that moment, Davis had been focused on Janie - suddenly, and without hesitation, his center of attention was diverted. With only a slight shift of his eyes his gaze zeroed in on Shawna.

Her hair was loose and blew gently in the breeze. Her smile was a perfect row of beautiful white pearls; caressed on either side by a soft dimple. Her green eyes glistened in the sun. She was just...so...beautiful, and she stared right back at him. Then she waved, "Hi boys."

Janie turned to see whatever it was that had pulled Davis away so hard and fast, but all she saw was...*Shawna?*

Then, as they joined together in the center of the yard - came the big highlight moment of the day. From the driver's side, Krys came into full view, and Jeff and Billy were watching, and, "Oh...My...God!" their voices rang in unison.

Watching their faces, realizing her breasts were about to become the center of attention (and loving every minute of it), *Stick them babies out,* she thought. And out they came. Then, with the added sway of her behind (which had always been a nice behind), she was suddenly not only sexy; she was Hot!

"Krystal!" Jeff exclaimed, "Davis said you were..." then he lost coherency, "...but I never thought...I mean...*Nice Tits!"* he sincerely meant it as a compliment. "I'm serious, Krys, really. Those are amazing tits." Suddenly Davis and Billy were howling wolf-calls. Tensions dropped and there was laughter. And except for Davis and Janie, everyone hugged each other.

Chapter 13

T hat night, the night of the first meeting - proved to be the beginning of something both miraculous and frightening. After a drink or two, and a little reminiscing (even Davis and Janie spoke some to each other), they all descended to the basement.

The furniture was pushed from the center of the room and a large bed comforter was spread out on the floor. Krys placed a candle in the center of it, lit the candle and turned off the other lights. Then they all sat cross-legged in a circle around the flame.

"What are we doing?" Shawna asked. It wasn't the first time she'd asked, but she wasn't getting an answer.

"Yes, Krys, exactly what *are* we doing?" Davis echoed.

Once they were adjusted to floor seating and got themselves comfortable, Krys looked at each of them individually, catching a brief eye-to-eye contact. Davis sat next to Shawna who sat next to Billy who was sitting next to Janie, then Jeff, and then Krys on around to Davis's other side.

"I believe..." she paused, gathering the right words to articulate her thought, "...we have acquired a kind of Supernatural Power. And I think I know how to tap into it."

All, except for Davis, lowered their heads in embarrassment for her. Janie actually became annoyed that she'd flown all the way there to hear that the alternative to her fear of dying was that she had a 'Supernatural Power.'

"Krys," Janie said, hoping her friend was going to *'get real'* real soon.

Krys had anticipated reluctance to her theory, and she saw the doubt on their faces, "Janie, please, give me some credit here." Then eyes rolled and she knew they thought she was full of shit. "Fine then," she said, "let me show you something that *is* real and *you* explain it."

She was wearing a large white, with light blue stripes, man's sleeveless casual shirt. It had belonged to an old boyfriend, but gotten left behind in the closet with a few other *old boyfriend souvenirs* she liked wearing around the house.

She reached into a breast pocket and pulled out a picture. "I'm sure you'll all remember this?" she grinned sarcastically and handed it to Jeff to pass around.

Jeff's eyes got big and a smile stretched across his face. It was one of the pictures Davis had taken *'that day'* out at the tree house - the day Krys and Bruce Edwards decided to *explore* each other. It was one where she was stomach down, palms to the floor, holding her head up and chest out, fully exposing the tiny mounds they all jokingly referred to as breasts.

Davis had taken the picture front on, so it was plain to see everything she had, and there just wasn't much there. "Remember that?" she asked flatly.

The guys nodded and smiled, the girls got hot and red, and the photo went around. "I thought you threw all those pictures away," Davis questioned, fiercely suppressing embarrassment.

Krys smiled, "Are you kidding? Those are some of the best pictures I ever took."

Unexpected snickers quickly rolled into laughter as Davis handed the picture back to her. Then she took another hesitant moment to look at each of them, searching for the trust and confidence of good friends. Until finally, she reached up and undid the top buttons on her shirt, "Well, my friends, *these* do not come from *those* without some kind of Supernatural Power," and she pulled the shirt open, causing the remaining buttons to slip from their holes.

As usual, she wore no brassiere, and her five closest friends stared with amazement at the full and exceptionally voluptuous bosom of their lifelong, *flat chested,* friend.

"They're beautiful." The statement came from Jeff, barely realizing that he'd said it out loud.

But they *were* beautiful, and as golden tan as the rest of her skin, not white like they'd been hiding in a bra their whole life. Krys looked at Jeff, "Touch them."

The depth of Krys's inhibition never ceased to amaze her friends, "Go on, Jeff, touch them, I want you to *know* that they're real."

He paused a moment and stared at them, *but only a moment*, and as he cupped his hands over her nipples, he felt not only the protruding nub in his palm, but the warmth of her flesh as well; they *were* real. He also felt his pants tightening. "Krys, this is amazing." He turned to his voyeuristic cohorts, "These are definitely, one hundred percent, give me an hour to stop this, Boobs," he told them.

Shawna and Janie were a little embarrassed, but they understood what she was trying to say. Then Janie asked, "So, how did this actually happen?"

As she explained, they were entranced by her story of candlelight and sizzling sweat and the mirror, right there in the basement, in the bedroom on the left, just her and *the power of concentration.* "I'm telling you we can manipulate this melting thing that's happening to us."

Then she realized she hadn't closed her shirt back yet, and Jeff was still ogling her. She smiled and brought both sides of the shirt together; making a minor adjustment that let one side momentarily slip away from her, Jeff, alone, got one last flash before buttoning up.

He knew she did it just for him, and suddenly, looking up into her eyes, his feelings took an emotional shift. There was a sense that perhaps they had always liked each other more than they ever admitted.

But, before there was time to question *Love or Lust,* Shawna redirected their attention, "So, what *is* this melting thing? And why is it happening to us?"

Davis looked at Jeff, "What did the Doctor say?"

Jeff lowered his eyes; self-conscious about the state of limbo he'd been in the past few days. "He said, everybody has a shit-load of brain cells in their head..."

Billy cut in, "The Doctor said *shit-load?*"

Ignoring him, Jeff went on, "...but most of them never get used. He said God gave us a gazillion of them, because he knew we'd destroy so many with all the stupid and abusive things we do to ourselves everyday.

The difference in *my* case is that, unlike the alcoholic whose brain cells are *killed* by alcohol, whatever is happening to me, the cells aren't dying. He said they're melting into a living fluid that's draining, in thin streams, to the center of my brain, where they're converging in a pool, forming one large cell in the middle of my head.

Billy's mouth dropped, "Are you serious?"

"That's what he said."

"Did he say what this could do to you?" Davis asked.

"Actually, he said he had never seen anything like it, and really had no idea what to expect. They want to keep me on observation for awhile."

The room was quiet. They were all scared and confused. Then Janie broke the silence, "So now were supposed to try and connect these two things? ...Jeff's brain and Krys's boobs?"

They looked around at each other, no one was prepared for the next level of thought process.

"Wow," Billy tried to make light, "Brains *and* boobs? Throw in some blonde hair and blue eyes and you've got the perfect woman." No one laughed. *Hey, Janie's got blonde hair and blue eyes,* he thought.

"When the melting begins," Krys said, "first you lose control of your muscles, you can't move. Then your face stretches all to hell...and your eyes get big..." she paused to think for a minute, "and...it's right about then that things start to get melty.

Like the whole world is made of ice cream and it's a really hot day. And your ice cream starts dripping, only...it doesn't drip off. It swirls around and around in one place, like...like a lava lamp continually running back into itself, forming and reforming the drips over and over." This description was met with unanimous agreement.

"But when it stops," she went on, "everything's normal again, nothing has changed, right?" They nodded. "So finally, I figured out that since the world is not melting, it had to be something in my head making it look that way, something all in my own mind. So, I started thinking, if my mind can just *do this to me* whenever it wants; stretch my skin and take control of my body, then why couldn't *I* take control and make it work *for me* instead of *against me*? And if it's going to change me, why not change me the way *I* want to change? That's when I started experimenting. Using the power of concentration beyond my own body, like on inanimate objects. And it worked, but it would end when I stopped concentrating. Then I discovered the crucially important ingredient."

She had their full attention.

"If you reform something and you *want* it to stay that way, you have to *will* it to be. You not only have to have the power and concentration, you have to have conviction and belief," she finished.

All eyes were on her, waiting for more. When there was no more, they sat back and took a deep breath. Krys looked at their distant and confused faces, "Do you want to try it?"

Heads whipped back and forth to see who would volunteer. Nobody did. Then Davis volunteered them all, "Ok," he said, "what do we do?"

"Davis, are you serious?" Janie snapped with reflex fear. "You really believe that all we have to do is just *want* something to be and *it will*?"

"It's not like the impossibility of trying to erase all the fuck-ups in a marriage, Janie," Davis bit back. "This is only *reshaping solid matter*." He felt his point was made. Janie was speechless. Everyone else tried to look away from the two and couldn't, anticipating the next verbal punch. But then it ended with a simple glare.

Krys felt a twinge of offense from both sides at the inference that her suggestion was ridiculously inconceivable, "I think you need to give it a chance, Janie, unless you've got a better explanation."

All eyes were on Janie, and she had no alternative. "Fine!" she said, "What the hell. Let's go fuck around with our brains and see what we come up with."

Billy smirked, trying to move things along, "Well, I'm glad to see were all in agreement."

"So..." Davis slowly looked away from Janie and back to Krys, repeating himself, "What do we do?"

"Yeah," Shawna jumped in, "like do we all hold hands or something?"

Krys smiled, "No, we don't have to hold hands. All you have to do is concentrate." Everyone but Janie seemed ready to try. "First, we need to find an object. Then we concentrate on trying to soften it and reshape it.

Around the room, they saw a television, a sofa, chairs, end tables, a phone, ...each other, and the one-foot-tall, three-inch-wide candle that burned right in front of them; and how hard could burning candle wax be to melt. "Well there's a baby step," Krys pointed out. They all looked and nodded with comfort that there was nothing to lose working on something that simple.

"Ok," she said, "everyone clear your head, stare at the candle - and focus." There were a few glances back and forth, no one sure if they could bring themselves to *believe* it would really work; *but then Krys's boobs did have to come from somewhere.* "All right," she said, "concentrate on melting out the middle of it, where it's not quite as warm."

It was only seconds before they conceded and gave in to it, seriously focusing and *trying* to make it work. Then the concentration became so thick you could cut it with a knife. All thought was on the center of the candle, and less than a minute later it was beading up with melty drops of wax. "Everyone see that?" Krys spoke in a low whisper.

The response was an astonished whisper back, "Yes." Their faces glowed from the flame dancing in their eyes, and the center of the candle was melting.

"Okay," Krys went on, "try to draw the wax to you. Pull it out like you're trying to pull a finger from it. Like making branches on a tree, stretch it out.

Their eyes gleamed intently as the concentration flowed from their minds, reaching out and pulling some of the candle back to them. It bubbled in a circle around the middle. The wax looked soft and oozy but stayed in place, it didn't run down the edge to the plate.

"This is fantastic, Krys!" Davis was in awe.

"No, Davis," she corrected, "this is good. My *boobs* are fantastic." There was a gentle round of laughter but their eyes never left the candle, except for the split second that Jeff and Krys glanced at each other. Suddenly the wax pulled out from all sides.

Their smiles suddenly turned to fascinated wonder, each watching their own little tree branch sprout. And when their concentration grew stronger, the branches grew bigger, eventually reaching a respectable size.

"Okay," Krys said, "now try to smooth it out. Stroke it with your mind as you would modeling-clay with your hands; try to get it as smooth as glass. I'd say, if you can do that, you probably have a good idea of how to manipulate control. Then start believing in the change and that it will stay the way you want it."

Their grins were big as they mentally fine-tuned the shape of the candle and smoothed it out. Davis was first to perfect his, it stretched about eight inches long and thin, and very smooth.

Krys had about seven inches, but thicker. Janie and the others all had similar variations of the same thing.

"All right," Krys said, "now believe and *want* it to stay there. Want it. Want it. Want it. Do you want it?" she cheered.

"Yes, we want it!" they chorused back.

"Ok, now...*Leave it!*" she ordered. "Look away from the candle." They all turned away and let out breath they didn't even know they'd been holding. "And...relax," she instructed. "Take a drink." They each snatched up their glass. "How do you feel?"

They looked curiously at each other with a half smile, as if coming out of a trance and having to get reacquainted with their surroundings.

Once full awareness set in, their smiles got bigger. Then Davis noticed Krys hadn't let up yet; she was still *into the candle*. "Krys?"

She stared hard while the others watched. Shawna looked at their creation and squealed with delight, "Our waxy branches are still there. We did it. We actually reshaped it."

"That's nothing," Krys announced. "Watch this." She widened her eyes, glaring at the candle, and like a flash of lightning, her one wax stem burst open with dozens of extensions. Spider-leg tree twigs all blooming from the main branch. Some were straight and some were twisted. One minute, nothing - the next: a whole damn tree.

And Krys fell backward laughing, "Was that great, or what?"

That was truly great," Jeff agreed. They all clinked glasses in a toast *'To Krystal and...Power Control!'*

Janie smiled, shaking her head, "Well, I don't understand it, but I guess it works." Krys flashed a smug grin. "But why?" Janie went on, "Why are we so special that this is happening to us? And what happens when *all* of our brain cells melt?"

Smiles began to fade.

"That's another thing," Jeff said, "The Doctor mentioned that the only time the cells were melting was during that...that stroke sucking coma thing I was in. He said when I came out of it the melting stopped, and that the cells would just live on in the pool they had formed.

So, they're not melting all the time. Only when your mind flips out and you become that ever-so-lovely wide-eyed creature of stretch and groan. He said, because we have so many cells, that comparatively speaking, I hadn't lost even a microscopic amount of enough to do me any harm.

"So," Janie repeated, "Why is this happening to us? Does anybody know?"

Billy looked at her, in her eyes, "I know," he said.

Davis hung his head, hoping Billy would say something, because he really didn't want to tell them what they were about to hear.

"What do you know?" Jeff asked.

"I know this isn't the first time it's happened to us," he said.

Jeff looked as though he were being accused of something, "I don't remember this happening before, and I'm sure I would, something like this.

Billy glared at him, "You don't?" There was a deathly silent pause. "You don't remember ten years ago when the six of us buried Jimmy Hagger, who, by the way, decided to come back to life last Christmas and kill my mom. You don't remember being down in that oozy pit of rats and snakes and toxic fumes? Shit! I can *still* smell the stench."

He stopped and looked at the horror on their faces; they remembered. "Remember when Krys fell over Jimmy's body? Remember how

Davis...stroked out and we had to slap him to get him out of it?" They remembered. "Remember, then it happened to each one of us?" They remembered.

"You think what happened ten years ago from breathing that toxic crap, is happening again?" Shawna blurted in a childish huff, then quickly reverted back to adult maturity, "So, this chemical contamination has been lying dormant in our systems for ten years and is now regenerating?"

Good answer, they thought, it was the most logical conclusion they could have come to.

Krys was grinning, "I wonder if the more times you stroke out and the bigger the pool gets, the more power you have."

They all looked at her like she was the alien in the crowd.

"I've stroked out four times," she said, amused. "Anyone want to arm wrestle?"

The joke broke the tension, they laughed. Then the realms of possibilities began to flow. Each of them was throwing out ideas on where this could take them. They could be famous, they could be rich, they could *save* the world, they could *destroy* the world. "Let's reshape something else," Davis said, "something bigger."

"I've got an idea," Shawna proposed, "let's go out back and see if we can turn the pool into a giant Hot Tub. We can concentrate on heating and bubbling the water." This was the suggestion of the decade.

"What do we use for swimsuits?" Janie asked.

"We can just wear our underwear," Billy said.

"I get the feeling Krys ain't wearing any," Jeff mused.

Then Krys hopped up, "Oh come on, it's never stopped me before," and she headed eagerly up the basement steps - the others followed, Shawna blew out the candle.

It was an above ground pool, four and a half feet deep, thirty feet long, fifteen feet wide, lined in basic blue and surrounded all the way around by pine wood decking. They climbed the steps to the pool's edge and stripped down.

Shawna was wearing, of all things, a matching pastel pink brassiere and lace-trimmed panties. The guys found, almost immediately, that if they didn't keep a good strong hold on some pure and clean thoughts, they could quickly develop a stiffening problem, in a situation they most likely couldn't do anything about.

Davis wore the standard white BVD's. Billy wore red bikini briefs, which pretty much displayed the man thing at rest. Jeff was a die-hard boxer wearer. He'd worn them all his life and had no intention of converting.

Janie had on the standard white cotton bra and panties, no lace trim, no silk, no pretty flowers. And Krys? Krys was just bare-ass naked and loving it. "Let's get in," she giggled. But the water was cooler than she thought, and instead, they found themselves sitting around the edge dangling their feet.

Krys stared into the water. There was a light submerged at the far end, spreading a field of clear blue before them. She focused on the center of the pool, "Jeff?" He looked up, she pointed to the far end, where the light was, "Concentrate there, warm it up. Davis, you do the right side, Janie, you do the left. Billy, you do all this right here in front of us." Then she stopped, momentarily lost in concentration.

"What about me?" Shawna asked.

"Shawna," Krys paused, "you focus here on the middle with me and let's warm this baby up." Shawna smiled and threw out a heavy burst of concentration.

It was late, the sky was black, and the only light coming from Krys Sanders' house was the glow of a backyard swimming pool, a glow that was about to get intense.

"Can you see it?" Krys asked. There was a light steamy spray rising six inches above the water.

"I see it," Billy said.

"Yeah, yeah, me too," the others chimed in.

"Let's get in," Krys instructed, and jumped in.

Each one lowered them self into the water, "It's warm, it's warmer than warm, it's close to hot. This is so cool!" Jeff said.

"Ok," said Davis, "it feels good like this, so we need to want it to stay this way and then...leave it. Like...*Now!*"

Krys dropped her concentration and turned to him, "No problem. How you feeling?" she asked with a smile. "Care to go for a swim?"

They all dropped their mental focus and let the water caress them as they swam through the steamy 100 degrees they'd created. It would turn their muscles to mush, but it felt great.

Somewhere in the next half hour, Jeff and Krys found themselves alone together in the dark end, while the others engaged in conversation, congregating around the light.

Through the steam, Jeff looked into her eyes and asked, "Why me?"

Krys's mouth turned up at the corners, "Why you, what?" she smirked. The water bubbled thick and hot over her reddening breasts.

He looked in her eyes, "Why did you choose me...to feel you?" His body was almost against hers; the water was hot between them.

Krys was feeling very attracted, her smile was gently fading to lustful hunger, "Because," she said, "you've always wanted to."

His neck stung from the hot spray spatters of the pool, his heart was beating hard against his chest, sweat rolled from his temples and his eyes locked on hers.

"And maybe I've always wanted you to," she whispered.

That was all he needed to hear, Jeff slid up next to her and took her in his arms. The fierce eye contact held for about ten seconds, then their mouths took over. They kissed as though neither of them had been kissed in years. Their lips slid together and their tongues licked and tasted, if two people could eat each other up with passion, Jeff and Krys would never need food again.

The water bubbled viciously around them, their blood sizzled as they clung to each other in a desperate longing to press their naked flesh into each other. Sweat rolled down their faces in streams. Jeff felt the crevice between her thighs with his growing erection and it throbbed hot and hard, "Oh Krys, you feel sooo good."

She bared her neck to him and let him bite and suck on her as she brought her burning legs up and wrapped them around him, "Oh Jeff, I'm so hot," she gasped a deep breath, marveling at the amount of sweat running through her hair.

"Krys, I want you. I want to be inside of you," his mouth slid up her neck to her cheek.

She bit his earlobe and whispered, "Make love to me, Jeff. Put yourself inside me."

At that moment, his penis was like stone, he would have gladly picked her up out of the water and taken her right there on the deck. But suddenly, he was light headed, and losing his balance.

"Jeff?"

Heavy bags of moisture hung from his eyes. Blotches of gray were spotting his vision. Then Krys started losing it.

"Jeff, my temples are pounding. I...I can't think. I don't feel right...like I miight paasssout." They both became nauseous.

"Krys, I'm burning up, I'm getting sick," he was dehydrating and slurring through dry lips. Then he pulled back from her, his face glowed red, "I caan't breathe," he gasped.

Her eyes drifted and closed, her face was luminously red.

"Jehhfff," she pushed the words out over a dry tongue. "Isss too hot, I'mm boilling, wee havvvetooo ghetouut." The water around them boiled, it snapped and hissed. Jeff tried to move, but it was like walking in fire, the pain made him scream, "Aaaauugghh, Davisss, help us!!"

The four at the other end looked up, startled, they had apparently forgotten all about the two deserters. Then they saw the water glowing bright white with bubbles, engulfing two red burning bodies.

Jeff was into his second cry for help by the time they hit the deck and ran. When they got there, boiling water was shooting small fountains into the air. Jeff and Krys were fire red and looked ready to explode. Their faces were scrunched, their eyes clamped shut, their jaws locked around grinding teeth.

Fortunately, they were next to the edge where Davis and Billy could lift them out. Unfortunately, Davis and Billy were forced to take the splatters of boiling water on their face and arms. "Aahh shit!" they yelled, and yanked the two bodies up. Janie and Shawna stood back, out of the way.

The pool gave one last fountain shot of water as their feet lifted out, the shot stretched ten feet into the air then dropped back to bubbles that would eventually simmer and fade.

Jeff and Krys lay on the deck, semi-conscious, the others were afraid to touch them; afraid their skin would be too sensitive. They figured it would be best for them to just lay there and cool off.

Finally, "Water," Jeff said. "Get us some water."

Shawna ran back to the other end of the pool and grabbed two half cans of beer.

"Jeff, are you ok?" Davis asked.

Shawna came back and gave them the drinks.

Jeff tried to pour enough in his mouth to be able to talk, "Yeah," he said, "I'm ok, how's Krys?"

Spilling her drink over her chin and down her neck, she grunted, "I'm all right."

With eyes closed, Jeff smiled, "Jeez you're hot, Krys."

It hurt, but she had to laugh, they all laughed. Davis looked at Krys, "So, I'm guessing, even *indirect* concentration changes things?"

She looked up over her head at him, "That's a very real possibility, Davis. Very real."

Eventually, Jeff and Krys were breathing something close to normal again. Jeff propped up on one arm and looked at her, flat on her back, taking deep breaths. He watched her beautiful new breasts move up and down with her lung action. Janie and Shawna noticed Davis and Billy watching them as well.

Now, the girls were not stupid, they knew that breasts were always a point of men's interest, but they didn't need a nice new, extra large pair, staring them right in the face as a reminder.

"Krys?" Janie finally spoke up, "If you're ok, why don't we get dried off and go inside?"

Krys nodded agreement, "Yeah, sounds good," she pulled herself up.

"Well, I'm going to sit out here and finish my drink," Davis told them.

"Yeah, me too," Billy said.

So the women ended up inside, while the men stayed at the pool.

"I don't know, Davis," Billy said, watching Janie's behind wiggle away, "I still think Janie's got the best ass of the three."

Davis scowled, "Then go for it, Billy. She fucked up. I don't want her. You can have her."

Billy and Jeff looked at each other with raised eyebrows, "Jeez, Davis, so she cheated on you *one* time, you guys have been together...like...forever, can't you just get over it?" Jeff asked.

Davis was suddenly very serious and a little embarrassed, "It wasn't just once," he said. "After I caught her *red-handed*, I moved out to a hotel for awhile. She tried for about a week to apologize, but when I called her at the house, guess who answered the phone, more than once. When I confronted her with it, she was forced to admit she was having an affair with him. And the kick in the ass is that *he* was married too. So, Fuck her, Billy. She's all yours."

Billy and Jeff looked away and drank, "Sorry, man, we didn't know," Jeff told him.

But Billy kept on, "Is she still seeing him?"

Davis half smiled, "Nope. *I* never said a word, but somehow his wife found out. Then all hell broke loose and he went crawling back begging her to forgive him, which she did. But he had to give up Janie in the process; he even ended up firing her. So now she's on her own and I couldn't care less.

I got a feeling we'll have to sell the house, cause I'm sure the hell not going to pay for a place I'm not living in, and I know *she* can't afford it...we'll probably both end up right back here where we started."

It was quiet. "How's things with you and Shawna?" Jeff asked.

Davis looked at him and grinned, "About the same as they are with you and Krys...Hot!"

The men drank and laughed.

Inside, the girls were in the living room, wrapped in towels. They'd opened a bottle of wine and, without glasses, passed it back and forth between themselves.

"Janie, I have something to tell you," Shawna said. Krys gulped on the bottle, she knew what was coming and wasn't sure she wanted to be sober for it.

"What is it?" Janie asked.

Shawna hesitated, obviously very uncomfortable, "Well," she began, "I really don't know exactly how it started, but since almost three weeks ago...I...well...it's just that..."

Janie interrupted, "What, Shawna? You can tell me. We're best friends, remember?"

Shawna rolled her eyes as the fangs of guilt gnawed at her, "Well...I'm sorry, Janie, but...Davis and I have been seeing each other. We've been dating."

The room went silent.

With the bottle stuck in her mouth, Krys's eyes darted back and forth between Janie and Shawna.

Shawna shrank back a little, almost cringing, waiting for the eruption.

Janie stared at her...speechless. Her eyes welled slowly with tears, tears that refused to let loose and run. She reached over and pulled the bottle away from Krys, downing the rest of it. Then, wiping her eyes, with a quivering voice, she said, "I'm glad, Shawna. He's a good person and you're a good person, I hope things go well for you both." Then she got up and went to the kitchen, "Krys, you got anything stronger than wine?"

Krys's mouth dropped and she and Shawna stared at each other, "Uh...yeah, sure, top cabinet on the left." There was a long moment of silence, then, "Janie? You ok?"

She walked back in with a tall mixed drink in one hand, and a cigarette in the other. She took up smoking when Davis left. "I'm fine," she whispered. Then she cried.

The girls came together in a hug, "I'm sorry," Shawna told her.

There was a sob and some sniffles, "It's ok, Shawny," her voice was wet and shaky, "I guess I totally screwed up. I'd take it all back if I could, you know, but it's too late, he doesn't want to have anything to do with me, and I guess I don't blame him." Then, more heavy sobbing into Krys's arms.

Eventually, she pulled back and wiped her face, "I'm ok." They all sat back down and Janie spilled a few guts, "I was in such a rut. I wasn't getting pregnant and I just got bored," she confessed. "Then I got stupid and went looking for some excitement. I had no idea it would turn out like this."

Krys and Shawna were both teary eyed. "I...I don't know what to say," Shawna sniffed, deeply sorrowful.

"Well, I guess I'm learning to deal with it," Janie admitted, "but it would help if I could get a life for myself, finding a decent job would even be nice." She looked at Shawna, "How about you? How were you after Kyle?"

It was something Shawna didn't particularly enjoy discussing, but she knew Janie could use the relativity.

When Shawna was twenty, she'd met a man she thought was her 'Prince Charming,' but after only a year and a half of marriage, she found out he was, what she called, a backdoor bisexual. And like Davis catching Janie, she caught Kyle, only he was with another man. Soon after, they were divorced.

"Screwed up," she said. "After a month of being a walking Zombie, reality set in. Things I never really thought about before suddenly began to make sense. Like, why he had those stupid muscle men magazines around, and why he never talked about the things he did when he was out with his friend Scott. It hurt. It hurt a lot. But I got over the little creep." They all smiled.

"You know, Janie, if you want to get away from...your life for awhile," Krys said, "we'd love to have you come back home. You could live here with Shawna and me while you get things together. I mean you don't sound like you really have anything keeping you in Florida, and part time at a furniture store isn't like you'd be giving up much."

Janie knew she was sincere. "Really, Janie," Shawna said, "it would be great, it would be like old times." Then Shawna shadowed over with a dark cloud and said, "I will probably continue to see Davis though, and that could be a problem. But I truly would love to have you back in Pleasure View with us.

"Janie looked in her eyes and saw the love of an old friend, she hesitated...then, "Are you sure it would be all right?"

Krys grinned and nodded and leaned over for another hug. Then a big three way hug, "Welcome home."

Chapter 14

Friday evening, *The Fantastic Six* reunited for more experimentation. This time, however, they were attempting a much bigger challenge.

They met at the tree house. None of them had been there in at least five years, and they were not surprised to find it very much dilapidated.

The wood was rotted, the sofa had been soaked through by many rainstorms, dried and re-soaked, and was rotted too. Most of the nails used to attach the steps leading up the tree house had rusted away and boards had fallen to the ground. Any boards remaining looked *ready* to fall.

The flooring sagged in all three of the rooms. The plank crossings from one tree to another were only partially there. And the roofs had all but caved in.

On the ground below, the six original owners of the *Robinson Crusoe* triplex stared up despondently. "Jeez, it sure went to hell didn't it," Billy sighed. Then they saw rats crawl and scurry around the edges and slip inside.

Krys was the only one who didn't appear discouraged, "Well gang, this looks like a challenge. Let's see what we can make of it."

Jeff turned to her, "You think we can rebuild this mess just by mental power?"

She smiled, "Don't you?"

He looked back at the ruined tree house, "It's gonna be hard."

"Ooohhhh," she moaned with a smirk, "it's sooo good when *it's hard.*"

Everyone else rolled their eyes and chose to overlook the obvious double entendre. Eventually, they all agreed to give it their best shot.

"Only, let's make it better than before," Krys said. "Let's be creative."

They walked in and around the trees looking up at the mess above them. "First of all," Shawna said, staring at the trunk of the tree and remaining ladder steps, "it needs a stairway."

And as she gazed at the top board, it began to soften. The rotty edges began to smooth over; cracks filled in as the wood came together. In minutes, it looked as melty as hot rubber, and in a seamless merge; the step actually became part of the body of the tree. You literally couldn't tell where the board ended and the tree began. Then, she pulled and brought it out toward her, changing the trunk and what was formerly a thin flat piece of wood, into the shape of a full and solid block step.

The others watched until they figured out what she was going for, then they joined in and helped create the rest of the steps.

Like statues, they were unmoving, engrossed in a metamorphic reshaping. With the stretching of the tree, they formed a second step, then a third, then forth...and so on.

"Let's spiral it," Shawna said, and suddenly, the steps were curving and winding around the tree, all the way down.

The gang slowly moved around with the steps, never letting up on it. Until, a most elaborate staircase was formed. When the last step met the ground and the job was complete, they closed their eyes and took a deep breath, then stepped back, and on Shawna's go ahead, opened their eyes and looked at it.

There before them, was a beautiful spiral staircase; each step was smooth and the same size as the step before it, a perfect two feet wide, one foot deep, eight inches high, and encircling the entire tree.

The outside wall of the trunk, however, was rough bark. This apparently dismayed Shawna, until she had another idea. "Hey, watch this," she told them and went back into focus.

The entire staircase suddenly began beading up and filming over with a glaze, like it had a coating of varnish making it all shiny. And once the gloss was high enough, and smoothed to her satisfaction, gleaming from the reflection of the sun, she stopped. "Now that's pretty!" she exclaimed.

They were all impressed, and a bit amazed.

"Now," Davis said, "let's fix those floorboards." And *the melting* started again.

Davis and Shawna took the main room floor, Billy and Jeff took the room behind it, Janie and Krys took the one on the right. Standing beneath their work areas, they focused intently on the conditioning of the wood and brought it together.

This was easier than the stairway; mostly because there was less shaping to do, they only had to solidify the wood, which, with the speed they were developing only took a few minutes. And when they finished, they went ahead and put Shawna's special gloss on it.

"This is awesome!" Billy exclaimed. "The tree house never looked so good," and he led the way up the *new* steps to the main room.

Inside, they could see how really grungy their old furniture had gotten, and there were rats crawling over everything.

"Aahh, I hate rats," Shawna snarled with disgust.

Davis and Jeff looked at each other and grinned, "Let's melt 'em," Jeff said. And the two began rat zapping around the room, eventually, Billy joined in.

When their eyes made contact with one of the furry little rodents, it immediately slowed down, seconds later, stopped. The rat would look up, clawing at its throat, trying to breathe. Suddenly its arms would drop and its head would fold, and it rolled into a ball of liquid. There would be one or two shrieking squeals before turning to something thick and muddy, then eyes popped and guts oozed, and the thing just dissolved to a gooey lump on the floor.

"Uh...terrific, boys," Janie said. "Now, what are we supposed to do with the puddles?"

They hadn't thought of that.

"Watch," Krys told them, and she glared at the spots on the floor. Seconds later, she had them running in a flow over the floorboards, connecting to each other and forming a small river of red and brown that streamed out the door and drained to the ground below. She continued the run until all puddles were gone. Then she relaxed. "Any other questions?"

"Well, Shee-it! I guess not," Janie laughed.

"Let's fix the walkways," Billy said, "so we can get across to work on the other rooms."

No sooner said, than done. They gathered at the entrance and turned on their brains.

The slat boards that had been held together by rope were now fusing to each other to become a single strip of wood. What used to be a rickety, swaying, walkway that would bend with every step taken was now one solid ramp. No longer just tied to the rooms, it had become an extension of the floor. "This is too good," Billy said.

"So," Krys started, "do we do this boy/girl or what?"

Jeff leered at her, "Sounds good to me," he said and grabbed her by the hand, running her out and over to the room on the right.

Billy shrugged, "I guess it's you and me, Janie, ok?"

She looked at Davis for a half a second, then turned to Billy, and with a deliberate lick of her tongue across her top lip, said "It's more than *ok*, Billy, let's go," and off they went to the other room.

Davis turned to Shawna, "Did you see that?"

She looked him in the eyes and smiled, "See what?"

He smiled back, "...Absolutely nothing." Then he reached around her, grabbed her ass with both hands and planted his mouth on her neck for a succulent Vampire kiss.

Over his shoulder, Shawna saw the sofa, it was ruined, "Let's fix that first," she said.

He turned and looked at it, a sudden flash of Janie, naked and on top of him shot down through his mind and thumped him in the chest. "...Yeah," he agreed, "time for something new," and then he turned back to her, entranced by her strawberry blonde waves and beautiful dimpled smile. The thump was forgotten. "Shawna, no pun intended, but when you smile, I swear, you make me melt. I could be falling very hard for you, you know."

She too faded to a longing smile, her eyes searched his, "I hope so, Davis. I know I am for you." They kissed with tender passion.

Eventually, Shawna pulled back, "Uh...can we work on the sofa now?"

"I think I'd rather work on you," he told her, then after another quick kiss, they went to the sofa.

If Shawna and Davis had been watching they would have seen tangible walls form on the other two rooms; the wood liquefying and sealing together, turning solid and finishing off with the glaze. A moment later, the roof was moving.

In working the sofa, they found they were able to reconstruct textures. They could take the material currently existing and, first; turn it to liquid, then solidify it in whatever other material they chose. By the time it was finished, they had virtually morphed it into a day bed. Then they continued making everything (sofa, chairs, table, etc.) look brand new.

Finally, as the others had done, Davis and Shawna rebuilt the walls and roof. And while admiring their handy work, they waited for the others to return. And waited...(played some grab ass) ...and waited. However, they were all playing grab ass. Even Billy and Janie.

"You know, Janie," Billy started, "I'm sure Davis has probably told you. Since way back, you know, when we were in High School, ...I always liked you best." he paused, searching her eyes for response; mostly they were filled with curiosity. "I used to get so jealous of him having you. I used to want you so much for myself." Suddenly, he realized he was confessing teenage fantasies directly to the object of his desire, and he became embarrassed.

As red heat crossed his face, he hung his head slightly, "Jeez, I'm sorry, I guess I shouldn't be telling you this. I mean, I know you probably want for you and him to get back together," he mumbled.

She looked at the shy man in front of her, "Billy," she said, lifting his head gently with soft fingers. "There is nowhere I'd rather be right now than right here with you."

He looked nervously into her eyes, trying to see through, into her mind, to see if she was just indulging a fantasy, or if perhaps she might really care for him.

"Billy, I've always liked you...a lot," she said with a smile, "and I've always thought you were *very* sexy."

He smiled (kept his red glow), "You did?"

"I *do*," she said, and took him in her arms, she put her mouth gently on his, soft and wet, and their lips slid hungrily together.

Eventually, the voice of interruption had to happen. "Hey, come and look!" Davis yelled out the window.

But they all wanted to show off. "No, you come and look?" Jeff shouted back. Suddenly, everyone was breaking away and running from room to room to see what the others had done.

Jeff and Krys had created a beautiful spider leg, Victorian style mahogany table and four matching chairs. The cushions in the center of each chair were covered with a fuchsia velvet material, while the wood reflected an intensely high gloss finish.

They fixed up a coffee table in the same style and worked in some small intricate detailing. They formed a snooty, uncomfortable looking love seat from the same era; the cushions very much resembled the ones on the chairs.

The walls of the room were done in high gloss mahogany, with thin intricate carvings in the border lining the edge around the ceiling.

Billy looked at the love seat and was amazed. "Did you make that from that beat up wooden crate we had?"

Krys and Jeff nodded proudly, "Yep!"

The entire room was very classy, very beautiful. They all stared a moment longer, in awe of the power, then went to see what the others had done.

After shining up their own new walls, Billy and Janie had shape-shifted a few old flattened beanbag chairs and a couple of tree stumps. The results were four large, round, thickly padded and cushy mushroom stools.

Next to the window was a stylish liquor cabinet...no liquor, but the bar looked damn good. And in the center of the room was a large oval Oriental rug.

"Jeez, Billy," Davis said, "there was basically nothing in here, how'd you do all that?"

Billy smiled, "We had to melt everything pretty much all the way down to liquid, then just kind of build it back up. Janie insisted on the bar." They laughed. "And wants it stocked before Sunday." They laughed some more and departed for the last room.

In the main room, Davis and Shawna had reshaped the table, making it round. It was butcher block with a shine. The chairs were butcher block too, but with cushions. The sofa/bed was bigger and softer than anything any of them ever remembered sleeping on. And where once was two wooden stick chairs, there were now two heavily padded leather recliners. And, as with the others, all walls were new and reflected a thick coat of varnish.

"Are we good or what!" Jeff stated.

They gazed silently around the room, taking it all in, and looking out the window to the other rooms. They smiled with pride. Eventually, they each took the nearest seat and flopped.

A few minutes later, Krys got up and went to the backpack she'd brought, "Well, there's not enough to stock up Janie's liquor cabinet," she said, "but I think it's time to celebrate." And with both arms in the bag, she pulled out two large bottles of *'J Roget American Spumante'* sparkling wine, "Party time!" She handed the bottles out, one for Davis to open, one for Billy, and then she went and sat next to Jeff.

A unanimous cheer followed by applause rang out for Krys, then cork popping and the toasting of each other on a job well done. And the bottles went 'round.

The following two weeks were filled with various smaller experiments, some as a group, some individually. The best ones were as couples, privately. With the power of control at their fingertips, there was no end to what they could do.

And except for Krys, they were each forced to experience another one or two, *out of control,* melting sessions. Their brains went into stroke drive, leaving them unable to move or talk. Their bodies became like thick stretching rubber.

But, a simple slap in the face brought them back and their power would be even greater, quicker, easier, and more precise than before.

Each of them pondered the notion, however, that supernatural gifts were usually only given with a price, or at the very least...a purpose.

THE
MELTDOWN

Chapter 1

Xanorse Chemicals Inc.

Ross Marxman: President.
Xanorse Chemicals Inc.
669 Lakeside Hwy.
Pleasure View, Kentucky
40117

Dear Mr. Hagger,

As the new President of Xanorse Chemicals, I wish to extend my apologies for not contacting you sooner regarding the purchase of the property on which you now reside.

However, with the brutal murders of so many of the company's executives this past winter, I'm sure you understand our recent turmoil, and the condition of certain projects having been placed on hold until proper administrative arrangements could be made.

Nevertheless, it has come to my attention, in reviewing our records concerning the property in question, that you were to have vacated the premises by this past December. And as such, we must, at present, insist that you comply with the legislated property appropriation no later than Friday, May 25th.

If you have not yet established a new residency, Xanorse Chemicals Human Resources Department will extend courtesies in the placement of your family with one of the local housing projects, at our expense, for thirty days.

We sincerely regret the inconvenience this may have caused. However, the situation is now urgent and must be resolved. Thank you for your cooperation.

Sincerely,

Ross Marxman

Ross Marxman: President,
Xanorse Chemicals Inc.

B ecky lowered the letter and stared back at the gruesome faces of her dead relatives. They had all gathered at the shack beyond the pasture and circled around a blazing bonfire.

They'd been telling old family stories and reminiscing for an hour before Bobby decided to reveal the letter and let Becky read it out loud.

"I can't believe they still think they're gonna come out here and throw us off our own land?" Jimmy stood, fury rising in his throat, "I guess they're just not getting the message. I guess we're gonna have to take care of them once and for all."

Everyone grunted agreement. Grandma Trudy came just short of making a speech, "They've destroyed the air, they've destroyed the land, and now they're trying to destroy our family. It's time for that damn chemycal company to come to an end."

The entire family cheered, Jimmy stood next to her, "I say we kill *everyone* who works there, and show them what real 'turmoil' is all about." The cheers became roars.

The fire flickered and glowed, highlighting deep-socket eyes and hollow noses. The gray and yellow of teeth and exposed jawbones lit up evil and slimy. Thick black-red blood pulsed hard, spurting through rotted openings. Lungs gurgled and overflowed with something thick and green when they laughed.

"Let's kill them all!" Jimmy shouted. Cheers rang through the trees and echoed into the black night.

Chapter 2

Monday, May 21st, began as regular a day as any Monday had for the past four months. Ross Marxman was always the first to arrive, always very early, and always followed by the new Vice President, Jerry Hammer.

Other executives that fell in with the early bird crowd were, Stephanie Newkirk (Director of Marketing), Josh Matthews (the new Head of Personnel), and Mark White (Chief of Quality Control); this was the 6:00 a.m. group.

Other administrative personnel began showing up between 6:30 and 7:00, including secretaries, which was what Shawna Taylor was to Mark White. As for the hundreds of working class peons, without whom the company would cease to exist, they didn't have to be at their stations until 7:30 when the morning whistle blew.

From 6:00 to 11:30 in the a.m., there seemed to be absolutely nothing unusual about the day, it was just another Monday. Then, at 11:40, an odd looking man with long black stringy hair, a scraggly beard, an old worn hat, old holey boots, overalls and in desperate need of a breath mint, showed up toting a long shiny double barreled shotgun.

He came out of nowhere, just turned the corner of the building and found himself at the employees' entrance, which was propped open while Security sat just inside at the monitors, enjoying the spring breeze.

367

The odd man stepped into the doorway and cocked the rifle, *Click!*

The Security Guard looked over, stunned and confused by the appearance of the stranger with a gun in his hands, "Can I help you?" he asked, standing quickly, letting his hand automatically fall to the butt of his own pistol.

The man with the long black hair looked the Guard in the eyes and smiled, "I don't think so," he said, flashing black gaps where teeth should be. "My name's Bobby Hagger, and I think I'll just help myself, thanks." Then he raised the gun point blank to the man's head.

The Guard panicked and tried jerking his revolver up in time to defend himself. *NOOO!* he almost had time to scream. But then the blast delivered an explosive little bombshell, and took his head clean off.

His brains plastered the wall behind him and only ribbons of cheek flesh were left stringing out from his neck. Blood sprayed everything in the room as his body banged spastically from side to side before throwing itself to the ground to jut around in a circle, until it realized it was dead, then decided to thump and twitch a few times before laying still.

"Ok," Bobby called from the doorway, "all's clear." He stepped back outside and looked off to the edge of the building to wave the family on in and do their worst.

Trudy and Jimmy led the pack, they marched through the first door, then Jimmy melted a large opening through the second. The whole family came for the fall of The Xanorse Empire; Moms, Dads, Brothers, Sisters, Aunts, Uncles, Nieces, Nephews and Cousins, reshaping and melting everything they could get their hands on.

Once inside, they took the metal stairway down to the main floor of operations. It wasn't long after before various machine operators noticed the offensive presence of intruders. One man rubbed his eyes, not believing what he was seeing. He'd been controlling the flow shaft that filled the concentrate vats with a steamy purple acid, when Charles Hagger limped up to him.

First, the man noticed the air around him turning from a mild sulfuric odor, to a putrid stench, and suddenly Charles was there in his face screaming at him, "Ya done messed with the wrong folks, mother fucker! Now it's time to die."

Eventually, his breath would have killed the man anyway, but Charles's fleshless bony hand shot out and grabbed him by the chest hairs beneath his shirt and oozed into his skin. The man was too shocked to move, then the pain of his chest melting shot through him and he screeched.

Blood gurgled up in his throat as Charles wrapped his fingers around the man's heart and yanked. The heart, of course, melted half gone before it was removed, it dripped down the outside of his shirt, and then he dropped dead to the ground.

"There's *one* heartless sumbitch out of the way," Charles laughed at his own pun, others chuckled low and raspy, then they spread out in different directions.

The building flourished with rows of large concentrate and mixing vats, big and round and metal, you had to go completely around one to see what was on the other side of it. There were dozens of scaffoldings and steel grate stairways that led to the various levels of processing. On the second floor were individual research labs, each with a large bay window.

The consistent operation of machinery; monstrous dryers, dehydrators, mixers, and processors, created a head throbbing noise of mechanical rock and roll; something as futile as a scream would not be heard.

Earl and Trudy rounded a corner together and came face to face with three men on their way from one station to another. They wore the standard employees white coveralls and red helmet (emblazoned with the Xanorse logo; a round sticker, tropic water blue with fizzy bubbles and a large solid red X in the center of it. The same logo was on the pocket of the coveralls), a pair of white rubber boots and white rubber gloves, protection requirements against chemical contact, and goggles.

"Evenin, fellers," Earl said and reached out taking one of the men by the hand, just a friendly shake...that cut through the meat to the bone, and dripped off at the wrist. The co-workers watched in horror as the man jerked around like an electroshock patient. Then Earl grabbed him further up on the arm and tore it off.

Trudy smiled a frightful tooth rot grin at one of the others, and said, "Give us a kiss, boy?" She clutched him on both sides of his head and pulled his face into hers, mashing their lips together.

At first the man was too shocked to react, and by the time he figured out what was happening, she was already *into* him and he was already *gone*. Her head had became one with his, she melted straight into his brain. Eventually, there was nothing left to hold on to and she grabbed his shoulders with a slight squeeze, his chest caved in. The man died dripping over himself, right down to the floor.

Earl looked at her, "Jeez, Trudy, let the man catch his breath, will ya."

She let go and pulled back, "Sorry...got carried away."

The third man suddenly regained motor reflexes and made no hesitation; busting ass to get far far away, down the hall. He screamed insanely, stopping only once to puke, then stumble around a corner.

Jimmy and some others climbed a set of steps, they got a little melty soft, but they were steel, and as long as nobody lingered too long on any one of them, they held out.

The stairway they were on wound around one of the circular mixing Vats, and led to a concrete walkway that crossed over and then went down a hallway. Once they were on top, they could slow down, concrete seem to melt slower and to a lesser degree than anything else...except dirt.

Jimmy stood over the Vat, he wiped at the endlessly rejuvenating oil that oozed from his body, and flung handfuls of it onto the huge cover of the container. It burned through; smoky little holes released toxic vapors from inside.

The family members with him watched and waited for direction. When Jimmy felt there were enough holes, he sneered, "Tip it over."

The Vat sat in a huge steel stirrup, held up by metal posts protruding from round securing cups on either side of it. The posts ran into the Vat through holes sealed with rubber stripping. This would allow the Vat to rotate from top to bottom.

The family reached out and rocked it back and forth, harder and harder, sloshing spills of hydrochloric acid and scorching the floor.

Two Vat operators, at their workstations, were caught off guard by the spilling acid.

When they were splashed and burned on the back of their necks, their screams disappeared in the jungle of mechanical noises. And when they whipped around to look up at the rocking Vat, they saw Jimmy and company, *"Holy Shit!"* cried one, and turned and ran. The other froze in place just a moment too long, the Vat flipped.

The acid poured over the man, completely. The sound that ripped from his throat was bloodcurdling but short, it gurgled out as he burned away.

The man who ran, was followed by a flood of acid racing across the floor at him, *"Help! Help!"* he cried. Other operators working diligently at their posts, turned to see what the commotion was; and without warning were taken themselves by the consuming flood. They didn't even hear *what* he was screaming about before the waves of death were upon them.

Jimmy stood at the center of the walkway and laughed, he watched the chain reaction of acid burning the base supports of *another* Vat, causing *it* to fall - crashing, splitting open and spewing contents of Sodium Metal. That Vat fell into another, which fell into another, each breaking open, until the entire floor in that section of the building was a pool of acid.

Suddenly, alarms were going off everywhere, the whole building rang with an ear piercing *'BUZZ! BUZZ! BUZZ!'*

"What in the hell is going on out there?" Ross Marxman pounded his desk and sprang from his seat. He turned and looked out through a two-way mirror, connected to his back wall, overlooking the mixing and drying stations, "Jesus Christ!" His mouth dropped, seeing his employees dissolving in the steamy pool. Then he heard the evacuation call over the intercom.

"This is an emergency, please evacuate all sections of the building in an orderly fashion. Repeat - This is not a test. This is an emergency, please evacuate!"

Ross turned to leave his office, when he found himself face to face with something dark and hellish. Earl's brother, Don, and daughter, Chrissy, stood with gaping flesh and squishy eyeballs, right in front of him...smiling.

"Afternoon, Boss-man," Don said.

Chrissy smiled, "Time to die!"

In the furnace room, Frank and June Hagger, Jack and Carol Sawder, and a few other cousins were imposing themselves on another crew, workers carefully weaving themselves through the maze of boilers and cylinders of Hydrogen gas.

The room had only two exit doors, and the Hagger clan was blocking one of them. The employees *here* were wearing hooded jumpsuits, boots and gloves. Their appearance surprised the creatures every bit as much as the creatures surprised them.

"What the hell are they?" Frank scoffed with an imitation of fear.

"I don't know," Carol said, "but *I'd* like to see 'em covered with their own mixtures," and she took off in a mad run directly at *the hooded ones*.

The Xanorse people stared at the dead and rotty group, until Carol was damn near upon them. Then reflex took over and they all jumped to the side and watched as she went to a huge Vat of boiling formic acid and embraced it with a melting hug.

Connecting with the wall of the Vat, it slowly disintegrated around her body, until she could slide in through the opening.

One man screamed a muffled cry through his hood, "Nooo!" But it was too late, the bubbling fluid was already pouring out at them.

The hooded ones turned and ran; right into the arms of Frank and June and company. There were seven creatures present, but with Carol still inside the holding tank, only six were available for killing, and there were quite a few plant employees coming at them.

In proportion, the employees out-numbered the creatures two to one, and with three members of the working team *already* in the arms of 'The Melters' (sizzling up lumpy pools of flesh), the rest thought, perhaps they could just run straight through, and by sheer force of body weight, get to the door and get out.

They were wrong.

Jack reached up and linked arms with June, who linked with Frank, and so on with the rest. "Make a wall," he ordered. And with dissolving swirls, they began to melt together.

Their deteriorated flesh softened like cake batter, spreading onto the skin of the one next to them. They attached and blended and became thicker. Eventually, their arm-*batter* stretched down from the bone, sliding into the flesh of their sides like wings. It oozed through holes and rot spots in their clothing, until the wings became a wall that was connected to the wall of the creature next to them.

When their sides were solidly together, and they were...one, they pulled out from each other and spread wide; a walking blockade of deadly flesh. And they were so well rehearsed at it; they made the transformation in all of about twenty seconds. And the Xanorse people were coming right at them. Followed by runaway acid...and Carol.

In the hallway of the executive offices, Mark White and other administrative staff were running frantically toward the exits. Directly behind Mark was his secretary, Shawna. Suddenly he stopped short and swore, "Shit!"

Shawna slammed into him. And when he turned to run back the other way, she found herself staring straight into the face of..."Jimmy!" his name fell from her lips like a lead weight, "Oh my God!"

From the doorway of Jerry Hammer's office, to her right, Dale gunner emerged, directly in front of her, *between* her and Jimmy. He reached for her neck, and with his hand coming at her she screamed, "NOOO!"

Then something new happened. Before his fingers could actually reach her, they began to droop and fold over, his whole hand folded over; it was melting.

She was staring at it, when it suddenly began to drip off. His fingers actually left his hand in drops. Then his hand dropped - fell off in a clump, on the floor.

As the thick black-red blood-oozing stump of his arm wavered in her face, Dale's eyes got big with surprise, "My hand! What have you done to my hand?" Then his arm dripped off, right up to his elbow, and eventually, his shoulder.

I did that, Shawna thought, *I can use* the power *on him.*

With her sudden revelation, she let herself fill with anger. And consumed by the idea that she was now the one in control, she felt very 'Wonder Womanly'.

So, with the Shawna Taylor stance of power, legs spread, hands on hips, head down and eyes up, she snarled, "Die, you creepy piece of shit!"

She zeroed in on his nose (or where his nose used to be), focused through to the center of his head, and concentrated for pure meltdown.

A second later, Dale's face opened up and the remainder of his brain, some facial muscle, some goopy blood, and portions of a crusty skull, poured out and ran thick onto his chest.

If I wasn't so pissed, she thought, *this would make me sick.*

Dale dropped to the ground; Shawna had turned him into a puddle, "This time, you're going to stay dead." Once she was convinced he was *un-returnable*, she relaxed and stared at the unbelievable mess she'd made, too stunned to move. Until brought back to reality by...growling. When she looked up, there at the end of the hallway, eight more family members had joined Jimmy.

"She killed Dale," he accused.

Wonder Woman stepped out, and terrified Shawna stepped back in, *there's no way I can stop them all, I've got to get help.* She turned and ran back down the hall.

Her first stop was Ross Marxman's office, she stuck her head in, "Mr. Marxman, I know who they a..." she stopped, confronted with a new and gruesome horror.

Ross lay in the middle of his floor, Don and Chrissy were on either side of him. They had melted off his hands and feet. And one handful at a time, were reaching into his body, pulling away chunks; tearing him apart bit by bit. The man was literally going to pieces. Don and Chrissy pushed out squirts of blood each time they went in for more.

Don looked up at Shawna and smiled, then clutched onto Ross's face. A finger in each eye, a thumb in the mouth; push, grasp, rip and pull, and he brought out a handful, "Come here, baby, let me give you some face."

Shawna puked - then pulled back and ran incoherently down the hall.

In the boiler room, attempting to break through the great wall of Hagger, to the door on the other side, were a group of frantic souls being wrapped in a blanket of dissolve.

On one side, the dead Hagger's and their *special touch* were melting away the protective Xanorse clothing they all wore, and burning the exposed skin. While on the other side, the bubbling flow of acid gnawed at their ankles.

There were only three employees still alive when Carol decided to reemerge from the Vat. She ran back at them, the same way she'd run through them the first time; *bloodthirsty!*

She jumped on the backs of two of them, threw an arm around each of their necks and squeezed until their heads popped off. The third passed out and fell victim to the disintegrating chemicals covering the floor.

The Hagger family wall tried to pull apart from each other, finding it a bit more difficult than fusing together; mostly because of the opposing chemicals they were standing in working against them with its own melting force. But they managed.

As Shawna rounded a corner at the end of the hallway, she saw others racing to get away, then she realized she was standing right next to a wall phone. She took a quick look around, saw no Hagger's, and grabbed the receiver.

At the other end of that corridor was another phone, she saw Stephanie Newkirk screaming insanely into it, and she heard the word police. Then she realized she didn't know who else to call, *Shit,* she thought, *I don't have time for anyone to put me on hold.* Then...*Janie! Yeah, I'll call Janie. She's at the house. She can get the gang together, while I try to get the hell out of here.*

She screwed up the number three times before finally getting it right. The call was almost incoherent, but Janie got the gist of it, told Shawna to get out, and that she would contact the others. They hung up, Shawna ran.

Chapter 3

D avis was beneath a Ford LTD when the call came through from Krys. He was head to toe with grease, having to use a rag to hold the phone. Krys was hysterical; he had to calm her down before she could pass on the message she just got from Janie. Once he understood, he slammed down the phone, wiped as much grime off as he could, and flew from the building.

She told him she'd pick up Janie, but he needed to get Jeff and Billy and they would all meet at Xanorse.

Pulling a towel from his trunk, he threw it over the car seat, swearing that he was going to be really pissed if he got grease all over everything. Then, squealing and sliding, left and right in half circles; he almost nailed a Volvo, a Pontiac and a Suzuki motorcycle getting out of the garage lot.

Jeff and Billy both worked construction; their current job had them out on Route 1. They were building a two story, five bedroom, two and a half bath, with basement and attic, home for a local Bank President.

They were on the second level pounding nails when Davis plowed onto what was still a dirt driveway; he almost disappeared in his own dust.

Jeff and Billy heard the horn blowing and waited for the cloud to settle to see who it was. Davis jumped out yelling at them to get down and get in.

It took him all of 25 seconds to tell them what was happening. They jumped in the car and fishtailed away.

Their Foreman, Stan Gamon, stood and cursed them the same way Davis's Boss had; yelling that they should *at least* finish the job they were in the middle of.

Krys rushed out of her beauty salon, so quickly, she left Mrs. Greenbush asleep under a dryer.

Three miles up the road, Route 1 emptied onto Lancaster Lane, five miles up from that was Short Cut. It was there that Davis and Krys almost slammed into each other, both coming from opposite directions. And then they raced, one behind the other to the Xanorse parking lot.

Barreling down Lakeside Highway were ten police cruisers, with gas pedal to the floor and sirens blaring. Everyone wanted the creatures before they disappeared into oblivion again. The cruisers barely made the turn onto Short Cut before they too were swerving into the Xanorse parking lot.

Each car went a different direction, lining up to surround the outer two sides of the building where the entrance and exit doors were located. Davis and Krys slid up next to each other as the squad cars whipped around them. The *Fantastic Five* piled out onto the asphalt. "Davis," Krys cried, "Shawna is still in there."

They ran up to the police blockade and tried to break through, but were stopped. "Sorry, son," the officer said to Davis, "those creatures are in there, we can't let anybody through."

Davis was quick to respond, "You don't understand, Officer, you can't stop them. Bullets won't kill them. They are already dead!"

As unexplainable as it was, *dead* was just not rational, "They're already dead? Yeah, ok sonny, if they're already dead and *we* can't stop them, what is it exactly you think *you* can do?"

Davis looked at the others, then back at the officer and smiled, "We're going to melt them," and he pushed past and took off running, the others followed.

"Stop!" The officer yelled. "Stop now, dammit, or I'll shoot!"

Davis stopped, then Krys, then the others. He turned back to look at the cop.

"What the hell do you mean, you're going to melt them?"

Davis smiled again and looked at the man's drawn pistol. A moment later the cop was watching oozing metal squish through his fingers as Davis melted the .38 magnum, bullets and all.

"Holy shit!" the cop was dumbfounded.

Davis and the others turned slowly then ran to the giant building.

Suddenly, *Click!...Click!...Click!* Nine police revolvers were pointed directly at the five of them...until the cop with the melted gun found his voice, "Let 'em go. Maybe they can do something we can't."

The Pleasure View Brat Pack never looked back.

Chapter 4

Inside, the ground floor was covered with thick purple acid. The boiler room fluids had run together with the main room concentrate fluids; anyone still on the ground floor was either dead or dying. If the acid itself didn't kill them, the fumes did.

Stairways and walkways were now few and far between; most of them had been disintegrated. The concrete hallways were really the only safe walks left to cross. Hagger family members were everywhere searching for anyone still alive, the mission was to 'kill them all.'

Most of the Laboratory rooms were destroyed. Technicians and assistants were almost all dead, one way or another. James Spinkton was found boiling in one of his own containers, his head bobbed up and down in the bubbles. Barbara Stein's backside had been burned off and pressed against a wall; she was stuck there in a three-dimensional form of artwork.

Bodies were half here and half there, draped over banisters and strewn across half dissolved stairways. Stephanie Newkirk made it from the wall phone to the break room, where she was eventually cornered on top a vending machine, captured and liquidated. There was Stephanie Newkirk all over the Reeses and Fritos.

Shawna, along with Josh Matthews, had discovered a loose grill on one of the air ducts; they pulled it off, crawled inside, and pulled it back on again. They sat quiet and frozen with fear, for what seemed like only seconds when Jimmy and cousins came down that particular hallway. Without realizing it, Shawna and Josh had both quit breathing; scared to make any noise.

Jimmy was only three feet past them when suddenly Shawna realized she needed oxygen, and all she could do was long thin slow sucks.

There were actually quite a few hiding places throughout the building; in cabinets, air ducts, the top of machinery, even behind stacked crates. The Hagger creatures hadn't really begun searching the obscure places yet; they were taking it easy plucking off the stupid ones who lingered in plain view. Billie Jo McClure for example, right there, dead center in the hall Jimmy had just entered. He smiled, extended his slimy hand, "You got a lot of guts, lady," and he plowed his fist into her stomach to bring them out and show them to her. She had only a moment to witness her red steaming intestines, then she too was among the deceased.

Jimmy was in mid-step over Billie Jo's body when a loud and sudden voice rang through the hall, echoing from one concrete wall to another. It was so unexpected, each member of the Hagger clan stopped still in their tracks to listen.

"I know you're in here Jimmy Hagger, and I'm going to put you back in the ground where you belong."

Shawna's eyes lit up, *Davis! It's Davis. Hail, hail, the gang's all here.*

Davis and Krys stood side by side with Jeff, Janie, and Billy behind them. They crossed slowly over the entry walk that led to the executive offices, looking down at the ground level below; it was a pool of chemicals, and bodies. Thankfully, they didn't see Shawna anywhere.

The path in front of them was a work of complete devastation. Broken glass, holes melted through walls, burned floorboards, blood, puddles of flesh, body parts, melted sections of the grate flooring from above.

"Jeez," Jeff choked, "do you really think we can stop them, Davis? We don't even know how many there are."

Davis stared at the gloomy mess, "We can stop them. We have to. We're the only ones with the power to stop them."

Just then, seventeen-year-old Patty Hagger stepped out into the hall of destruction from one of the offices, she had a man's genitals slowly dissolving in her hand, "Down here, Jimmy," she called out, "there's five live ones."

The sight of the dead rotty girl, exposing bone and muscle through holey flesh, shocked all five of them. "Melt her, Krys," Janie whispered.

And without realizing it, Krys took the obstinate Shawna stance (legs spread, hands on hips, head down, eyes up) and threw out some heavy concentration, "Melt, you Bitch!"

Until that moment, Patty Hagger had been smiling, it was toothless, but it was a smile none-the-less, "Come on, Jimmy, they think they're going to sto..." her words suddenly cut short, she felt her blood boiling, snapping, popping, "What are you doing to me?" Her gravely voice sounded scared, then her shoulders drooped, her arms were stretching. "How can you dooooo..." her voice snarled viciously and quickly trailed off. Her face suddenly began dripping, then her whole head turned to mush. In seconds, Patty had run all over herself and shrunk to a stub. Eventually, she was just another puddle.

"Patty? PAAATTYYY!" Jimmy cried out.

Davis looked at Krys, "Now they're really gonna be pissed."

Jeff looked over her shoulder, "Nice job, Krys. And quick. In a hurry, were you?"

As the five moved down the walk, cautiously looking in each wreck of an office along the way, they heard the faint shuffling of dead Hagger's moving about. The machinery had stopped, the evacuation alarm had *finally* shut off; the building was completely silent of all operations. The only sounds still in the air were body movements. "Shawna, where are you?" Davis called out in a loud whisper.

The gang reached the end of executive row at the same time Erwin and June came around the corner right in front of them. Janie screamed, Erwin grinned and reached for her. He grabbed her wrist, and when it began to burn, she screamed louder. Davis shot a quick glare to Janie's wrist and concentrated on holding it together.

Erwin looked down at his grip and realized he wasn't melting through in the way he'd grown accustomed to, "What the..." he started angrily, then Billy began working on his hand, melting it off almost instantly.

Davis brought Janie's wrist back to normal. Erwin looked surprised, June looked at him, "What's the matter, Erwin?"

Then Erwin saw his arm begin to drip and looked at Billy, Billy looked pissed and on a mission.

"Run, June, they've got some kind of power. *Run!*"

Well, June wasn't a complete idiot, and when she saw Erwin turn into a fountain of bubbling rot, she turned and did the creature hustle as best as she could in the opposite direction.

Janie stepped into the hallway after her, "Wrong, Bitch!" And aimed her focus at June's feet. Unfortunately, June had already made it to the next hallway and was turning by the time Janie could do any real damage. She did, however, dissolve a foot. Which, after making the turn, June quickly bent down and formed a stub to hobble on.

"You ok, Janie?" Billy asked.

She flexed her wrist a little, "It's weird," she said. "I don't feel anything different, it's like it didn't really happen. Thanks Davis...and Billy."

Davis gave an obligatory smile, "No problem." Then he turned to face the hallway, "Where are you, Jimmy? Come on out you slimy piece of chicken shit." They all stood motionless and waited.

Then, right above them, a heavy metal door slid open with a loud screech, "Come and get me, asshole!" It was Jimmy's gravely voice.

The gang froze, riddled with goose bumps, and they listened to the shuffling of not one, not two, but a whole troop of dead moving Hagger's. "They're right above us," Davis whispered. He looked around for a stairway that was still intact, "Look," he pointed to where June had run, there were steps leading up.

The shuffling above continued, the Hagger's moved across the metal grate. "Let's go," Krys instructed, and she took off for the stairway, she stopped at the corridor June had gone into, making sure no one was going to spring out at them. No one did.

Some of the steps had been partially burned; they took them two at a time.

Jimmy was listening intently, to know from which direction they would be coming. He led the family across the walk onto another concrete floor, a small floor, in fact, it was just a ten-foot square slab surrounded by lead pipe railings. On the other side was a door with a large 'Roof Exit' sign. Jimmy grabbed the handle - it burned off in his hand, "Shit," he grumbled and melted his own opening.

When Krys and the others reached the level Jimmy and family were on, it was just in time to see the last Hagger corpse step out to a mid-level section of roof.

The building had three roof levels; each made of concrete and covered with pebble rock. The Hagger's were on level two, sizzling gravel like hot coals.

In the parking lot, the entire police force, waiting to hear or see something...anything, were suddenly alert to the emerging figures on the second level roof. "That's them," said the officer in charge, and he raised a bullhorn, "The Creature's are on the roof. Prepare to fire. Shoot to kill!" The sound of cocking rifles cut through the warm still air of the afternoon with a harsh stainless steel chill. "Ready...aim...fire!"

The entire force opened up on them.

The explosion of gunfire seemed endless. In reality, it was less than a minute, and a lot of bullets went into the building, but even more went into the Hagger's...only to pass through. The police watched, helplessly, as the shooting didn't even phase them, not one of them fell, not even a stagger. Finally, a cease-fire was called.

The Hagger's moved to the center of the roof and spread out in a line. Then, one by one, Davis, Krys, Jeff, Janie, and Billy came out forming their own line.

For a moment, it was a stare down. Davis and company were awe-struck by the gruesomeness of each and every member of the family. Thick black-red blood oozed from the gaping holes in their decayed flesh. Teeth and jawbones dangled from their faces. Yellow pus ran from their eyeballs. Where noses were missing was slimy red and white swirls of over exposed brain-rot. And they stood ready for battle, on the gravel that slowly sizzled beneath their toxic feet.

Jimmy stood in the center of the line up and looked at the only threats to his existence. First he glared at Davis and a sudden flash-back to the woods streaked through his mind; he was carrying a magazine, then the vision was gone. He looked at Jeff, something was familiar but it wasn't clear. Then Krys, and his throat closed in for a hard choking swallow, his blood pumped a few spurts from his chest. *I know her,* he thought, and stared.

The rabbit hopped, I'm taking you home for supper, Mr.Rabbit. *The words ran through his head as he lifted his rifle and shot. The rabbit had crossed the road before it was hit. The cartridge sent the little bunny flying into the air, a pinwheel of spraying blood, and Jimmy ran out of the bushes to fetch his prize.* Oh Shit! A car!

Jimmy was dead center of the road with only enough time to turn briefly from his rabbit dinner and stare directly at the little yellow beetle coming at him. It's that girl from the tree house, the one that was naked that day. Gosh she's purty.

'Thump! Thump!' The car exploded into his body, and everything went black!!!

It was her, he thought, standing paralyzed on the roof. This was the girl who killed him. But she was so beautiful; he could even love her, how could someone this beautiful be the one who, apparently, was responsible for what he'd become. "It was you," he said. "You're the one what killed me," he took a step toward her.

Krys's eyes filled with tears, "It was an accident, Jimmy."

Trudy stepped forward, "You killed my grandbaby?"

Suddenly, Krys was defensive, "It was an accident. The damn fool ran into the middle of the road, he didn't even look where he was going."

"Kill them!" Jimmy commanded.

The entire family moved in on the five. Frank and Verna were the closest and leapt at Davis. He managed to duck Frank who flew over and landed on a metal ventilation pipe protruding from the roof. The pipe was two feet tall and went directly through Frank's stomach as he dropped straight on to it. When it punctured its way out his back, there was what *used* to be a vital organ stuck to the end of it.

Verna, on the other hand, landed directly on top of Davis and immediately began burning. Davis felt flesh searing on his arms, and his clothes began to stick to him. All he could think quick enough to do was to concentrate on his original body form, hoping *his* melt power was stronger than *hers* and would hold him together long enough to get her off.

Billy focused on Verna, and with unbelievably rapid speed he burned her right down to liquid. He dropped her to a pool of melt in ten seconds. Of course Davis was covered with *that* melt until it ran off, but he remained intact.

Meanwhile, Frank had rolled over. The pipe slid out of his side and he oozed himself back together. And as Janie, Jeff, and Krys began flinging out burning glares - the battle began.

The Fantastic Five were darting back and forth, dodging the sweeping arms of burning Hagger's. They knew all it would take was one good swipe at the neck and they could lose their head, *and then where would they be.*

Jimmy flung acid oil in every direction, Billy and Krys were hit a few times and burned hellaciously, but they kept fighting, then Billy tripped and went down flat on his back.

Chrissy stepped over his face, one leg on either side, "Eat me," she said, "and make it good," then she dropped to her knees to grind her hot crotch onto his mouth.

Suddenly, Chrissy got an ass full of Janie's foot and flew forward. "He's mine, Bitch!" Janie snarled, and her eyes drilled the rotted girl. Janie was furious, and taken completely by surprise by what that fury did to her power; glaring at Chrissy, expecting no more than to dissolve her, she watched the dead girl's head...blow up. It exploded right in front of her. So stunned with this new and startling revelation, Janie lost focus of her concentration and Chrissy's body was left writhing on the gravel. Billy finally rolled over and turned the rest of her to mush.

Davis and Jeff had backed up to each other, encircled by a string of the *undead*. The odds were two to ten, and all they really had time to do was to shoot burning glances at their feet, one at a time, trying to slow them down. Spending too much time on any one of them would leave the others to rush in. But they managed to hold their own, and gradually disintegrated the legs of several attackers.

Krys dodged dropping building parts, as Charles and Don scaled the roof structures, tearing off protruding pipes and beams and throwing them at her.

"We need to make a break for it," Jeff told Davis. "This circle is getting tighter, they're going to get us."

Davis agreed, "On the count of three, just cut and run for it, I think we can jump over them," and he began to count.

Janie and Billy were dealing with Frank and Henry, and Frank and Henry were swinging so violently hard that Janie and Billy barely had time to duck their flailing arms, let alone take time to retaliate.

Then it happened. Frank got Billy by the arm, at the elbow...and squeezed.

Billy's arm came off without a hitch.

His cry of anguish echoed through the trees, and his blood ran like water from a drain spout.

Janie watched in horror, and screamed. Seeing his blood, she delved quickly into her rational mind, *What do I do?* The answer came, *seal him up...Now!* And she stared at Billy's arm, closing the opening until the bleeding stopped.

Davis and Jeff leapt over the circle of now stubby legged Hagger's, and found themselves joining Krys in the dodge of falling building materials, "Jesus, Krys," Jeff said, "why don't you melt those two assholes?"

And between the three of them, they turned both Charles and Don into a flesh-tone liquid that spread over the roof rock.

"Nice paint job, Blake," Davis told Jeff, "a bit runny perhaps..."

Then they saw Billy and Janie about to be consumed by the swinging Frank and Henry, *"Janie, look out!"* Krys yelled. Janie's instant reaction was to leap out of the way, unfortunately, Billy was still laying behind her; and when she was gone, Frank and Henry came right down on top of him.

Billy *tried* to send out *burn* signals on them, and was able to cause a little damage; they went soft, which in the long run made it easier for Davis and Jeff to finish them off. But they were on Billy for too long, they'd burned too far into him. And though he tried to *think* it away, the pain was too great; his body had succumbed to the meltdown of Frank and Henry.

Billy Dunes...died on the roof of Xanorse Chemicals Inc.

It took the others a moment to grasp the reality of what had just happened, then they became enraged. Davis, Krys, Jeff, and Janie, *all* with tears in their eyes, turned on the stubby legged group of Cousins, Aunts and Uncles, and began blowing them apart. There was a second of oozy slime at the focus point, then an explosion. And the gruesome beings blew up. Body and bone parts sprayed over the gravel.

Eventually, all that was left of the Hagger's was Jimmy, Trudy, Earl, Lila, and little Molly. And the four remaining *heroes* were circling them. "I killed you once, Jimmy Hagger, and I'll kill you again, you and your whole damn demented family," Krys told him.

She was standing in front of the doorway they'd come through to the roof; but as she lowered her head, lifted her eyes, and focused on the demolition of the slimy creature who's life should have ended ten years before, she was suddenly thrown forward when June Hagger, who'd stayed inside during the fight, burst through and jumped on Krys's back.

Krys felt an immediate burn sensation as she dropped to the ground in front of Jimmy. June remained on her briefly, "You've killed enough of my family, you Bitch," she growled.

Caught off guard and too stunned to move, Davis, Jeff, and Janie were watching, when Shawna flew through the door behind June. First, she grabbed her by the shoulders and rolled her off of Krys, "*Your* family is just not dead enough," Shawna shouted. And standing over her, melted her onto the roof gravel like cheese on a hamburger.

"Kill the others," Jimmy commanded and he turned to Krys, she was critically wounded and wavered painfully in and out of consciousness. He dropped down to her side and scooped her up in his arms.

The remaining Hagger family turned on the other four so quick; they didn't have time to get to Krys before having to fend for themselves. And as Jimmy lifted her, his arms began to come through, "I wanted you," he said. "I thought you were so beautiful. But, you killed me."

In her last and dying breath, Krys looked into his dead eyes, "It was an accident, Jimmy," then her tear streaked face went void of all expression, her eyes glazed over and her body fell into three pieces from where his arms cut through. Krys Sanders was dead.

Shawna had been able to escape the attention of Earl Hagger long enough to see her best friend die. Abruptly, filled with rage, she screamed loud and guttural (not a shriek), as if she were possessed, "Aaaauuugghhh, die, Jimmy Hagger, die!"

Her eyes glowed red, with a line of power from her mind to his body that was physically visible. And after burning for only a short moment, he suddenly...blew up. Immediately followed by the explosions of Earl, Trudy, Lila, and the little puff of smoke known as Molly. The Hagger's were all finally dead...again.

Billy and Krys's head and upper torso were about all that was left of them, laying three feet from each other on the second level rooftop of the Xanorse building, surrounded by the puddles that were their killers.

Davis held Shawna tight, her face buried in his chest. Neither of them could believe they'd just lost two of their best friends at the same time.

Shawna's body shook; she couldn't bring herself to look back at what was left of them. And the harder the reality hit, the heavier her mind dumped memory flashes; Krys's eighth birthday party, she got play make-up and Shawna was the only one allowed in the bathroom to share putting it on with her – both of them thought they were Beauty Queens. And then a couple of weeks ago, her life-long dream of having a bust-line finally came true. She was on top of the world and ready to conquer it, and just like that...her life was snatched away.

And just when Shawna didn't think she could take anymore; all the old feelings of her crush on Billy came storming back to her, until her sobbing became inconsolable.

Davis just stared; tears ran rivers from his eyes. Billy was one of the greatest guys he ever knew, he was always there for him. *How can this be? ...Oh my God,* he thought, *How can Billy's dad take another loss like this?* With anguish, Davis dropped his head to Shawna's shoulder.

Trembling with a new and sudden heartbreaking loss, Janie knelt down and pressed her cheek to Billy's, "You're a truly wonderful man, Billy," and she sobbed. Her hands clutched his head, her fingers wove through his sweaty-wet curly blonde hair, and she gave him a last gentle kiss on his mouth, "I already miss you," she cried. And with her face next to his, as the tears flowed, she turned to look at her dead best friend in the arms of what could have been a great future.

Jeff, too, was crumpled with a broken heart, holding Krys's remains. He lifted her head and leaned her shoulders against his leg, gently stroking her hair, kissing her forehead, "I'm sorry it took us so long to come around, Krys," he whispered. "I just always thought there would be more time." He buried his wet face in her hair and wept, "I love you."

As the police moved to the roof, the surviving members of the Pleasure View Brat Pack were numb and unmoving, their faces stained with tears. "We're going to need statements from all of you," they were told. "We're going to need to know who the creatures were and what this power is you all seem to have."

Davis brought his streaked face around to look at the officer, "Their power was different than ours." His three remaining friends looked at him.

"How is it different?" the Cop asked.

"Our brains are still intact," he said. "We have control over it. These creatures were all dead, their brains had been eaten away; their power was released to their bodies through their bloodstream. They had no control."

The officer took off his hat and scratched his head, "And how did you all acquire this *power*?"

Davis thought for a minute then turned to the man and shrugged, "I don't know, ...too many chemicals in the pool I guess."

The silence that afternoon, on a beautifully blue, clear and sunny day out on Lakeside Highway was deafening. And four life-long friends, who would never give up *The Pact* they'd made; the bonding secret that at one time had been the alliance of six best friends in the prime of their youth - discovered a depth of grief that would forever shadow their lives.

THE END

And now...a slice from

TROPAES

The next spine tingling Book from Author

Brad Rieman

Mary picked up the gravy boat and handed it over to me, "Sure, here."

I was taking it from her, thinking I had a good grip on it, but when she started to let go, the dish wobbled and gravy sloshed out. Mary and I each made a quick jerking attempt to rescue the situation; save it from more spilling or dropping it all together, and our hands met - mine on top of hers.

Suddenly, like the time on the front porch steps outside the home of her childhood, there was a flash of blinding whiteness and the thunderous sound of lightning cracking. All at once, I was in a different reality:

I was on board 'Sweet Rayne,' my sailboat. It was nighttime; the boat was adrift on the sea. I stood at the back port side and was stunned silent by the image in front of me.

There was only the light of the moon, but it was full and lit things quite well. Enough that I could see, from tiller to companionway, everything was covered in blood. There was so much blood, I was afraid to walk for chance of slipping.

The boat rocked gently with the ocean, at first there didn't seem to be anyone aboard. Then a dim flickering light stretched up from the cabin below.

I called out for whoever might be there to identify themselves. When there was no answer, it dawned on me, that if this was the same kind of location transportation I did with Mary the first time; I was once again, simply a ghost looking in on her memory - *Mary's memory*. But how could this bloody mess on *my boat* be part of *her* memory?

I had to get to the cabin and see what was going on.

I stepped carefully around the splotches and puddles, into the dry spots, slowly making my way across the deck. With the full moon overhead, there were no shadows; it was as if the whole bloody scene had a spotlight on it.

When I reached the cabin, I took a deep breath and went down. But as I hit the floorboard, I was almost run over, I had to leap out of the way. What came at me simply snapped my mind. But by the glow of a burning Lantern, I saw Mary head straight up the steps. Her face was tense and sweaty, there was blood splattered on her. She moved anxiously with hard pumping adrenaline; and on her shoulder was a body.

The bottom half of the person was in front of her, the top half lay over her back. It looked like a woman but it was hard to tell; the legs and clothing were so torn up and blood soaked.

I stepped out of the way, the vision focused when she passed me, and I saw the top half of the woman hanging behind her; head down, bobbing, barely attached. It was Autumn.

I shivered with a start; Mary and I both dropped the gravy boat. It wasn't that far off the table, but it did splatter a mess.

I was back in my own reality at the dinner table with Rayne and Mary; I was shocked and fell back to my seat. All I could do was stare at her. *Mary, what have you done?* my brain pounded.

Mary stared back at me, "Dad? Are you okay?"

"John?" Larayna's hand was on my arm.

I looked at her and realized *I* must have looked frightening; my whole body was twisted, repulsed and fearful of what I'd just seen.

"Dad?" Mary said again.

I looked in her sweet face, not a single flicker of meanness there whatsoever. I decided I would investigate the matter later, on my own - before I said anything about it.

I tried easing into a smile, "Sorry," I said, "everything just kind of went white for a moment. Maybe the unexpected jump for the gravy caught my equilibrium off guard or something. I'm fine...really."

"Are you sure?" Larayna was concerned.

Mary stared at me, curiously. I smiled at each of them, "Yes, yes I'm sure. Really."

Later that night, when they were both sleeping, I got up and went to Mary's room - she was out like a light.

I sat on the edge of her bed and looked at the peacefulness of her sleep. I knew I wasn't going to want to see what I was about to see. But I had to know what happened.

Mary lie on her side, her arm made a V on the mattress; her hand was palm down in front of her face. I slid my hand smoothly into hers

- palm to palm. My heart quickened, and I gently wrapped my fingers in a grip.

'*Crack!*'

The white light blinded me just for a second, I jerked around, and suddenly I was standing...somewhere else.

It was the week before, on the beach with Mary. She had just read me Darlene Raintree's poem about '*the glow from hell.*'

"Hey," she suddenly changed the subject, "I was thinking about going out sailing for a bit. You want to come?"

The smile on her face held just long enough to mark its impression in my mind, and suddenly the white light flashed. Not long enough to blind me, but enough to pass me from one reality to another; and again, I was somewhere else.

I was back at the dock, looking down on my own boat. It was that same night, but later; just before I went and destroyed Karen White.

From where I stood, I could see Autumn and...*Myself* onboard. I had just walked away from her, I saw myself turn back and say, *"Let me give you some understanding. Let me give you something to think about between now and the next time I see you."*

There were a few more words and then my eyes were glowing, spitting green and gold sparks. I unfurled my black cape and lifted to the air. Autumn dropped to the chair beneath her.

I watched myself rise in front of a cloud. In the night, I appeared as a large black bird.

When I reached the center of the cloud, I spread the wings of my cape and let it blow behind me. I caused a furious wind to rise, whipping wickedly through my hair and snapping the curtain of my cape.

I closed my arms in a cross and brought my head down, my eyes put out green beams of light, which together, went to her, forcing her to look back at me through the glow.

Then I began to spin; slowly at first, round and round. The lights of my eyes turning circles like the rotating lamp of a Lighthouse out of control. I spun faster and created a tornado of wind; Autumn's hair whipped across her face.

And in a grand exit, I spun full speed in a black blur at the center of my own cyclone, bursting with rods of electricity, exploding in a spectacle of power and force. Then the narrow end of the cone lifted itself to the cloud and drilled in.

Twenty seconds later, I was gone.

Standing back, with third-person perspective, I must say, it was quite impressive. So, I know where *I* went when I left, but *what became of Autumn?* Now I would find out.

I watched her, she was stunned, trying to make herself stand from the chair; not that she was ready to go anywhere, but she needed to stabilize her body.

Then to my complete surprise *and horror*, I saw Mary race up from the cabin through the companionway, with a skinning knife in hand, and screaming some indefinable sound of anguish.

She had been down there the whole time! She heard everything!

Autumn was only conscious enough to be aware that something else was coming at her; she slowly brought her eyes around to Mary's direction. But her reaction time was delayed and Mary was on her with the knife, lunging for its first jab before Autumn could process what was happening. The pain captured her full attention

Autumn screamed, and by the second thrust, she had her hands on Mary's arm. But Mary was strong, and Autumn was still in too much shock to be worth anything. Her hands clung weakly to Mary's arm - pumping back and forth, pulling the knife out, then ramming it back in again. And as Autumn screamed, Mary yelled, and she had no trouble finding words.

"The Evil must die! You will never hurt my family again. Never!" And with each word cried, came another plunge of the knife. She stabbed every part of her body. *"Never!"* ...in the chest. *"Never!"* ...in the groin. "Never!" ...in the eye...

In her attempt to escape the *killing machine* Mary had become; Autumn staggered and bled...and died all over the deck.

When Mary's temporary loss of sanity ended, there were slices of flesh and fingers and...parts, scattered from port to starboard, sliding around in a pool of bright red.

Autumn's body was a ragged mop of lifelessness. Mary finally stopped and stood still, breathing heavy, trying to regain composure - remember who and where she was.

Eventually, she looked around at the mess she'd made. Then she looked in my direction, though I was invisible to her; she was looking back at the dock to see if anybody was watching. There was no one in sight.

About the Author

Brad Rieman was born in southern California and raised on the beach; the author of many poems, song lyrics, and short stories - he headed for a change of scenery and wound up in Louisville Kentucky. Eventually, the writing grew to novels and screenplays; *The Melting* is his first novel. He lives with his lovely wife, Pamela, and whichever children may currently be occupying a bedroom. Hard at work on his next book - *Tropaes*, the fictional biography of a Warlock, his goals are 'success as a writer,' and to 'get back to the beach!'